PATHOG

A Click Your Poison book

by
James Schannep

The eAversion Version

Second Print Edition

This book is a work of fiction. Names, characters, businesses, organizations, places, events, and incidents are either the product of the author's imagination or are used fictitiously. Any resemblance to actual persons, living, dead, or undead, events, or locales is entirely coincidental. Certain public figures were used either satirically or for parody, and no connection to their real-life personas was intended nor should be inferred.

The chapters "Carp's Lesson in Perseverance" and "Battle of the Bees" are adapted from *Ancient Tales and Folklore of Japan* by Richard Gordon Smith, London, A. & C. Black, 1918—a book that is now in the public domain.

Author's Note: *INFECTED* was published in late 2012, which means that's the year the world ended in *PATHOGENS*. Still, you might find a pop-culture reference or two that stems from our "non-nom'd" future. These errors you might find were intentional, because I wanted the humor to be relevant. That said, I did my best to keep the story pre-2012 in all practical ways. See: the Lady Gaga's meat-suit reference.

Choice-order powered by *Random.org*.

Copyright © 2016 by James Schannep

All rights reserved.
Print Edition
www.jamesschannep.com

Library of Congress Cataloging-in-Publication Data
Schannep, James, 1984—
PATHOGENS: a Click Your Poison book / James Schannep

1. Apocalyptic & Post-Apocalyptic—Science Fiction—Fiction.
2. Horror—Fiction. I. Title

COVER ART BY BRIAN SILVEIRA

This book has been modified from its original version. It has been formatted to fit this page.

ISBN-10: 1537256769
ISBN-13: 978-1537256764

Here's how it works: You, Dear Reader, are the main character of this story. Ready to put your zombie survival strategies to the test? Your decisions can lead to bashing-in undead brains or getting your face eaten off.; the choice is yours. Do not read this book front to back. Instead, follow the options presented at the end of each chapter to the next section. The story evolves based on your decisions, so choose wisely.

Click Your Poison books

INFECTED—Will YOU Survive the Zombie Apocalypse?
MURDERED—Can YOU Solve the Mystery?
SUPERPOWERED—Will YOU Be a Hero or a Villain?
PATHOGENS—More Zombocalypse Survival Stories!
MAROONED—Can YOU Endure Treachery and Survival on the High Seas?
SPIED (coming in 2019)—Can YOU Save the World as a Secret Agent?

* More titles coming soon! *
Sign up for the new release mailing list at: http://eepurl.com/bdWUBb
Or visit the author's blog at www.jameschannep.com

For Melissa, Sarah, Alison, Amy, and Samantha, my wonderfully supportive sisters who showed me that six different characters (like us!) will see the same event from six different perspectives—and for teaching me why that's a good thing. Love you all.

P.S.– You'll find the names of many from our family in here. Please note that all names were assigned randomly and no inferences should be made based on character names. Seriously.

Acknowledgements

I am in awe of my wife Michaela for somehow managing to read this book even while you were swamped with work. You truly have the tenacity of an apocalypse survivor. As always, thank you for your sacrifices that allow me to be able to do what I love for a living.

A big thanks to my Alpha Reader, Fred Buckley, for playing along as I wrote. Expect a GIF soon, bud.

Special thanks to my Beta Readers, many of whom I've never met, yet nonetheless gave me your time and insights, for which I am both indebted and extremely grateful: Mike Beeson, Sean Miller, Andy Ross, Steven Slaughter, Maria Mountokalaki, Sara Pearson, R. L. Meyer, Brian Yoakam, Elizabeth Wright, Sarah Briggs, Kari Cowell, and Ben van Gastel.

To my copyeditor: Linda Jay, cover artist: Brian Silveira, and to Paul Salvette and the team at BB eBooks. Thank you all for your generosity and professionalism.

And to my friends and family, for your unyielding encouragement, enthusiasm and support.

PATHOGENS

Here's the sitch: With the breakthrough wonder drug known as *Gilgazyme®*, Big Pharma has finally ended human aging. Newly improved genes enter your bloodstream on a viral vector; these new pathogens then replicate and alter your genetic code so you can live forever. You can probably guess where this is going. Hint: It rhymes with *Mombie Dapocalypse*.

And it's your job, Dear Reader, to survive.

Read the chapter and see if you've got what it takes. Unlike other *Click Your Poison*™ books, this is the first one where you don't "play" as yourself. Instead, you can choose a character and see how that person survived the initial outbreak. Think of this page as your "character-select screen" in this gamebook.

Each of these characters first appeared in *INFECTED*, but you don't need to have that book memorized (or even have read it, truth be told), to enjoy *PATHOGENS*. Instead, pick a persona and learn the story as only one who experienced it truly can. Each character has his or her own perspective, strengths and weaknesses, and it's likely you'll connect with some more than others, so make sure you try the story multiple times.

But beware—since these characters appear in another book, if you take the wrong path and end up bitten, mangled, or dead, you'll rip the very fabric of the space/time continuum and your adventure will be over. Good luck!

Sims

Technical Sergeant Robert Sims, National Guardsman and electrician in the greatest Air Force in the goddamned world. Divorced, no kids, fourteen years of service given to your nation thus far. You're a "Prepper" (a dedicated survivalist), and you've been looking forward to the *zombocalypse* for as long as you can remember. Your unit was mobilized, and now you find yourself at the tip of the spear. When it comes to idioms, you're not the smartest crayon in the box, but you're an electrical genius.

Select Sims Go to page 8

Rosie

Smart, cute, spunky redhead. 17-year-old high school student. Your father is a combat-veteran Marine and you work weekends at the family-owned shooting range. Sarah is your real name and, truth be told, you're more interested in boys and music than you are bug-out-bags and MREs, but you play along for dad's sake. Ever since mom died, he's had a hard time, and he's not the type to get a pedicure, so for quality time you learn about pyrotechnics. Unfortunately, Sarah's world is about to end, and you'll have to fully embrace his training to become the "Rosie the Riveter" of the apocalyptic wasteland.

Select Rosie Go to page 7

Lucas

Lucas Tesshu, middle-aged man who handles crises with the same serenity a stone handles the river. As a child of Japanese immigrants, you've lived much of your life as an outsider, making solitude a revered mentor and friend. As a Kendo instructor and master of swordplay, you're more than capable of defending yourself, but as a disciple of Bushido, you're committed to helping those in need. So the question becomes: Can a man unable to leave someone for dead still survive the Zombie Apocalypse?

Select Lucas <u>Go to page 6</u>

Hefty

Poor as dirt, good ole southern boy. Thin as a rail, and yeah, the nickname is ironic. Known to the State as inmate #: 080620-06. They say money doesn't grow on trees, but you can cook some up in your kitchen using a few household ingredients as fertilizer. Like literal fertilizer, for one. But you're over that now, clean, back on the straight and narrow, and ready to be a productive member of society once you get released from the Big House. A day that's about to come early, courtesy of the Apocalypse.

Select Hefty <u>Go to page 5</u>

Tyberius

Work nights at the call center, days at the bank. Sleep? Yeah, right. It's all you can do to provide for you and Mama, who lost her own job in the recession. She still hopes you'll find a nice girl and settle down, but you'd settle for an apartment in the better part of town. So you use any spare moment; while eating, even while shitting, to take online courses on a smartphone, angling for a promotion at the bank. But all that effort is about to be in vain when the global economy tanks in 3, 2, 1...

Select Tyberius <u>Go to page 9</u>

Cooper

Kaeden Cooper, known as "Kay" to your friends. Daughter of a NASCAR driver who turned to the bottle and lost his shot at stardom. You've since done your fair share of racing on the motorbike circuit, but it's still very much a man's world, and no one wanted to give you sponsorship unless you posed by the bike in a bikini. Instead, you turn wrenches for a living, waiting for the weekend until you can ride again. Little do you know that this shift under the hood will be your last. Soon the world will learn it's those who know how to change their own oil who will survive.

Select Cooper <u>Go to page 3</u>

Cooper

Idling at a stoplight, you tip your helmet up, grab the Big Gulp of Mountain Dew from its handlebar cupholder attachment, and take a long pull from the straw. *Sweet nectar of life.* The morning ride is usually the best part of your day, but it's an unseasonably cold Saturday morning and your lower back is throbbing.

A homeless man sits on a nearby bus stop bench, picking at a disgusting sore on his forearm. The flesh is raised and puffy, but the skin is white rather than the normal irritated red. The veins surrounding his wound appear black. Like he's got oil for blood.

Preoccupied with thoughts of just how much you're not looking forward to a day full of oil changes, the light turns green and the driver behind you blares his horn. You respond by flipping him an over-the-shoulder bird. Drink stowed and helmet down, your bike purrs as you twist the throttle. Despite your back acting up, you enjoy the thrill of over-accelerating down the road. Front wheel almost comes off the ground, but not quite.

Up ahead, two men stumble drunkenly along the side of the road. *Christ, this city,* you think as one of them runs into traffic. The second man appears worse off and tries to follow his friend, but he's much slower and probably won't make it across the road in time. You give him a toot of your horn and his head stops lolling on his shoulders; snapping into place with surprising intensity. His eyes glisten in your headlights like an animal's.

Then he lunges at you.

Your first instinct is to brake, but instead you increase the throttle, using the added momentum to swerve around him. He sees the danger, and reaches out, as if to catch you. Pushing the turn further, his fingertips only barely scrape across your leather jacket. Once clear of him, you release the throttle and squeeze the brakes, causing the bike to skid to a stop. The rear wheel fishtails, but you control the slide just like you might coming off a jump on the Motocross circuit.

The Big Gulp is nowhere to be found, but Dew has splashed all over your helmet and jacket. Pulling the helmet off, you look back—but the man is gone. Like he disappeared into thin air. Must've instantly sobered up and realized the impending lawsuit against him if you crashed.

"Asshole!" you scream.

Motorcycle parked in front of the garage, you head inside and throw your sopping wet, sticky jacket and helmet in the corner. After clocking-in, you notice Owen already at the waiting room coffeemaker.

"Fuck this city and everyone in it. I wish they'd all just curl up and die," you say, walking past him to check the overnight drop-box.

"Morning, Kay," he replies, just as the aroma of his coffee hits you. You're still not sure if he brews the stuff to smell like burnt shit intentionally, as a cost-saving technique so the customers won't drink it, but either way, it's nauseating.

The drop-box reveals that several early risers left their cars before the garage opened at the crack of dawn. You've got more than a dozen cars waiting for you today. Oil changes, mostly.

"Seriously, boss. We need to have a no-oil-change policy on Saturdays."

"Yeah, well…" he says, pointing to the wall behind you.

The sign reads, "Management's Suggestion Bin," with an arrow pointing straight down to the trash can positioned below.

"Hardy har har."

"Hey, you can always hop behind the desk. Less customer complaints for a pretty face."

"So you keep telling me. And my answer always remains…?"

"To go fuck myself?"

"Your words, boss. Your words," you say, pushing through the door from the lobby and into the garage.

The lights come on automatically in response to the motion, and the sweet smell of motor oil fills your nostrils. As the shift lead, you're the first to arrive, but as you boot up your workstation, your back tweaks in pain again.

The bottle of Oxycodone in your desk only has three tabs left. *Damn.* This month's supply went fast. Taking all three, you use the last few minutes of quiet to distribute starting assignments to the staff's workstation inboxes.

Stephen is tall, if not a little gangly, and overly talkative. So why not let him wrap his arms around a trio of motorcycles brought out from storage, ready for a tune-up and oil change?

Josh has an odd sense of humor, interrupted only by his frequent cigarette breaks. H1 Humvee 4x4 scheduled for tire rotation? There you go, Josh. Let's put you under the hummer so I can't see you stroke your goatee while offering sage wisdom. The bumpersticker reads *Ad Vitam Paramus,* so I'm sure you'll tell us all what that means before the little hand hits ten.

Ooh, a police cruiser in need of new brake pads? Make that a priority, Brian. Despite being a white guy of average build and social status, he likes to rag on the police. Maybe that perpetual buzz cut of his is really a *woulda-shoulda-coulda* military cut.

And then there's Craig. Mr. Reliable. Station wagon here for its 120,000-mile service? Have at it, Craig. Reliable, not sexy, overlooked, but trusty. Won't let you down. Just like the station wagon.

As for you? It's entirely possible that Owen made you shift lead so the other guys would stop hitting on you. But rank has its privileges. Like setting your own schedule and priorities. Which means if you want to, you can decide:

- ➤ Meds haven't kicked in yet. I'll browse the internet for a bit until the guys start flowing in. <u>Go to page 366</u>
- ➤ Guess I'll get a jump on the rest of the pile. List isn't getting any shorter; what's up next? <u>Go to page 190</u>

Hefty

Go Fish is a game with incredibly high stakes. Especially when it's played in prison, modified so the rules, risks, and rewards are more akin to poker. Which is exactly why you don't play. Plenty of other opportunities to get yourself shanked in here.

Instead, you sit at the table in front of the breakroom TV. Every table has six chairs welded to it, along with a chess/checker board printed on the center of its chrome metal surface. Though no one actually plays chess in here, the cardmongers have devised a way to set the pieces so they look like they're mid-game, but they're actually staged to signify the bet on the next hand. It's similar to the betting system in roulette, but you don't know the details because, again, you don't play.

Your cellmate, a hulking Mexican gang-banger and self-described *cholo*, whom you affectionately call "Celly," throws his cards down, grins, and rearranges the chess pieces to indicate his win.

"Bullshit," Bobby the skinhead says. "I call bullshit. That's three full schools of fish in as many hands."

"Be careful what you accuse a man of, *cabron*."

"C'mon, guys. Today's laundry day," you remind them in your slow Southern drawl.

Laundry day, in inmate terms, is contraband delivery day. Shouldn't be much longer before you're sent back to your cell to trade soiled bedding for new, with a fresh batch of lotto scratch tickets tucked inside. After all, you don't play cards, but you've got the itch to gamble as much as any man in here. An itch that you like to scratch in the literal sense.

"Hefty, I suggest you turn the fuck around and watch TV, like a good boy," Celly says.

No mixed message there. The TV is muted, but a special news bulletin catches your eye. Some reality TV paternity-test program was interrupted for genuine breaking news. The screen shows a handsome man in a lab coat giving a press conference, smiling brightly against the flash of cameras.

The headline reads, "Will YOU Live Forever?" and the closed captions below say: *Dr. Lewis Deleon and his revolutionary new gene therapy promise to end aging after one dose with the patented Gilgazyme® inhaler.*

"Nobody calls me a liar, *pendejo*!"

Out of nowhere, Bobby the skinhead comes crashing into the TV, knocking it off the stand. You jump up and out of the way as Celly rushes in for another haymaker, but the fist fight is quickly broken up by the guards, who take both Celly and Bobby the skinhead away. Celly is certainly a liar, though it's true that no one calls him one. Hell, just look at the guy.

"Everyone else, line up!" a prison guard shouts. "Laundry detail, who's pushing the delivery cart today?"

➤ Volunteer. Go to page 344
➤ Head back to your cell. Go to page 220

Lucas

After morning exercise you take a few minutes to sit and meditate before the students arrive for class. Breathing is measured, calm. The vitality in your muscles slowly fades, blood flowing, finally leaving your fists and feet to a more even flow. To the center—to calm. *Be mindful of your surroundings,* you tell yourself. *Of who you are today, at this brief stop on the journey of life.*

The mat beneath your sit bones feels firm, with springs just below the surface, waiting. Like you. *Ding!* the door chime announces your first student. Your eyes almost open in reflex, but you keep them shut.

"Good morning, Master Tesshu," a demure young voice says, huffing with excited breath.

"Haley, welcome. Please sit. Find your *Ki*."

You hear the shuffling of feet, a bag tossed to the side. The mat rocks slightly as the girl plops onto the floor on your right side.

"See you after," her mother says before the door chime dings once more.

They flow in like this; a stream of students. Nathanael, Christian, Mason, Nolan, and the twins: Liam and Stella. They may be the water, but you are the boulder that guides their path, and in return they too, shape you. Life made smooth by decades of students flowing through.

Finally, you open your eyes. Some students have theirs closed, emulating you. Nathanael makes eye contact, then quickly breaks it, blushing. He is the eldest in this youth Kendo class. He turns eighteen next week, when he will have to switch to adult Kendo Wednesday evenings. But for today, on a peaceful Saturday morning, he can blush like a schoolboy.

"Fascinating stuff," a woman says from the doorway. She's a young mother, not even thirty, and a small boy hides in her shadow. She continues, "Hi, there. I talked with the old man. This is Salvator; first day. Do you mind if I sit in?"

You smile. "Today. But today only. An atmosphere free of parental expectation is essential for growing confidence."

"You won't even know I'm here," she says, then finds a seat at the far wall.

"Sit, listen, learn," you say to the boy, who joins the others.

You let time pass, listening to the breath of the room. The calmness evaporates as commuter traffic out front erupts into a cacophony of screeching tires and car horns at the advent of a traffic jam.

"Mason, music, if you please."

The boy hops up, jogs over to the stereo, and presses "Play" on the ancient boombox. The pre-loaded CD doesn't try to drown out the traffic sounds, but instead blends recordings of running water, birds chirping, and meditation bells to create a more pleasant atmosphere.

"Much better. Now then...."

- "Around the room, what do you hope to learn today?" Go to page 346
- "The Kendo concept and purpose—do you remember them? Let's see." Go to page 206

Rosie

You run, crouched in a three-quarter squat, keeping your head down as best you can. The dirt kicks up beneath your heels and you slide into position behind the dilapidated barrier, like you're stealing home. The whole place screams *apocalypse*—rusted-out cars, paint-chipped walls, broken windows. You huff labored breaths behind your paintball mask, the condensation building up on the visor. It's not much in the way of protection, but it's better than nothing.

Once you're able to control your breathing, you realize there's another rasping sound—right behind you. You turn to see your younger brother Jason, his own mask upturned and a blank look on his face. His jaw is slack, showing off his braces-covered maw, tongue out slightly, his *moan* permeating the air. His arms rise up like Boris Karloff's mummy, and he staggers toward you.

- Brother or not, shoot him in the head. Go to page 162
- Rack him in the nuts, that'll make him snap out of it. Go to page 249

Sims

The belly of the C-17 rumbles over the Pacific as you rise from a nap, hoisting yourself up by the nylon webbing straps that run along the metal hull, and stretch your legs. Situated around the plane in other states of boredom-prevention are an odd jumble of soldiers, marines, SEALs, seamen, and airmen.

It's a strange collection of US military personnel, to be sure. In fact, no one onboard is from the same unit—even the flight crew, which is highly against regulations. The Top Secret classification of the mission, along with the extremely unusual nature of said mission, led to a joint operation where not one soul knew another. Which is how a USAF National Guard electrician ended up on this particular mission.

Makes it harder to drop the beans, you think.

Operation RAS-Putin: The mission, in which you helped give a free dose of *Gilgazyme®* to the Russki President, or Prime Minister, or whatever they're calling their elected dictator these days. Your job, simple as it was, involved showing the spooks how to cut security system wires and avoid the generic systems, like lighting. Then they planted the inhaler as if it were a gift from the founders of *Human Infinite Technologies*, and the megalomaniac did the rest himself. Bingo! Instant regime change.

Your stomach drops and you stumble with unsure footing. The C-17 is banking, you realize. What the hell? It should be a straight flight from Russia back home to the US. Why are they turning?

➤ Go ask the flight crew. Go to page 253
➤ Stay back here and ask the mission commander. Go to page 155

Tyberius

Shit, shit, shit! You only closed your eyes for a second, but you must've dosed off. Extra hours at the midnight call-center mean a few extra dollars come payday, but if you show up late to the bank (again), it'll mean your ass. That bank teller job is your bread-and-butter right now.

You slide on a new pair of undershorts and tank-top undershirt, spray Febreze on your workshirt, then pull on yesterday's slacks—all the while swishing mouthwash around. Shoes, money clip, bank ID, cell phone, and it's time to run out the door. The TV is on in the living room, but the couch sits empty.

"Mama?" you say, buttoning your white, Walmart-brand business shirt.

You flip off the TV and rush outside. There she is, back turned, bent down over the stoop, huddled over something you can't quite see. Shoulders straining, she digs with an intensity you're not used to; whatever she's after makes a wet, sucking sound as she pulls at it. She's filthy, you can see that, with some kind of dark muck caking her skin.

"Mama…?"

She turns slowly, giving you a good look at the open plot of ground. In one hand, there's a large kitchen spoon, full of fresh dirt. The stub of her right wrist is coated in the stuff. She sets down the spoon and wipes her left hand and her amputated right limb on her apron.

"Mama, what're you doing?"

"Gard'nin'," she says, drawing the word out in her thick Rwandan accent. "City-man waters this here. Gotta get up early if we want to replace them bushes with berry plants."

Have to hand it to her; the woman could fold a dollar in half and spend it as two. You laugh, then turn just in time to see your bus pass by. *Damn!*

"I'm makin' chicken and manioc tonight, okay?" she says, then seeing your panic, smiles and adds, "Go on, now. Best hurry! That bank can't run proper without my handsome boy."

You start to run, then dart back, kiss her on the cheek, and sprint back after the bus. It takes full, Olympian strides to catch up. Hurdling fire hydrants and juking past pedestrians, you fly down the sidewalk. The bus's emergency flashers come on as it prepares for the next stop.

"Wait! Hold the bus!" you cry.

A stuffy-looking old man glances your way, then quickly boards the bus in silence. You arrive just as it pulls away from the curb. Frantic, seeing the best-paying job you ever had disappear, you slap on the side of the bus and cry for it to wait. By some miracle, the bus stops. The door opens and you try to catch your breath as you board.

"Hey, thanks—" you start.

"Hit my bus again and it'll be your last ride," the bus driver says angrily. "Well? Let's go!"

The bus is nearly full; only two benches are empty. The first is two rows in, right by the asshole who ignored your calls for help. The other is in the last row in the back, just across from a sleeping homeless dude bundled up in a nest of blankets.

- ➤ Head to the back and get some sleep. It's a twenty-minute ride, so might as well take advantage. Go to page 176
- ➤ Stay up front, and make the guy who didn't say anything even more uncomfortable. Go to page 13

17 Forever

As you pull at the double doors, Nathanael turns to face you. His skin is sickly, with a decidedly anemic pallor. Even his eyes seem to have faded from blue to gray. You look to the wound on his side, but he keeps his gaze fixed on you.

Slowly, gently, like a doubting Thomas, you reach out and touch the hole in his ribcage. The boy makes no reaction. Indeed, there isn't even a rise and fall in his chest from breathing. He puts his hand on yours. You're shocked by the icy-cold touch of his skin, so you pull back in reflex.

He doesn't let go. Maybe you're projecting, but he looks concerned. Not nervous, like he often did over the years in class, but maybe…apologetic? He opens his mouth, and you expect him to say sorry, but it's a growling moan that comes out. Then, faster than he's ever moved while sparring, he pulls you toward that open mouth and whips his neck towards you.

You react quickly and execute a perfect break of the hold. Or what should have been a perfect escape maneuver, but his pain receptors must not be working, because he doesn't let go. Instead, he bites you right on the cheek. A fitting kiss goodbye.

You're INFECTED!

Access Denied

"Don't you need me to come in and pay?" the guy asks.

"Consider it an IOU," Owen says. "Good luck out there."

"Wait a sec. My boys out here dropped off some motorcycles. Can we get those too?"

"At least one of those is still in the garage," Stephen says in a voice low enough so the men outside can't hear.

Owen grimaces, unsure.

"You guys okay in there? Listen, we all need to help each other out, right? I've got a place with food and shelter. I could use some guys who know how to turn an engine," the man says.

"We don't have much food, boss. Let's strike a deal," Craig says.

Owen sighs, then looks to you.

- "Open it up. We can't stay in here alone forever. Josh needs a doctor anyway." Go to page 208
- "We already said no. Stick to your guns, boss." Go to page 319

Affronted

The guy makes a point to stare out the window, as if just looking at you might be dangerous. People suck, but you're used to it. Being tall, athletic, and black means dealing with people who cross the street when you approach. You see it as kind of like being a Rottweiler or a pit bull. Not dangerous by nature, but given a bad rap after a few highly-publicized incidents.

After a while you notice the bus isn't moving. You're not at a stop, you're just…stopped. When you look out the front, you see it's not a traffic signal. It's a sea of traffic. Beyond are military Humvees and police cruisers.

"Ah, hell," the driver says.

You have the same thought. Your boss won't stand for another day late, no matter the excuse. The bus driver opens the door and you look forward as a uniformed police officer boards the bus.

"What's goin' on?" the driver asks.

"This area is under military quarantine," the cop says in a low voice. The closest passengers murmur, but most of the others don't hear.

"Oh, lord. *Terrorists?*" the driver asks.

"I bet it's Anthrax," the old guy next to you says.

Someone stands up.

"Everyone remain in your seats!" the cop shouts, a hand on his piece. He looks scared. "We're evacuating the area in an orderly fashion," the cop tells the driver, his voice low again. "Stay on the bus, lock your doors, and you'll be safe."

The homeless dude in the back stirs, growling with anger. Or is that hunger? Then he lunges at the nearest passenger, who screams out. Yet instead of moving to help, the cop just goes for his radio.

"I'm on the Red B-Line bus now. Looks like they've already got infected on board, over," he says.

"Roger that. Take the driver's keys and we'll notify the National Guard to send in a containment team."

You've seen enough TV to pick up on the buzzwords and that conversation terrified you. No way you're staying on this bus.

➢ Head to the rear emergency exit and duck out. Go to page 119
➢ Rush past the cop. Go to page 77

Agh! Mazing*

You reach the entrance to *The Bramble,* a man-made wrought-iron "hedge-maze" with a sign boasting that this is the most difficult man-made labyrinth. *Great.* In order to keep the solution top-secret, the maze is covered so it can't be seen from the famous Ferris wheel or from any of the park's sky-high roller coasters.

The maze gets its name from the briar-patch theme, which gives you the ability to see movement from one path through the next, but you've got no chance of breaking through from one path to another. You're going to have to make it through the old-fashioned way—by getting lucky.

The opening forks with an immediate turn to the left, or a path straight ahead. You glance both ways, hoping for a clue, and see that they both appear to end in a bend, with more maze around each corner. With a full horde of the undead on your heels, you'd better get going. Where to?

➢ Left. (Go to #10)
➢ Straight. (Go to #2)

* *The subsequent numerical maze choices were randomly ordered for added difficulty. Good luck.*

1

Looking over your shoulder, you sprint down the long hallway, leading dozens of ghouls behind you. When you round the bend, you come to an end. The maze simply stops, but through the gaps in the metal briar you can see the way out from the other side. Freedom was almost in your grasp, but there's no way through the hardened barrier.

And no way back, either. The horde is upon you, and when they stumble-run into you with the force of a stampede, you're crushed against the brambles. You bleed out, but not before the ghouls make a meal of you. Don't worry, though, there won't be enough left of you to rise again.

THE END

2

You take great strides down the straightaway, then follow the path's bend around to the right. This leads to another immediate right and another straightaway. A forced left turn doubles into another, which opens into a long straight path. You sprint hard to the end of the hallway, expecting another bend, but it's an optical illusion.

The hallway's end looks just like those that lead to a bend in the maze, but this one's a dead end. You can see through the bramble into another path beyond, but there's no way to cut through. Instead, you have to run back in the opposite direction.

It's a long, flat path, then a winding snake of four turns before you finally make it back from the way you've come. By now, the hungry masses have flooded into the maze behind you, completely clogging the other routes. With a roof above you, there's no way out. The survivors have followed you in, but so have hundreds of zombies.

THE END

3

This path gives way to an abrupt right-hand turn. Once you round the bend, you're greeted with a flat wall—a dead end. Luckily, it was a short enough detour not to have cost you too much time, so you sprint back into the hall. Angelica sprints past, left to right. She clearly sees you, but keeps right on. Is she going the right way? Are you? Where to?

- Double-back left. (Go to #2)
- Double-back right. (Go to #12)
- Continue on right. (Go to #5)

4

Looking over your shoulder, you sprint down the long hallway, leading dozens of ghouls behind you. When you round the bend, you come to an end. The maze simply stops, but when you go to look through the gaps in the metal briar, you see it's just a hard left, half-hidden by the bramble.

"An obstacle illusion!" Sims shouts. And he's right, even if he did blunder the phrase. The truth is, if you hadn't practically stumbled into it, you'd never have seen the way out!

As you round the corner and free yourself from the maze, the undead masses plow into the bramble, skewering themselves upon the iron thorns. You can hardly believe you've made it out, but it's true! And you can see some others from your group, heading for the parking lot.

- Time to leave *The Funtastic Rockencoaster Adventure Park* for good. Go to page 94

5

The hallway ends with a forced bend around to the left, and then you're directly presented with a fork. Both paths curl away from one another, like a pair of opposing ram's horns. Behind you, throngs of zombies close in and the wretched brambles tear flesh off those who scrape against the maze wall. Better keep going—but which way?

- Left. (Go to #7)
- Right. (Go to #9)

6

The turn brings you to an end in the hall, and you're about to turn back when you realize that it's just a hard left, half-hidden by the bramble. *An optical illusion*, you think. You press forward, following the path around, and when you turn the corner—you're met head-on by a frenzied zombie.

He grabs hold of you, wrestling for your very life. When you're pulled against the scraping walls of the bramble, your uniform ripping in protest, it gives you an idea. You slam the ghoul's head against one of the enormous thorns, imploding his skull against the maze wall like a pumpkin dropped off a balcony.

If he beat you to this path, that means he was in the maze before you opened the emergency tunnels and let loose the horde. How long has that bastard been lost in here?

You check for the tears in your clothing and realize you've been bitten. Somehow, during the adrenaline-fueled struggle, you didn't even notice the pain. But the bite-marks are undeniable.

You're INFECTED!

7

This is the longest straightaway you've encountered so far, save for a new path to the right that opens about halfway down the hall. Should you keep going, or turn now?

- Straight. (Go to #5)
- Right. (Go to #3)

8

When you turn left, the path continues further and further, spiraling further to the left. It's like being trapped in one of those giant swirl lollipops. The trail narrows as you get closer to the center, the concentric circle spiraling inwards in a dizzying, hypnotist's path. As you're flushed to the inevitable middle, all you can hope for is a drain to release you from this turn.

Sorry, no such luck. It's a dead end, and you can already hear the marching hordes following your footsteps, coming ever closer. There's no way out, save for being carried out in the engorged stomachs of the undead.

THE END

9

The zombie horde is catching up now, with every moment's hesitation. The ghouls don't pause to make decisions; they go on *every* path, for they are Legion. The maze curls around to an immediate left, or a long lingering straightaway. One more decision, one more second lost to hesitation.

- Left. (Go to #6)
- Straight. (Go to #11)

10

The green-painted metallic vines that form the walls glitter under the artificial lights of the maze as you sprint forward. Before you make it to the end of this stretch, you pass a turn leading to the right. It's a longer straightaway than what lies before you, but also appears to end in a turn. Do you want to keep going or take this new path?

- Keep going. (Go to #12)
- Turn right. (Go to #7)

11

Dashing down the path, you're greeted by a winding curl in the maze. In true labyrinthine fashion, the hall curves alternately left and right, but you're never given a choice to leave. You must be making it!

All the while the horde is gaining on you. Each corner forces you to slow your run, while the ghouls simply slam against the brambles and bounce off of one another. Your running has them frenzied, and they fall over themselves at the excited prospect of catching you.

Finally, the hall opens up. There's a fork at the end, a wishbone with symmetrical paths leading in opposite directions. With the massive crowd of ghouls hot on your heels, you'd better pray that this coin-toss of a decision goes in your favor.

- Left. (Go to #4)
- Right. (Go to #1)

12

You rush forward and veer right around a bend in the maze, going the only way the path will allow. This leads to another immediate right turn in what is effectively a candy cane-shaped path. Once you make this second right, you're met with a dead end. Dammit! The undead fiends are certainly in the maze with you now, but you have no choice but to turn back.

Sprinting faster than you've ever run, you take two lefts to go back into the straightaway, where you see the flow of the dead enter the maze. You plow into the first zombie like a linebacker, knocking the 95-lb. woman onto her back. They crowd is still thin enough that you could blow past them and take the first path to the right, or you can turn left now and avoid them altogether.

➢ Straight/right. (Go to #2)
➢ Left. (Go to #7)

Agonizing

As fast as you can, you sprint off into the woods, as if you could run away from the images of Jason and blood seared onto your retinas. A *boom* sounds from the Ranger Station and you know that Jason did what you couldn't.

The agony, it's just…almost too much to bear. *No, keep running. Run, goddammit!*

Your jaw snaps together and you nip your tongue as you lose footing and step into a hole. Blinding pain rips through your right leg—your body tries to continue forward at a running pace, the heavy rucksack on your back helping propel you forward, while your foot is immobilized in the hole.

Flat on your face, tears streaming down into the dead leaves of the forest floor, you realize your leg is most likely broken. If not, then it's seriously sprained with multiple torn ligaments. Possibly all of the above.

You try to push yourself off the ground, but that just hurts too damn much. Crawling is nearly impossible with your pack on, and yet it contains all your food, all your ammo. There's no way you'll make it out here alone, broken, and without hope.

THE END

All the Light

You leave the dojo by yourself, knowing full well that Captain Delozier wouldn't appreciate this unauthorized stroll through the neighborhood. So you keep low and out of sight, and there are enough parked cars and obstacles that you're able to make it across the street without detection.

"What're you up to, bud?" a man calls down from the roof of the hardware store.

"Same as you, actually," you say with a grin. "Can I borrow a ladder? I want to get on top of my dojo."

The man is tall and lean, with coal-black hair. He's holding a rifle and doesn't respond right away, but after some thought says, "Yeah, I'm sure we've got an extra one downstairs. Hang on."

After a few minutes, the metal barrier that the man has erected behind the storefront glass opens and the man passes a ladder through. It's a small, telescoping model, but should extend enough to do the trick.

You thank the man, return to the dojo storefront, and set up the ladder. Once up on top, you're greeted with a different view of the city. There are no city sounds like traffic, just the occasional *pop* of distant gunfire. On the horizon, you see St. Mary's Hospital with a plume of smoke coming from one of the upper floors.

Your heart sinks, but then you remember why you're here. The boom box runs on auxiliary batteries, and as soon as you so much as touch the radio antenna to the larger roof structure, the message blooms with clarity.

"…it won't be our last, God willing. Any and all survivors are welcome to join us at the old reformatory off Route 14. I repeat, this is a transmission-only message; we are not currently capable of two-way communication. If anyone is out there, know that you're not alone. This is Colonel Arthur Gray of the civilian camp, Salvation, broadcasting in the blind. We have food and shelter and weapons. This may be humanity's greatest threat, but it won't be our last, God willing.…"

The message repeats on loop.

"I don't get it," Liam says in a whine.

"Me neeeev'r," Stella adds.

"Well, it means two things," you explain to the group. "First, the military isn't fully in control. If there are civilian camps broadcasting a general notice, they don't have everything contained. But—the good news—people are fighting back. Defending themselves, just like you were trained to do."

"And there will be a place to go when your parents come get you," Master Hanzo adds.

"It's where I'll find my sister," you say.

There's a tapping on the glass doors—dinner. You motion for the boys nearest the front to open the door, but as they do, Captain Delozier waves you over.

"A word," he says.

Hmm, does he know you broke out? Should you tell him about the message?

➢ Tell him. Go to page 36
➢ Don't tell him. Go to page 365

Always Faithful

"You know the Corps?" the man asks, his posture slackening ever so slightly.

You nod. "My Dad. And he's bit. We're trying to find a doc to help out."

The man sighs, then gestures toward the hallway beyond with a jerk of his head over his shoulder. "Go help your old man, and I'll pretend I didn't see you. I think I've got my hands full anyway."

You look to the two junkies, then back to the man, and nod your thanks. Where to next?

- ➤ The Morgue. When the dead are rising, it'll likely be the safest place here. Go to page 150
- ➤ ER. This is an emergency! Go to page 326
- ➤ Cafeteria. Maybe you can catch a doctor on break? Go to page 149

Anarchy in the Streets

"People are starting to panic. It's like a city-wide traffic stop, except enforced on the honor system because there aren't enough cops to go around. No one is allowed to move. People are staying in their cars, for now, but you can tell it's temporary. Some have already left. Started looting. Fighting each other for no reason."

"It's like *The Purge*," Nathanael says.

"Cool," Christian adds.

"How did you get through?" you ask, ignoring the teens.

"You're not the only ninja in the family, bro," she says, a glimmer of humor in her eyes that never fully manifests on her lips. "I got lucky, I really did. They're bringing in the military, Luke. The big guns—and they're using them."

"Shooting civilians?"

She shakes her head. "Not like that. The corpses…I don't know how else to explain it. The corpses came to life, or not life, I dunno. That's not my department, but when security managed to pin one down, the docs said no heartbeat, no blood flow, no pain, no emotion. Only hunger."

"Living corpses? Come on…"

"Yes, that's exactly what they are! You can stab one in the heart and it'll keep coming. The only way is to crush the skull," she says.

You close your eyes and think back to the homeless man. The way he didn't feel pain. His eyes—the only thing you saw in them—pure animal instinct. *Hunger.*

"Once bitten, it only takes someone six hours before they're a 'living corpse' themselves. I don't think the hospital will be there tomorrow, Luke. And we need to leave now before this barricade traps us all. Let's go!"

"Go? Go where?" You almost laugh at the sheer ridiculousness of it all.

"Haven't you been listening?! Away. Away from *people!*"

"Melissa, these kids' parents will come looking for them. We can't just—"

"Leave them here, then! Or put a note on the door. I don't care what you do, just come with me. Do you have any idea how dangerous it was for me to get here? The military is already setting up outside your front door!"

You can't just leave the kids here, you know that much.

➢ These are just kids! And you've got an old man with you. There's no way you can run. Go to page 136
➢ But maybe she's right? If you all gather and run for it while there's still time…. Go to page 29

An Offering

A dozen nuns (at least three of whom are named Sister Mary) wearing habits rummage through donations in the annex. A cursory inspection of the wares shows that most of the supplies are clothes and children's books. Not much that'll help, save for the canned food. But that won't last long when "homeless, sick, and needy" is becoming a bigger category by the minute.

"Are you here to help us sort?" one Mary asks.

"Or to protect the flock?" asks another Mary, eyes on your rifle.

"And maybe tend the wounded. Didn't you recently get certified, dear?" asks the third Mary.

You nod. "First aid. Mostly for drowning, but I can do basic triage."

"Is this all you've got?" Jason balks. "No real emergency supplies? No sandbags or flares? Surely you guys have a disaster preparation kit here somewhere."

Disappointment overtakes the nuns. At length, one says, "There is something...."

She steps to the back and gingerly lifts several layers of neatly folded cloth before she finds a smallish box, about the size of a cigar humidor. The nun carries the box with reverence, holding it up as if she's found the Holy Grail.

The box is sleek and modern, gun-metal blue. The word *Gilgazyme*® is etched on the metal and when she lifts the lid, a cool light shines from within. There's a single inhaler inside, though the perfectly sculpted velvet inlays tell you there used to be more.

"Thirteen of them," the sister says. "Each of us has taken one as a sacrament, and now one is left for you, Sarah. Join us as an immortal Bride of Christ. It will prevent the ravages of disease, and God willing, we'll be able to help the wounded without fear."

"Where'd you get it?" Jason asks with awe. He's right to hold the box in high esteem. There must have been a billion dollars' worth of product in there.

"It was here, in the donation bin, when we showed up this morning. Like manna from Heaven. We were meant to have it. We've prayed for help and guidance, and this is the answer to those prayers. Do you feel this is the path the Lord has for you? To help heal the sick?" she asks, taking your wrist, and placing the *Gilgazyme*® in your palm.

The inhaler is minimally decorated; no words, only the symbol of infinity, ∞, repeated and interlocking like chain mail in shining silver décor around its light blue slender body. Over the mouthpiece is a red cap labeled, "Remove before use."

➢ Say, "I'd better, ummm, pray about this first. C'mon, Jay. Let's check the main hall." Go to page 287
➢ Politely decline, then find the priest and check on Dad. Go to page 272
➢ Take it. Immunity to the plague? This is divine providence. Go to page 130

The Art of Words

"**E**xcuse me?" Delozier says.

"With respect, I would be betraying the trust of these children's parents if I simply handed them over. No matter how pure your motives, Captain."

"I don't think you grasp what we're fighting here. This is an infection that creates—and I don't use this word lightly—*zombies*. People come back from the dead—and again, being literal here—they then try to eat each other. I'm offering the protection of soldiers."

"And I am politely declining. Would it not be easier for you if we stay here? Less to protect, less to watch over. I am capable of defending this dojo, and would be more than happy to give you a demonstration if you persist in your demands."

He presses his pointer finger against your chest. You can picture snatching it, pulling his arm taut, twisting it over and delivering a blow with your other hand to help his elbow find a new direction to bend. Instead, you wait and listen.

"This is on you, then," he says at length.

"It is the same life, whether we choose to spend it laughing or crying."

The proverb hangs in the air and the man shakes his head before turning to leave. One of the soldiers gives you a nod of respect before following his boss outside. Once the doors are closed, Nolan locks up.

"Oh, em, gee," Haley says. "That guy was like, ready to shoot us."

"And sensei told him to screw off," Nathanael adds.

"Language!" you scold.

"That was *awesome!*" Christian says.

"Enough. I will take responsibility for you, but ultimately, you must protect yourself. We must train. Back to positions."

Later that night, Captain Delozier returns with a peace offering: Boxed meals.

"That took a set of brass ones," he says. "But it was the right call."

"Thank you, sir."

"Since you can't leave, I've added you to my headcount for meals. We'll bring food rations for breakfast and dinner. There's a couple staying in the hardware store across the street as well, and they owe that generosity to you. Oh, and do us both a favor. Turn out the lights for the night. Tends to attract these things like skeeters to a bug zapper. G'night," the man says before leaving.

"I think we have some candles in the office," Master Hanzo says.

"We can roll out the pads and use them as sleeping mats. It will be like camping," you say, keeping a smile for the children.

"Can we tell ghost stories?" Mason asks.

"Master Hanzo knows many traditional stories. Grandfather, tell us…

- ➢ "…about the carp's lesson in perseverance?" Go to page 58
- ➢ "…about the Emperor consumed by his own greed?" Go to page 102
- ➢ "…how the warrior Yogodayu won his battle?" Go to page 30

Assault and Prepper

FROM: PreppyLongStalking69
TO: Distro-all; zombiefiend.com
SUBJECT: See? I wasn't crazy!
TEXT: To all you doubters, nay-sayers, and haters, prepare to be shrugged off. I knew this would happen. I fucking knew it! When you're being eaten alive by the living dead, just remember, if you wouldn't have been such a dick, you might have survived too. Sent from my compound.
TL;DR: I told you so!

So yeah, that's waiting for you in your inbox. Makes it easy to find the thread from the username, and *PreppyLongStalking69* left Google maps images of said compound online. What. An. Idiot. In two clicks, you're on your way. The waypoint takes you, as expected, out in the middle of nowhere.

The Camry doesn't have the best off-road clearance, but hey, you're a divorced sergeant. Money is tight. Or was, back when money was important. Now, all that matters is being prepared. So in a sense, you're rich now. *Silver linens!* The dirt road isn't too bad, even in the dark, and you bump along with ease before the compound comes into view.

A large, newly plowed and seeded tract of land and a modular home sit like a glorious beacon in the moonlight. It's got everything—a well, horse stables, remote location, even solar paneling. Guy was certainly prepared.

A dozen para-military vehicles sit parked out front; looks like a few others had the same idea. There's a Jeep in the ditch alongside the road with a shattered windshield and bloody interior. When you park and step out of the Camry, you see several of the vehicles parked out front have bullet-holes as well. Just off to the side are several large mounds of fresh dirt; each one is about 7'x3'.

"Nice gas-mask," a voice calls from upstairs. "What was your username?"

He's standing up on the balcony, assault rifle in hand. More survivalists come out from the compound. You swallow hard and say, "*Ninja-Guidon*."

"Ahhh, I remember arguing with you a few times. I'm *Rebel_Yell_1997*, but you can call me Duke," he says. When you don't respond, he continues, "Look, *Ninja-G*, I'll level with you, we got enough fat white guys here already."

"No, I totally get it. That being the case, I'll just be on my way, so…"

"Not so fast. We can always use more supplies, and from what I recall, you were a regular. I'm guessing you brought us a nice care-package, yeah?"

"Is that all this was?" you say, trying to buy time, and angle towards the M4. "You invented *Preppy Long Stalking* and catfished other survivors into bringing you their gear?"

The man grins. "Nah, *the Prepster* was real, and served as the bait, we just came and put the hook on. You're the third forum member to show up."

His eyes go to the mounds of dirt. There's no way you're getting out of here alive, so you might as well take out as many asshole rednecks as you can. He wants a donation? *Time to donate some lead to this motherfucker!* You claim the M4 and go down in a blaze of glory.

THE END

At a Loss

After a few hours' walk on a beautiful sunny day, you arrive at the Ranger Station. The parking lot has several official park vehicles, as well as a school bus and a decked-out Cadillac Escalade. The bus is gray with red trim and has "Boy Scout Troop 1408" stenciled on the side. The Caddie is midnight-blue and fresh from a detail; clean even in the wilderness, it looks like something off *Pimp My Ride*.

That's when you hear the crying. It's wailing; a weeping despair that permeates the still of nature. For some reason, you think of a mother who's lost a child. Jason shivers and rubs away goosebumps.

The front door is unlocked; a simple push/pull—no handle or knob. You're not sure how smart Zulu are, but part of you hopes that any inside pushed their way out, and any outside couldn't figure out how to pull their way in.

When you slowly open the door, the weeping grows in intensity. Despite the sunshine out in nature, it's dark and cold inside the building.

"Do Zulu cry?" Jason whispers. "Because I need to shoot whoever that is."

You clear a lump from your throat, ready your weapon, and say, "Hello?"

The crying stops. *Great*, you think, the lump returning.

"If there's someone here, show yourself," you say.

"We're here to help, but we're armed," Jason adds.

There's a sniffling from the back office and then a meek voice says, "Please, it's not safe. They're still here."

You step over to the office door, which has a chest-high section of safety glass. A woman appears before you, and you try not to jump. She's a park ranger, her uniform smattered with gore and her face red from crying.

"That rap star guy—his people brought him here. He was sick. He took that new drug, and… They brought him here. Then the children, oh God…."

You turn back to gauge Jason's reaction and catch sight of a small shadow behind him. A kid hiding under the table? Your heart jumps.

"Look out!" you cry.

Jason flips around with his shotgun shouldered, but too high. The kid lunges at your brother's legs. Jason stumbles back, kicking at the kid.

When the hellion comes back, you finally get a good look at him in the light from the doorway. He's a scout, in uniform, and definitely Zulu. Trying to earn his devour-the-flesh-of-the-living merit badge.

You dart forward and raise your rifle. The kid chews on a section of fabric torn from Jason's pants. Dead-eyed, but enjoying the taste of your brother's scent. *Crack*—you shoot the tyke in the head. The Ranger screams from the office.

Jason clutches his thigh, where blood pools out between his fingers. He looks up to you and says, "Awww, fuck monkeys. Now what?"

➢ Don't draw it out, like with Daddy. Shoot your brother and be done with it.
  Go to page 116
➢ Ask the Ranger for a first-aid kit. It might just be a scratch…right?
  Go to page 268

Away from the Herd

"Christ, lady. You got a death wish, that's on you," Hefty says. "C'mon, Ty. We ain't wanted here."

Tyberius looks saddened, but follows his friend away. Angelica has the same *lost puppy* look, though she follows you as the group splits ways. Jose simply waits patiently for your next move. You could use a dozen like him, that's for sure.

"I don't know that we need to be *that* careful," Angelica says.

"Exactly. You don't know. But I'll tell you this: Good, gentle people were probably the first to die. If you're the kind of person who sticks your neck out to help your neighbor, you'll get a bite to the jugular as thanks."

You continue walking through the zoo in silence until a zebra crosses in front of you.

"*Qué?*" Jose says.

The zebra looks back, then takes off in the opposite direction. How the hell did a zebra get out? You look to the zebra, to Jose and Angelica, then to the shadow on the pavement. You turn back just in time to see something yellow and black leap from the top of the ice cream shack. As the leopard pounces, you raise the wrench to defend yourself, but you've got no chance against this apex predator.

Oh, and poor choice of last words.

THE END

B&E

The pipe goes through the glass like you're only clearing cobwebs. Once it's shattered, you can simply reach in, unlock the doors, and let yourself in. After you smash the glass of the inner set of doors, an alarm kicks off. *Dee-doo, dee-doo, doo-doo. Shit, shit, shit.*

You step in with the pipe raised, ready for more nutters, but your senses are thrown off by the wailing alarm and the darkened store. Better get that turned off posthaste.

When you open the doors and head in, a shadow steps forward, arm raised, a police baton in his hand. It's too dark to get any details.

- Fuck him up. Shoot first, ask questions later. Go to page 339
- Call out for a truce. Nutters don't hold weapons. Go to page 35

Backing Out

You lock the dojo from the inside and consider leaving a note, but Melissa's impatience wears on you. Breathing deeply, you find a measure of calm, but that evaporates as soon as you head out the back door.

It's a thin road, the kind that's perpetually wet and cold from a lack of sunlight and natural drainage, built to house each of the business's dumpsters. If you were to run to the left, it would lead toward St. Mary's Hospital.

Heading right, the alley opens into another street full of shops: a tattoo parlor, a payday loans building, a strip club, and a liquor store. You don't often see this side, and less often do you *really* look at it. When you were a child, coming to this very spot for your own Kendo training, you rode a bicycle to and from class. On the day you passed the level three test, you celebrated at an ice cream parlor where the tattoo shop now sits. Not long ago, the strip club was an arcade. Before that, it was a dressmaker. *Change is the way of the world*, you tell yourself.

"Damn, we're too late!" your sister yells.

Snapping out of it, you see that the area is already barricaded by the military, and now the National Guard soldiers head towards you.

"Stay where you are!" one booms from behind his gasmask.

"Our only chance is to run for it," she says.

"Melissa, look around you! Master Hanzo can't run. We have children!"

"They can't catch us all."

"*No*," you growl. Then to the children, "Stay together, live together."

"Obey your sensei," Hanzo adds.

A terrible sadness washes over your sister's face. "We'll meet again, Luke. In this life or the next."

"Don't...."

"Come find me," she says, then takes off running.

"*Imouto!*"

The soldiers are upon you now, but their attention turns to Melissa. One frightened young man raises his rifle. Not even thinking, you step in front of his weapon.

"Outta the way!" the man shouts.

"Infected don't run," another soldier says.

That seems to work, and the first soldier lowers his rifle.

"We're taking you to the containment camp," a third says. "You'll be safe there."

➤ *Go quietly, for the sake of your group.* Go to page 183

Battle of the Bees

The students gather in a semi-circle while Master Hanzo bites on his empty pipe. He clears his throat, closes his eyes, and begins, "This story takes place almost a thousand years ago, when Japan was very much a wild place. To this day, the mountains of Kasagi remain wild, and with it, the memory of Yogodayu's victory. But victory was not always assured. Yogodayu had a feud with his wife's brother, who attacked Yogodayu's fort and sent him, badly beaten, into the mountains for safety. Yogodayu—"

"That's a funny name," Liam says.

"Shhh!" some of the other kids say before you have the chance to shush him yourself.

"Yogodayu had only twenty-some warriors with him, and he greatly feared that his brother-in-law would come to finish him off. While he was hiding in the caves, he found a bee trapped in a spider's web struggling to get free. But no matter how much the bee tried, it only seemed to become tangled further.

"Yogodayu took pity on the bee, and, as he cut it loose, said, 'Be free! It is always good to grant freedom to others, even when you yourself are pursued.'

"That night, Yogodayu dreamt of a man in yellow and black robes who came to him and said, 'It is I, the bee you rescued! And now I want to help. Collect as many jars as you can, and the next time your enemies attack, the bees of the wild will be with you.'"

"I knew it was the bee," Haley says.

"So Yogodayu told his men of the dream and they each went to their home villages to recruit more warriors and to bring back jars to the fort. They gathered eighty men, but thousands of jars, and the bees came down from the mountains to live in the jars. Yogodayu's brother-in-law heard word of the gathering warriors and came to attack again.

"This time, they released the bees. There were three thousand bees per enemy and the attackers quickly fled, some losing their minds."

"The moral," you add, "is to always help those in need, for you too will need help one day."

"Goodnight," Master Hanzo says.

The old man abruptly extinguishes the candles with a sweep of his robe, and the room goes dark. The children whisper to themselves for a time, but eventually you all fall fast asleep.

Sometime in the middle of the night, you're awakened by an urgent pounding on the doors. It takes only a brief moment to exit the dream-state of sleep before the memories of what's out there come flooding back.

It's an urgent, almost animal-like intensity, rapping upon the door, pulling at the handles and groping for a way in. With no streetlights, you can't see who it is—or *how many*—out in the shadowy black of night. A huffing voice shouts something, but you can't make out any words, or be certain there are any to make out.

➢ Leave the doors closed. You can't defend against a mob with a wooden sword. Go to page 341

➢ Open the doors. Bushido demands you help any way you can. Go to page 408

Bearing Down

Turns out there are no Humvees with military bearing. Not any with open seats, anyway. If you don't want to get left behind, you'll have to find an alternate form of transportation. Time being of the essence, you end up taking your trusty old Toyota Camry.

You manage to pull in behind the last Hummer just as the convoy departs. The gunner swivels around to aim the .50 cal your way, and you frantically wave so the team will ID you as friendly. It's Captain Nobody and his psychotic gunner, Simecek. *Great.*

Luckily, he doesn't shoot. At you, anyway. He does, however, open fire at a crowd of fleshies too far off in the distance, wasting ammo and drawing more undead to the commotion.

"Jackass!" you cry.

A figure stands on the roof of a hardware store, a hunting rifle in one hand, slashing a *Kill the commotion!* gesture with the other. Simecek opens fire at him as well. That's when you notice the woman on the roof. In one smooth motion, Hardware Man drops to one knee, aims down the scope, and hits Simecek with a headshot.

It's chaos. Other Guardsmen open fire at the hardware store, and the drivers all take evasive action. The bulk of the convoy runs into a concrete flood drain. Keeping your head down, you follow.

The Hummers take the concrete canyon easily enough, but no such luck for your Camry. The tires can't find purchase on the algae sludge that coats the base of the runoff, and your front-wheel-drive sedan spins sidewise and gets caught against the edges of the drain, pinned bumper-to-bumper.

The convoy leaves without you.

Not ready to accept that your car is caput, you gun the engine. Terrible shrieks come from the tires, but no traction. Might as well be a dinner bell. The undead come tumbling down the sides of the steeply-sloped ditch, but they're quick to rise again.

Taking the M4 in hand, you stay hunkered down in the ravine, not sure if Hardware Man is still up there taking headshots or not. Would it be so bad if he were? Better than being eaten alive, surely.

You sprint up the side of the ditch, but the scum coating the ravine sends you sliding back into the arms of two dozen ghouls. There won't be enough left of you to rise again.

THE END

Beaten

You flip the cot and disconnect one of the legs. The cot was designed to be collapsible, so the metal beams separate with ease. You weigh the beam in your hand to assess the possibility of the new bludgeon. That'll do.

By now the fiend is right on top of you, so you lash out with an uppercut to the jaw. The former woman staggers back, then moans. Not with pain, but excitement. She wants you, and she wants you *bad*. Her movements are random, though predictable—she's coming right for you.

You leap off the ground, adding as much of your weight to the blow as you can, and slam the club against her head. Other people in the tent are awake now, and a few are screaming.

The screams bring in the guard from outside, and he stands with his rifle at the ready. "Another two *Turned*," he says into a chest-radio. "Go for a transfer to aggressor tent."

In response, four more soldiers rush in. The woman is already down—you've seen to that—so the soldiers focus on you. One drags her corpse while the others fight to immobilize you. You think they're just trying to break up the conflict, so you don't put your full effort into resisting, but it's enough that they switch to beating you with their rifles.

The three men drag you out of the tent and through the military compound, back to an alley where two other guards let you pass. Once you make it through, you find yourself among dozens of bodies—some charred and burned, but most freshly dead.

"Wait..." you cry, but they're not listening. Apparently they're unable to make any discernment between an aggressor and one who's *Turned*. Either that or they just don't care.

The men open fire.

THE END

Be Careful What You Wish For

The doctor nods, still obviously shaken, then leaves the tent without another word. Ten minutes later, a dozen soldiers enter, each carrying a set of vehicle strap-downs. One man shouts, "Listen up! For your own protection, lie down on your cot, arms by your side and *do not move*. Any movement will be taken as aggression and will be dealt with harshly."

This is *not* what you had in mind. But with a dozen armed men, what choice do you have? They use their straps to bind you to your cots, despite your protests that you're not infected. They're the kind of thick nylon belts you usually see securing goods on the back of flatbed trucks, and the soldiers ratchet them down tight.

Once finished, they turn off the lights and leave you in darkness, nothing for comfort but the labored breathing of your fellow patients. Eventually, that just becomes white noise. At some point, as boredom sinks in and adrenaline sails off, you fall asleep. You really weren't planning on sleeping tonight, but despite your best efforts, sleep comes. Exhaustion has a way of doing that.

You have a nightmare that you're in church with mama and the choir is singing, but you can't understand the words. You know she wants you to sing along, and you don't want to disappoint, but you can't tell what they're saying. It's not even in English; it's not in any language. It's *moaning*. A chorus of the damned.

When you wake up, everything is still dark, but the soft low moans from your dream are here with you. At least they can't get to you, right?

…right?

- ➤ Call out for the doctor. Go to page 261
- ➤ Stay quiet, don't move. Go to page 128

Bell of the Ball

You give the man your best *sultry eyes* and rise from the table. Sashaying over, you say, "You're right. I am impressed. You must have big brass balls to pull off something like this."

"Well...thanks," Duke says, surprised.

"It might just be the wine going to my head, but—can I see them?"

"What?"

"Those big balls of yours."

"Look, I can tell you're fucking with me," he says, laughing nervously, his tone suggesting he can't tell. At all.

You're his dream girl; he has clearly fantasized about you, so it doesn't take much to be putty in your hands. When you get on your knees and go for his belt buckle, his eyes go wide. Focused on his own swelling manhood, he doesn't notice when you go for the toenail clippers from your boot.

"God, I've waited for this moment," Duke groans.

"Ever since you said...what was it?"

"Give my left nut for a date with you."

"Consider the debt paid," you say, severing the connecting flesh with the nail clippers.

Duke howls out in pain while blood and other clear fluid pools out from the wound. His hands go to his crotch in pain and then he tries to punch at you, but the strain makes it worse and he tips his chair and falls to the floor.

The door opens just as you take Duke's steak knife and tuck it into your boot. Bud has his handgun drawn and aimed at you. You offer your hands and a confused look.

"I don't know what happened; he just fell," you say.

Bud holsters the handgun and goes for his boss. As Bud kneels, Duke groans in pain, trying to tell Bud to kill you through pained, gritted teeth. So you put the steak knife in Bud's spine before the message sinks in. Bud falls atop Duke in an almost humorous position. Might make the other men who find them pause.

Time to go.

➤ Straight out into the woods, right now. A dress isn't best, but time is of the essence. Go to page 370
➤ Back to the stalls. Take Bud's key and get back in your riding clothes before you go. Go to page 397

Besties

"Christ, you almost gave me a heart attack," the man shouts over the alarm.

You keep backing up until your prison tennis shoes crunch on the entry glass. He follows and finally, you get a good look at the guy. He's a young black man with strikingly intelligent eyes. He wears a businessman's shirt and holds a policeman's baton in his right hand.

"You some kinda cop? Like security, errr…."

"Fuck, no," he says. Then, noting your prison jumpsuit, adds, "You some kinda psycho killer?"

"Ain't psycho, but I've had to put some a' them nutters down."

"The infected?" he asks.

You nod. He looks away and swallows hard. "Guess we all have."

"Can we shut this goddamned alarm off?"

"Lemme see your pipe," he answers.

You hesitate, but if he wanted to hit you, he would have already. There was a lot of racism back in prison, but everyone had to do what they did to survive. Out here, survival means one race—human. He takes the pipe and steps over to the side, where there's a locked fuse box. With a great slam of the pipe, he unlocks it, finds the right switch, and shuts off the wailing alarm.

"How'd you know to do that?" you ask.

"We have the same setup at my job," he says, handing back the pipe. "Thanks. I'm Ty, by the way. Tyberius, but to my friends it's just Ty."

"Mine call me Hefty," you say, though in truth, you haven't had a real friend in over two years.

He nods. "When's the last time you ate?"

"Today, why? Oh…yeah, I always been this skinny. I could use some sleep though. We could run together, if the jumpsuit don't put you off. I'll watch your back, you watch mine. Deal?"

The man thinks about it for a minute, then his eyes grow distant. He says, "My brother wore one of those once, so no, I don't mind. But I'd need a favor. I need to drop off a dress somewhere. We can look out for each other, and if you don't ask me what it's for, I won't ask about what you did to survive, neither. We leave the past where it belongs."

A dress? He doesn't seem to want to elaborate, so you don't push it. Oh well. You're beyond exhausted, and if he makes sure you don't get chomped by nutters while you sleep, then it's worth an errand. Besides, what else you got planned?

The future, for the first time in a coon's age, seems bright. Funny that it took the world falling apart to feel that way. It's almost like being reborn, in a sense. You can have a new life—one in which you were never a con. This Tyberius guy seems ready to let the past stay buried, so why not?

"I'd best get a change of clothes, then," you say.

Go to page 160

The Best Policy

As soon as you've stepped outside and closed the doors, you go right into it. "I know, I went outside while we're supposed to be under quarantine, but—"

"Wait, you did *what*?"

"—but if you'll listen to why—"

"Un-fucking-believable," he says, not listening, "My guys have been shooting to kill in areas we've already cleared of survivors. The only people dumb enough to walk through a hot zone are the infected. But you know what? Doesn't matter anymore."

He looks to you, but you decide not to humor him with the "Why not?" he so desperately craves. At length, he continues, "We're leaving tomorrow."

"Oh? The quarantine is being lifted?"

"The quarantine has *failed*," he says, shaking his head. "The whole city is screwed, maybe elsewhere too. You'll get breakfast, then we're evacuating to the hospital and pulling out."

The man stares, hoping for a reaction, but you've trained hard to be the stone that lets the water flow past.

"There is a survivor camp outside of town, I heard them broadcast on the radio."

"Yeah? You should probably go."

"My responsibility is to my students."

"Their parents are probably dead," he says, unblinking.

You look back through the glass doors into the dojo, where the children are watching. Hopefully they can't hear, but just in case, you decide to cut it short. "Thank you for letting me know, Captain. Good luck with your evacuation."

"Sure. See you in the morning."

One last supper, one last breakfast. Then what?

➢ Stay in the dojo and wait for the parents to come. Go to page 201
➢ Head out once the barricades are lifted and take your pupils home. Go to page 282
➢ Go straight for this "Salvation." He's right; the parents are probably dead. Go to page 126

Best Served Cold

You don't own a car (hence taking the bus to work), so it looks like you'll have to borrow one. Mrs. Alaina next door owns a large Buick, so it should be worth your time to stop by. Besides, seeing as how she's the one that got mama infected, you owe her a visit anyhow.

But when you arrive outside her apartment, you're struck with hesitation; your hand hovers over the door handle—coated in your mother's blood.

Turning your pants pocket inside-out, you use it as a handkerchief to grab the handle, which sticks to the fabric. The door groans as you open it, a sound that blends with the moan of the occupant. She's not trying to hide or trick you; she stands right on the other side of the door, waiting. Only, it's not Mrs. Alaina. It's your mother. Mama comes for you once more.

When she raises two hands, the illusion breaks. You crack her in the forehead with the police baton just in time and she stumbles back under the blow, but that doesn't stop her.

When she comes back you shove the black baton in her mouth. She bites down, so you release the weapon, take her head in your hands, and lift her into the air. With the same ease as handling a doll, you aim at a corner of the kitchen counter and slam her head down against it, ending the woman.

The corpse falls limply to the floor. When you take your baton, it has teeth marks on it. Mrs. Alaina is your mother again, so you look away. *What's the point anymore?* She screams. *How can you live with yourself after this?*

You shake your head to clear it. It's not her yelling at you. Still, you feel hollow. If you didn't have this funeral idea, you'd probably still be back home, numb, not sure what to do next.

You see one of those pill containers, split by day of the week, holding all of Mrs. Alaina's medication. She was an older woman, so there are a *lot* of pills. How hard would it be to wash the whole collection down with a glass of water from her sink? End the pain once and for all. Rejoin mama.

No, you tell yourself. If you go now, who will bury her? So you continue searching, trying not to listen to the voice that says, *But maybe after...? Wouldn't it be nice just to sleep and never wake up?*

Bingo—keys are in the woman's purse by the door and ready to go.

By the time you arrive at the outskirts of the mall, the sun is setting. You'll probably have to stay the night here, especially with that crowd still following. It should be defensible, though, because this mall sits outside of town, purchased while land was still cheap. Several construction sites are under development and just beyond that awaits the shopping mall with a large "Grand Opening!!!" sign. Brand-spanking new.

The nearest part of the mall happens to be a department store, and you figure they're all basically the same, so long as they have a menswear department for your suit and a place to get mama a nice dress.

- ➢ Go for the service entrance, where they unload new items. It's out of the way and should have less chance of trouble. Go to page 324
- ➢ Go for the main doors. The double-wide glass doors should let you see if anyone's inside. Go to page 301

Big Bad Piggies

The National Guard soldiers rush in and smoke fills the store. No, not smoke, *tear gas*. A canister lands dead center of the helpdesk you're hiding behind. Immediately your eyes burn and a gallon of mucous pours out of your nose.

You need to get outside—now! With a wailing cry, you rush past the gasmask-clad men and out into the open. Though you're no longer in the cloud of tear gas, it sticks to your skin and face. You bend over, hands on your knees, and vomit.

Someone comes over to comfort you and puts an arm around you. Then they bite into you.

You're INFECTED!

Blazing Irony

You use the fire extinguisher to start a fire. It doesn't take much, once the chemical reaction gets going and liquid flames pour out over the floor in a flood. The overhead sprinklers kick on, but after a moment they sputter, then groan and quit. Someone must have shut off the main water line.

That slight kick of H_2O seems only to have made the fire angrier. You rush forward now, keeping the fire extinguisher handy.

There's a clear path up ahead, relatively speaking, as the nutters rush in from the eaves with every second. You can see the front door leading out of the infirmary. It's a secure barrier with a small window of mesh-inlaid safety glass.

Off to the right a trio of undead paw at an office—with a guard and a doctor captive within.

- Help the guys out. Burning alive is a fate no man deserves. Go to page 111
- Keep going! It'll only be clear for a few more moments. Go to page 50

Bloodbath

Once the doctor leaves, you formulate your plan. The woman in the corner is going to *Turn* first, so she's priority one. With all those blankets, you could just suffocate the infected lady, hopefully without raising too much attention. Most everyone in here is asleep or otherwise highly incapacitated.

Still, you'll need a weapon for the others.

They've done their best to rid the tent of exactly that, so you'll have to get creative. The vomiter's metal pail could do some damage, but probably just as much to you with its contents. The wall barriers are metal too, but a quick inspection shows the welding is much too strong to pull apart bare-handed.

Leaning back on your cot, you feel the metal crossbeam shift under your thighs. You flip the cot and disconnect one of the legs. The cot was designed to be collapsible, so the metal beams separate with ease. You weigh the beam in your hand to assess the possibility of the new bludgeon. That'll do.

When you walk across the tent towards the infected woman, many eyes turn to follow you, so you make a show of asking after the woman's well-being. Under the guise of a caring soul, the other occupants of the tent go back to ignoring you.

To keep up the ruse, you talk to the woman as you bunch up the thick woolen blankets and smash them down over the woman's mouth. After a few quiet seconds, she starts to thrash, so you press harder.

"What's going on?" the guy behind you asks.

"Uhhh…seizure…"

"I'll get the doctor."

"No, don't! I got it under control. Here, uhhh, come help."

The man comes to your side just as the woman goes limp. He looks to you, slowly putting it together. That's when you lash out with the cot leg and catch the man on his temple. He doesn't even have a chance to scream, he just falls to the ground. Two more quick thumps with the club and the man's legs twitch with his death rattle.

That's when other people in the tent start to scream.

You attack the nearest woman and the cheap, hollow aluminum bends under the blow. Frustrated, you go for another club from the nearest cot while the others run from you.

A gasmask-clad guard rushes in, then clutches his chest radio. "One of the infected is *Turned*; I'm on it."

He raises his rifle and fires. You flinch, but you're unharmed. When he shoots again, you see he's aimed past you. Looking back, you see the woman you just suffocated has risen from her cot and now takes a bullet in the head as the guard finally shoots her.

"The black guy! He's *Turned* too!" someone shouts. Others agree.

The guard swings his rifle to you and you open your mouth to speak, but before you get a chance, the muzzle sends out a plume of flame as he fires.

THE END

Blow Your House Down

You flip the light switch and drop behind the desk. For a split-second, you think you actually turned some lights on because of the bright flash, but then the ear-splitting roar of the explosion registers.

It's like the air has been sucked from the room, and you gasp for breath. Pressure differential? Maybe, but either way you're wheezing like someone punched you in the chest, and your ears are ringing. When you look up, there's just a heap of rubble where the metal doors once stood, and the linoleum floor is coated in debris—both from the storefront and from those who stood here only a few moments ago.

There's a finger lying on the countertop of the helpdesk, pointing right at you. Bile rises in your throat and you rush upstairs for some fresh air. Sam Colt reloads his rifle while Lily sits by one of your garden boxes, closely examining the soil.

Sam says, "They had it coming. They were deserters, and they wanted the store."

"Deserters?" you parrot dumbly.

"They were assigned to the hospital, but it's overrun. They only wanted to help themselves—to what's ours."

"To what we stole first, you mean," Lily says, not looking up from the garden.

"It was us or them," he says, though it's directed at you.

"It *is* us or them," Lily says, standing up and dusting her hands off on her pants. "But the 'them' should be the fucking fifty-percent infected and the 'us' should be *people*."

"Should be."

The air hangs silent.

"If the hospital is gone, and the military just…quit," you say. "How long will it be fifty-percent? What's the next increment or whatever?"

Lily laughs, a cold, bitter laugh. "There isn't one. The next order of magnitude is one-hundred-percent infected."

"That's not true, and you know it. We can hold out," Sam says.

"Sure. It's not a hundred. But it's ninety-nine-point-nine, nine, nine, nine, nine—"

"Okay, we get it!" Sam yells.

"We need to stick together," you say, at barely a whisper.

And it hits you hard that mama is out there, alone, with no one to help her while the whole city falls apart.

"I need to get my mom," you say, adding:

- ➤ "I'm going now, while the soldiers are distracted." Go to page 170
- ➤ "I'm going tonight, under the cover of darkness." Go to page 139

Boob Tube

You follow Sam and Lily back down to the hardware store and into the manager's office. It has a TV mounted on the wall and Lily offers the boss's chair for you to sit in. The screen comes to life and FOX News plays, mid-broadcast. TV personality Bill O'Reilly is giving his opinion on hand-picked news, as usual.

"...you know that I did, I always said he was a bit strange. Still, I can't say I saw *this* coming. If there are children in the room, I recommend not watching. We did our best to clean up the footage, but it's still graphic. The following has never aired and is a FOX News exclusive. Our source says this was recorded in preparation for tonight's broadcast."

Meanwhile, the ticker at the bottom of the screen is listing states where the governors have declared a state of emergency and cities that are now under martial law. You look for your city as you listen. When the screen changes to show Stephen Colbert at his desk addressing the camera, your attention shifts off the ticker and onto his face.

His skin is pale, eyes sallow. There's something odd about his expression, like he can't decide if he's angry or just bored. It's the face of someone waiting at the DMV who just found out they'd been waiting in the wrong line all morning.

Jennifer Lawrence sits in the guest seat, nervous. She's looking around as if for help. The camera zooms in on Colbert, who sits unblinking.

"Stephen? We're rolling," a voice says from somewhere off-screen. "Stephen, don't you want to ask about *X-men? Hunger Games? The Oscars*, maybe?"

Colbert's lips part and his voice comes out as a hoarse whisper. The news broadcast provides subtitles, because it's nearly impossible to hear. He says, "Live forever? Why? What...is there? At some point it's just eat, sleep, sh—t. Eat, sleep, sh—t. Eat...sleep...sh—t...."

"...eat...

"...sleep...

"...sh—t...."

FOX bleeps his curse words as Colbert continues the phrase like a mantra. His words become less like speech and more like growls with each utterance. Finally, he just *wheezes* and his eyes glaze over. It looks like the man had a tiny, almost imperceptible stroke.

"Stephen?" Jennifer says.

The camera pulls back and Colbert turns to face his guest, and both motions occur eerily at the same speed.

"Are you—" she says, putting a hand on his.

Suddenly he's got her wrist and is pulling, hard. At the same time, he lunges over the desk, trying to get to her. She screams and punches the TV host with her free hand. She's got a mean left hook, but it doesn't even register, and Colbert claws at the starlet with his own free hand.

The TV crew rushes in too late. He gains purchase at the front of her dress and that part of the screen blurs as he pulls apart the thinly constructed designer gown. When he bites into her neck, the rest of the screen becomes a red-and-flesh-toned blur, and the audio is simply a series of bleeps.

The feed cuts back to O'Reilly.

"Motherfucker ate J-Law…" Lily says.

"This isn't even here," Sam says. "This is New York, or Hollywood, or wherever they film his show."

"It's…everywhere?" you say. It's a question, but you know the answer.

"From what I've seen, it only takes a few hours to spread," Sam says.

A strange tone sounds as the television is suddenly taken into local control and your community Sheriff appears on the screen.

"The Governor has declared a state of emergency," the Sheriff announces. "But we are as of yet unprepared for any sort of mass evacuation. We're working as hard as we can to set up aid stations and sanctuaries. In the meantime, work with friends and neighbors. Find a group. Nobody can beat this thing alone. And… we need all the help we can get."

"*Mama*—I need to get home!" you say.

"I don't think that's happening anytime soon, Ty," Sam answers.

Before you can reply, there's a heavy pounding on the metal doors from outside. It's definitely a "cop knock" and it sends a chill down your spine.

"I'll handle it," Sam says. He steps over to the doors and slides open an eye-level panel. "Captain Delozier, what can I do you for?"

"We're here for the runner, Sam," a man says. The voice is stern, even muffled by the National Guardsman's gasmask.

"I'll take responsibility for him. You have bigger problems, I'm sure."

There's a tense moment and Lily shifts, taking the pistol in both hands.

After what feels like ages, the Captain says, "How's Daisy? Need anything? Water?"

"*Lily* is fine, thanks. We're good here, Captain."

➢ Wait! Tell the Captain he has to let you go. You need to get home and protect your mother. Go to page 91

➢ Stay quiet, but try to call home as soon as they leave. Go to page 409

Bound by Compassion

"First, we need to treat his wound," Owen says.

"Fine by me, boss. Just so long as I'm not on the menu for a midnight snack," you add.

"Tourniquet," Craig says. "It's the only way to stop the bleeding and—with any luck—stop infection. Sorry, bud, but I think you might lose that arm."

Brian nods, stoically accepting this part of his fate. Stephen takes Josh's belt from his corpse, then closes the trunk. He ties down Brian's arm, and that gives you an idea.

"Into the Honda," you say.

Brian does so while Owen finds the keys to crack the windows. Craig takes all the blankets you can spare to make Brian comfortable, which isn't much. Still, Brian could easily let himself out of the car, so it's time for that tie-down idea.

Once he's inside, you wrap the entire car with nylon tie-downs, then ratchet the doors shut. One set gets strapped across both rear doors, and another set over the front. There's no way he's getting out.

"What if I have to piss?" Brian says.

"Use an empty water bottle," Stephen replies.

"What if...what if I have to shit?"

"Don't," Owen says. "If you make it a day, we'll let you out. Once you make it, I mean." The man looks away, knowing he doesn't even have himself convinced. You raise the car on the auto platform, just to be safe.

It's hard to sleep with a dead guy in the trunk and an infected co-worker above your head, groaning in pain. The occasional *pop* of distant gunfire and the collective din of the moaning undead doesn't help, either.

Stephen's fast asleep and sawing logs, Owen writes something in a journal, and Craig stares out into the night through a porthole window on the rolling garage door. You check your computer. Surfing the Internet in the middle of the night when you can't sleep almost makes the world feel normal. But, no, you can't even have that—your computer shows "Installing Updates, Please Do Not Shut Off Or Unplug Your Machine."

Craig's workstation is active, glowing softly in the dark garage. He must've been on it recently, because the screensaver isn't even active. He won't mind if you check the news.

When you get to the screen, you see he's been on one of his chat message boards. He's signed in as user *NotTNelson* and the most recent comment posted at this computer says, "they r all sleep. quiet out. good time for package pickup." There's a reply right after from *Rebel_Yell_1997*: "Rog. En route. ETA: 10 mike."

You scroll up to see the original post, which was also posted by *Rebel_Yell_1997*. It says:

> By now you've seen this email, I'm sure.
>
>   FROM: PreppyLongStalking69
>   TO: Distro-all; zombiefiend.com
>   SUBJECT: See? I wasn't crazy!

> TEXT: To all you doubters, nay-sayers, and haters, prepare to be shrugged off. I knew this would happen. I fucking knew it! When you're being eaten alive by the living dead, just remember, if you wouldn't have been such a dick, you might have survived too. Sent from my compound.
> TL;DR: I told you so!
>
> *So the Prepster has a compound, wants to rub it in our faces, but was stupid enough to complete his message with attached map coordinates. If you're seeing this private post, it's because I trust you. You're part of my ZA survival team. We knew this day would come.*
> *Get your gear and weapons. Prepster's about to have a lot of visitors, and a new Mayor in yours truly. We're gathering up breeding stock now. Don't worry, the righteous shall be rewarded and the faithful will inherit.*
> *Ad Vitam Paramus*

"The fuck..." you mutter to yourself, scrolling along. From the looks of it, they've already taken *Prepster's* compound and killed the guy. *Christ.*

There are a lot of replies from people talking about when and where to meet, then one from *Rebel_Yell_1997* directed at *NotTNelson* reading, "You got my girl at that garage, right? If you deliver, you've got a place in paradise."

And a response: "kay's here alright. come get her."

Your spine tingles and you quickly scroll back down to the bottom. "ETA: 10 mike" is timestamped exactly ten minutes ago. That's when you realize the sound of gunfire has been slowly growing louder. Now you hear engines outside. Sounds like a couple motorcycles and something big, like a Humvee.

Craig punches the red plunger-style button in the garage and the doors start to open.

➢ Quick! Warn Owen and Stephen that you've been betrayed. That gang is back! Go to page 46
➢ That bastard! Grab my wrench and get the jump on them. Go to page 189

The Boys Are Back

You get Owen's attention and Stephen comes out of the haze of sleep rather quickly, but it's too late. The men from outside stand in the garage doorway with firearms drawn. Craig avoids eye contact with the lot of you.

"You should have let us in when you had the chance," the leader says. "Take the breeding stock and shoot the men."

You're not going without a fight. You take your trusty wrench and swing it at the nearest man.

He flinches, so you miss his head, but he screams out as you hit his shoulder. The leader rushes in and knocks the wrench away with a machete, then he punches you in the gut. As his men bind your wrists behind your back with zip-ties, he says, "I like the feisty ones. Boys, I formally call dibs. This one goes to my personal breeding stockade."

Then they blindfold you.

➢ *Go limp, but plan an escape as soon as you can.* Go to page 56

Broker

The man's eyes grow wide when he sees you charge in. He was hoping to shoot his prey in the back as you ran away; he wasn't expecting another predator. Moving with new urgency, he claims a long brass rifle shell from the box resting between the bars of the pawn shop window.

Something glints on the street in the morning sun, and you see an empty bottle; a fifth of whiskey. *God bless the homeless!* You scoop the bottle up in mid-stride, and as the rifleman slides the bolt-action forward, sling the bottle at him.

It hits the barred window, which works perfectly. The bottle explodes and the man takes a glass rain-shower full in the face as a result. He fires blindly and the rifle sets off a car alarm in the distance. You make it to the shop as the man rubs the shards from his eyes.

The metal is ungodly hot, but you grab the rifle by the barrel and pull it free of the building.

"That's enough, goddammit! Drop the weapon, and turn slowly," a man says from behind, his voice muffled by a gasmask.

➢ It is enough. Hands up, go quietly. Go to page 374
➢ Take the rifle and run! They won't shoot you in the back. Go to page 112

Bug-out

With new passengers turning into fleshies and the situation in the C-17 growing worse by the minute, as soon as the plane touches down, you sneak out the back without anyone noticing. The base is under attack, just like in Manaus, except here the soldiers are shooting at each other too. *Time to get the fuck out with a Dodge*, you think. Or, in your case, a Toyota.

The Camry is easy enough to spot, what with its chipped maroon paint and veteran bumper-stickers: support our troops ribbon, American flag, "If you can read this, thank a teacher. If you can read this in English, thank a soldier," and your personal favorite, "I'll keep my money, my guns, and my freedom...you can keep your *CHANGE*."

That last one is especially true now that the world's going to shit, right? If you relied solely on a nanny-state, you wouldn't be ready. Those begging for Change are now changing. But you? You're ready.

You pop the trunk and pull out *Bob* (bug-out-bag; get it? B-O-B.) to switch out a few choice items from your ruck. You've got dehydrated food, bottled water and a filter for more, a sleeping bag, extra undies and socks, utility tools, and a handgun to complement your M4. Which, unfortunately, only has fourteen rounds left. *Damn.*

A pang of regret washes over you. Why couldn't this have happened ten years from now? You're only six years from retirement and were planning a completely off-the-grid compound. The survival forums you frequent would've helped you develop a detailed plan.

Closing the trunk with a sigh, you go for the driver's seat and start 'er up. Where to?

- It's getting late, and the streets are the most dangerous place you can be. Get off base and find somewhere to *hole up* for the night. Go to page 288
- Wait, didn't somebody on the forums post about a nearby compound? It probably has room for two! Pull up the thread on your phone and head for Prepper Paradise. Go to page 25

Building an Offense

It's still in the framing stage, so you're not sure what this building will be, once fully constructed. Actually, scratch that. The world is crumbling, right? This nutter plague is only going to get worse. So this place will forevermore be a construction site until it rots and eventually becomes nothing at all. Job finished! Pack it up, guys.

You claim a nice, baseball-bat-sized chunk of wood, give it a few test swings and move on in search of something better. There's plenty of rebar but none of the metal rods are short enough to be useful. Best keep looking.

One of the rooms in the back is in the plumbing stage and you step down into the foundation to manually wrench free a length of pipe. It's not easy, but leverage is on your side. With the final tug, you kick something tucked under the half-finished floor and get the pipe free.

Bending lower, you see someone has stashed a nail gun under the boards—*jackpot*. A quick inspection shows the nail gun has roughly a hundred nails in reserve and a heavy-duty battery pack sits fully charged on its cradle. You waste one nail test-firing into a board, but yep, it works!

Now, strolling back across the parking lot with the pipe held over your left shoulder and the nail gun at the ready in your right hand, several nutters approach. They start at you first with curiosity, but when the closest fiend starts to *moan*, the other ghouls grow genuinely excited.

"Sir, can I get ya to look here?" you say, raising the nail gun to the first zombie's brow.

His dead eyes cross as he looks up, then he wraps cold, claw-like fingers around your arm. With a pull of the trigger, his head snaps back and he falls like a sack of dead meat.

"Hefty's *Nailers for Nutters* is open for business!"

The next two go down just as easily, happy to allow you the chance to get close enough to press the nail gun flush against their skulls. The two after that, however, come in unison, and you opt for the pipe here. After setting the nail gun down, you're free to use it two-handed.

First ducking to the side, you nearly decapitate the first ghoul with a firm swing, leaving her head as only mush. You're quick to recover, stepping away from the dead nutter and offering another kiss of pipe to her friend.

Teeth rain onto the pavement with the cadence of loose change, but even without a lower jaw, still the bastard comes. You line up with one of the twice-dead corpses on the ground, aiming to trip him, and bring the pipe straight in; shoving the ghoul by his ribcage. Once the undead man falls to the ground, you end him with a few quick strokes from the pipe.

After the parking lot grows still once more and adrenaline wears off, you realize just how exhausted you are. That all-night hike took its toll. Better rest up in the mall for a spell. The nearest entrance is one of the department stores, but the glass double-doors are locked.

- ➢ Kick your way in. Go to page 195
- ➢ Smash the door open with the pipe. Go to page 28

Burned

You run past the men, not looking back. They most certainly see you dart past, but you don't need to see the look on their faces. You quickly make it to the end of the hall, grab the doorknob, and turn.

It's locked. By a keypad, no less.

You slam the fire extinguisher against the door handle again and again, exhausting yourself, but it doesn't budge. Secure entry is limited in the infirmary, in or out, and you're exactly the class of person this door discriminates against. You turn back, thinking maybe there's time to help those guys out and use their keycards, but you're greeted by a wall of fire.

In defeat, you slump against the door. That's when the flaming zombies rush towards you. Melting skin, and teeth so hot they burst. This is going to be an agonizing death.

THE END

Burning Bright

Even in broad daylight, it is incredibly creepy to have the living dead follow your every move. They're not very fast, but they don't take breaks, and it's exhausting to look over your shoulder every other second.

The park itself is green and lush, a verdant oasis in a city of brick and steel. This Garden of Eden has already been corrupted by sins of the flesh, however, in the form of a mostly devoured hobo who crawls your way.

There's no muscle-tissue left on his legs, so it's just a torso of a man dragging behind gristle, bone, and connective tissue. He starts to moan, so you better not waste any time. You flip him over on his back with a swift kick to the ribs, then jab Isabelle up under his chin and into the brain cavity.

That's when you hear a rustle in the bushes.

You wipe Isabelle off on your pant-leg, bringing her back to glimmering steel. It won't intimidate a fleshie, but it might deter a human scavenger. Squinting hard, you can just make out something inside. The bushes glow with a fiery-orange light, giving you a better feel for the shape of the thing: It's huge.

It's a goddamned tiger.

The zoo is on the other side of the park, but how the hell did it get out? Moving almost too fast for your brain to process, the beast bounds out of the brush and leaps with a swat of its paw—which hits like a catcher's mitt filled with concrete.

You're eaten alive, but hey, look on the bright side. You're not infected.

THE END

Busy Streets

Nolan accepts the explanation that his parents simply aren't home more easily than you expected, but you can tell that the state of the house weighs on Nathanael in particular. It's difficult not to dwell on *why* the boy's parents aren't home.

You continue hiking towards Haley's neighborhood in near-silence. Any human noise, and speech in particular, seems to rile up the dead to a frenzied level. A small group of walking corpses clusters on the street ahead of you, though from the look of it, they're wandering in the same direction you are—towards something else.

That's when you hear the squeal of tires.

"Out of sight, stay down!" you hiss.

Your three pupils obey your command, ducking behind an abandoned car. From this vantage point, you watch an SUV and three motorcycles come driving like mad. As you get a better look, you see the SUV is actually a Humvee, but civilian-owned. With a barrage of gunfire, they mow down the small crowd of walking corpses.

- ➢ Wave them down. If they have room in that Hummer, this whole thing will go a lot quicker. Go to page 60
- ➢ Duck inside the nearest house. They may be killing walking corpses, but that doesn't make them good people. Go to page 254

The Cables Guy

The Marines form a four-man, side-by-side wall between the Ambassador and the zombie horde, carefully aiming and firing at the wave of former men, women, and children. The collective undead *moan* is deafening against the reverberating walls of the terminal.

You shake your head to clear it, doing your best to ignore the sounds of combat and terror. When you open your eyes and focus, the keypad stares back at you with cold indifference, but you can overcome. It looks like an older model, so hopefully there are a few outmoded security features.

Skinning *Isabelle*—your 9" razor-sharp officially-licensed knife from *Rambo: First Blood*—you slide the tip of the blade behind the panel and pry it off. This reveals an array of wires and a circuit board. Just need to follow the wiring, find the right connection, and manually override the system.

Letting instinct take over, your fingers dance across the wires. You clip and reverse their connections. *Beep*—just like that, the door opens. The crowd is all relieved smiles.

"Did I mention God bless the Air Force?" the Ambassador says.

Everyone floods onto the jetway, just in time. Once it's just you and the Marines, you cut the wires again and lock the doorway between freedom and the terminal horde. A sense of pride swells in your chest as you hurry back towards the C-17.

Out on the tarmac, two of the stern-looking men in suits who escort the Ambassador break off and approach you. One is slightly taller, thinner, with razor burn on the creases of his neck. The other is broad-chested and has a trimmed, manicured beard.

The tall one says, "That was impressive back there. Quick thinking."

"No problem. Or thanks, I guess," you reply.

"I'm Special Agent Danly," the man continues, producing a badge, "and this is Special Agent Bertram. We're with the United States Diplomatic Security Service."

Bertram nods his thick, ruddy beard in greeting.

"Bob Sims," you say.

"Well, Bob Sims. We're taking one of these private planes, and we'd like to invite you to come along," Agent Danly says.

"What? Where?"

"Mercury City," Agent Bertram says. "There's a guy we know from training."

"I dunno. I'm supposed to meet up with my unit after this mission, so...."

They both look to the chaos surrounding the runway, then back to you. Bertram shrugs and says, "Suit yourself, but if there's anyone prepared for surviving something like this, it's Brendan Droakam."

You look to the C-17, nearly finished loading, then across the runway to the scattered private planes and small hangars, and finally back to the pair of agents.

➤ "You know what? Screw it. Let's go find your pal and then hit a private island."
Go to page 306

➤ "Yeah, I appreciate the offer, but I can't just go AWOL with complete strangers, so...." Go to page 135

Cagey

"Not everyone in here will get an offer like that, you know," Angelica says after Craig leaves.

"So?"

"So…maybe you should have considered it."

"Fuck off."

She shakes her head. Using her *mom-voice*, she says, "None of us want to be here, young lady. But you won't find anyone else in here with a friend out there. Much less anyone the boss actually fancies. Maybe you'll regret it? Or maybe you'll cool off and put on that dress before Bud comes back."

"Never kowtowed to a man yet."

"I don't think you have much of a choice."

"Listen, bitch, I get it. You had a husband and he made the money. Before that, your daddy made the money. You? You spent the money. And in exchange you cooked, you cleaned, you fucked. Or hell, maybe there was a maid who did all three for you."

Something in her eyes says you struck a nerve. Was it a bit harsh? Maybe. But she struck a nerve with you too. Turning away, you pace your cell, thinking, *Do I really not have a choice?*

The last time you saw your mom stand up to dad's drinking, she said, "You always have a choice." Then he chose to hit her. After that, she chose not to speak up anymore. But that stuck with you: *Always a choice.*

So you look around the horse stall for choices. There's a bucket in the corner for you to "do your business." There's a thick woolen blanket on a pile of hay. Then, up on the wall you see a mounted push-broom. Bet they expect you to use it to keep your stall clean.

Taking the broom, you angle your boot on the wide broomhead and *snap* the handle off. Where the wood connected is now a jagged end. Your very own spear. Taking the broomhead, which looks very much like a foot-long subway sandwich with bristles coming out, you go to the door. Shoving it through the handle so that it extends beyond the door frame, you lock yourself inside.

Footsteps sound through the barn—someone's coming. You step back and position the spear behind your back. Angelica was watching you; now she looks away.

"Christ, you're stubborn," Bud says upon seeing you. "It's just a dress. If it was me, I'd have made you put on lingerie."

You smile.

"Or maybe you just want me to come in there and put you in that dress myself?"

"Bud, I'll wear the dress, okay?" Angelica says.

"Shut up. This doesn't concern you," you snap.

"Oooh, got a soft spot for blondie, do ya?" Bud says. "Maybe you don't care if I slap you around, but maybe you'll put that dress on to stop me from hurting her?"

- ➤ "Takes a big man to hit a little woman. Know this, you touch her and I will kill you." Go to page 399
- ➤ "Do what you want, but I know the truth: You just don't have the balls to come in here." Go to page 395

Cannot See

The back alley is clear, but the dumpster in question rests against the building opposite yours. Thankfully, it's on wheels, so you can move it. The bin is nearly empty, so the task doesn't take much strength. The big green trash receptacle squeals loudly on rusted joints when you pull and push it into place, and your hands are sticky from touching the filthy surface.

"Climb up," you say, before doing the same. The dumpster wobbles on its wheels, and you grab the wall for balance. "Okay, boost me up first, then I'll pull you up from the roof."

Nathanael looks to the side, and you follow his gaze to see a pair of the gasmask-clad soldiers running down the alley towards you.

"If you're alive, stay where you are with your hands up!" one of the soldiers shouts.

"Quickly, we're almost there!" you whisper urgently.

Nathanael nods, then interlocks his fingers so you can use them as a stair-step. You climb up, your fingers only inches from the rooftop. Nathanael groans and tries to lift you higher.

"Oh, shit—is it—are they infected?" one of the soldiers asks.

"They've learned how to do that termite thing!" the other shouts, raising his rifle.

They open fire, letting off multiple bursts from their rifles in panic, and you drop down to shield Nathanael from the hail of gunfire. Perhaps it works; perhaps you save the boy, but you'll never know. Blinding pain sends your vision to white, then to black. Your eyes close, never to open again.

THE END

Captivity/Depravity

Serial killers, rapists, psychopaths. There are still animals in the world, just no cages. As civilization's fire goes out, the darkness creeps back in. You ride in that darkness, bound and blindfolded and tossed in the back of the Humvee.

It's impossible to tell how far you've gone or even where you're going, but that hardly matters. You just keep hearing the man's words echo through your head. He called you *breeding stock*. All you can do is wait…and plot. If they assume that you're mere property, it means they underestimate you. And you've been proving men who underestimate you wrong all your life.

The Humvee stops, the doors open, and the men take off your blindfold. A horse barn. That's where the men take you. It's modern, with individual stalls that have locking doors; your own personal prison. As you're led inside, you see that most of the stalls have a woman or young girl inside, sometimes with a bunkmate or two. More are being led in by the minute.

You're tossed inside before the men lock the door and leave. Your back sings out in pain and you lie there for several minutes before you can muster the strength to stand up and look around. In the cell next to you, there's a blonde woman in her fifties. She's well-dressed in white pants and a floral blouse, bedazzled in gold jewelry. After a second look, you notice the material is blood-flecked. She was a privileged housewife, but those days are behind her now.

You start to chew on your bindings and she approaches the bars that separate your stalls. She puts a hand through and opens it to reveal a set of fingernail clippers sitting atop her palm. Thanking her, you take the clippers and cut your bonds. It's almost funny how such a simple tool could free your hands so easily.

"Angelica," she says. "That's my name." You simply stare at her. What does she think this is? Pledge week at a sorority? "Cooper, is it?" she says, noting the embroidered nametag on your workshirt.

"I've seen kids in the other stalls. Little girls," you say.

She looks out to the other cells and you slip the clippers into one of your boots. A simple tool, but one that could prove useful. Angelica turns back, shakes her head, and says, "God, I hope not. I think they're just planning ahead; it's what they do. If we do our jobs right, maybe they'll leave them alone?"

"Our *jobs*?"

"Why do you think we're here, sweetheart?"

You're actually speechless. How do you explain to someone that rape is about the farthest thing there is from a job? But by the same token, is she right that it's up to you to protect the girls through self-sacrifice? *It won't come to that,* you promise yourself.

Days go by. Three? Four? It's hard to keep track. You don't talk with Angelica much after that first night, though you can hear her mumbling to herself at various times, either in prayer or perhaps losing her mind. Maybe both. She has an ornate, gaudy candlestick a little over a foot long that she polishes day and night until its golden gleam rivals sunlight.

You're given food, but left to sleep on a pile of hay and an itchy blanket. A bucket sits in the corner where you can relieve yourself, but the food guy won't take it from you and you're forced to dump it out through the window bars. Well, you threw it at the food guy once, but you didn't eat for a full day after that. If you're going to escape, you'll need your strength.

Men come for the women in the night. Makes it hard to sleep. Some consummate their urges right there in the stalls, probably getting off on having an audience, while others "check out" women for an hour or the night. One thing you've learned: The stalls don't have unique locks, they seem to operate from a universal skeleton key.

As each night goes by, the women get more visitors. From the pillow-talk, you've heard that more and more of the living dead attack the compound every day, usually at night. So it is that those with close-calls find the need to express their "biological imperative" after a survival situation. Or, even worse, some of those who've been bitten come for some sexual healing in their last hours of life. With any luck, the plague isn't an STD as well.

For some reason, they've left you alone. Until now, anyway. The door to your stall suddenly opens and a dress is thrown in. "Duke wants you to join him for dinner," the guy at the door says.

"You and 'Duke' can go fuck yourselves," you reply, harsh as you can muster.

"Now why would we do that when there are so many pretty faces in here? Dinner's in an hour. If you're willin' to play nice, you get a shower and a shave first."

The man locks your stall again and pauses, staring at you. It's a hot night and sweat drips down his bicep and over his tattoo: stylized-calligraphy that reads, "*Ad Vitam Paramus.*"

Eventually he leaves.

"That's Bud," Angelica says. "He's the one who brought me here."

- ➢ Put on the dress; see how this plays out. Go to page 89
- ➢ Refuse. You won't play their games. Go to page 330

Carp's Lesson in Perseverance

The students gather in a semi-circle while Master Hanzo bites on his empty pipe. He clears his throat, closes his eyes, and begins, "This story takes place in Kyoto, Japan, over 200 years ago. There was a master painter named Okyo, who was rich and famous, which was rare for an artist at the time. He was so successful that students would leave their homes to come study with Okyo. The greatest pupil he ever had was named Rosetsu, who became one of Japan's greatest artists of all time, but that would have never happened if not for the lesson he learned from a carp."

"What's carp?" Stella asks.

"A big fish with whiskers like Grandfather Hanzo who makes kissy faces like this," you say, puckering up in a silly carp impression. The kids laugh, and Master Hanzo clears his throat for silence before continuing.

"When Rosetsu first left home and travelled to study under Master Okyo, he was overjoyed. But when he tried to learn the secrets of the great artist, it was like the gods were conspiring against him; like he had a block against learning. No matter how many times he heard a lesson, it didn't stick. Okyo never had a dumber pupil than Rosetsu."

"Sounds like Mason," Nathanael says to Christian, and they both chuckle.

"Hey!" Mason says, before he jumps up to hit the eldest boy.

"Enough!" you chide.

"For three years, Rosetsu stayed to study with his master, watching other pupils come and go, each learning the trade and going back home to live as successful artists. Eventually, Rosetsu feared he would never learn the secrets of Okyo, and so in the middle of the night, he left. He did not want to face his master and tell him that he quit, so he walked all night until he was too exhausted to walk anymore.

"When Rosetsu awoke the next morning, it was to a splashing sound. He went to investigate and found a carp in the frozen river, trying to get a biscuit that lay atop a large piece of ice. The carp would batter its own body against the ice, breaking away piece by piece, losing scales and hurting itself in the process. Rosetsu watched for three full hours, fascinated by the persistence of the carp, until the carp—bloody and wounded—finally grabbed the biscuit and swam away.

"Rosetsu knew the lesson right away, and said, 'I will be like this carp. I will learn the secrets of Okyo or I will die trying!' and returned to his master to tell him what he saw. Rosetsu worked harder than ever and eventually surpassed his master in skill. He took a leaping carp as his sigil so his family would never forget the lesson that he learned."

"And so each of you are my Rosetsus, if only you keep in mind the lesson of the carp," you say.

"Goodnight," Master Hanzo says.

The old man abruptly extinguishes the candles with a sweep of his robe, and the room goes dark. The children whisper to themselves for a time, but eventually you all fall fast asleep.

Sometime in the middle of the night, you're awakened by an urgent pounding on the doors. It takes only a brief moment to exit the dream-state of sleep before the memories of what's out there come flooding back.

It's an urgent, almost animal-like intensity, rapping upon the door, pulling at the handles and groping for a way in. With no streetlights, you can't see who it is—or *how many*—out in the shadowy black of night. A huffing voice shouts something, but you can't make out any words, or be certain there are any to make out.

- ➤ Open the doors. Bushido demands you help any way you can. Go to page 408
- ➤ Leave the doors closed. You can't defend against a mob with a wooden sword. Go to page 341

Chaotic Evil

You shout and wave the men down, which certainly gets their attention. Having dealt with the living dead, they rev their engines, peel out, and head straight for you. The children still hide next to the car, but when the gang pulls up, they're within full view.

"What the hell? Is it Halloween already?" one of the bikers says, noting your kendo armor.

"Every day's Halloween now; didn't you get the memo?" another asks.

"Good point. But is it a trick? Or is it a treat?" the first responds.

"We could use your help," you say. "I'm trying to get these children to their parents."

"Yeah? Where you been hidin' em these last few days?" the third biker asks.

You look to the driver of the Humvee. It's usually the silent one who's in charge. Finally, he speaks up. "Take the girl for breeding stock, kill the rest."

Before he's even finished speaking, you unsheathe the sword and cut down the first biker. By the time they raise their weapons, you've dispatched the second. And just as you're engaging the third, you learn that kendo armor doesn't stop bullets.

Is this what humanity has come to? And in such a short time?

THE END

Chaotic Good

Down the aisle, cell by cell, you free the others from their stalls. Angelica takes the opposite side of the horse barn, and you toss the keys back and forth for maximum efficiency. In only a matter of minutes, roughly fifty women and girls are set free.

Mothers are reunited with daughters, sisters weep in each other's arms, complete strangers fall at your feet, pleading for God to bless you and thanking you for your kindness.

"Everyone shut up and quit your damn blubbering!" you shout. "We've got a small lead here; we don't need someone hearing the lamentations of the women and coming in here to investigate."

"It'll be okay. Everything will be okay," Angelica adds.

"What now? Where will we go?" a mother who holds a young daughter under each arm asks.

All eyes go to you.

"The good news is that these men don't want to kill you. The bad news is that they'll want to lock you back up in here. Use it to your advantage. Run; they won't shoot you. But if you get the chance, take a few of the bastards out. We can't face them as a gang and win, but if we flee now, they can't catch us all."

"Every woman for herself," a college-age woman says. Looks like a runner.

"Pretty much," you reply. "Good luck and all that."

With that, you turn to go. Angelica follows and says, "You should consider a career as a motivational speaker."

"Funny. Good luck to you too," you say, hoping she'll get the hint.

"You're not getting rid of me that easily," she says. "Besides, I snatched Bud's key to the Humvee."

You look back to see she's brought her candlestick, and in the other hand she's holding up the keyring. "Fine. You can come with me, but what I say goes. Got a problem with that?"

She shakes her head. Hounds bay, much like during a prison break. Which, in a sense, it is. Powerful flashlight beams sweep the fields and one comes to rest on a pocket of the escaping women.

"Breeders are out!" a man shouts.

"*Keys*," you say, hand out.

Angelica hands them over and you hit the lock button on the FOB, listening for the horn. It's close. You run towards the garage where the Humvee's parked, which is a maintenance shed for vehicles. Probably where they would have had you working when you weren't in the barn.

"Grab anything that looks like it could break a skull," you say.

Taking only a minute, you shove a large wrench, a motorcycle chain, a tire iron, and a long-neck screwdriver in the back of the Hummer. Then the sound of voices approaching makes you turn back.

"Hey!" a man shouts. His eyes roll back into his head and he hits the floor in a heap. Angelica stands behind him, a spot of crimson shining at the base of her golden candlestick. Maybe she'll prove useful after all.

"Quick!" you say, jumping in the car.

The Humvee starts up with a growl and you slam on the accelerator. The shed doors swing open when you smash into them, sending men flying at the periphery. Under the glow of the headlights, you swerve towards as many of the search parties as you can, giving the fleeing women the best chance you can.

"Where are we going?" Angelica asks.

"No idea. I was blindfolded when they brought me here."

She nods. "Maybe the GPS? I'll try the recent destinations."

"Good thinking," you say, just as the front of the Hummer knocks a man with a rifle out of your way.

Most of the recent POIs were random GPS coordinates, so you're not sure where they lead, but one was an address you easily recognized: Owen's Garage. There was a twinge of pain in your chest when Angelica selected the garage, but thoughts of claiming your motorcycle and hitting the open road keep you driving.

Say what you will about the assholes back at the compound, but they were certainly prepared. The Hummer was topped off with gas before they stored it, so you've got a full tank to get back to town. You groan and a hand goes to your back before you can stop it.

"What's wrong?" Angelica asks.

"Nothing," you say. Though in truth, you're half-considering turning back to the compound to search for Oxycodone. "An old riding injury. I'm fine, don't bring it up again."

She reaches over and flips on the toggle switch for your heated seat, then smiles meekly. A smile that quickly drops as you re-enter civilization. The city is in chaos. Burning buildings, dead bodies everywhere—walking or otherwise. The Humvee isn't as agile as your motorcycle, but the cattleguard on the front proves useful nearly every block. You're only a few miles from the garage when you reach a military blockade.

A young soldier, probably not even of drinking age, waves you down. He's in full battle gear, and despite his fresh face, you can tell he's seen a lot of action in the last few days.

"Couldn't help but notice your bumper sticker," he says.

> "Just scavenged this rig, to be honest. You know how it is out there."
> Go to page 391
> "Yep, *Ad Vitam Paramus*, that's us. What's with the barricade?" Go to page 289

Chaotic Neutral

Captain Nobody and Simecek both seem on the edge of mania, and you get the feeling that it takes a concerted effort on their parts to fall in line with the convoy. Hoping not to set them off, you turn up the tactical radio as a distraction.

"—a full-scale retreat from St Mary's Hospital. Where the hell is that damn convoy?"

"Sir? This is Sergeant Sims," you say, keying the mike. "Convoy is putting down *en routes*. What is the situation down there? Do you have an extraction point? Over."

"Sergeant, get your asses down here! We're overrun. The bastards are *eating*—"

Gunfire erupts on the radio, along with men screaming in the background, then the line goes dead.

"Hello? Come again, over," you hail, to no avail.

Then gunfire erupts from behind. You turn to see Simecek blasting away on the .50 cal at a crowd of fleshies too far off in the distance, wasting ammo and drawing more undead to the commotion.

"What the hell—" you start when Simecek's head snaps back from a headshot. "*SNIPER!!!*"

The other gunners in the convoy open fire on surrounding buildings and Captain Nobody takes evasive action, pulling away and down a sidestreet.

"Where are you going?" you ask.

"The hell away from here!"

"We need to stay with the convoy, the hospital—"

"Is overrun!" he screams, cutting you off.

You take a moment, composing yourself. "Soldier, this is a direct order. Those men need our help, goddammit! The hospital may have fallen, but we'll burn that bridge when we come to it."

He looks at you, sizing you up, before coming to a conclusion. "No way to change your mind, Sarge?"

"No. When someone signals rescue, you come, so…."

"Well, in that case, I'm sorry," he says.

He swings at you, and you duck, but too slowly.

Everything goes black.

You wake up, the morning light pouring in through the storefront window, head pounding. As the fuzziness starts to dissipate, you take stock.

You're in a clothing shop, lying on a pile of sweaters, gasmask still on, firearms gone. The bastard left your rucksack and Isabelle in her sheath, but not much else.

➤ *Better see just where you are…* Go to page 327

Civil Liberties

"Stay put!" the cop shouts as you rush forward.

He draws his gun, sinks into a quarter-squat, and aims right at you—both hands, center mass. It's textbook hostile-engagement position.

"That guy's crazy!" you shout.

"I said *stop!*"

No way. You continue forward, sprinting to put the cop between you and the crazed homeless man, when you're suddenly thrown on your back. The gunshot echoes through the bus with powerful reverberations and the shock is so great, it takes a few seconds for the truth to set in.

The bastard shot you. Hopefully somebody got it on their smartphone, because that would definitely go viral.

THE END

Clean Room

Tyberius opens the men's room and an obese man with a fanny-pack and a bib-shaped vomit stain on his shirt rushes out with a gurgling moan. Pale hands raised for feeding and, ultimately, disappointment. You swing your wrench from the left while Hefty swings his pipe from the right; the blunt instruments meeting in the epicenter of the man's skull.

It's a disgusting amount of damage, but the smell coming from the bathroom is worse.

"Let's try the women's," you suggest.

The ladies' room is spotless by comparison. Hell, you could eat off the floor if you had any food. Hefty pulls down the baby-changing station tray and uses it as a hammock. The rest of you are forced to catch what few z's you can on the cold tile floor.

The next morning, you regroup at the front.

"Okay, I'm thinking we'll split the park right down the center, east and west, north and south, as viewed from the Ferris wheel," you say. "Report back for lunch. We're looking for flashlights, food, anything useful."

"Haven't you ever seen a horror movie?" Angelica asks.

You cross your arms across your chest. After a terrible night's sleep on the stiff, cold floor, it's too early for this crap. "Yeah, I have. And in case you didn't notice, it's broad daylight outside. There's no full moon. No thunderstorm. No goddamned eclipse. And you're no virgin in peril, lady."

"I'm putting up with your 'leadership' so I don't have to be alone," she says, firmly.

Tyberius and Hefty avoid eye contact, waiting to see what you'll say. After a moment, you go with:

> ➢ *"You're putting up with it because you'd be dead without me. We're splitting up. You three go together, I'll take Jose. Meet back here."* Go to page 336

Cold

You run past the men, not looking back. They most certainly see you dart past, but you don't need to see the look on their faces. You quickly make it to the end of the hall, grab the doorknob, and turn.

It's locked. By a keypad, no less.

You slam the fire extinguisher against the door handle again and again, exhausting yourself, but it doesn't budge. Secure entry is limited in the infirmary, in or out, and you're exactly the class of person this door discriminates against. You turn back, thinking maybe there's time to help those guys out and use their keycards, but you're greeted by a shambling horde of undead Aryans. Even the trio at the office, flummoxed by something as simple as a door handle, now come for you.

You fight, using the fire extinguisher, but it's hopeless. Icy-cold hands grab hold while teeth cut deep. You're eaten alive.

THE END

Cold Cuts

The man looks at you with tears welling in his eyes, but simply sinks back into the crowd. For a moment, there is only silence, the crowd staring at you as if waiting for direction. You look to Jason, but the disappointment is clear on his face.

"Don't look at me like that," you say, hushed yet firm.

"You know," Jason says to the crowd. "You guys might want to disconnect the automatic doors, if you're going to barricade yourself in here. Kinda defeats the point."

You pick up on his direction. "Speaking of, why not use some of those knives to sharpen your broom and mop handles? A blunt instrument won't do much against raging Zulu."

"You'll stay here and show us, right? Protect us?" an older woman asks, desperation in her voice.

Will you help them, or continue your search for a doctor?

- ➢ ER. This is an emergency! Go to page 326
- ➢ "Uhhh…sure. But y'all have to do whatever I say. Got it?" Go to page 157
- ➢ Pharmacy. If there's something that'll help Dad, that's where it will be held. Go to page 285
- ➢ The Morgue. When the dead are rising, it'll likely be the safest place here. Go to page 150

Collateral Damage

A good night's sleep is exactly what you need. You're up at the crack of dawn, ready to beat the heat of the day on the road back into town. You just need to re-hike what you did yesterday, and then do about the same after a ninety-degree turn to find the twins' neighborhood.

You're walking a wide-open patch of road, watching a few walking corpses on the horizon, when suddenly you hear a procession of incredible cracking booms. Like an entire forest of trees being snapped in half one after another in rapid succession.

You turn just in time to see the dirt on the side of the road leaping into the air with impact strikes as a fifty-caliber machine gun traces its way towards you. With no time to run or signal the driver that you're a living, breathing man, the enormous bullets rip you apart.

Apparently only corpses wander the middle of nowhere these days.

THE END

Committed

The following six hours and twenty-nine minutes are some of the worst in your life. The thought that *your* government would allow its own people to knowingly take poison is a hard rock to swallow and the guilt that you might be a part of it sits in your stomach like lead paint.

You never gave any credence or clear water to those who suggested we faked the moon landing or the "Truthers" who think 9/11 was an inside job. Sure, you follow the same message boards as other preppers who think Sandy Hook was invented to help pass anti-second-amendment legislation, but paranoia comes with the territory. You always figured they just didn't know the government like you.

Now you don't know what to think. Are aliens real? Is there a secret base under the Denver Airport? Do the Freemasons and the Illuminati rule the world? Were cancer meds suppressed by Big Pharma? Christ, do *lizard people* walk among us?

The whole flight passes like this, in a flash of panic. It only makes things worse when two more civilians attack and are subsequently put down. Then the LT freaks out at the six-hour mark and bites three of his men while they try to strap him to a gurney. Did any of the civvies bite their own before they were killed?

As soon as the C-17 touches down and the bay door lowers, you're the first one out. Gasmask securely pulled over your sweaty head, ruck slung, and rifle at the ready. Keeping your head down, you head for your reserve unit.

The base is insane. Total chaos. You've never seen anything like it. The entry gates have been breached, most likely by semi-truck drivers looking for answers; looking for sanctuary. The airport in Manaus was insane, but here the mental patients have taken over the asylum.

Inside the reserve office there's a measure of calm relative to the hellscape outside. At the manning desk sits a young Airman whose nametag reads "Fanuzzi." He looks at you wearily as you approach, probably because you're still wearing a gasmask.

"Just touched down from *Operation RAS-Putin*," you say. "Is the Group Commander in?"

"Sorry, Sergeant. All guard members have been mobilized. We're assisting the Army with a humanitarian something or other."

"Where? How long ago?" you ask.

"Ahh, all day, as far as I know." He consults his log book. "We've got one bird still in the area, and I can get you a seat if you're ready for it. Otherwise, the Army is putting together crews for Humvees at the Armory."

The kid clearly has no idea what's going on, so you'll have to get a mission brief en route. Last time you checked, you had less than half a full magazine for your M4, and the armory might be a good spot for a refill. Then again, a bird in the hand gets the worm, and a helicopter ride to front lines would be significantly faster than a Humvee ride through clogged streets.

➤ I think I'll stick with Air Power and take that last seat on the helicopter. Go to page 140
➤ Strength in numbers: both people and bullets. Humvee it up! Go to page 152

The Con

You step into the visitation room, spin around, and spray the fire extinguisher at the doctor and guard. They cough and stumble back into the hungry arms of the Aryan Brotherhood. The men scream, and once you've blown your load of chemical foam, you see the keycard on the ground.

You sweep the card back with your foot, then slam the door closed, leaving you alone in the visitation room.

Taking the keycard, you're able to let yourself right out the front door. Sure, that was a dick move, but you're alive. And you're free.

The night is dark, and the parking lot is empty, but you're alone. Funny, the damage doesn't look so bad from here.

➤ *Take one last look, then start walking towards the city, a free man.* Go to page 138

Concealed Weapons

Solitary *snaps* open the Asp baton and you look around for something to arm yourself with, but fall woefully short. They don't just leave weapons lying about the prison, after all. They keep all the good stuff locked away in the armory. Which, you realize, is exactly where Solitary is headed.

He ducks out of the SHU complex, keeping close to the sides of the building. With one eye on Solitary, you look around the prison once you're outside. Just what happened while you were locked away? It's already dark out and you're offered little in the way of information. Still, the lights of the cell block shine brightly, so you can orient yourself. The searchlights from the guard towers sweep across the prison grounds.

The armory is located next to the SHU complex, both kept away from the cellblocks and in the most secure wing of the prison. Just beyond the armory is the motorpool, then the outer fence, and beyond that—freedom.

Solitary shuffles through the keyring, trying all the ones that look like they'll fit the locked front door of the armory. When you turn back to provide a lookout, you're met by an approaching guard.

"Oh, shit," you mutter.

Then the guard *moans*. He reaches out for you and you push back, keeping him at arm's length. He snaps hungry jaws, making wet noises from deep inside his throat. A hideous bite wound on his neck froths from the effort.

Solitary readies the Asp and you shove the guard up against the wall. With the man pinned in this way, he's an easy target for your new partner, and Solitary bashes the guard's brains out with three fierce blows from the weapon.

"Thanks," you huff, out of breath from wrestling the nutter.

In response, Solitary bends down, unclasps the dead guard's belt, and offers it to you. You gratefully accept the gift and put it on while Solitary continues with the door.

A moment later, he's got it open and you follow him inside. Enormous stockpiles of weapons wait for you within, lethal and non-lethal, as well as four prison guards. The men are in the middle of suiting up in riot gear when you barge in, and there's an awkward moment where no one moves.

"So…ya'll come here often?" you say.

Then Solitary turns and runs back outside. One of the guards bum fires, the bullet exploding off the wall just over your head. The rest of the men scramble to claim their armaments while you take the hint and sprint away.

Solitary runs away from this set of buildings, towards the laundry, machine shop, cafeteria, and infirmary.

- ➢ Chase after him! Go to page 231
- ➢ Split up—head for the motorpool! Go to page 228

Consumed by Guilt

You go for the first hiding spot you can think of—the confessional booth. It's not much of a barrier, but it has a door you can close, and maybe if you sit still, they're forget you're in here. The screams coming from out there are horrendous, and you can almost see the chaos through the ornate slats of the confessional door.

While you're inside, furiously praying for redemption, wondering what the hell you did that was so bad as to get to this point in life, you hear a scraping on the other side. You're not alone in here—there's someone on the other side of the partition.

"Father?" you ask in a meek whisper.

Then the partition explodes in and a hideous ghoul claws its way to you. The nutter came through face-first, so his mouth and gums are a bloody mess of splinters.

You fall back and out the confessional door, but the fiend rides you down to the floor and tumbles out with you. There they are, the whole frenzied gang of them, gums smattered with gore like they're wearing nightmarish clown makeup.

They close in just as the first bites you. This isn't going to be pleasant.

THE END

Contra

Your heart beats furiously. Next to these young gun operators, you're a fat old man. But you'll be okay; you're only providing runway security, and your brand-new M4 carbine is in great shape. The tactical helmet and vest you checked out from the National Guard's para-rescue unit helps bolster your confidence too.

Still, you can't shake the feeling that you're like a bride on her wedding night. The USAF combat virgin. Heh, look at that—something old, something new, something borrowed, something blue.

"Our last op was a milk-run," Lt. Dosa, the Marine Corps mission commander, says. "But tonight, we have American lives at stake. These chickenshits down here let their dictator walk all over them. Literally. We know this drug turns people into flesh-eating bastards, but it looks like they make more fleshies with just one bite and now it's spreading, *fast*. We're authorized live ammunition and have a general kill order for any combatant *or non-combatant* threatening the mission. *Comprende?*"

It takes a moment for that to sink in. A general kill order...against civilians? The intel brief back home mentioned the potential side-effects of *Gilgazyme®* but could it really be that bad? Could all of Venezuela be...*undead*?

The loadmaster steps out from the cockpit and shouts, "Gentlemen, time to strap the fuck down! The runway, ah, isn't clear."

As he disappears, you buckle yourself into the webbing, then check your ammo for the fifteenth time. You pop out the magazine and rap it against your helmet—the old basic training trick to keep your ammo flush—before popping it back in.

The interior goes dark, letting your eyes adjust. First combat mission is a night op. *Great*, you think, dropping the night-vision goggles over your helmet.

A minute later, the C17 hits the runway, *hard*. You bite the tip of your tongue and taste iron. Lt. Dosa shouts something, but the belly of the beast screeches open and you can't make him out. The men leap up and move in a coordinated response and you follow. Almost immediately; shots fired.

The flight line in Manaus is crowded by hundreds—no, *thousands*—of people. Unlike most US airports, this one isn't fenced off. In fact, its border to the north is simply jungle and it looks like half the population of Venezuela has arrived to greet you.

Green figures sprint, shamble, or hobble towards you on sprained or broken ankles. The night-vision paints the whole area sickly green and makes human eyes shine out hungrily like a pack of rabid dogs in the moonlight. It's nearly impossible to tell friendlies from fleshies.

A group of about fifty children flank in from the side, previously hidden by the tall grass, but something seems off about them. Is that shock and fear you're seeing? Or (*gulp*) hunger? Are they excited by the thought of rescue or by the thought of feeding?

They rush in with open arms towards an Army Ranger near the front of the formation.

➤ Dash forward to warn him; you can't risk shooting a bunch of kids. Go to page 197
➤ Open fire! Mow down the *Children in the Corn*. Go to page 328

Convenient

There's a convenience store nearby, so you duck in to check for refreshments. The place must have been evacuated for the quarantine, because the door is unlocked and no one is home. Even the drink case is nearly untouched. You take a water, down the bottle, then sip on a sports drink.

"Water or something with electrolytes," you say. "No soda or tea."

While the kids drink their fill and look for snacks, you find an area map near the cash register. Spreading it out on the counter, you compare it to the class roster you brought from the dojo and plot a course from house to house. Nolan lives closest, then Haley is down the street and Nathanael is a few miles away from there. The twins lived on the outskirts of town, where you'll stop last to see if you can notify their parents that the children are safe at the dojo.

"Looks like closest-to-furthest is the same order as youngest-to-oldest," you say.

"That's convenient," Haley says.

"Indeed. Ready?"

Leaving the convenience store towards Nolan's house, you're struck by how fast everything has occurred. The city feels practically abandoned, though you know that can't be the case. The greater metro-area tops two million citizens. Where is everyone? The quarantine would account for some missing from their homes, but not nearly enough.

As you approach the boy's house, a hand on your sword hilt, you see that the door jamb used to be white, but is smeared with gore.

"It's that one," Nolan says, "with the red door."

The door that sits open.

- ➢ "Stay here while I check it out. Nathanael is in charge while I'm gone."
  Go to page 269
- ➢ "Stay behind me, move like shadows. We must be extra careful inside."
  Go to page 181

Cooped Up

"What?" Cooper says, answering the knock on her door.

"Good evening to you too," you say. She doesn't respond, so you go on. "It's just too weird, you know? All that going on out there, and us in here with all this. It almost doesn't seem fair. I just couldn't sleep, so…"

"So, what? You thought you'd swing over and I'd fuck your brains out?"

"Uhh, I…"

"You've gotta be fucking kidding me. Go back to your room, jerk off, and be ready to work in the morning. I'll forget we ever had this conversation, provided we never have to have it again. Got it?"

"Yes, ma'am."

She closes the door, leaving you alone and bewildered.

- Go check on Angelica. Go to page 165
- Go check on Jose. Go to page 127
- Go check on Tyberius and Hefty. Go to page 362
- Head back to your room and get some sleep. Go to page 396

Crack the Whip

"Everyone, on your feet. No eye contact, try to look big and threatening," you say.

You step out in front of the group and slide the motorcycle chain off your shoulder, letting one end drop against the pavement. The beast's eyes lock onto the sound, then back up at you. Snarling, it pads forward on gigantic paws.

Taking one of the patio chairs like a lion tamer, you crack the chain against the ground like a whip. Somehow your legs propel you forward and you *crack* the chain once more.

The lion crouches, ears folded back and growling, so you crack the makeshift whip again. Then it backs away. You shout and press the advantage. The lion turns and sprints around the corner, joined by several hidden lionesses, leaving you with a cold sweat.

"Hole…*eee*…shit…" Hefty says.

"Coop, that was amazing," Tyberius says.

So you press the advantage with them too, saying, "You can come with us if you want. But what I say goes, got it?"

"Yes, ma'am," they say in unison, brows raised in shock.

"Good. Let's hope that amusement park isn't totally fucked."

"Coop, do you think we could make a pit stop? I met some people at a hardware store that I had to leave. I was hoping to check on 'em. It's more or less on the way," Tyberius says.

➢ Fine. But let's hurry. I don't want to wait around and see if that lion finds his courage. Go to page 313
➢ No. Straight to the park. I'm not running an orphanage. Go to page 86

Crowd Control

Something is deeply wrong, and it's panic-fueled instinct that propels you forward. You smash into the cop, sending the man faltering into the bus driver's lap, but the door is still open from when the officer came aboard, so you dash out before he can recover.

You look about, wild-eyed, knowing that you don't have much time to escape before that cop comes after you. He's already getting up, but that crazed homeless guy might be a bigger distraction. Other passengers scream and blood sprays against one of the back windows.

"Hey! Stay put. We have infected in the area," shouts a street cop, brandishing a baton.

Infected? What the hell does that mean? Beyond the man there's a line of National Guardsmen defending a wooden barrier, the kind of thing they put up at events for crowd control. But these are armed soldiers, not event security rent-a-cops. What's going on here? You're trying to think, but the cop shouting in your face makes it nearly impossible.

- Cooperate. Tell him there was a crazed guy on the bus! Go to page 294
- Knock him out; that'll give you some time to think. Go to page 242
- Run past the soldiers. Run home. Just…run. Go to page 308

The Crying Gang

The armory is locked up tight, but that doesn't much matter when there are a dozen highly-motivated, 250-pound men desperate to get inside. It doesn't take long to break the door down, and you rush in with the crowd like Black Friday shoppers at a Walmart that just opened the path to the Blu-ray players.

Thunk thunk! Hisssssss.

Inside, you're greeted by three prison guards fully decked out in riot gear. Your eyes go from the men in gas masks to the multiple canisters of tear gas they just activated in the tiny room. Then your vision goes blurry as your mucous membranes burst and tear ducts overflow.

Lungs burning, you bounce against other inmates and the walls, trying to get back outside and away from the teargas. This stuff is potent, and from all appearances, they unloaded their full supply.

You finally make it outside, just in time to vomit on the ground. All but blind, you stumble until you're found by a rogue wandering nutter. It's almost a relief to feel something other than burning when the ghoul bites into you.

You're INFECTED!

Cut the Cord

She comes at you, groping and clawing, growling and snapping her teeth. Mama isn't the one behind those eyes; who—or *what*—is back there isn't even human. It's just hungry. But even if this *thing* isn't your mother, can you kill her? The one who gave you life and fed you? She doesn't leave you with much choice. Now you'll have to give her death before she feeds on you.

Stop! You want to cry. *Don't make me do this!*

But the words don't come. Instead, she comes. The infected woman lunges out with both arms, as if she forgot she had one amputated as a child. You take her wrist in your hand, and swing her around—sending the woman flailing towards the living room floor. The coffee table explodes beneath her, but she doesn't even notice. She gets up without using her hand to stabilize herself, almost like a snake.

When she comes for you, it's with the exact same movements, and so you anticipate catching her wrist once more. Taking her right hand in your left, you squeeze tight. Despite her small, frail body, she moves with incredible, hellish strength. She comes in for a bite and you take her throat with your right hand. Adrenaline pulses through you, and you're much, much stronger. She can barely move against your grip.

"*Stop!*" you hiss through your teeth but, of course, she does not.

You squeeze tighter, cutting off the guttural moan in her throat. *Tighter.* Trying to choke out the fiend inside her by sheer strength alone.

Her eyes bulge, but she shows no sign of giving up. You take her and slam her against the wall, hard. The fiend's teeth chatter, but her eyes don't even blink. She squirms, trying to get you, so you slam her against the wall once more. Again and again. In this macabre dance you move down the hallway towards the bedrooms, knocking family portraits off the wall as you go.

Tears flowing freely, it's hard to see, and you hit against the hall table, then step on one of the downed picture frames and lose your balance. Together, you both fall into her bedroom, and for a panicked moment, you think she might get free, or get her teeth close enough for a bite. She rises first and launches at you, so you kick directly into her chest, flinging her back into her closet.

She thrashes, becoming tangled within the dresses and blouses hanging there, and it gives you a moment to wipe the tears away and try to control your breathing. It turns the momentum of battle against her, but just barely. Time to end this.

When she comes for you this time, you throw her onto her bed and come after her. Taking her singular arm, you pin it beneath your leg so you can get two hands around her neck. You plant your other knee against her chest and push hard, squeezing until there's a *snap*. You don't hear it so much as feel it, and her body goes limp.

But when you pull away, her mouth is still moving, masticating air or chewing her own tongue. You snapped her spinal column, but that doesn't stop her from wanting to eat you, nor her eyes from watching you.

In one final burst of energy, you take her head in both hands and slam it into the headboard. Over and over and over again, until red and white and grey pus flows down the wall.

She's not moving. It's over.

You fall back off the bed, weak in the legs, stumbling to find your footing. It feels like you're going to faint. No, like you're going to be sick. Dashing into her bathroom, you throw up. After several minutes of retching, you compose yourself and come back out. She's still there, twice-dead.

"Can't just leave her like this," you hear yourself say.

This is not a fitting end. You look to the closet and realize she just ruined all her good Sunday dresses. But you can do that for her. You can go to a department store, pick out a fancy dress, and send mama off right. With a real funeral, and everything. You can get yourself a nice suit. You can lay her to rest proper.

- ➤ Find a car to drive to the mall. Go to page 37
- ➤ Get walking. Go to page 403

Cut Your Losses

You make a break for it, sprinting as fast as your out-of-shape legs will carry you. Why, oh why, didn't you try harder on your biannual fitness tests? You shoot one ghoul mid-stride, and go for another—*click*. That's it, the M4 is empty.

That second zombie reaches for you and you slam the butt of the rifle hard against its head. Which does nothing. It's not even stunned. The thing grabs hold of your rifle and you shove it away, losing your M4 in the process. They don't call it a *death grip* for nothing.

Feeling naked and defenseless, you keep running, but you're over halfway there. Just at the entrance to the shop, several bony hands grab hold and pull you back.

Struggling frantically, you manage to slip out of your body armor and their grasp. You lunge into the sandwich shop entrance, and pull down the security gate. At the last second, you *Indiana Jones* grab your rucksack and pull it in.

By some miracle, the shop door is unlocked and you rush inside, throw the deadbolt and turn to face any threats within. The corpse of an employee is sprawled out on the floor, blood splattered and pooled everywhere. You plant both feet for a quick stop, but her bodily fluids lubricate your boots and the linoleum goes out from under you.

When your forehead slams against the counter, everything goes black.

You wake up, the morning light pouring in through the storefront window, head pounding. As the fuzziness starts to dissipate, you take stock.

You're in the sandwich shop, lying on the linoleum floor, gasmask still on. Isabelle is still in her sheath, and it looks like the security gate must have held, because you concussion-slept all night without being eaten. Speaking of which, the memory of the corpse comes back and you look over to see the sandwich shop employee lying next to you with a bloody mouth and a sandwich knife *inside* her head. In the back room, the manager is dead and eaten.

Despite the terrible scene and pounding headache, you keep your wits enough to grab a bite to eat before you get going. You got lucky. Better be more careful next time.

➤ *Time to see what's left outside…* Go to page 327

Cynicism

While you take the motorcycle chain and giant monkey wrench, Angelica opts only for her candlestick. Not what you would pick in a fight, though there's something to be said for the weapon you know. In a running crouch, you head from the parking lot to the front doors but the entrance is filled with ghouls; dead end.

Barely able to think, with the sounds of gunfire and men's screams all around you, you look for an alternate route. Around the side, there's a wing under construction and a welcome sight: a great, shining behemoth. A red dragon, inviting you to ride on its back, slaying your enemies like a fantasy warrior-queen.

It's a construction vehicle with a backhoe claw serving as its spiked tail, and a trenching tool—what appears to be a gigantic chainsaw—serving as your fire-breathing front. Stenciled on the side of the vehicle is his name: DITCH WITCH® RT80 QUAD.

"Let's go," you say.

There are two seats on the thing, one for the driver and one to operate the rear claw. Once mounted, you'll ride atop four tank-tread-style limbs. You take the reins, telling Angelica just to play with the levers to get the hang of the claw. No need to worry about collateral damage here. The seat is bloodied, but the keys are still in the ignition. You'll have to make sure you aren't pulled off, like the poor sap who rode it last.

With a mighty roar, your chariot growls to life and you propel it forward. The chainsaw front engages and you tear through the construction and into the hospital. Immediately, you're faced with several of the hungry dead, but your dragon is hungrier. It paints the walls with viscera and tears the ghouls apart.

The floor tiles crack under the weight of your beast, but no matter. You continue on. A quick glance back to Angelica shows the woman swinging the claw around like mad, battering any undead who might try to follow. The sheer mass of the claw deals brutal damage, but nearly all of the ghouls find their footing again to follow.

The hallway ahead is cordoned off with waiting-room couches and coffee tables, secretaries' desks and filing cabinets. There must be a couple thousand pounds of office furniture between you and the next area of the hospital: the cafeteria.

And more shocking still, there're people on the other side. Living people. You can see their blood-stained faces looking at you with terror through the glass portholes in the double doors beyond the barricade. Men, women, and children.

They've locked themselves in, but they're really trapped, due to the wall of undead. Even if they wanted out, they couldn't possibly fight off that many infected hospital patients.

➢ Take the group of corpses down. The only good zombie is a twice-dead zombie. Go to page 279
➢ They made their choice. Mine? Find a way up to the roof and that chopper. Go to page 307

Daddy's Girl

The road home is darker than normal, as only about half of the streetlights are working. A few have been knocked over from all the haphazard driving accidents, but a few more are simply dark. This part of the grid must be down already, but some sections are still intact.

Despite the figures constantly darting out towards your headlights, and the need to weave the Jeep in a zig-zag pattern, you drive home in silence, the new knowledge you gained from the hospital weighing heavily on your heart. Jason, on the other hand, is fast asleep in the passenger seat. Poor kid.

You pull into the driveway, wake your brother, and take your rifle. Time to say goodbye. Power's still on here; half the lights are on inside your house. You pause at the front door—there's a bullet hole at chest-height, the interior light shining through.

"Look alive," you tell Jason. "Could be looters."

The door is locked, so you use your key and slowly head inside. There's blood everywhere. Dad's handgun lies in the center of the room, and a trail of red leads towards the kitchen. Panic swelling in your chest, you follow the trail, where there's a man lying face first on the linoleum.

Despite seeing a corpse with the back of his head blown out, your heart soars. It's the stranger, not Dad. There are several footprints in the blood, the tread matching dad's boots. Following the limping gait with your eyes, you see a figure in the hallway by Dad's room.

"Daddy?" you say, slowly stepping forward.

The man stumbles with odd, cavorting steps. Despite the slack jaw and glazed eyes, you'd know that face anywhere. His skin is ashen gray, almost like marble, and his fingers are contorted claws.

"Oh, shit..." Jason says.

Dad's head snaps towards your brother and a low, guttural growl comes from his throat. The metal of your rifle is cold in your sweat-drenched palms. *Oh, God. This isn't happening!* You're frozen, paralyzed. Time creeps by, each second lasting a decade. *He can't be dead, he can't. He can't be one of those things!*

"No...!" Jason cries as Dad's hands rise up to embrace his son.

- ➤ You can't do it—you know you can't. Scream for Jason to run! Go to page 115
- ➤ That's not your Daddy. It's Zulu. Put him down. Go to page 270

Damage is Done

You grab a scarf from your closet and tie it tightly around Jason's bicep, cutting off the circulation, and then inspect the wound. It's bad—really bad. The bite is deep, and the flesh around it is puffy and rended.

"Cut it off! Cut it off!" Jason screams.

"...don't..." Dad croaks from the doorway. He looks like death warmed over—pale and slick with sweat, eyes bloodshot, skin around them dark and bruised. "Circulation...takes under...a minute.... Infected..."

He's right, and you know it. Fresh from that lifeguard course, you know it takes under a minute for blood to flow from the heart and do a full circulation lap throughout the body. If the infection is transmitted from a bite, it left Jason's arm and flowed into his body in only seconds.

"Jay," you say, the name catching in your throat. "It's too late."

"No, it'll work, cut it off!"

The old man stumbles back against the door jamb like a drunk, his eyelids heavy. "...blade...not sterile..."

You remember back to your AP History class. Civil War amputations had, what, a fifty-percent mortality rate? You'd probably do more damage than good. Slowly, you look to Jason and shake your head no. He sinks against the bed, looks at his wound, and starts to cry.

Now your own tears flow freely. "Daddy, what do we do?"

His eyes blink open and with renewed clarity, he hisses, "*Leave us!*"

"No! I won't. I won't leave you."

"Once bitten...soon biting...."

"You won't turn. I'll stop it, somehow."

Jason wipes his eyes, inadvertently painting himself in a bright-red, bloody bandit's mask. "If you want to stop it, you'll have to shoot us. In the head, like that guy. I shot him in the chest first, but—"

"Jay, no!"

Dad stumbles forward, then gathers himself. With extreme effort, he says, "If you live...we live...with you..."

➢ Do the merciful thing; put them out of their misery. Go to page 204
➢ Refuse. Barricade them in the house, get in the Jeep and leave. Go to page 315

Dancing Partner

"You want me to be submissive; is that it?" you ask.

"I want you to *want* to please me, like I want to please you," Duke says.

You stand up, saunter across to his side of the table, bringing your knife and fork. "Well, let me cut your meat, dear," you say, plunging the fork into his steak.

You position the knife to cut his filet, then swing the blade up to cut his throat instead. But the attack stops short. You're nothing less than astounded when his hand clenches tightly around your forearm, halting the blow. Blood oozes from his self-inflicted carving wound, but he doesn't seem to care.

"Do you think I'm stupid?" he says.

"I...wanted to see how good you are. If you're a worthy king."

Duke grins and releases his grip. He says, "And? What did we decide?"

Taking a moment to think, you decide:

➢ I can seduce him, fairly easily, then make my escape once he falls asleep. Go to page 124
➢ Yes, I do think he's stupid, and I can play him like a fiddle. Time for some mind games. Go to page 297

The Dark Ages

The Ferris wheel was visible on the horizon once you passed the skyscrapers of downtown and since then has served as your North Star to navigate you safely into port. Your legs ache from jogging/hiking all day, and the sun went below the horizon about an hour ago, but you've finally arrived.

Automatic lights beam at the entrance, which is designed to look like a castle, complete with a drawbridge permanently welded in the open position. Though the walls may be built of plaster atop rebar, they're better than nothing.

The Funtastic Rockencoaster Adventure Park is full of kitsch, from the streaming banners to the inflatable princess ready for photos. From the looks of it, this was a *Medieval Funtimes* park that was bought out, updated, and bastardized into what lies before you.

"Welcome home, m'lady," Hefty says.

"What kind of bullshit place is this?" you say.

"Parents never brought you?" Tyberius asks. "I only came once, after my brother…well, never wanted to come again after that; guess it always reminds me of him."

It sounds like someone is trapped inside the ticket booth, groaning and growling in hell's version of snoring, but you're too tired to start clearing out the dead now. After looking at the front map, you say, "There's a hotel with a restaurant. Let's secure the building, eat, and get some rest. We can take the park tomorrow."

The group nods and follows you towards the hotel. It's near the front entrance, presumably so people can check in on a Friday night before exploring the park over the weekend. Still, you have to put down three ghouls on the way, one of whom still dutifully clutches a selfie-stick.

The hotel exterior is that of a gigantic castle, and, in case you didn't get the theme—there's a gigantic *CASTLELOT!* logo above the entrance. The lobby's centerpiece is an enormous sword sticking from a boulder and the directory boasts: The Canterbury Theatre, Round Table Restaurant, Lady-of-the-lake Pool and Spa, and other Arthurian-inspired attractions.

The hotel is a bona fide resort. Several pools with swim-up bars. A mini-golf course for guests. In short, it's the kind of place that would cost you half a month's pay for a night's stay. Which means the beds are going to feel amazing.

You open the doors only to be met by darkness. Your stomach sinks—can't explore a hotel in complete darkness. There's power to the park; the entrance taught you that much, but the hotel must be on a separate circuit.

"Goddammit," you say. Then with a sigh, add, "We'll find some flashlights and clear it out tomorrow."

The group lets out a collective weary groan, but they know you're right. Okay, where are you spending the night?

➢ The public restrooms. Small enough to secure in the dark. Go to page 65
➢ The gift shops. Eat some candy and sleep on top of a giant teddy bear. Go to page 267

Dead of Night

Despite Sam and Lily's insistence that this is not a good idea, you ready yourself for departure. Sam offers everything short of his rifle. "Want me to make you a shield? Forge a spear?"

"Nah, I'm faster when I'm not weighed down. Besides, I still got this pigstick," you say, showing off the baton.

"Goodbye, Ty," Lily says.

"See you later," you correct.

Not wanting to attract the soldiers' attention, you use one of the spools of rope in the store and rappel your way off the rooftop. Once on the street, you duck behind a parked car and scout your route. The driver of the car slaps the windshield and chomps his jaws, psychotically trying to get to you from inside. The man's growls are barely muffled.

Down the street, the soldiers go car-to-car, tapping on windows and collecting car keys from the frightened occupants within. Those that are still living, anyway. The undead man accidentally presses his chest against the steering wheel while trying to get to you, and the horn beeps loudly.

"*Shit,*" you mutter. Knowing you'll need to make a break for it, you turn to leave, but you're stuck on something. When you look down, you see that a gray, ashen fist holds your pant leg. The arm comes from the sewage drain and suddenly the other arm grabs around your ankle and pulls.

You slam the baton down on the wrists over and over, but they don't even flinch. Instead, your leg is dragged into the gutter and you experience excruciating pain as teeth pierce your work socks. You manage to pull away, losing a strip of flesh and a good chunk of your slacks.

Doesn't matter, though. It's not a clean getaway.

You're INFECTED!

Death of Reason

"They're just a coupla kids!" the woman shrieks.

The man rubs his eyes with the back of his pistol hand, then resumes pointing the gun at you. He steps forward, blinking rapidly. "Where'd you get all that?" he says, pointing the pistol at your weapons and gear.

"It's ours."

"Yeah? Give it here."

"Can't do that," you reply coolly.

He shakes the pistol at you, and you shake your head back. He scratches at his chest and looks back at the pharmacy window. "You don't open this door, I'm gonna shoot these kids!"

Whatever the pharmacist says, the man doesn't like it. The pharmacist's voice is muffled by the security window, but the junkie thumbs the hammer back, and there's no mistake there.

The next few seconds go by in a flash. Jason steps forward, the blond junkie turns toward you with wide eyes, and the woman screams out as a barrage of gunshots erupt inside the room.

The junkie man gets peppered by pellets from Jason's 16-gauge, as well as three sucking chest wounds courtesy of your .22. He drops the pistol, falls to the floor, and touches his wounds with surprise. It looks like he wants to speak, but only rasping, wheezing breath comes out.

You look to your own chest, touching a similar spot, but your fingers come away with dark, almost black, blood. You fall to your knees, then black out.

THE END

Debutante's Ball

The dress fits perfectly. Like it was tailored for you, in fact. But the guy forgot shoes, so you're wearing your biker boots underneath. And yeah, though you hate to admit it, cleaning up a bit felt amazing after a few days in that horse stall. *At least he didn't drop off a curling iron and makeup compact,* you think. Just in case you end up zip-tied again, you keep Angelica's fingernail clippers tucked into the left boot.

"Hot diggity," Bud says with a whistle when he returns. "Guess I can see why Duke wanted you in that dress so bad. Okay, almost dinner time, let's go."

You can't even remember the last time you wore a dress, and despite the warm night, it's breezier than you'd like. Bud walks with the swagger of a man not threatened by you in the least. That'll help with escape.

The constant armed patrols, however, will not. There are far more people here than you'd expected, both infected and healthy. As you walk to "the big house," you can see several pockets of dead in the distance and men moving to fight them. This isn't a clean-up action, it's a battle.

"You'll come to realize you're lucky. It's safe here," Bud says, noting your gaze.

You don't acknowledge the man. Is he saying that for your benefit, or trying to convince himself? Things must be really bad in the city at the rate the dead are flowing into the camp. *Worse every day,* you think. How many days are left?

A candlelight dinner for two. You down the glass of wine set in front of you, meant for sipping as you wait for dinner. Seated across the table is the man you recognize as the owner of the Hummer. The man the others are calling Duke.

"Is this supposed to be a romantic gesture?" you ask. "Not likely to make me forget that I just came from a horse stall."

"I'm sorry about that, really. I'd like it if you stayed up here, with me. I figured you could use some time to cool off and to ponder the alternative, but I didn't want to be presumptuous."

That gets a laugh. "I have to ask…why me? It's clear you singled me out, but I have to be honest. I don't get it."

"Number 10. The perfect 10! How could I let the world end and not save you?"

Your number from the motorbike circuit? *Oh, God. A fan,* you think, heart sinking.

"Big into Motocross?"

"You really don't remember me, do you?" he says, seemingly amused with the situation.

"I'm sorry, I sign a lot of autographs, but—"

"Let me refresh your memory. You, after a race, me, stupidly saying, 'I'd give my left nut for a date with you.'"

You can't help but laugh again; this is unbelievable. "I meet a lot of drunk fans."

"I wasn't drunk!" he screams, slamming his palms on the table, making you jump at the sudden outburst. Then, just as suddenly, he calms down completely and says in a low voice, "I was in love."

"And you really thought that was the best way to get my attention?"

"I said it was stupid, didn't I? That's why I wanted to do it better this time, not fuck it up…"

"You can't force someone to love you."

He growls to himself and takes his steak knife, carving it into his opposite forearm while he groans "Stupid!" over and over. The whole display lasts about a minute and then he is calm once more.

"I want you to *learn* to love me. I'm king of this castle, and you can be my queen. I have bikes and a garage for you to work in. You can have anything you want!"

He becomes quiet as Bud brings out dinner—steak. Bud refills your wine, then leaves and shuts the door behind him. This Duke guy is clearly a nut job. Time to act.

- ➤ Give him a "nut job." Make him redeem that date offer, the hard way.
  Go to page 34
- ➤ His knife is dirty. Play nice, offer to cut his steak, then go for the jugular.
  Go to page 85

Demanding

"Out of the question," Captain Delozier says after you've finished your appeal.

"Due respect, sir, but you need to get her. I'll go with you."

"Look, I get it. We all love our mothers. But this is a secure perimeter around the hospital and nothing more."

"Just let me through, then! I'll go get her."

"Ty, bud, let it go," Sam says.

"She's all I got, man. Picture Lily alone, not knowing what's coming."

"I suggest you listen to your friend," Delozier says. "If she stays home, she'll be fine. In a day or two you'll be back together. Now if you'll excuse me…"

"Fucking coward!" you cry, not ready to admit defeat.

"I'm letting you stay here out of respect for the Colts. But if you push me, I'll be forced to—"

"What, huh? What're you gonna do? Nothing, that's what. You don't give a shit, do you?"

"That's it. Open the doors, Sam. Not a request."

Sam sighs and Lily looks away. "I'm sorry, Ty," he says, before pulling open the doors.

Not much of a choice here:

➢ *Looks like you're now property of the US Army.* Go to page 374

Devoured

The pain of having lost everyone you know—and worse, not knowing their fates—eats at you. You feel like a walking corpse yourself. Each city block that you pass has an abandoned military containment section. Yours was the epicenter, with the grocery store parking lot allowing room for tents, while the store itself must have provided your daily meal rations. How many people were quarantined? Did they run out of food? Or run out of hope for safety?

As you continue on, you see that this small command post was in fact a fiefdom to a larger, central kingdom. Soon, you approach suburbia, and with it a more fortified, yet equally abandoned, wall. In the vast distances you still hear gunfire and sirens.

Turning back, you see the hospital on the horizon, caught ablaze. *Walking corpses,* you think again. If your sister was right, the quarantine at the dojo was only meant to slow the march of the dead, while this must be what they were protecting: the command center. The castle of this new military kingdom.

That's when you hear the moaning. It had mixed into the wind, like an Old West ghost town. Or, perhaps more likely, your shock at seeing the dead city had dulled your senses.

That doesn't matter now. All that matters are the half-dozen people who stumble forward. Seeing them up close, all your skepticism of the concept of the living dead vanishes. One man has seven bullet holes in his chest, yet stumbles and gropes at you all the same. There's a woman whose lower jaw is missing; completely ripped off. Her tongue lolls out of her exposed throat, like a dog on a hot day. Each walking corpse has injuries that don't bleed and skin so pale, it could glow.

As they come, you suddenly feel very vulnerable. You wish you'd brought your Kendo armor, and what's more—a weapon. Your martial arts training should serve you well, but it's been far too long since you've faced an opponent while unarmed.

With your back to the wall, they come from all directions, converging like an eclipsing crescent moon. You lash out with strong blocks against their grasp, but sensing the life in you, they simply grow more excited. Most opponents tire after a few attempted strikes, but every time the dead come for you, it is with a never-fading intensity.

Their moans and growls are answered in chorus by dozens more voices on the other side of the wall behind you. Your mind scrambles for a way out, for a way to break through their ranks, when you're taken from behind.

Several hungry arms have broken through the canvas skin of the barrier, forcing their way in-between the wire frame and grasping onto your limbs. If only you could cut through! Instead, they hold you in place with the collective strength of legion while those out front eat you alive.

THE END

Dinner is Served

There will be hell to pay, that's for sure. The guards will certainly find a file out in the open, especially when it's the size of Ron Jeremy's penis. Are there cameras outside that could have recorded the contraband dump? How did you just now think of that? *Dammit.*

By the time the dinner call goes out, you're shitting bricks from nervousness. Your undershirt is soaked with sweat to the point of bleeding through to your inmate jumpsuit. *Why did I have to look?* you think over and over again on the way to the cafeteria. *Curiosity killed the cat.*

You arrive, surprised to see a few inmates already seated. One is your cellmate. Looks like they opened the SHU and dumped out the contents. Celly nods at you in recognition.

Damn it! your voice roars inside your head. What're the odds he was getting out tonight? He's going to be expecting that file. You look away, figuring if you break eye contact, he's less likely to see the guilt all over your face.

The other inmate you recognize is simply known as Solitary. He's the guy everyone in here recognizes. A lifer who prefers solitary to the yard, they say. Even now, he wears wrist and ankle cuffs, the two shackled together so the man can't raise his hands over his head—the price of being a repeat violent offender.

You sit, pretending to focus on dinner, thinking only of how screwed you are, when someone starts screaming. The cafeteria forms a ring around the fighters, just like high school. Only something is terribly different. It's not two men fighting, it's one man *biting* another.

The guards rush in and pull the victim away, and the aggressor snaps his jaws and lunges at the guards, managing to catch one, who screams. There's a blur of movement in your peripheral vision, and you flinch as Solitary darts past. Despite the shackles limiting his movement, the man moves like quicksilver.

Solitary sweeps the frenzied attacker's legs out from beneath him, then stomps on the man's head, again and again, until he stops moving.

Celly shaves his head at the sink, completely bald, down to the skin. The whole time, you can't help but think about that nutter eating the other guy. *Jesus,* you think. *I mean—*

"What the fuck?" Celly says, rifling through his blankets. "I thought today was contraband day, *hombre*?"

He steps towards you, and his hulking frame would be scary enough, but seeing his ink up close makes it worse. Three tear tattoos drip down from under his right eye. You swallow, hard. He rubs the Christian cross tattooed on his chin in contemplation.

"You know something about this, *esse*?"

- ➢ It's just a white lie: Deny, deny, counter-accuse, deny. Go to page 274
- ➢ Once they find the file outside, he'll know. Tell him you did it to be on the safe side. Offer to buy him another…shank maker. Go to page 376

The Dirty Half-dozen

Once you make it out and past the walls, you're able to think clearly once again. Those walls that would have helped keep the undead hordes out should now serve to keep them in. For a little while, anyway. Long enough for you to find a new safe place, far, far away from here.

After running for a few minutes, you direct the group to a gas station convenience store. It's been broken open and raided, but there are still a few sundries left within. Everyone grabs a drink and a snack. Sims snags a tin of chewing tobacco. Angelica looks for feminine products, trying to be discreet.

"That's a nasty habit," Angelica says to Sims, scrunching her nose.

"Yeah? Well, you know what they say, *Old Habits and Die Hard.*"

"We're moving out. The sun's going down and this place isn't secure. Any ideas?" you ask.

"The hospital is FUBAR," Sims says.

"No churches," Angelica adds.

"I done used up my ideas," Hefty says.

"Yeah, whatever you think is best, Coop," Tyberius replies.

"As long as we find a radio. I'm going to signal rescue, at all costs. So…" Sims says.

All eyes are on you, trusting your leadership. It takes an effort not to smile. Even though the park went to shit, you've got something better than a wall. You've got your very own group of survivors.

"Let's move out," you say. "We'll find somewhere safe enough for tonight, then somewhere safer tomorrow. We stick together, we stay alive."

<u>Go to page 160</u>

Ditch

You leap from the tram into the lazy river just before the first car smashes into the crashed cart. It's a soft landing—mostly. The moat isn't very wide, and you hit your shoulder against the concrete wall, which hurts but isn't a debilitating wound.

The gasmask starts to try to filter the water, but it's not designed as a SCUBA mask, so you pull the thing off to breathe. The current isn't very strong, but all the same, you can't stand in one place, so you have to go with the flow.

The sides of the lazy river are impossible to climb out of "for your own safety," but there's bound to be a bank downstream where you can get out. And indeed there is, but it's completely clogged. With no lifeguard to fish out the extra tubes and various detritus, there's a natural dam formed in the moat.

And it's filled with corpses, some of them undead fleshies.

You swim as fast as you can against the current, but with all your sodden battle gear, it's no use. Like a sloth of bears (yep, "sloth" is the name of a group of bears), waiting for spawning salmon, the zombies grab hold once you're forced by the stream into their midst.

With any luck, you'll drown before you're eaten.

THE END

Doesn't Add Up

"Call in the goddamn chopper!" you scream.

Belliveau nods and makes the call. You cover him while he does so and fire on two zombies. The first goes down with a *bang*, but then your slide stays open. That's it, mag's empty. In that moment of surprise, the second fleshie grabs you. Before you can bring out your knife, it digs in with its teeth.

Belliveau shoots the zombie and it falls off you.

"Evac is inbound!" he says.

But it's too late…

You're INFECTED!

Dojo

You rush over to the building with its glass front and pull on the double-doors. Locked. Frustrated, you shake them, rattling their hinges. The children inside range from maybe seven-year-olds to high schoolers, and they shrink back at the sight of you. The master of the dojo is a middle-aged Japanese man. His face is placid, sad even, and he shakes his head at you.

You nod back. *Yes, let me in!* But the man doesn't budge. Then, fearing that a rifle shot is imminent, you back away and look for cover behind a stalled car. The National Guard soldiers jog towards you.

Locking eyes with the man in the dojo, you sprint at the glass doors, ready to break them down. He gets it, and rushes to disengage the door lock and let you in, precisely when you would have smashed through.

"Good call," you say.

The man wears a classic white karate-gi and holds a large wooden staff, a mock-sword, you realize. The way he holds it tells you he knows what he's doing.

"I am sorry," the man says. "But I cannot allow you to endanger my pupils."

Slowly and deliberately, he raises the wooden sword.

- ➤ Prepare to defend yourself. His 5'8" and 150 pounds versus your 6'3" and 225. Go to page 233
- ➤ Appeal to his humanity and plea for help. He doesn't want trouble any more than you do. Go to page 265

Do the Right Thing

You rush in to help open the inner doors just as the convict smashes through the glass. Not wanting to get cut, you step back, police baton at the ready, should any of the fiends follow the guy inside.

As he pushes through, the store's alarm goes off—*Dee-doo, dee-doo, doo-doo*—must be battery-operated. Seeing you, the convict shouts, "Same team, same team!" and you back away, realizing he's taken you for a threat.

He spins back, then holds up a nail gun to address the pair of infected that have followed him into the entrance way. He puts the nail gun up against the first ghoul's head and it drops, with a steel *Bindi* dotting her forehead. Equally as fast and effectively, he puts down the second undead.

"Christ, you almost gave me a heart attack," you shout over the alarm.

The guy is skinny, thin as a rail, really, and his orange jumpsuit hangs off his lean frame. His eyes go to your police baton and he says, "You some kinda cop? Like security, errr...."

"Fuck, no. You some kinda psycho killer?"

"Ain't psycho, but I've had to put some a' them nutters down," he says in a thick Southern drawl.

"The infected?"

He nods and you look away, swallowing a knot of emotion as the memories of your mother boil to the surface. At length, you say, "Guess we all have."

"Can we shut this goddamned alarm off?"

"Lemme see your pipe," you say.

He hesitates, but hands the weapon over. With a great slam of the pipe, you break open the cover to the alarm fuse box, find the right switch, and shut off the wailing alarm.

"How'd you know to do that?"

"We have the same setup at my job," you say, handing back the pipe. "Thanks. I'm Ty, by the way. Tyberius, but to my friends it's just Ty."

"Mine call me Hefty."

You nod. "When's the last time you ate?"

"Today, why? Oh...yeah, I always been this skinny. I could use some sleep though. We could run together, if the jumpsuit don't put you off. I'll watch your back, you watch mine. Deal?"

"My brother wore one of those once, so no, I don't mind. But I'd need a favor. I need to drop off a dress somewhere. We can look out for each other, and if you don't ask me what it's for, I won't ask about what you did to survive, neither. We leave the past where it belongs."

"I'd best get a change of clothes, then," he says.

"There are other department stores in here. And a mattress store. You look like you could use a few hours first."

"Then what?" he asks all of a sudden. "After you drop off your dress, I mean."

Probably just kill myself, a voice inside says, shocking you, even though you know it's the truth. After the funeral, you didn't have any plans, because you didn't have anything left to live for.

He continues, "Once the past is past, we stick together, yeah? Find someplace safe?"

That's really what mama would want—for you to survive. As long as you remember her, she'll live on. Like one of those movie stars in the black-and-white movies she used to watch. Long gone, but remembered and beloved.

You put out a hand for him to shake. He grins and takes it. "Just came from a construction site near here; could probably get you somethin' suited to a man of your stature. Sledgehammer, maybe. Those nutters won't even know what hit 'em."

Sounds good to you.

Go to page 160

Down with the Sickness

The streets leading to the hospital are absolute chaos and grow worse, the closer you get to downtown. Cars flipped over and burning. Police cruisers, ambulances, and fire trucks litter the suburban roads; sirens blazing, but seemingly abandoned. Pedestrians chase one another to and fro. Lions lay with lambs, pigs fly, and politicians tell the truth—you know, the end times. They're nigh.

"How did it get so bad so fast?" Jason wonders aloud.

"It already was bad, right under our noses," you say. "Denial is a dangerous foe."

"Thanks, Freud."

The road ahead is completely barricaded, but you can see the hospital just beyond. "Hang on," you say, flipping the Jeep over to manual 4x4. Jason grabs the *oh-shit bar* above the passenger window as the Jeep hops the curb and rips across the green median. The back tires throw up chunks of sod in your wake as the Jeep slides around the barricade and back to the road.

"Badass," Jason says.

As tires squeal against pavement, a woman rushes onto the road. You floor the accelerator and gun the engine, but she frantically stumbles forward, trying to get you to stop, waving her arms in panicked mania. You weave away from her, but at the last second she lunges—and *slaps* off the front bumper.

You let out a squeal. "*Omigod*, is she okay?"

"Doubt it."

"Should we stop?"

Jason looks back. "Nope. She's fine."

In the rear-view mirror, you see the woman slowly rise from the road, despite the odd angles at which her limbs now bend. Yep, better keep moving.

Ahead, the hospital parking lot is the epicenter of social decay—over-packed with cars, most having ignored the lines and signs of the lot. Doing the same, you pull onto a flower bed and park atop the daisies at the entrance. With all the chaos, you figure it's best to bring your firearms with you.

When you run inside the automatic doors, you're greeted with a directional sign. Where to?

- Pharmacy. If there's something that'll help Dad, that's where it will be held. Go to page 285
- ER. This is an emergency! Go to page 326
- The Morgue. When the dead are rising, it'll likely be the safest place here. Go to page 150
- Cafeteria. Maybe you can catch a doctor on break? Go to page 149

Draconian

"Get inside or get left behind!" you shout, running back in. You slam your hand on the plunger switch and yell, "*NOW!!!*"

The door begins on its course, rattling down the tracks on rollers that have long needed replacing. Owen sprints in, then Stephen. Craig and Brian come running, but a lifetime of saying "fuck you" to cardio doesn't give Craig much of a chance, while having his arm chewed like a hungry dog on a rawhide bone has sapped Brian's strength.

Still, Brian was closer, and it looks like he'll make it. So you lunge forward, turn, and kick him in the chest. He falls back towards Craig and the door closes. The moaning grows louder, and then the two men's screams drown out all sound from outside.

"You goddamned bitch!" Stephen yells.

You turn to face him, almost confused by his anger. "Brian was bitten. Didn't you see what happened to Josh?"

"And Craig?!" he shouts, spittle hitting you in the face.

"You're still alive, you ignorant fool!"

Stephen punches you in the stomach. It's a sucker-punch, the breath shoots from your abdomen and you stumble back to Josh's work station. You grab a large chrome wrench from the desk and turn in a wild swing.

He's further back than you thought, and you hit only air. You're still sucking for breath when he swings. You bring the wrench up and he punches metal, buying you a moment of time as he screams out in pain and grabs his bruised knuckles.

"Guys, stop!" Owen shouts, stepping between the two of you.

Stephen elbows his boss in the face and the man falls back. Then Stephen grabs a lug nut off his workstation and hurls it at you like a fastball pitch. You duck down and the next thing you know, he's tackled you. His fingers wrap around your neck.

Everything goes dull, then red. Your vision tunnels like you're about to pass out. Then suddenly you can breathe again. When you look up, you see Owen standing over you, with one hand outstretched and the other holding a bloody wrench.

"It was the only choice we had. You did the right thing," he says.

You take his hand and he helps you up. Stephen isn't moving. The garage door starts opening again, meaning either Craig or Brian used the employee keypad entrance. Damn them! The dead flood into the garage and with a welded door at your back, there's nowhere to go. You grab the wrench to fight, but you know this won't end well.

THE END

Dragon Emperor

The students gather in a semi-circle while Master Hanzo bites on his empty pipe. He clears his throat, closes his eyes, and begins, "This story takes place in ancient China, Zhou dynasty. Before the Silk Road, there was some trade, usually by exiles and hermits. Well, one such was a priestess who wandered all the way from a great civilization in Egypt. She was traveling through China, lost, and found she was without water. She asked a man for a drink, and he scolded her. In those days, women did not speak to men, and this man was a nobleman—so her blunder was double. But she pleaded for mercy.

"She said, 'All I want in this world is a cup of water!'

"But the man, born to riches, did not know true thirst. 'I don't care,' he said. 'No one can give me all I want in the world, so why should I help you?'"

Nolan shifts on the floor and whispers, "He's not very nice."

The other children nod solemnly.

"'But, I can give you your desires!' the woman said. 'If you give me water, I will give you the power of the dragon, which is the power to have all your wishes granted!'

"The man, who was actually a prince, agreed. He was turned into a dragon, and destroyed all of his enemies. This man became the Emperor of China, uniting the many kingdoms into one, but since he was so cruel to the Egyptian priestess—his gift was actually a curse. His own thirst for greatness could never be quenched.

"The Dragon Emperor began to consume. First, the prize livestock and best crops, but then he desired *more*. When a master painter completed a great work of art, the dragon would come and swallow it whole. If a tapestry took four or more years to complete, the dragon would come and eat it! If a mother who was unable to have children prayed and prayed and finally got pregnant, the dragon would come and eat—"

"Ewww," Christian says.

Haley punches him in the arm, and that silences the teen.

Master Hanzo continues, "The people prayed for an end to the terror of the dragon. The Emperor's own son was coming of age, and the priests were afraid the dragon would consume their future ruler. One man, known for his wisdom, said he would make a gift—the greatest blade that man had ever seen. He took years to complete the dagger, and it was never equalled.

"Just as expected, at completion, the dragon showed up. The wise man offered the blade, and the dragon ate it—but the dagger was made to the exact right size, and caught in the dragon's throat, killing the Dragon Emperor and allowing his more just and peaceful son to inherit the land."

Master Hanzo opens his eyes, chews on his pipe and looks around at the students.

"The lesson," you ask, "Is it to always be generous with your gifts, or your gifts will consume you?"

"What happened to the wise man?" asks Mason. "The one who killed the dragon?"

"Some say he turned into a tiger and left China, never to return. Goodnight," Master Hanzo says.

The old man abruptly extinguishes the candles with a sweep of his robe, and the room goes dark. The children whisper to themselves for a time, but eventually you all fall fast asleep.

Sometime in the middle of the night, you're awakened by an urgent pounding on the doors. It takes only a brief moment to exit the dream-state of sleep before the memories of what's out there come flooding back.

It's an urgent, almost animal-like intensity, rapping upon the door, pulling at the handles and groping for a way in. With no streetlights, you can't see who it is—or *how many*—out in the shadowy black of night. A huffing voice shouts something, but you can't make out any words, or be certain there are any to make out.

- ➤ Leave the doors closed. You can't defend against a mob with a wooden sword. Go to page 341
- ➤ Open the doors. Bushido demands you help any way you can. Go to page 408

Drooling

Okay, so that was all a dream. As in, none of that happened after you saved the Ambassador. In fact, right now you're asleep on the C-17, headed back to the States. Still, that would be cool, wouldn't it? To be a zombie-slaying badass superhero? You wish, Sims. You wish.

But you're to be congratulated on finding this book's major Easter Egg!

If you want to join Agent Droakam and be a superhero for real, check out *SUPERPOWERED*. If you want to hang out with agents Bertram and Danly in a non-zombie environment, check out *MURDERED* and put your detective skills to the test.

For now:

Time to wake up. Go to page 120

Early Bird

You jog through the parking lot, which, even in the morning light, catches the attention of five nutters close enough to see you. They give stumbling chase and you go for the nearest entrance—a department store.

Bad news: shit must have gone down after closing time, because the doors are locked. You can see through them to another set of double doors and the darkened store beyond.

- Find another way in! Go to page 198
- Kick 'em down! Go to page 195

Eaten

Hefty shakes his head, but doesn't protest, so as a group of five, you head towards the cafeteria. It's not hard to find—there are large mural-sized maps with a "You Are Here!" at every trail junction. Getting inside, however, might be a different story.

The entry has been barricaded from within. The front of the building is almost entirely made of glass, but every square inch is covered with stacked tables and chairs. Sure would be nice to have that Ditch Witch right about now.

"Think there might be survivors?" Angelica asks.

"Only one way to find out," Hefty answers.

"Not the front," you say. "There will be a back way in, and it'll be less protected." They follow you around to an EMPLOYEE ONLY entrance. It's locked, of course. "Ty, take off the doorknob," you order.

The big man nods and hefts the sledgehammer up over his head like he's doing the strongman test at a carnival. He brings it down cleanly on the door handle, shearing if off in one swipe. You knock the rest away, then push the door open. This door wasn't barricaded, but from this angle you can see just how crazy the front is—it would have taken hours to clear it from the entrance.

"Smart, Cooper. Nicely done," Tyberius says.

When you head in, you're greeted with a terrible stench. It's impossibly dark and you can't see very far, what with the barricade blocking the sun from the glass façade. But it's the *moan* that raises the hair on the back of your neck.

"Hefty, take the left. Tyberius, right. Jose, with me. Angelica, watch our rear!" you shout.

Moving quickly, the gang rushes in. Hefty proves his worth with that lead pipe, while Tyberius does terrible damage with his sledgehammer. Jose is quick and efficient, trapping heads between the frying pan and cleaver. Your wrench is more than capable of collapsing a skull, and Angelica even manages to batter a former nine-year-old with her candlestick. In a matter of moments, you've dispatched more than a dozen ghouls and the cafeteria is silent, save for your heavy breathing.

"Nice work, everyone," you say. It's true. Could you have taken that many alone? "This is where the survivors holed up. Let's check for food."

The survivors didn't leave much, and with no power, what little food was left in the refrigerators didn't hold. Must've been a massive blackout in the city while you were trapped at that compound. Still, they died and turned before they ate everything, so you're able to scrounge up enough for one meal. A meal you're happy to eat out on the patio.

"That was some good shit, Coop," Tyberius says, taking a seat next to you. "Where'd you learn to be so cool under pressure?"

"Try running a pit crew sometime," you say.

"No shit, that was like some *Rainbow Six*, *Call of Duty*-level badassery," Hefty adds.

You don't respond, instead taking another bite of potato chips. You can barely taste their overly salty goodness through the throbbing in your lower back.

"You'll have to excuse her," Angelica says. "She doesn't trust you because the last men we met—"

You lash out, slapping Angelica across the face, silencing the woman. "If you ever say another word about that place, I swear to God it'll be your last!"

The sudden outburst surprises even you, but if you're going to lead these men, you can't have them thinking of you in terms of *breeding stock*. No one at the table speaks, much less eats. Everyone sits frozen, staring at some detail on the tables.

Calmly, you continue, "We all did what we had to do to survive, didn't we? Doesn't mean we have to talk about it."

"Fine by me..." Tyberius says.

Hefty nods. "I'm good with that."

The group goes back to eating, and you finish your makeshift meal without another word.

"We might be wise to consider the zoo animals," you say afterwards. "For food, I mean."

"Ummm, yeah, about that," Hefty says.

"You object?"

"Unless you're talking about the seals, it's a no-go. I...uhhh...we let most of the animals out this morning."

"You did *what*?"

"Seemed wrong just to leave them incarcerated, considering they'd all starve to death," Hefty says with a shrug. "And I figured maybe a bull elephant would take a few nutters down on its way out."

"We're walking around with wild animals?" Angelica asks.

"Not yet. We just opened the cages. Most were too scared to come out, or too used to the bars to try," Tyberius explains.

"Kinda like people, come to think of it," Hefty adds.

"What about the carnivores?" you ask.

"All of 'em."

"Christ," you say. "Frightened, hungry predators *and* the dead? We're getting out of here."

"To go where?" Angelica asks.

You don't answer. Frankly, because you don't know.

"My next idea was the theme park," Hefty says. "Used to work there, and I know where they store the extra food. Lots and lots of extra food. Got a wall too, but I doubt many would think of it as a shelter. Which means we should have it to ourselves. Safe as can be."

"Like it was here...before you *Jurassic Park*'ed the place," you say.

"Uhhh, guys," Tyberius says.

He points towards a stroller parking area—and a lion. The king of the jungle takes a cautious step towards you. The scale of the animal is something you didn't appreciate from afar. He's gigantic. His nostrils flare as he smells your food.

➢ Run! Go to page 292
➢ Stand tall, scare it off. Go to page 76

Eat Me

"I've got a better idea," the guard says. "Why don't you fuck yourself? You know what? *If* we do come back, I'm making sure we visit this cell last. But hey, if you get hungry, there's some big Mexican chorizo right there you can choke on."

And with that, the guard is off. He leaves the food cart right in front of your cell and abandons the prison. The other inmates he hadn't yet visited howl with anger. But that's nothing compared to what's locked in here with you.

"You dumb, white, *loco*..." he growls.

Celly takes your food tray for himself, and you don't bother to argue. If you hadn't tossed his file, things might be different.

Three more days pass, and you're weak with hunger. The food trays are tantalizingly just out of reach, and starting to smell. What's worse, Celly's starting to look at you *funny*. Any time you fall asleep, he nudges you to see if you're only sleeping.

Then you don't wake up. Celly puts a pillow over your face and that's that. A starving man is at his most dangerous, and you're the only food within arm's reach.

THE END

Emergency Exit

You hop up, and the homeless guy does the same. Your arms go to the big red handle on the back door, while the vagrant's arms go to you. He grabs you firmly by the shirtsleeves, so you switch focus. You try to shove the guy away, but he's got a death grip on your arms. He's frothing at the mouth and repeatedly snapping his teeth.

Other passengers on the bus start screaming.

Leaning back, you plant a foot on the homeless guy's chest and kick him back. He tears your shirtsleeves to tatters, but then falls away. Not wasting any time, you open the back door and jump out.

Someone screams, and you see that the crazed vagrant now holds a new passenger hostage.

"Hey! Stay put. We have infected in the area," shouts a street cop, brandishing a baton.

Infected? What the hell does that mean? Beyond the man there's a line of National Guardsmen defending a wooden barrier, the kind of thing they put up at events for crowd control. But these are armed soldiers, not event security rent-a-cops. What's going on here? You're trying to think, but the cop shouting in your face makes it nearly impossible.

- ➤ Run past the soldiers. Run home. Just…run. Go to page 308
- ➤ Cooperate. Tell him there was a crazed guy on the bus! Go to page 294
- ➤ Knock him out; that'll give you some time to think. Go to page 242

Encroaching

Everyone thinks you're crazy for hiking through the swamps at night, but you explain the urgency. Reluctantly, they nod their heads, say goodbyes, and promise to meet you at Salvation. Still, as you presently slog through the muck, you can't help but agree with their original assessment.

Where the Kendo armor was hot and muggy during the day, your sweat chills you at night, and the helmet obscures what little night vision the cloudy sky affords. Something moves in the brackish waters and you freeze, your hand on the pommel of your sword.

There it is again—you're not imagining it. You spring the sword out into the night sky and the steel blade shimmers in the pale moonlight. Focused on the rippling swamp ahead, a shape just beneath the surface catches your eye.

You plunge the blade into the water, if only to slow your would-be attacker. You can't make out the walking corpse's head in the murky black, but your armor should protect you. That confidence wavers when your sword glances off the body below, like you've just struck a boulder.

That's when something latches onto your leg. Something *big*. Then it wrenches you off your feet and pins you underwater until you drown. The big gators don't usually come this far towards civilization, but something must be displacing them north.

THE END

Enemy of My Enemy

You rush the trio of nutters, slamming the butt of the fire extinguisher as hard as you can into the skull of the nearest one.

"Come on!" you shout.

The office door swings open and the guard smashes into one of the ghouls with his Asp baton. The doctor cowers behind the correctional officer, so you and the guard finish off the third flesh-eating bastard together.

Once their undead bodies stop twitching, the guard looks you over. He removes a pair of handcuffs and you raise your hands, shaking your head and back away.

"I'll get the two of you out of here," the cop says. "But we can't have inmates running amok. If the warden sees us…"

Say:

➢ "Fuck you, and fuck the warden. You ain't cuffin' me." Go to page 163
➢ "Gimme your word and I'll go along." Go to page 207

Enough

You take off running, knowing full well that since these guys are weighed down by tactical gear (and gasmasks, no less), they have no chance of catching you. They shout warnings for you to stop; the classic empty threat, "Stop or I'll shoot!"

But this time it's different.

You stumble forward as something painfully stings you in the back. It hurts so much that you barely register the deafening *boom* that accompanied the shot. You fall forward on your chest, wheezing for breath. Whatever just hit you, you can no longer feel your legs. Guess you won't be running anymore.

THE END

Excommunicated

"Jason, help me with Dad," you say. Together, you lift your father from his spot against the altar and head down the aisle towards the front doors. "Dad? Daddy, can you hear me? We're leaving."

The man looks over to you with glossy eyes and a slack jaw. A flicker of understanding lights behind his eyes. It's small, but you can tell that something you said registered. He licks his lips, his tongue dry and his gums smacking because of cotton mouth. "Before…" Dad croaks. "Mil…chest…"

Your eyes sting with tears at seeing the strongest man you've ever known barely able to speak. But you get what he means—his foot locker from his Marine days. It's been at the foot of his bed for as long as you can remember, though you've never seen it opened.

"I'll take care of it. You just rest now, okay, Daddy?"

Though they're busy with the stranger—who thrashes and bites at them from behind the sheet—Father Thomas rises to stop you.

"Where are you going?"

"Somewhere else, just leave us alone!" Jason shouts.

"No…" your father croaks. "Leave…me…"

"You see? He wants to stay," Father Thomas says.

Dad stumbles forward, then gathers himself. With extreme effort, he says, "If you live…we live…with you…"

Dad's head snaps towards your brother and a low, guttural growl comes from his throat. The metal of your rifle is cold in your sweat-drenched palms. *Oh, God. This isn't happening!* You're frozen, paralyzed. Time creeps by, each second lasting a decade. *He can't be dead, he can't. He can't be one of those things!*

"No…!" Jason cries as Dad's hands rise up to embrace his son.

"I'm sorry," you say, then raise the rifle.

Crack—the Zulu that was once your father falls to the floor, twice-dead.

"Enough!" Father Thomas cries. "You are no longer welcome here! Leave us!"

You barely hear him over the pain of losing your father. Jason takes you by the arm and practically drags you outside and into the Jeep.

"C'mon, Sarah. This place is fucked six ways to Sunday, let's skedaddle."

You drive away just as a Humvee pulls up to the cathedral parking lot. Several armed men hop out and walk towards the front doors. *Good luck with the crazies,* you think to yourself.

"Where are we headed?" Jason asks.

- "We need to distance ourselves from this city. Like you said, skedaddle." Go to page 114
- "Dad mentioned his mil locker. Let's head home and get supplies before we go." Go to page 177

Exit Lane

There's only one main road out of town and into the woods—and that tunnel to freedom is up ahead. A police barricade was set in place to prevent a mass exodus from town, but plenty of people ran the barricade, and so can you.

The only light comes from the sirens of abandoned patrol cruisers. You scan the area, but find no sign of the police officers. The Jeep's headlights suddenly glint off something on the road, and you slam on the brakes, but too late. The tires scream and hiss when they hit the spike strip, and you skid to the side, the Jeep threatening to flip. You hold your breath, turn into the skid, and close your eyes. The Jeep comes to a stop and after a moment, you head out to check the wheels.

They're fucked; you'll have to continue on foot.

"Conserve ammo. We need it to last and we don't—"

"Yeah, I get it. I'm not a kid, you know."

The first figure to come clear in the headlights is a man in a business suit, his necktie pulled so tight that his eyes literally bulge from his head. The white oxford shirt he wears is smattered in gore up to his nose.

More follow. Mothers, fathers, children. Truck drivers, cops, commuters. They all come for you.

"There's…so many…" Jason says in awe.

"Only shoot the ones you have to! Keep moving!"

"Maybe we should pick off these ones and find a hiding spot until first light?"

➤ Great idea. Cab of a semi-truck should work well. High off the ground and roomy enough. Go to page 323

➤ No way. Keep moving, and eventually take guard shifts somewhere less hot. Go to page 142

Failure to Launch

Your throat is hoarse and dry, and doesn't obey when you tell it to shout. Your arms are leaden, and the rifle feels like it weighs a hundred pounds. The front of Jason's pants darken and you can tell he's going through the same terror-stalled body shutdown.

Until dad bites into him.

Jason screams and can suddenly move again, but the old man holds Jason tight. Bite after bite, and there's nothing Jason can do about it. You force yourself forward, raise the rifle, and put them both down.

In the silence that follows, you're alone in this world for the first time. Well, that's not totally true, is it? You'll always have your guilt with you. Guilt, and bad memories.

> *Leave this cursed home. Go, and never look back.* Go to page 315

Familicide

A simple squeeze of the trigger, and Jason is dead. His eyes stay wide-open; his last expression was one of surprise. A sick feeling overtakes your whole body and you heave a silent, dry sob of anguish. In the back of your mind, you hear the office door open and turn back towards the ranger.

"Monster!" she cries. She holds a can of bear spray—basically mace on steroids—and blasts you in the face.

Nothing has ever hurt like this. Bear spray is so potent, it's actually illegal to use on humans. It's designed to stop a charging grizzly from an effective range of up to 35 feet. So what happens when it's sprayed in the face of a teenage girl at point-blank range?

Such searing pain that it's literally blinding. Yes, you're blind now, permanently.

You bum-fire the 10/20 at the shrieking woman, and either you kill her or she's smart enough to go silent. Still, without your eyesight and no friends or family to help you, there's no possible way you can survive.

THE END

Family Reunion

You rest in the living room while the parents fawn over their children. They thank you profusely through tear-streaked smiles, but delivering the students safely to their families is reward enough. Now your thoughts go to Master Hanzo and the twins.

At dinner, the adults tell you about how congested the city is, and how they tried so hard to make it to the dojo. The quarantine blocked all routes. And their own homes? The dead and the desperate made Nathanael's mom and Nolan's parents flee. It was the mutual fear of their children's safety that brought them together. As a group, they'd been planning an excursion to the dojo, but you beat them to the punch.

Then you tell them all about "Salvation" and suggest that they meet you there. After helping plot their route to safety, you plot your own path to the twins' home. Now that you don't have to stop by Nathanael's house, you could possibly hike through the swampland. It's a straight shot from one new development to another, through a large area of uninhabitable marsh. Still, it would be a major shortcut compared to taking the roads.

Over after-dinner tea, it's time to ponder your options:

➤ Stay the night, then follow the paved roads when you have good visibility. Go to page 68
➤ Go now, through the swamp, lest the twins' parents mount their own rescue effort before you reach them. Go to page 110
➤ Head out now and take the long, paved road to find the last set of parents. Go to page 381
➤ Scrap the plan and head back. If these parents were coming to the dojo, maybe you can protect the twins while you wait for their parents? Go to page 295
➤ Get a good night's sleep, then trek through the marshes at first light. Go to page 230

Family Values

The man is ecstatic. He pushes his way through the crowd and says, "I'm Chris. You won't regret this!"

"See that we don't," Jason says, trying to act tough.

"The rest of you, I'd recommend heading somewhere more defensible," you say. With that, you leave the cafeteria and head towards the NICU.

"What're we walking into, Chris?" you ask.

"I came down to get some food for my wife, and when I tried to go back, they said it was on lock-down. It's probably the most secure place in the hospital. They keep high-risk and immune-compromised babies in there, so they limit access. Plus, you know, people steal babies…so they don't let you in unless you're on the guest list."

"How do you get in? Escort? Key card?" Jason asks.

"Entry area has a camera. You show an ID and they buzz you in. That's the door," Chris says.

He points to the door labeled, "NEONATAL INTENSIVE CARE UNIT." As luck would have it, a nurse not much older than you opens the door and steps out. Rifle in hand, you charge forward.

"Hold the door! Guy just wants to be reunited with his family! Let us in, Nurse Betty, or I'm not afraid to use your body as a door prop!"

She holds the door open and Chris pushes his way through. You follow with Jason and your new hostage, just in case. Chris runs to find his wife and kid, but you don't waste time on a touching reunion.

"Doctors, now!" you shout.

Three middle-aged men in lab coats come forward, with some hesitation.

"One of you is coming with us; we've got a sick man."

All three shake their heads, and the man in the middle says, "You can't just threaten violence and expect to get what you want—we're needed *here*."

- ➢ Back up the threat with action. You only need one doctor. Go to page 185
- ➢ Explain your situation. Go to page 359

Fast Food

You run down the bus aisle, past terrified passengers who duck away from you, and past the cop shouting for you to stay put. The only other person moving on the bus is the vagrant in the back, who snarls and stumbles forward.

Lowering your shoulder, you blast into the homeless man, sending him sprawling. You probably have fifty pounds on the guy, so it's easy to force your way through. You pull on the big red handle of the emergency exit, swing the door open, then stumble as something grabs your leg.

You pull hard, dragging the homeless man with you, but he finds an ankle and bites through your business socks with incredible force.

You're INFECTED!

Fatigue

You're penned shoulder-to-shoulder with dozens of farm animals. Literally. Burly cows heave their distressed bodies against you, while geese dart between your feet and nip at your heels. You're in line for the slaughterhouse; somehow you just know, and there's no way but forward. The ground is a mixture of mud and excrement, and you catch your reflection in a foul puddle—you're a pig.

When you look up, you're face-to-face with a goat, its dreadful eyes wide and angry, the flat, rectangular pupils drifting like an alien spacecraft before a brilliant sun. The goat's ears lower with agitation, then it lets out a terribly shrill scream, piercing your subconscious.

You shoot awake to see Lt. Dosa, eyes like saucers, screaming, as a woman sucks against his chest. He shoves her away and something that was once a part of him comes away with her. He looks at the arterial blood spurting from his chest and screams again.

She was probably someone's grandmother; sweet and kind and hardworking in life, now a feral powerhouse of hunger in afterlife. She pulls at him with inhuman ferocity while everyone suddenly wakes up with a mix of confusion and shock.

Lt. Dosa levels a punch at the woman's jaw and she opens her mouth to accept the gift. Then, fast as a striking viper, a Navy SEAL opens the woman's neck from ear to ear. Yet almost no blood comes out, like slicing into a cadaver on the autopsy table.

No blood pressure means...no heartbeat? A fact she's bothered by no more than this arterial wound. Her moaning changes to something more like a sucking sound as she turns towards this new threat.

You raise your rifle, but an Army Ranger next to you pushes the muzzle back down. "Not in flight," he says.

Unsheathing *Isabelle*, you stand and approach the woman from behind, then stick nine inches of cold steel against the base of her skull and up into her head. She falls limply and your knife comes out black and sticky.

It's a long moment of silence as everyone processes what just happened.

"We can't establish contact with the base," the loadmaster says at last. Looking at Lt. Dosa, he adds, "You're all on your own once we touch down."

"Is there something wrong with our comm?" you ask.

The loadmaster looks to the floor, sighs, then turns back into the cockpit without answering. You stand and follow him, your brain not willing to accept what he's saying.

"What do you mean we're 'on our own'? What orders do we have? Who are we debriefing?"

"Just *what* don't you get? There isn't a base anymore!" the loadmaster shouts back.

"How...how is that possible?"

The co-pilot turns and says, "It's Venezuela all over again, man."

"No, we wouldn't dose ourselves," you say, shaking your head.

The pilot laughs in disgust. "We didn't have to. Think about it. How would it look if we gave this *Gilga*-shit to a bunch of dick-head dictators, but no one in America got sick? They had to turn a blind eye in order to have plausible deniability, and if a

Kardashian or two died and ate her brain-dead fans, no big loss. Only…we waited too long to intervene."

"Are you saying we knew this would happen?"

"No," the co-pilot says. "We're saying we *made sure* it would happen. Who do you think funded this little project?"

"How…how do you know all this?"

"Need-to-know basis, and we needed to fucking know."

"The first *celebutard* was infected a couple of weeks ago. Containment has failed, Sergeant," the pilot adds.

Your head swirls and stomach turns—*I'm going to be sick*, you think. Vision narrowing, knees weak, you stumble out of the cockpit back into the loading bay, where the soldiers now have their weapons trained on the civilian passengers.

The infection, it's everywhere. You find your bag, dig into it, and pull out a black gasmask. You pull the thing on, sucking in deep breaths, and see the world anew through a plastic visor. The effect is calming, like breathing into a paper bag for a panic attack. It gives you a few minutes to think clearly, to plot out your next move.

So…what's next?

➢ This can't be all there is. I'll find my guard unit. There has to be a contingency plan, and I'm better off working with the military. Go to page 69
➢ As soon as we touch down, I'm out of here. I've got my bug-out bag in the car ready to go. I'm ready for this, even if Uncle Sam wasn't. Go to page 48

Feast

At the center of the park, the three survivors meet up with two more: A black-haired woman in a mechanic's overshirt who carries a chain and a wrench, and a man in kitchen whites who carries a butcher's knife and a frying pan. The group confers for a minute before the mechanic steps forward.

"I'm Cooper," she says, offering a hand to shake. "I'm sure they told you that I'm the leader of this merry band of misfits."

"Sergeant Sims. US Air Force electrical maintenance specialist."

"A pleasure. This here is Jose, man doesn't *habla mucho,* but he's good in a fight. I'm Cooper, and I guess you can think of me as your new commanding officer."

Trying to buy a moment to think, you say, "I'm going to signal rescue, at all costs. So…"

"Yeah, sure. Whatever. In the meantime, any chance you can get the power back on in the hotel? There's a restaurant on-site, and it'd be nice to have a real meal, don't you think?"

"Listen, Cooper, you seem…nice, but I'm not one to take orders from random strangers, so…."

Cooper sighs. "I was trying to be civil…" She wraps an arm around you, taking you into her confidence. Her voice grows hushed, and harsh. "Truth is, I think you could be useful, Sims. I really do, but I don't take chances. I protect my friends and my friends protect me, but if we're going to travel together, I need to know I can trust that you'll do what I say."

Out of nowhere she applies pressure to your wounded shoulder, sweeps your feet out from under you, and before you know what's happened, you're face-first on the ground, in agonizing pain.

"So what's it going to be, *cuntfuck?* Are we going to be friends or not?"

"*YES!!!*" you scream.

"And what I say goes?"

"Yes, yes! *Goddammit,* yes!"

She releases you. After a humiliated moment, you climb back onto your feet. Cooper stares at Angelica, an unspoken agreement passing between them. You look away in shame and see Jose smiling. Tyberius and Hefty simply shrug. That's just the way it is, it would seem. Until you can signal rescue, it looks like you're stuck with Tyberius, Hefty, Jose, Mega-bitch Cooper, and Angelica the Meek.

You've never been bullied before, but with a wounded shoulder and no real weapon, what choice do you have? Truth be told, you feel safe under the wing of such a strong leader. The walk to the hotel passes in silence, and so does the dinner that follows. The hotel is in immaculate condition, with zero fleshies, ample power, and running water. Flip a few breakers and you're in business.

There's a maintenance radio down here that crackles to life once you get the power going. It's a weak transmission, but it's something. You crank up the volume, tune the station manually, and listen closely to the man's voice on the other end. "…threat…God…and all…are…at the…off…." the man says through bursts of static. It's so hard to make out, but maybe you can boost the signal? This kind of thing used to be your job, after all.

After a moment, the message comes back with, "anyone…alone…Salvation…

blind…" and continues where you found it with "…threat." It's looping. Some kind of distress call? Someone's last words?

Then the cheering starts. The group calls out to you from upstairs, thrilled that you turned the power on, and ready to eat a feast, with you as the guest of honor. Even Cooper seems truly happy.

"Sims, you magnificent son-of-a-bitch, come on up! Dinner and drinks are on me," she says.

"Okay, here's everyone's room key," Cooper says after the meal. "We're in the suites. Take the night, get your head on straight, and tomorrow we're checking out the park in earnest. We might be here a while, and we're going to make the best of it. This is a great place to be—and this hotel is miraculously free of those *things,* so I want you to count your blessings and wake up with a smile on your faces. Got it?"

The hotel suite is somewhere a king or pop star would stay—a level of luxury you could never afford after a million years in the National Guard. Taking off your gasmask and uniform for the night, you prepare to unwind. After pillaging the minibar, you fill up the private Jacuzzi and take a soak.

Now, sprawled out in a bathrobe on a bed big enough to sleep triplets, you cruise the pay-per-view channels, which asks for a credit card. You laugh aloud. The whole thing is surreal. No, not the fact that there are porno rentals at a family-friendly resort, but that here you are, all these luxurious amenities at your fingertips, while the world crumbles outside….

Wonder what everyone else is up to? Tyberius and Hefty opted to share the multi-bedroom "family penthouse," but everyone else is just down the hall.

- ➤ Go check on Angelica. Go to page 165
- ➤ Go check on Cooper. Go to page 75
- ➤ Go check on Jose. Go to page 127
- ➤ Go check on Tyberius and Hefty. Go to page 362
- ➤ Nope. Stay in for a quiet night alone. Go to page 396

Feminine Wiles

"Haven't decided yet," you say as you lower the knife and cut his steak in earnest.

You slice off a bite, bring the fork towards his mouth, but when he opens his mouth—take the bite for yourself. You then sip his wine, with a devious smirk curling around the edges of the glass.

You sway your hips as you go back to your seat, the fabric clinging, then sliding; knowing full well what the visual is doing to the man. You finish the meal in silence, feeling his gaze on you, but not meeting it. That smirk, however, remains a constant feature.

"How about dessert?" you say, one eyebrow rising.

He swallows. "What did you have in mind?"

"I remember you saying something about a garage? I'm ready to be impressed."

Duke nods and rises from his seat. He leads you out of the big house and off to a prefab metal shelter—a garage built just for you, so he says. You can't help but notice Bud trailing as a shadow.

"He's not coming with us, is he?"

"He'll stay outside. You won't even know he's there."

The inside of the garage is truly impressive. Several bikes and a full set-up to work on them, along with several posters of you in your racing days. It looks like what you might have had in Motocross if your contract hadn't gone to shit. Ironic, in a way. You weren't willing to whore yourself out to magazines for all this, but look how you got it in the end. Well, screw irony.

You sit on one of the bikes, knees high, letting the little black dress fall up your thighs; give the man what he wants to see. "All this for little ole me?" you say, demurely.

"The world," he says. "Last we met you said to me, 'not if I were the last man on earth.' Thought you might rethink it, now that we're at the end of the world."

He steps forward and rubs your leg. His hands are sweaty. You pull him close and kiss the man, suppressing the bile in the back of your throat and playing the sex-kitten act to full force. Stepping off the bike, you shove him away, *hard*.

He hits against a worktable, where there's an electric wench used to strap down motorcycles and immobilize them for easy work. It's built-in, right there on the end of the table. When you pull out a length of nylon cable, it makes a loud whirring sound as it unspools, and Duke's eyes grow wide with fear.

You laugh, playfully, and then in a husky voice say, "Trust me..."

Taking the nylon around one wrist, you feel his muscles tighten with resistance. But when you rub against his chest, his fight dies down. Working quickly, you thread the tie-down cable around his wrists, pinning him to the table like it's a medieval torture rack.

Duke tries to sit up when you flip the electric wench on. He reaches out, wasting the few precious seconds where he might have freed himself before it was too late. You watch the man's face as he realizes you've betrayed him, savoring the moment. He opens his mouth to speak, but instead screams as the wench pulls the cord tight.

The electric motor strains, but his body gives out first. He cries bloody murder as his bones, joints, and tendons do the same with sickening crunches and snaps. Then you claim a fifteen-inch tire iron, feeling the curved steel in your hands before heading to the front door. When you open it, you see Bud rushing forward.

"Help! Duke is stuck!" Bud looks at you, trying to comprehend what you're saying. Inside, he looks at Duke on the table, then back to you. "It was a sex thing. I can't get him out!"

Bud growls, then rushes to Duke's side. From behind, you smash the man in the back of his knees and he collapses to the floor. Then you smash the back of his head and he falls, still. Duke's arms bend the wrong way as he's drawn further into the wench. He might live, but he'll never have full use of his arms again. Besides, leaving him alive might slow the other guards as you escape.

Time to go.

- ➢ Back to the stalls. Take Bud's key and get back in your riding clothes before you go. Go to page 397
- ➢ Straight out into the woods, right now. A dress isn't best, but time is of the essence. Go to page 370

Field Trip

The National Guardsmen leave; they're off to defend the hospital. You leave too, your students and Master Hanzo in tow, defending them as you make the trek across the city. The day threatens to be a warm one, made warmer still by all the hiking. You'll want to check convenience stores for water bottles along the way.

Though you instructed the group that they'll have to travel in silence, somehow the walking corpses know where to find you. Some instinct, perhaps? Just the movement of people walking? Either way, they come for you. Though they stumble, they're gaining on you. A shambling corpse never tires, while an aged man quickly does so.

Still, he's virile, for someone who spends most of his days drinking tea, reading poetry, and meditating.

"I'm ti-awwwww'd," Liam complains.

"No!" Stella shouts. "The bad people!"

Tears stream down her face as she points back to the growing crowd of walking corpses. You pick Liam up and carry him for the time being. Stella rushes to your side, puts her arms up to be held, and Nathanael takes her. He's the eldest, at seventeen, but his post-growth-spurt lean frame will tire quickly.

When a group of undead come around the corner in front of you, Master Hanzo gasps and clutches his chest, then falls to his knees.

"Leave me!" he shouts.

You prepare to fight off the group up front by setting Liam down and assessing the threat of the group when Liam suddenly screams and runs towards a nearby second-hand bookstore—THE BOOKWORM. Stella wriggles her way free from Nathanael and follows her brother. The door is unlocked and they disappear inside.

You take Master Hanzo under one arm and Nathanael takes his other arm. As a group, you amble towards the bookshop, hoping it might provide refuge.

"Find a back door!" you shout.

Haley quickly reports back that there is only a store room and toilet. No other way out. It's an older store; a relic of a different age. But the front of the shop is primarily glass, and you're not sure how long that will hold.

That's when the group of undead smashes against the glass doors. It's unlike the strange curiosity the early attempts displayed. This is pure, rabid hunger. They know people are inside, and they burn with desire to join you. Some leave bloody smears on the glass as they break their fists on the doors.

Their greedy, hungry teeth come for you all. With no back exit, there's no way you'll make it out of this alive. But at least there won't be enough of you left to rise again.

THE END

¡ Fiesta!

Jose opens the door, frying pan and cleaver at the ready.

"No, no! I just wanted to say hi. *Hola?*" you say, hands raised in supplication.

"*Hola...*" he responds, looking past you and into the hall.

You pull a handful of tiny alcohol bottles from your bathrobe pockets and hold them up as a peace offering. His eyes light up in understanding, and he rattles something off in rapid-fire Spanish, ushering you into the room.

It's basically the same as yours—right down to the porno up on the pay-per-view. Guillermo opens his own mini-bar, then mixes some of the alcohol with a tiny can of pineapple juice into two tumblers and hands you one of the cocktails.

"*Arriba, abajo, al centro, adentro...salud,*" he says. As he does so, he raises the glass, lowers it, brings it in, then downs the drink.

"Uhhh... 'May the girls with itty bitties at least let you pet their pretty kitties!'" you say, before downing your own beverage.

Though the language barrier is high, man-code proves universal. You drink the night away, but eventually, what goes up must come down. At some point you wake up, still drunk, the TV on its loop of advertisements for on-demand entertainment, and Guillermo passed out next to you on the couch.

- ➢ Go check on Tyberius and Hefty. Go to page 362
- ➢ Go check on Cooper. Go to page 75
- ➢ Go check on Angelica. Go to page 165
- ➢ Head back to your room and get some sleep. Go to page 396

Final Solution

You stay quiet in the dark, hoping against hope that the *Turned* patients in here with you won't pick up on your presence. That you won't get them in a frenzy. Because they don't care if the straps cut through their skin. They would break their own arms to get free. To get to you.

Panic settles in, so you try to focus on something outside of the tent. There are car engines in the distance—a sound you haven't heard in a full day. Is the army leaving? Is the quarantine over?

That's when the main tent flap opens. There's some light from outside, so you can see the silhouette of a gasmask-clad soldier. He's muttering something that sounds religious in tone, but you're pretty sure he's speaking Spanish. You recognize the word "Maria." Sounds like the Hail Mary prayer.

Now the *Turned* in the room grow restless. Frenzied. The room erupts with the brightness of a lightning strike; it's the muzzle of the soldier's rifle as he shoots the first infected in the head. A moment later, the crack of gunfire shakes the tent and illuminates the scene once more at the next cot over.

He's going person-to-person, one bullet for each. Now your screams blend with the groans and growls of the damned, but it doesn't make him stop. Eventually your turn comes up too.

THE END

Finding Mr. Right

It's already dark out and the searchlights from the guard towers sweep across the prison grounds. You move quickly, darting from building to building to keep clear of the searchlight beam.

The armory waits up ahead. Just beyond the armory is the motorpool, then the outer fence, and beyond that—freedom. You're considering the armory as a possible "pit stop" when you see another figure in the darkness.

You creep closer, hoping not to alert a nutter. But as you get closer to the armory, you see it's Solitary, the prison's resident violent offender. He wears a guard's utility belt and rifles through a set of keyrings, trying to let himself into the secure building.

After a few moments, he finds the right key and opens the armory door. You step forward, but a second later, Solitary comes sprinting back out. A gunshot *cracks* from inside the armory and the inmate runs away from whoever is inside, away from this set of buildings, towards the laundry, machine shop, cafeteria, and infirmary.

> ➢ Chase after him—he might know another way out! Go to page 309
> ➢ Use him as a welcome distraction—head for the motorpool! Go to page 228

The Fine Print

"I'm in," you say.

"Sarah, what the fuck?!" Jason screams.

One of the nuns produces a yardstick from somewhere deep within her robes and slaps your brother with it. She follows after him, swatting Jason for his foul mouth, until he's forced from the room.

After the commotion, Sister Mary III passes out the rest of the inhalers to the superfluity of nuns while she sing-song chants, *"In nomine Patris et Filii et Spiritus Sancti."*

Without hesitation, you pop the cap and suck down the cool solution from within. As you depress the injector, the formula forces itself into your throat and lungs. You can't tell if it's liquid or gas, but it coats your esophagus in a viscous embrace. The effervescent tingling spreads throughout your body and eventually dissipates altogether.

The Mother Superior then says, *"Ite ad Evangelium Domini nuntiandum."*

"Deo gratias," her sisters reply in unison.

"Amen," you say.

Disinformation can be just as deadly as a lie, and you've just been fed the forbidden fruit. Gilgazyme® doesn't prevent the plague, it *is* the plague. But you'll find that out soon enough once feeling gives way to instinct. Then you'll help the helpless in the most merciful way possible, by releasing them from their suffering.

You're INFECTED![1]

---

1. Just a guess: You didn't read INFECTED, right? Either that, or you thought, Heh, I'm going to be a zombie! Not this time. Different book, different rules.

Fire in the Hole!

"This is where the shit hits the road, gentlemen. Look alive!" you say.

Finding cover behind a food services cart with the other Marines, you hunker down while the corporal readies his M203 grenade launcher. A hollow *thunk* announces the shot, and a moment later, there's a satisfying *KABOOOOOM!!!*

When you bring your head up, you see an enormous hole where once there was a barrier. Unfortunately, so do most of the zombies on the tarmac. More of the fiends come out of the woodwork, and you've got a quarter-million or so hungry eyes looking your way.

Better hurry.

Flaming debris dots the landscape, and there's a ring of fire that marks your entrance. In the middle of the pack of Marines, you rush inside the opening and into the terminal. A smear of cooked flesh paints the walls within, followed by more bits and pieces of something that was once human. A torso and head twitches just outside that line of gore and beyond that—more fleshies.

"Ambassador!" you scream.

"Up here," a meek voice cries in the distance.

Time to find a way up to the second level. You do your best to step around the...*squick*...that paints the linoleum floor. It seems the barricades weren't foolproof, as evidenced by the dozens of zombies that already wander the airport's interior.

With your fireteam of Marines, you quickly cut your way through the crowds and upstairs. Jogging over towards the shops, you focus on one store in particular where the security gate has been rolled down and two dozen people cower within.

"Get this gate up, quick. We have a way out, but we can't stay here long," you say.

Several tough-looking men in suits start to comply and raise the barrier, but a tall, thin man with razor burn on the creases of his neck interrupts them.

"Don't," he says, stepping forward and gripping the gate.

You're about to protest, but then he points behind you. The rear stairwell is thick with the shambling horde. A few quick strides to the rail show more gathered below. They flood in through the hole Corporal Gardner blew open, like shoppers on Black Friday. And you're the last Blu-ray player.

You look back towards the Ambassador's staff and all you see are pained, cold stares. Like they're looking at a dead man. Slowly, they all turn away. They don't want to watch you die.

The four Marines open fire, but there are far too many of the things. This won't end well.

THE END

Firepower

"Sounds good to me," Sam says, then, after Lily is out of earshot, "Just be careful not to blow us up."

"Uhhh…."

"See these metal doors up front? It's a decent barricade—for now. But let's say tomorrow, a dozen of those infected bastards want in. Will it hold up? Or if a hundred come to find us the day after that? Or worse, what if Pawnshop Guy's buddies show up and they want our supplies? How do you think we'd fare if somebody strapped a tow truck to the front and gave this door a good tug?"

You nod. "Makes sense. So how do we…make it better?"

"Well, we don't. No door can stop an army. Not a door I can make here, anyway. No, we're not making a bigger door. Our plan is to make *no* door, should the need arise."

"I'm not sure—"

"Hear me out. We're going to set the door to blow up in the event of an all-out attack. The front of the store will collapse, and that's when we'll start living up on the roof. So go back to the BBQ section and look for propane."

You do as requested, but the propane area is under lock and key. Lucky for you, you're in a hardware store and they sell bolt cutters here. On one of your many treks from the front to deliver propane canisters, you see a garden section. A display of seeds and, behind that, several dozen stacks of fertilizer.

"Hey, Unabomber, what about fertilizer? That can make bombs or whatever, right?" you say.

Sam grins. "Do you know how lucky we are that this crisis hit in spring? If it were the start of fall, this store would be full of leaf rakes and snow shovels. We're gonna need those seeds in the long term. Humanity, I mean. If nothing else, we've got that on our side."

"Why not start now? Plant some carrots, potatoes…."

"You want to stand out there and be a scarecrow?"

You point up. "Green roof. Ain't that a thing these days?"

He's nodding now. "Ty, I knew I had a good feeling about you. Know anything about gardening?"

"Some. My mom's always watching those TV shows. Hell, it's half of what she talks about too."

"Good—I think you've got your own project now," Sam adds.

➤ *Start a rooftop garden.* Go to page 304

Flame Retardant

You grab the fire extinguisher anyway, just in case you have to use the thing as a bludgeoning weapon. With even a quick pit-stop, the nutters are gaining ground. There's a clear path up ahead, relatively speaking, as the nutters rush in from the eaves with every second. You can see the front door leading out of the infirmary. It's a secure barrier with a small window of mesh-inlaid safety glass.

Off to the right a trio of undead paw at an office—with a guard and a doctor captive within.

- Help the guys out. Being eaten alive is a fate no man deserves. Go to page 349
- Keep going! It'll only be clear for a few more moments. Go to page 66

Flower Power

Lily smiles. "Okay, mister, but I'm afraid that makes you my heavy lifter." *Good*, you think, ready to work out some frustration. She bids you follow her to aisle eight, where you find some 50-gallon drums. "Bring all of these to the back; I'll meet you by the bathrooms."

They're fairly easy to move, especially while empty, since you can just roll them on their sides. Once you bring the last, Lily meets you with a hose stretching from the women's restroom. She places it in a smaller bucket next to an identical hose connected to the men's room. The walls are lined with collapsible shelving, each shelf with a smaller mop-sized bucket or flower pot on top.

Noticing your look, she explains, "Sam says it's only a matter of time before the infrastructure shuts down. So we need to maximize drinking water while we still have a chance. Put the biggest barrels in the corner, then out from there. Should be hard to move once full."

"How long you been here?"

"Just today."

"Don't plan on leavin' anytime soon?"

"The way Sam puts it, this is our new home. Until it isn't." You nod and your stomach growls loud enough for Lily to hear. "Good point, we haven't thought much about food. There's some beef jerky at the register?" the statement lilts at the end, making it a question.

"Yeah, I could use a lunch break. Woke up late and skipped breakfast."

"Guess humanity is just having 'one of those days.' C'mon."

Up front, Sam uses welding equipment to add reinforced pylons to the barrier. Lily goes for the snacks, and Sam stops to see what you're doing.

Pushing his welder's mask up, he says, "Hey, save those. National Guard should have some rations for us tonight."

"These are snacks, Sam. Not real food," Lily protests.

"Calories are calories."

You look around while they continue to argue, and your eyes come to rest on a display of garden seeds. Behind that, there are a few dozen bags of soil. "Why not plant a garden?"

They both turn to you, then Sam says, "You want to stand out there and be a scarecrow?"

You point up. "Green roof. Ain't that a thing these days?"

"Hey, now that's a good idea," Lily says. "We can ration out this stuff and whatever we get from the Army in the meantime."

Sam nods, "I've already been thinking one day we'll end up on the roof for good. Doesn't matter how strong I make the entrance. If a couple dozen undead bastards want in bad enough…or, God forbid, somebody with a truck. Figured I'd set it to blow as a fail-safe."

"I've got a brown thumb," Lily says with an exaggerated frown. "Know anything about gardening?"

"Some. My mom's always watching those TV shows. Hell, it's half of what she talks about too."

"Good—I think you've got your own project now," Sam adds.

➢ *Start a rooftop garden.* <u>Go to page 304</u>

Follower

Shortly after the Ambassador and his staff enter the C17, the loadmaster comes out to tell you that you're approaching maximum capacity.

"Pack it in, Marines! We're done here," Lt. Dosa shouts. He swirls his finger in the air to signal rendezvous and the gathered soldiers turn to board the aircraft. No one seems concerned that he called them all Marines. *Old habits and Die Hard*, you think.

The call to action successfully averted, you head back to your seat, which is now filled by refugees. The whole plane is filled wall-to-wall with dirty, destitute survivors, happy enough just to have a chance at a full life. If "Coyotes" brought illegal immigrants over in a C17, this is what it would look like.

One of the boys offers his seat against the wall and you gladly take it. There's nothing quite like the post-climax that comes from surviving combat. The calm that follows is a bit like falling asleep after sex and a sandwich, only somehow better. You've just completed a biological imperative of the highest order: Surviving, despite the odds stacked against you.

It's like a drug, and you're on the wonderful high that only a first-timer can experience. When the plane takes off and the combat adrenaline has officially worn off, your eyelids seem to weigh about a thousand pounds each.

➤ *Fall into the deepest sleep you've ever known.* Go to page 120

Fortified Position

"Melissa, stay with us here! The military will handle things. It's safer here."

A terrible sadness washes over your sister's face. "We'll meet again, Luke. In this life or the next."

"Don't…."

"Come find me," she says, then takes off running.

"*Imouto!*"

She flees out the back door, leaving you reeling. Your heart aches, but when you turn back and see the wide-eyed stares of your students, you know you made the right choice. You stand up tall, clear your throat, and put on a brave face.

"My sister is frightened, and I'm sure you'll long remember this day, but look outside—the army is setting up tents, see? They're going to stay here and keep out any more crazies. And until your parents come to claim you, guess what? It is still Saturday, and we're still having class."

You cast a glance to Master Hanzo, who gives a nod of approval before retreating to the office. If Melissa is right, and all it takes is one bite, you need to get the idea of avoiding contact drilled into the children's heads.

"Gear up. We're going to run *Ohji Waza*—parry and counterattack. Form a line, you will each be fending off attacks from me, and I will *not* be going easy on you."

"Even the kids?" Stella asks.

"You're too strong," Mason complains.

"A *motodachi* is what we call fighting a more advanced sparring partner. Why do you think we use this technique in training Kendo?"

"So we'll become better?" Haley asks.

"After a rainstorm, the soil hardens," you say, making a fist to emphasize the aphorism.

That's when the National Guard soldiers show up at your door. With a gesture, you have Nolan open it for them. They wear full battle armor, complete with tactical vests. They're covered head to toe, and the glare from the dojo lights on their gasmasks makes it difficult to see their faces.

The leader steps forward and says, "Good morning. My name is Captain Delozier and this area is now under military quarantine. Has anyone here been bitten?"

"I am Lucas Tesshu, master of this dojo. No one here has been bitten."

"Okay, sure. That's good news. But I'll still need you all to come with me so we can keep you safe. There's food, water, and a place to sleep."

"Sleep? How long will we be gone?" Nolan asks.

"Not sure, little buddy. Until we've cleared the city of infected. Leave your sticks here; let's go."

➤ Refuse to leave. The children are *your* responsibility. Go to page 24
➤ Go along quietly. The military will protect you all. Go to page 183

Get Busy Drivin'

The modified school bus chugs to life when you turn the engine. *I think I can (escape), I think I can (escape)*...When you pull out of the garage, a massive gate sits between you and freedom. Do you have room to gain speed in this behemoth? Probably not. Unless you make room! You keep the bus in reverse and head towards the crowd behind.

They dart out of the way, with the exception of a few nutters that bounce off your rear bumper. Skidding to a stop, you shift to drive and floor the accelerator.

It takes a while for the bus to build up steam, but you're soon up to ramming speed. By the time you make it to the inner gate, the barrier doesn't stand a chance. You have to correct an involuntary fish-tail, but it barely slows you.

The second fence, the outermost barrier, is more formidable. Still, in this giant hunk of metal, you easily smash through the second fence. It catches something under the bus, and your side mirrors show a shower of sparks in your wake.

The police cruisers follow you out, the men inside honking horns and turning on the *whoop whoop!* of the siren in celebration.

Not far down the road, the scraps of gate trapped under the bus start to do serious damage. Thick, black smoke comes from under the hood and you can be sure you're at the beginning stages of an engine fire.

You slam on the brakes, sliding across the road, and bring the bus to a stop. When you run outside, the police cruisers blast past you. The third and final car slows down and Celly leans out.

"*Vaya con Dios!*" he cries before gunning the engine and peeling away.

That's it. You're free of the prison, but you're alone in the dead of the night. Better put some distance between you and that prison. Funny, the damage doesn't look so bad from here.

➤ *Take one last look, then start walking towards the city, a free man.* Go to page 138

Get Busy Livin'

Right along the rural highway, dead of night, you walk. The state penitentiary is damn near thirty miles away from town, a short drive on an open highway, but far enough that a prison break is supposed to be easily contained. That is, of course, when there are still authorities to contain a break.

You've been walking for about three hours when you make it to a roadside rest area. Several signs still read: PRISON AREA—DO NOT PICK UP HITCHHIKERS. After taking advantage of the men's room and smashing open the vending machines, it's time to continue on.

Walking the rest of the night, with the first hints of dawn on the horizon, you finally reach the outskirts of town. Several construction sites are under development and just beyond that awaits a shopping mall with a large "Grand Opening!!!" sign. Brand-spanking new. This area wasn't even under construction yet when you rode from the courthouse to the prison.

Still, this is one of those moments where the sky metaphorically opens and a beam of sunlight shows the mall as a gift from God. Your dogs are barking and there's nothing you'd rather do right now than find a Serta mattress, slip out of your shoes and jumpsuit, and experience the best night of sleep you've had in years. But before that can happen, there's just one problem:

Several figures mill about the near-empty parking lot. Though you suspected as much, looks like the nutter scourge wasn't just restricted to the prison. That's why there was no police response sent to the Big House. They were busy enough here.

Great; now what?

➤ Scavenge the construction sites for something useful before heading over. Go to page 49
➤ They aren't that many. Go now, before more show up, and find what you need in the mall. Go to page 105

Getting Late

The rest of the National Guardsmen depart, block by block, to go join the hospital fight. Rattled gunfire and wailing sirens tell of their struggle, but you have no way of knowing if the tide of battle favors the living or the dead.

With the quarantine abandoned, and thus effectively lifted, the streets empty out. Any living persons are long gone, and there's the occasional wandering ghoul, but if you stay quiet, they move along. All that noise from the hospital appears to interest them more.

As the sun wanes, you prepare for departure. Eat a snack, drink plenty of water, but you don't take anything Sam offers. No armor or shield, nothing to weigh you down. Home can't be more than an hour away on foot, even if you do encounter undead on the way.

"Guess that's it," you say. "I'll come back in the morning with my mom."

"Goodbye, Ty," Lily says.

"See you later," you correct.

"Motherfucker," Sam says.

You turn and see he's got his eye in the rifle's scope, looking down the street—looking the direction you're headed.

It doesn't take long to see what's got his attention. Without the normal daily commuters, the street is all but silent, so you can hear the approaching convoy even from several miles away. Engines roar and radios blare as the Humvees approach.

"Reinforcements, no doubt," Sam says after he lowers the rifle.

The street around the store fills with ghouls attracted by the noise. Where did they even come from? One crawls out from the sewer drainage ditch, a trio come from the alley, and more come from every recess in the city block.

Moaning. You thought it was your imagination, or maybe just an echo of the engines, but no, it's a chorus of the damned.

The convoy makes it to your block now, headed for the hospital. One of the gunners standing behind a massive machine gun opens fire into the growing crowd of dead, which brings more from the recesses. A car window shatters and a once-dead thing crawls out.

"Cut it out!" Sam shouts. He frantically slashes at his throat in the "kill" sign.

The gunner, a shirtless man, brings the machine gun around towards the store—with enormous artillery rounds ripping the street to shreds—and Sam raises his rifle. As soon as Sam fires, a dozen other soldiers open fire on the hardware store. Instinctively, you step in front of Lily, then fall into one of the garden boxes and fertilize the crop with your life blood.

THE END

Get to the Choppa!

The helicopter's blades spin in a blur, and you get the feeling they were about to take off when the pilot saw you jogging towards the helipad. As soon as you climb aboard, an Airman in the back points out your seat and the chopper takes off.

The Airman, whose nametag reads BELLIVEAU, hands you a headset and says, "Welcome, Sergeant. ETA to the St. Mary's LZ is ten Mike."

"What's the mission?" you call out after switching your gasmask for a headset.

The man cocks his head, as if confused, but answers, "Extraction. This is a one-way ticket; weren't you told?"

A knot forms in your throat. You slowly shake your head.

"The hospital is lost. We're bringing back the unit commanders, but it's a hot-swap. We go in, they come back. Then we find our own way out," Airman Belliveau says.

Damn. What kind of suicide mission did you sign up for? Looking around at the specialty badges around the helicopter, all you see are combat rescue and para rescue; half a dozen badasses. You fold your arms across your "Communications Electrician Maintenance" badge, but no one seems to care. Are they really that undermanned already?

Looking out the side, you see dozens of black, fiery plumes on the horizon. The sun wanes behind them and the streets below are clogged with wrecks. People, living, dead, and undead, litter the city. Your eyes are drawn to the high-rises, as whole buildings and streets go dark one after another, a rolling blackout, like electrical dominoes.

St. Mary's Hospital comes into view as a *bona fide* war zone. In a massive epidemic where everyone thought their loved ones were just *sick*, the biggest hospital in the city became ground zero. When the dead rise again, beware the morgue.

"We can't touch down," the pilot calls from up front. "The LZ is too hot!"

Looking down, you can't help but agree. It's chaos in the hospital parking lot. Still, there's gotta be a way. When you pull your gasmask back on, the six-man crew in the back dons their own. What's the plan?

➢ All these cables and pulleys on the sides—isn't fast-roping the default for combat rescue? Go to page 213
➢ This is the biggest hospital in the city—shouldn't there be a helipad up top? Go to page 275

Gimme Shelter

"Jay, the door," you say, rifle at the ready.

He nods, and walks across the living room. Your mind goes back to one of Dad's heart-to-hearts when he said, "There's no worse feeling than killing a man, even one who deserves it. But dead men don't feel. So if it's you or the enemy, you'll have to learn to live with that feeling or not live at all."

I'm not ready, you think, heart sinking.

But before you can finish, "Jay, wait!" it's open and the panicked man stumbles into your living room, falling to the floor in a bloody heap. His attacker rushes in right behind him, snarling and reaching out with frenzied arms. Whatever instinct possesses the man sends him straight toward Jason.

Suddenly, a red mist sprays out of the far side of the lunatic's head and he collapses, dead. You realize you've shouldered your rifle and the gunshot was yours. You don't even remember moving, you just remember one thought entered your head as the crazed attacker moved toward your brother. One word, really: *No*.

A quick glance to the other man shows that he is unconscious on the ground. The tension gone from the moment, you lower your rifle. *Oh, God,* you think. That was as easy as one of Jay's paintball games, easier even.

"I just killed a man," you say, but it sounds disconnected. Like someone else is speaking.

"You killed the enemy," Dad says. "Charlie."

"It was a z—zom…" Jason can't bring himself to say it.

"Zulu…the enemy," you say.

"Right," Dad confirms. "It was either him or Jay."

➤ Drag the dead body outside and lock up. Go to page 357
➤ Check on the unconscious man. Go to page 266

Gnawing at You

In the dream, you're standing amidst a sea of uniform white crosses marking the graves of all those who served this country and paid the ultimate price. Despite the lack of inscriptions, you know the gravestone before you is Dad's. Jason lies nearby, curled in the fetal position, weeping.

All at once, the crosses start sinking into the earth, just like quicksand, all save your father's. Jason sinks into the ground and you go to save him, but Dad climbs out of the earth, the green grass oozing away like swamp water.

"Let's be together, Sport. *Forever.*" He grabs you and brings you down into the muck.

You scream out, and just like that, you're awake. With a Zulu right on top of you. The undead construction worker bites at your arms, his teeth sinking into your exposed flesh.

Jason shoots awake at the sound of your screams, then, with a deafening *KA-BOOM!* he blasts the man point-blank in the face with his shotgun.

"Asshole!" you cry. "You were supposed to be on watch!"

"Look away. I—I have to shoot you..."

You're INFECTED!

Goodbyes

It's surprisingly easy to carry Master Hanzo back to the dojo. He was a frail man in life, and it takes no more effort than it would to heft a bag of rice as it does to carry the man in death. The dojo itself is silent and empty, as it shall remain.

You lay Master Hanzo to rest in the office on one of his reclining chairs. Brushing your hand down his face, you close the man's eyes for him. You've never given a proper eulogy, but you do remember the poem quoted at your father's funeral.

"*Blow if you will, fall wind—the flowers have all faded.* Sleep well, my friend."

With that, you leave him, and prepare to go. The hallway gives you a clear view of the front, and of the person standing at the glass doors. The shock of dirty blond hair is unmistakable—it is your eldest student, Nathanael.

He's not looking directly at you, so you can't see his face, but the gaping wound in his rib cage tells you he's in trouble. In fact, you're not even sure how he's standing.

- ➢ Tend to your student. He's only a boy; you can't leave him when he might need your help. Go to page 11
- ➢ There's only one reason he's still on his feet—and nothing you can do about it. Head out the back door and leave this accursed place. Go to page 92

Good Move

Let's face it; you know there's something wrong with Harrison Ford. This is the most unnatural he's looked since *Kingdom of the Crystal Skull, and* the way hunger has replaced the boredom in his eyes is off-putting, to say the least. Still, these men are paid for protection, so it's best not to attack Mr. *Air Force One* while his security is on-site.

His guys do their best to restrain the raging celebrity, but he moves with the ferocity of someone half his age and rips off one man's sunglasses with an attempted bite. Some of the teeth strike home, and crimson pours out from just beneath the man's eye.

"Get that maniac out of here!" your father yells, thrusting a forceful point towards the door with his good hand.

It takes all six security guards to do so, each of them suffering bites and scrapes as they drag the crazed actor outside and into the limousine. The three of you watch from the window as they shove him inside, jump in, gun the engine, and spray gravel while fishtailing out of the parking lot.

A rising dust cloud shows the limo disappear in the distance.

At length, dad says, "Now's a good time to practice those sewing skills, Sport."

"It looks pretty deep," you say. "Shouldn't we go to a hospital?"

"What if we were in the backcountry, three days away from the nearest hospital? You need to know how to do this stuff."

You nod, and Jason brings the first aid kit before you can even ask for it. You've had first-aid training, but don't have any real-trauma experience yet. With a deep breath and a hard swallow, you look to your father's bite wound.

Careful to disinfect the area, you fumble with needle and thread through latex gloves. Your father does his best not to wince, but his nerves are exposed and your hand is not as sure as you'd like. Finally, it's done.

"Not bad," Dad says.

"Ummm, guys?" Jason asks.

Your brother's eyes are glued on the store TV and Fox News. The anchor's saying, "It also appears that Shia LaBeouf, best known for the *Transformers* series, who was reported to have died yesterday is…still alive. The first reports came through Twitter, but sightings of the young star have been confirmed in downtown Los Angeles. Onlookers say he's in a blood-spattered hospital robe, evidently mocking his supposed death—stumbling and shambling after the gathered crowd with animal growls. Is it an elaborate stunt for a movie, or just more celebrity mania? On the phone we're joined by…."

"I saw that on YouTube earlier," Jason says. "Everybody in the comments was all like 'faaaaaake.'"

"Are we going to acknowledge that this seems like more than just *normal* Hollywood crazy?" you ask.

"Turn it off," your father says, gruff determination in his voice. After an extended moment, he comes to a decision. "Start packing up. This thing is bigger than we're being told; I just hope to God we're not too late. I'd bet this has been going on for weeks. Typical media—treat us like a mushroom, keep us in the dark and shit on us. Grab a rifle and plenty of ammo. Jay, get a shotgun—16-gauge—and fill the hunting vest with shells."

"I'm old enough for a 12-gauge, pops."

"Less weight, more room for extra shells."

Jason simply nods, then heads off to arm himself.

"Wait, where are we going?" you ask. "I have school tomorrow, I need to—"

"School's over, Sport. I wish I could have taught you more, but…" he says, trailing off. Finally adding, "With this bum hand, I'll have to be support. I'll carry the food, water, radio…and a pistol too, just in case."

Is this what Dad's always been predicting? The day when it all hits the fan?

Knowing there's gravity to this moment, you head to the weapons locker to claim a rifle. You can only take one, but the decision is easy enough. A .22 caliber is lightweight and allows plenty of ammo. You grab the rifle you always called "the little one" when Dad gave shooting lessons, but have since qualified as expert-rated on several times over: The Ruger 10/22 semiautomatic rifle.

You arrive at home, only two hours later, having taken all you could from the gun range. Traffic on the streets is starting to get a little crazy. From the looks of it, looting has already begun. What was the tipping point? Did you miss something on TV?

Your father is pale, his skin slick with sweat. He's clearly lost a lot of blood, so you check his bandage, but it's not even red. The bleeding has completely stopped. When you remove the bandage, you see only exposed flesh, cut deep, like a pig ready for roasting.

"Daddy, I don't think I did the stitches right. Maybe we should get you to a doctor?" you ask.

"I'm fine. Let's keep packing. It's not safe here."

You're about to respond, but then there's a sudden and furious pounding on the door. Dad nods, resting his good hand on his 9mm handgun. The pounding continues, along with a muffled plea. You look through the peephole and see a bloodied man, fear in his eyes, checking back over his shoulder between pounds on your door.

He looks harmless enough, *a typical suburban sheep*, as dad would say. Somewhat overweight, balding, with a neatly-trimmed goatee. Completely unprepared. Didn't you sell him Girl Scout cookies a few years back?

"Please, he's trying to kill me," the man whimpers. *"Please!"*

- ➢ Keep watching, but stay quiet. Go to page 390
- ➢ Open it. He needs your help. Go to page 141

Going Psycho

You reach for the guard's Asp, the baton he dropped when the group overwhelmed him, then scramble to your feet and use the weapon to crack the nearest nutter in the shoulder. It's a blow that would send any man reeling, but the fiend doesn't even seem to notice.

The next time you strike the skinhead in his forehead, where he has the scar of a pentagram carved in his flesh. There's a sickening *crunch* and the man falls back from the blow and something black seeps from the pentagram, but still the nutter attacks. It's hard to get a good shot with him bobbing around like a coke fiend.

The fiend stops in his tracks, still reaching out for you, but unable to move forward. Not wasting any time, you wind up for a full swing and smash the Asp against the pentagram once more. This time you puncture the skull and dip your baton into the fiend's inky head-well.

The nutter falls to the ground and you see Solitary standing behind the dead fiend. Looks like he held the skinhead for you, and now the man gives a nod of respect. Solitary turns away to fight more of the crazed gang and you do the same, but when you turn back, it's into the arms of a guard—and the Taser he shoves into your rib cage. You fall limp.

When you come to, it's in the SHU. Yep, they threw you in solitary confinement despite the fact that you're pretty damn sure *they know you helped*, yet here you are. Rules are rules, and you attacked a fellow inmate during a "riot." It's bullshit, but at least you're safe. If there's some kind of *super-rabies* spreading through the prison population, this might be the best place to be.

Still, you can't help but wonder if it's getting better or worse, and no one answers your questions about the outside world. What happened to all those people? Are they sick? Are there still riots? Is everything under control?

That's part of the punishment: no human contact whatsoever. Even your food comes from an unseen hand. With such Spartan conditions, the minutes tick by like hours. It feels like days later when the door finally opens. Solitary stands before you.

"What...?" you try.

Then you see the unconscious guard at his feet. Solitary unshackles himself using the guard's keys and takes the guard's utility belt for his own. It's got the keyring, a handheld radio, a pair of handcuffs, and a telescoping Asp baton.

"How...?"

Solitary simply turns to leave.

➤ Stay with him. Guy may be a psycho, but he's clearly got a soft spot for good ole Hefty. Strength in numbers—even Solitary must realize that. Go to page 71
➤ Head out into the Yard to get a better look at the state of things. You need to know the big picture before you plan your next move. Go to page 245
➤ Go it alone and sneak out the front door. Passing through the infirmary won't be easy, but you'll be careful. Go to page 387

Going Terminal

Lt. Dosa looks you up and down, and the edge of his mouth twitches in what might be a smile. "Corporal Gardner!" he barks. "Grab your fireteam and follow Sergeant Sims into the airport. He's the lead, but look smart."

"Sir, just one fireteam?" the Corporal asks, unsure.

"How many Marines does it take to fuck a lightbulb?"

"*Hoorah*, LT!"

Marines, you think with a shake of your head as the pair exchange salutes. Dosa turns back to command the rest of the unit while Gardner and his fireteam—a whopping three other men—look to you for leadership. Well, this is what you volunteered for, isn't it?

"Okay, quick in and out. Grab the Ambassador and hustle back here before they even notice we're gone," you say.

"*Hoorah!*" the four Marines shout in unison.

Adrenaline courses through your veins, slowing everything down, and the hundred yards to the terminal feels like an eternity.

The terminal is heavily illuminated, so you flip off and stow your night-vision. There are (to put it in technical terms) a metric shit-ton of zombies surrounding the place. It looks like the survivors within have barricaded the whole area, which makes finding an entrance problematic.

"Orders?" Corporal Gardner asks.

You look at the man—and at the M203 grenade launcher attachment he has equipped. Decisions, decisions. If this is a rescue mission, you might not want to turn the evacuees' barricade into molten slag. Then again, when else are you going to get an opportunity to command a Marine to bring fiery hell onto earth? And it's already all broken loose, come hell or hot water.

➢ "Secure a staircar. We're going in through the jetway." Go to page 168
➢ "Make a hole, Corporal! Blast your way through the barricade." Go to page 131

Gossip Girls

You call out to Angelica, who comes to join you and Jose while Tyberius and Hefty stay with the new guy.

"What's going on here?" you ask. "Everything okay?"

"What do you mean?"

"Soldier boy. Where'd you find him? Is he alone? Pretend this is a sewing circle and let's talk behind his back."

"He seems like a good man. Not like…those others we met."

"How do you know?"

"I think I know when someone's trying to rape me, Cooper," she says, icily.

"Keep it down," you hiss back.

You look to Jose, but he's not listening.

"I just wanted to make sure you're not, I don't know, being held hostage or something. Do you think we should trust him?"

"You're asking me?" she says, taken aback. "Well, yeah, I do. Sims injured his shoulder back there, so he might need us more than we need him right now, but I think he could help in the long run. And if we run into any other military types? It'd be good to have one on our side, right?"

"Thanks," you say with a nod.

Maybe Angelica is right and the new guy isn't like the others. Maybe he's a survivalist, but a good one. Either way, it's probably a good idea to keep him close. But first…you need to assert dominance. Or maybe get a second opinion from one of the others?

- ➤ Introduce yourself. Make sure he knows you're the boss. Go to page 383
- ➤ Take Tyberius aside, ask him for the low-down. Go to page 348
- ➤ Take Hefty aside, ask him for the skinny. Go to page 182

Grabbing a Bite

The cafeteria is buttressed by glass walls with a set of automatic double doors for the entry. As you approach, you see dozens of terrified figures huddled within, crowded in the center of the mess hall behind a few overturned tables.

The doors open for you, and the cow-eyed crowd simply watches. Some hold brooms and mops, or kitchen wares as makeshift weapons. One man, a middle-aged Latino in stained kitchen whites, holds a pot and a cleaver.

"*Mordido?*" he asks, punctuating the question with a double-chomp of his teeth.

Your brain searches through the High School Spanish archives. *Morder*...to bite? Ahh, you get it.

"Bitten? No. *Todos bien,*" you say. *All good.* At least, that's what you think you say. Spanish was never your best subject. They teach to the test, and your spoken language skills are *que terrible.*

"You have guns?" a frightened man asks. "Where did you get guns?"

"God-given right," Jason says, deliberately dodging the question.

"Please," the man says. "My wife...my newborn son. They've locked down the NICU—please help me get to my family."

"Anyone in here a doctor?" you ask.

Most break your gaze, but all shake their heads.

"There are doctors in the NICU!" the man presses.

➢ "Yeah, okay. I'll get you in, but there sure as hell better be plenty of doctors in there." Go to page 118

➢ "No, sorry. I'm not looking for an OB-GYN. Which way to virology and infectious diseases?" Go to page 67

Gray Anatomy

You have to take an elevator deep into the bowels of the hospital to reach the morgue. The basement level is oddly silent compared to the upper levels. In a word? Dead. It's down in this windowless cavern where autopsies are performed, John and Jane Does are kept on ice, and those wishing for cremation are offered up to the flame.

You push open the double doors to the morgue and let yourself in. Dozens of bodies are on display; some hang from the ceiling, blood draining like some cannibalistic butcher shop, but many more are bound onto the slab tables. On the nearest table lies a, ummm, *person*—you can't tell if it's a man or a woman—who's been flayed open. Their skin is peeled away and pinned back to show off the inner workings. You step closer, and the muscle tissue starts...*twitching*.

"Nightmare fuel," Jason says.

"Please don't disturb the patients," a man interjects.

You turn to see a slight, hunched, bald man in a lab coat. He wears large goggles that magnify his eyes and push his features towards reptilian and elbow-length black rubber gloves. His fingertips rest in a steeple shape just beneath his angular chin.

"Have the field trips begun already?" he asks, eyebrow rising. Is that supposed to be humor?

"Are you...*studying* them?" you ask.

"But of course! This is an historic opportunity. My colleagues are focused on *saving* them, would you believe that? Incredibly short-sighted, when you consider the potential. Just look at this," he says, stepping over to an industrial-sized refrigerator.

He reaches in and returns with a five-gallon jar. Suspended in fluid inside is a floating human head. The eyes are wide open with lips parted. Jason steps closer and the head's eyes suddenly turn towards your brother. The mouth snaps open and closed.

"Look at that—mastication! This head has been detached from the body for nearly twenty-four hours and shows no signs of muscular degeneration. Incredible!"

"Is there..." you say, trying to properly order your thoughts, "a way to *stop* the transformation?"

"Have you been bitten? Exposed in any way? A scrape or a cut?" the man asks, stepping forward, his lizard eyes blinking with sudden, intense focus.

"Our dad," Jason offers.

"I see. No, not that I'm aware of. But if you wanted to bring your father *here*, I'd be more than happy to examine him. How fresh is his infection?"

"He was bitten early this afternoon," you say.

The man shakes his head. "Pity. I'm sure his incubation is nearly complete. I'd love to see how a patient experiences the world right from the moment of infection."

He looks to the head in his hands, then to your brother. Something flashes across his face that you don't like. You raise the rifle one-handed, pulling Jason away with the other.

"Back off, Umbrella Corporation. I won't hesitate to put down every last *patient* in here before you get a chance to *Human Centipede* them together or whatever fucked-up plans you've got."

The man skulks away, muttering something about "mixed metaphors" to the head as he goes to store it in the refrigerator. Time to leave the creep with his creepers.

- ➤ How about a second opinion? To the cafeteria. Maybe you can catch another doctor on break? Go to page 149
- ➤ Pharmacy. You have to try! Get some antibiotics or something. Go to page 285
- ➤ Better head home. If nothing else…to say goodbye. Go to page 83
- ➤ To the ER! This guy only knows the dead; time to find someone who knows the dying. Go to page 326

A Great Big Convoy

Good news: The armory has plenty of ammo for your M4, and the motorpool still has about a dozen Humvees ready for checkout. Bad news: There's almost no organization down here. No one knows who's in charge, and what's worse, no one cares.

"Whoever's in charge must already be down at the hospital," an Army Sergeant says, "otherwise, how would everyone know to meet there?"

"Looking for a ride, Sarge?" another young soldier asks.

He might not even be twenty years old, yet he looks like he was born into his desert-cammo uniform. He's unmistakably a soldier, with that high-and-tight haircut, but his thick, ruddy handlebar mustache is definitely not in regs. Most likely, he just got home from deployment.

"What's your name, Soldier?" you ask, noting he doesn't wear his uniform jacket.

He touches his undershirt where the nametag would normally sit and says, "Can't you see? I'm No-body. I changed it once I heard that *nobody* makes it out of this thing alive."

"Okay, Nobody, do you also have no rank?"

"Of course I have rank, Sarge. This is the Army, after all. I'm Captain of this here ship," he says, patting the Humvee on its hood.

Another soldier, this one not even bothering to wear the undershirt of his uniform, hops up on the gunner turret of the Humvee. He's covered in war-paint, and the whites of his crazed eyes pop against his painted face.

"And him?" you ask.

"No rank, but I got a name. Simecek," the shirtless man says. "Convoy's movin' out, pops. Get in or get lost."

Captain Nobody shrugs and gets in the driver seat.

- ➤ I suppose you have to be half-crazy to fight legions of undead. Get in the front passenger seat. Go to page 63
- ➤ This is FUBAR—find a different ride; one with some sense of military bearing. Go to page 31

Green Dreams

You're late for work again, though this time mama was good enough to wake you. Your eyelids are heavy, and no matter how much you strain, you can't quite open them. Gritting your teeth and stretching your eyebrows up to the top of your head lifts your eyelids ever so slightly. Just enough to see her standing next to your bed. That's odd...she never comes into your room. Not since you turned thirteen and—

She has two arms! Her amputated limb is a new arm, freshly made of packed mud and earth. Thick, woody roots wrap around the phantom limb like varicose veins, and bits of stone dot the skin like sylvan warts.

It's so shocking that you try to pull away, to sit up in bed and bring the covers up, but you're paralyzed. Like you're the one encased in the same mud, and everything pushes back against your efforts.

Straining, you finally manage to sit up a bit. Her eyes are blank, and her mouth hangs open. It's not her face, though, it's that homeless guy on the bus. But it's her too, somehow, in a way that makes sense only in dreams. She growls and her arms come up slowly, like the mummy monster in one of those black-and-white horror movies mama leaves on the TV.

You try to scream, to tell her to stop, but you can't. Her arms come up around your neck, the new golem-arm crumbling from effort. Red, wet earthworms pulse forth from the earthen limb as white, mealy maggots rip through the ebony flesh of her true arm.

Dirt and worms and maggots fall into your open mouth and—

—you shoot awake with a scream, a face full of potting soil. You spit dirt, and blink to get your bearings. Somehow you managed to fall asleep on the rooftop, using a half-empty soil bag as a pillow. There's a canvas painter's tarp atop you for a blanket, most likely Lily's doing.

Head pounding, you get up, accidentally kick the empty whiskey bottle, and stumble over to the side alley for an urgent morning piss. You let out a groan of relief as your stream arcs out over the roof's edge, and the alley echoes back at you with a cacophony of moans.

Squinting hard in the morning light, you see a man and woman down below reaching up towards the source of the waterfall. They have dead, blank eyes and hungry mouths.

You stumble away and fall on your back, lucky not to piss yourself.

"Uhhh, Ty?" It's Lily, and you quickly get to your feet and zip up before you turn around. She's blushing, holding three more Styrofoam boxes.

Sam comes up behind her with a thermos. "I found some coffee in the break— what's up?"

You just point to the alley. They set the food down and go for a look.

"Jesus," Sam says.

"Why are they just out in the open?" Lily asks. "Shouldn't the soldiers take care of them?"

Sam moves to the edge of the roof over the storefront and you follow. The street is clear now, with no cars blocking the way. A lone infected man stumbles through the open streets below.

"When did *that* happen?" you ask.

He doesn't answer, so Lily prods. At length, Sam says, "If they cleared the street, it means they're preparing to move out. Things are moving a lot faster than we thought."

"Well, what did Delozier say? Six-hour infection rate? Based on the number of infected we've seen, we can assume that patient zero probably hit this city a few weeks ago," Lily says, doing some mental math. "Three at most. If you have one infected individual on the loose, averaging one bite per hour, with new biters joining the pool hourly starting at the six-hour point...."

She trails off, her thoughts going internal. Sam sees your look and says, "Algebra teacher."

"Holy shit. We've already passed the tipping point. Yesterday, if my math holds. Fifty-percent of the population already infected."

A series of *pops* sound in the distance, like someone launching fireworks. You look towards the source and see a plume of dark smoke coming from the hospital.

"What if it's more than one guy? Like, maybe a jumbo jet got sick and landed here? How does that change things?" you ask.

Lily swallows. "If there were three hundred patient zeroes? Well, in that case...we're already fucked."

More rifle *pops* sound from the hospital. The three of you hold silent, weighing your fate and more generally, that of humanity. Your thoughts are just going towards your mother when the radio on Sam's hip goes off.

"This is Colt, go ahead," he answers.

"Colt, this is Captain Delozier. Good and bad, bud. At least depending on where you're sitting. We're disbanding the quarantine. It failed, and that is bad news all around. All troops are needed at the hospital, but I'm setting up a temporary HQ in the area—and you're sitting on it."

Sam doesn't reply, but something in his expression hardens.

"They're coming here?" Lily says.

"Colt, do you copy?"

Sam looks to Lily, then to you.

- ➢ "No way. Tell that war pig to find his own farm." Go to page 172
- ➢ "Not a bad idea...Might be nice to have a guard dog, no?" Go to page 345

Grunts

"Did you guys feel that?" you ask.

A few of the combat veterans in the C-17 belly nod or make some sort of growl in acknowledgment, but most ignore you. Aside from the flight crew, you're the only Air Force guy on the mission. Even *you* questioned why you were brought along, so can you really blame them?

One of the men, Army Special Forces from the look of him, shakes a can of black spray-paint, then begins to tag over his cammo body armor. He paints, "I-D-G-A-F."

"Id-gaf?" you say.

He shakes his head. "I-don't-give-a-fuck. Reminds me not to hold back in combat."

You swallow hard, suddenly feeling very naked. You squeak out something like, "Awesome," and go find the mission commander. *Combat?* Please, God, no....

"Hey, LT," you say.

The Marine in question, Lieutenant Dosa, is a young man, to be sure, but his features go beyond hardened. His eyes are gray and cold, and he's one of the few men present who doesn't sport a spec-ops beard. Most Air Force LTs are spoiled kids two or three years outside of college, with no clue how the military works. Not this guy. He has the gravity of an Air Force Colonel.

"Sergeant."

"Ummm, Sir, it looks like the men are getting ready for—well, I thought we were heading home, but now...."

"Right. Hope you're rested up. We've been tasked to fly into Manaus and evacuate essential US personnel."

"Brazil?"

"That's the one. I'm sure the Russians will have no qualms about shooting their own leadership once they switch from vodka to human flesh, but there's been no contact with Venezuela for three days now."

"Like...the whole country?" you say dumbly.

With a smirk he says, "We'll be there soon, so get ready."

You get that sinking feeling again, only this time the plane's not turning. Time to...

➢ Find your weapons and battle-rattle. Time to shoot some undead commies! Go to page 73

➢ Find somewhere to hide. You're an electrician! And you don't want to lose your seat. Go to page 186

Handled

"You hit that yet?" a nearby soldier asks, trouble in his eyes.

You say nothing, just stare back.

"Nah, didn't think so," the man says after a beat.

There's a loud *slap* from the back of the store and several of the soldiers up front howl with laughter. When you turn, you see the aggressor holding his cheek and Lily fuming red.

"Lucky I don't hit bitches!" the man cries.

"What's going on here?" Captain Delozier demands, stepping out from the stairwell.

"Your men need to keep it in their pants if they don't want it shot off," Lily says.

Sam unslings his rifle. "What happened?"

"I didn't do nothing. Tell your buddy to keep his bitch on a leash, Captain."

Now Sam's rifle is at the ready, not quite pointed at the soldier, but close.

"What. The fuck. Is going on?" Delozier reiterates.

"Nothing!" the soldier says. "I was just being friendly, but the bitch can't take a joke."

"Call her a bitch one more time," Sam says, cool. "And I'll cut—"

"Bitch."

Sam pulls a knife and the soldier raises his weapon. Then there's a *BOOM* and you flinch from the sound. Another two shots ring out, and three more in response to that. Before you even know what's happened, you see Lily holds her pistol in the air, smoke curling from the barrel. Her chest blooms crimson from the soldier's itchy trigger finger, and that man lies on the floor dead from Sam's rifle.

You instinctively step forward, and the nearby soldier shoots a round into your chest. Too much pressure, such a small space. All it took was one spark to set off the powder keg.

THE END

Hard-Boiled Defender

"Okay, let's get this place defensible. Clip the wires to the door sensors; move this barricade right up against the glass. And build it high—we don't want to be seen by Zulu, or we might attract unwanted curiosity. Let's do a food check; eat anything perishable right now. Like eggs—dig in."

And so it goes, using your survival skills and know-how to lock down the cafeteria. Hours go by, and despite your best efforts, the shamblers find their way here. Did they remember where to go when hungry? Smell you through the air vents? Catch a glimpse of movement through the barrier cracks? Doesn't matter, because it only takes one to notice and call in the rest.

The multitudes. They bang, claw, punch, scrape, and slap at the glass, first leaving fluids, then leaving cracks.

"Get ready!" you shout.

Then all goes quiet. Several gunshots thud dully from further down the hospital corridors. You pop up and peer over the barricade, only to see the police SWAT team engaging the enemy alongside regular, uniformed cops.

"We're saved!" someone yells.

"Keep quiet!" you snap.

There may be dozens of police officers, but there are hundreds of undead out there. It's only a few minutes before the gunshots cease. The horde returns to your battlements, but this time they're already in a frenzied state and make short work of the glass walls, the ghouls pouring through the barricade like a collective battering ram.

You hadn't originally planned a siege when you came to the hospital, so you don't have much in the way of ammo. Still, this is your Alamo, behind you are your 300 Spartans, and you don't go down without a fight.

THE END

Hardened

You sprint towards the hardware store, eyes locked on the man on the roof. He's backlit by the morning sun, so you don't get more than a silhouette, but you can see him sling a rifle over his shoulder, then turn away.

As you get closer to the hardware store and the sun's respective angle sinks behind the building, the storefront comes into sharp clarity. On either side of the entrance are consumer displays. Get the perfect BBQ for summer. While you're at it, why not install a pool and get some loungers? Above the doors, a sign reads, "Honeydew Supplies—*We make hardware easy on your melon!*"

"Fucking puns," you groan.

The double doors slide open in response to your approach, but you skid to a halt. It looked just like a glare in the morning sun, but now that they're open, you see the doorway is reinforced by metal siding.

"Fuck," you groan, then remember the gunman.

You duck behind the nearest car just as a rifle blast screams out against the metal doorway of the store. The pawnshop guy is reloading again, and you're considering running again when a metallic shriek catches your attention. When you turn back, you see the barricade doors have parted and a man stands in the breach with rifle raised.

He fires over your head, aimed across the street.

"Coming?!" he shouts.

Not wasting another breath, you sprint towards the opening and help the guy pull the sliding metal panels closed behind you. Once inside, he engages several locks and latches while you get a good look at him.

The man is younger than you expected; early 20s, most likely, and tall, like you. Easily over six-foot but lean. You've probably got fifty pounds of muscle on the guy. Still, with coal-black hair that offsets his pale skin and a firm, stubbled jawline he looks like he could hold his own. Finally finished locking up, he turns back to you.

"Welcome to the store. Name's Sam Colt. And that little lady goes by Lily."

You turn back as a woman steps out from behind the first aisle of the hardware store. Strawberry blonde, about the same age as Sam and fit, she looks at you through soft brown eyes. Her air of sweet innocence is offset by a cold, dark handgun hanging in her left hand.

A man named after a gun, and a woman named after a flower; funny, that.

"Tyberius. My friends call me Ty, and you two certainly qualify. Not sure why you helped me out, but if I there's anything I can do…"

"You tell us. Is there anything you can do?" Lily asks.

You laugh at the absurd nature of it all. "I can help you deposit a check."

"I'd bet you can bash a skull pretty easily too," Sam says.

"Excuse me?"

"Don't tell me you ain't fought one yet," Lily says.

You look to her, then to Sam for some kind of explanation.

"Guess you're gonna want to see for yourself," Sam says with a sigh. "Up to the roof, let's go."

The rooftop of the hardware store is the equivalent of looking out a second-story window, but it's enough. You can see a city block in any direction, each barricaded with gridlocked traffic. The high-rises of downtown surround your periphery, and there's the big "H" on the hospital in the distance. Further on the horizon, opposite downtown, a Ferris wheel sits unmoving. A commotion draws your attention down to the storefront, where the National Guard is raiding the pawn shop. They can't get into the front door, so they drop tear gas canisters through the barred windows.

"That's what happens when you take potshots at civvies," Sam says.

"Guess the soldiers ain't all bad," you say with a shrug.

"Look! It's happening," Lily urges, tugging on your shirt sleeve.

The block you came from, the one with the stalled city bus, comes alive with excited shouts. You walk to the nearest edge of the roof and crane your neck to get a better view. A thin man in black tights groans in pain and stumbles towards the line.

"Here," Sam says, passing a pair of binoculars.

Through the lenses you see it's actually a woman, but she's been badly burned and no longer has any hair. She's not wearing tights at all; her clothing is mostly burned away and her skin is blackened like BBQ. Her jaw hangs open, slack.

The soldiers prepare to open fire, but a man exits his car and comes to stand between them. You can tell the man is confused and panicked, unable to understand why the National Guard isn't helping her. You're about to ask the same question when she reaches the Good Samaritan and lunges at him.

He tries to hold her off and she brings his hands into her mouth.

"Holy shit!" you cry as the soldiers open fire. "What the…what…?"

Sam and Lily say nothing.

➢ "I—I need a minute. Is this shit on the news?" Go to page 42
➢ "What the fuck is going on? Tell me everything!" Go to page 358

Hard Part's Over

That's it! You did it. Stepped into another person's shoes and survived the zombie apocalypse. Well, at least the initial outbreak. *PATHOGENS* has one "best ending" for every character, so if you're satisfied you made it, why not help someone else survive?

If you enjoyed the book, it would mean a lot to me as an author if you were to leave a review on Amazon or Goodreads. As an indie writer, word-of-mouth is my best survival strategy, and reviews are the #1 way to help Amazon promote a book to new readers.

When you're done, don't forget to check out the other exciting titles in the *Click Your Poison*™ multiverse!

INFECTED—*Will YOU Survive the Zombie Apocalypse?*
MURDERED—*Can YOU Solve the Mystery?*
SUPERPOWERED—*Will YOU Be a Hero or a Villain?*
PATHOGENS—*More Zombocalypse Survival Stories!*
MAROONED—*Can YOU Endure Treachery and Survival on the High Seas?*
SPIED (coming in 2019)—*Can YOU Save the World as a Secret Agent?*

* More titles coming soon! *

Sign up for the new release mailing list at: http://eepurl.com/bdWUBb
Or visit the author's blog at www.jameschannep.com

Hatchet Job

Without hesitation, you pull Jason into his room next door, jump on the bed, reach up over the poster of Danny Trejo (posing and showing off a massive knife collection tucked inside a leather duster), and pull the machete off your brother's wall.

"Jay, grab the bedpost and shut your eyes. Bite down on this," you say, grabbing a leather belt from a pair of jeans on the floor. His room has always been messy, but it's about to get a lot worse.

Your brother complies with a whimper, fearing the pain to come. The machete is real, and sharp. Still, you have to steel yourself. *Take a deep breath.*

"*DO IT!!!*" Jason screams, before biting back down on the belt.

You bring the blade down just above the bite wound as hard as you can, cleanly shearing through the flesh of his bicep. But the blade catches on bone. Jason screams out in pain, thick gobs of spittle flying around the belt and tears streaming down his face.

You wrench the blade free from his arm, then slam it back down as hard as you can. The *crack* of metal on bone turns your stomach and your own biceps scream out empathetically. Jason sobs freely, but you can't stop now.

You jump onto his bed, raise the blade up over your head, leap into the air, and *slam* the machete onto his arm with your full body weight.

His arm falls limply to the floor and blood spurts from the wound in tune to a quickened heartbeat. Acting as fast as you can, you take the belt from your brother's mouth, and tighten it around his arm, cutting off the circulation from the wound. Jason falls to his bed; the shock is too much for his system.

Your own nerves shot, you fall back into his desk chair. Your arms spasm uncontrollably and your shoulders heave up and down with dry sobs.

"…that…was foolish," Dad chastises hoarsely from the doorway. He looks like death warmed over—pale and slick with sweat, eyes bloodshot, skin around them dark and bruised. "Circulation…takes under…a minute…. Infected…"

The old man stumbles back against the door jamb like a drunk, his eyelids heavy. "…blade…not sterile…"

Now your own tears flow freely. "Daddy, what do we do?"

His eyes blink open and with renewed clarity, he hisses, "*Leave us!*"

- ➢ Run now, take the Jeep keys, don't look back. Go to page 315
- ➢ Do the merciful thing; put them out of their misery. Go to page 204

Headshot

You depress the trigger and watch Jason's head flinch back in reflex as the splatter from your shot ripples out across his forehead.

"Ah, fuck monkeys. Goddamn son-of-a…what the hell, Sarah? Headshots are against the rules!" your brother complains. Bright green paint covers the rising welt on his brow.

"Jay, language!" you say, turning the situation on him.

"I don't give a shit, that hurt," the fourteen-year-old groans.

"You shouldn't try to scare your sister," you say with a shrug, "Especially when she's armed."

"I'll get you back," he says, rubbing the paint off with the back of his sleeve. There's a halo of blood from where the paintball broke his flesh.

You turn and start walking out of the paintball arena. "Doubt it. C'mon, I'm late for my shift at the range."

➢ *Get driving before dad calls.* <u>Go to page 167</u>

Heated Exchange

The guard raises the bloodied Asp, but the doctor pushes his way between the two of you.

"We need his help as much he needs ours," the doc says. "I'll go on record as such, once this riot is over."

You can't help but laugh. "Paperwork? C'mon Doc, look around. The dead is risin'."

The doctor bobbles his head uncertainly. "Technically, the patients' hearts *have* stopped beating, but it isn't until true brain death—as you've seen—that I would qualify the infected as 'dead.'"

"I'm not sure that matters so much as how the fuck we're supposed to get out of here," the guard says, pointing towards the blaze with his baton.

It's true, the fire is spreading at such a rate that you can no longer reach the front door. The doctor steps out of the office and points to the ceiling tiles.

"Up and over?"

"It won't take us through the doorway," the guard says.

"But it'll take us thru the fire. C'mon!" you shout.

The three of you drag the desk from the office to the hall, then one-by-one hop on and pull each other into the ceiling. It's hard to see from inside the crawl space, but the smoke that seeps through the tiles helps orient you past danger.

On the other side, you drop down, and the guard opens the door with his key card. Once you're through, it locks again behind you. Rushing down the hall, you make it out past the visitation area, and the guard lets you out front.

"If it wasn't for the fire, I'd lock you to one of these chairs. But you didn't let us burn alive, so consider us even. I don't suppose I can count on you to stay put?" he asks.

You shake your head. "You shouldn't, neither."

"We can't just abandon our posts," the doctor says.

You can only sigh.

➢ *Wish them luck and be on your way. If they want to get busy dyin', that's their business.* <u>Go to page 138</u>

Heeding the Call

The rolling garage door opens with a mighty shriek. The whole time Josh's eyes stare at nothing, unblinking. Shouldn't somebody do that *hand-down-the-face* thing people always do in movies to close his eyes? Yet there's something behind those dead eyes. Like a growing recognition. Is he "seeing" something in the afterlife?

"Brian, you and Stephen take him out. Put him in the dumpster for now. It's not the best place, I know, but maybe that'll stop those *things* from eating him. We'll bury the man proper when this is all over," Owen says.

Brian nods and Stephen simply gets to it, but when they grab Josh, his corpse suddenly moves.

"He's not dead!" you shout without thinking.

Realizing your error, you clamp your hands over your mouth. Too late. Both men look to you, and in that instant Josh grabs hold of Brian's arm and bites into it with a ferocity the man never had in life.

Brian screams bloody murder; high-pitched like a child. It must hurt to high hell, having someone burrow into your flesh with their incisors. Stephen and Owen tug at Josh to get the undead man off of Brian, while Craig looks out to the dusky streets.

"Shut him up!" Craig shouts. "There's more out here...they, they *hear* him...they're coming!!!"

You look out to the horizon and see that Craig's right. Already, there are a dozen shambling figures. Heads lolling about on uneven shoulders, arms outstretched, moaning with flesh-eating greed.

➤ Close the garage. Those who can make it back, make it back. Go to page 101
➤ Grab a wrench and prepare to fight the bastards off. Go to page 369

Helluva Thanks

The booze from the mini-bar bolstering your confidence, you knock on Angelica's suite. She opens the door wearing her hotel bathrobe, most likely spending her night just like you are spending yours.

"Milady, how are you this fine evening?"

"My knight in camo armor," Angelica says in a thick, boozy voice.

You grin. Then, after a beat, look past her and say, "So, are all the rooms the same, or…?"

She doesn't respond, instead simply tugs at her bathrobe's belt. She's nude underneath the fine Egyptian cotton, and though she's in her 40s or 50s, there's clearly been a strict Pilates and yoga regimen in her past. She drops the robe, turns slowly, and walks back into the room, giving you a good look at her firm, golden-bronzed body. That is definitely the ass of a 20-year-old and you suddenly find your blood flowing in response.

"You coming?" she asks.

And indeed you are, far too quickly, if pride will allow you to admit it. Leaving no room for argument, Angelica throws you onto the bed, pulls your robe open and takes you. The excitement of knowing this night could be your last, coupled with the complete lack of coyness in her almost feral lovemaking brings you to an intense, shuddering climax.

All you can do is pant in breathless response. She falls beside you on the bed and says, "So you're taking me with you, right? We could go tonight. Meet up with your army friends at whatever secret base. Or tell them a spot to pick us up. I won't take up much room or food, and I can pitch in. I'll cook or clean or—"

"Hey, hey, slow down a minute. I haven't signaled rescue yet, but I will, I promise. We'll all go."

"We have to go now. It's not safe. Cooper and the others don't know what they're doing. She's just an auto mechanic! We've got to get out of here, Sims."

"Leave tonight? You're joking, right? This park is an incredible find! Hell, I'd bet the military will want to use this as a camp. They'll probably come here. And in the meantime, we're safer together, so…"

Her face suddenly goes blank, like she just received a *botoxic injection*. After a moment, she leaves the bed and says, "Okay. Well, I guess we'd better get some rest. See you tomorrow."

Then she heads into the bathroom and closes the door before you can respond.

- ➤ Go check on Tyberius and Hefty. Go to page 362
- ➤ Go check on Jose. Go to page 127
- ➤ Go check on Cooper. Go to page 75
- ➤ Head back to your room and get some sleep. Go to page 396

Herd Immunity

It's a dark, moonless night, which makes the riot all the more dangerous. The yard is barely illuminated by the lights of the cell blocks, but even so, you can see several bodies sprawled out on the grass. Searchlights sweep from the guard towers and as soon as they come across the flood of inmates, a piercing klaxon rings out, as if the prison itself were mourning.

Then the tower guards open fire.

They shoot indiscriminately into the crowd, hoping to cow the inmate population and stop the riots. Instead, that sends the men into even more of a frenzy. The bolder ones climb the guard towers by the dozen, ready to overtake the lone gunmen at the top.

The rest of the prisoners naturally segregate, as they do every time they head to the yard, each gang pressing their way through the yard fences and out to the larger prison beyond.

The gunshots cease, giving way to screams as the tower guards are thrown over the edge. In one tower, the shooting starts up again, a bloodthirsty inmate having fun at everyone else's expense.

"Hefty, come on!" shouts an inmate, recognizable as a member of the Aryan Brotherhood by his swastika tattoos. He waves you towards the group of white inmates who've broken through and are heading towards the side of the prison that has the chapel, hospital, visitation ward, and main entrance.

With a look back, you see your giant *cholo* cellmate join the Mexican cartel and the black gangs in pushing down the fence towards the more secure wing of the prison: the SHU, the armory, and the motorpool.

- ➢ Birds of a feather, right? Racist assholes or not, go with the group looking out for you. Go to page 338
- ➢ There's only the human race now, and two gangs of cons are better than one. Follow Celly. Go to page 364

Home on the Range

You pull up to "OPEN FIRE," your family-owned shooting range, only minutes before you're supposed to take over for Dad. Jason skulks out of the car, baseball cap pulled down low over his brow, causing his ears to stick out at the sides.

"Sorry, sorry, sorry," you say as the shop door *dings* open, avoiding eye contact and moving straight into the unisex restroom to change for work. You don't even give Dad time to speak, employing battle-tested tactics used by teenagers for thousands of years. In less than two minutes, you're changed clothes, hair pulled back into a ponytail, and you're back out in the shop, ready for work.

"Cutting it awfully close, Sport," Dad says, running a hand over his ruddy, high-and-tight ex-Marine haircut—his signature, *keeping-my-anger-bottled-up* move.

"I know, I'm sorry. I—" Your voice has suddenly stopped working. Standing before you, cradling an IMI Galil assault rifle, is none other than the legendary actor Harrison Ford. He notices you staring, and his iconic grin spreads across his face, making you feel warm inside.

"Mr. Ford and his friends have been waiting," your father continues.

That's when you notice he's not alone. His entourage, looking much like Secret Service agents, mill about, inspecting the wares. There are six guards, a bit much for a celebrity; he must've beefed up his security detail in the wake of recent celebrity murders. That's when you notice he wasn't grinning at all. In fact, his face is blank; expressionless. It's not like he's angry, just…bored.

"Can I have your autograph?" It's Jason. He's finally noticed Indiana Jones too.

And yet Harrison Ford doesn't move, doesn't speak, doesn't even blink. At length, his head turns, his gaze finally landing upon Jason. You share a concerned look with your father.

One of the men steps forward. "I'll level with you," he says. "We met the Docs at *Human Infinite*. You know, the *Gilgazyme* guys? Anyway, Mr. Ford—"

A clatter rings out. Harrison Ford has dropped the assault rifle. Dad rushes in, lifts the weapon, and inspects it before he hands it back to the movie star. Ford's movements are slow, as he raises his arms to receive the weapon. But the Galil just rolls off his fingers once more. It's as if his hands are numb.

"I think he's having a stroke," you say. You've been training as a lifeguard for a summer, and you can tell something's not right.

"Looks more like shell shock to me," your father says. "Only…"

Dad slowly waves his hand in front of Harrison's face, trying to gauge his mental acuity. No reaction. Not even a dilated pupil. Dad snaps his fingers.

Suddenly able to move like lightning, the Oscar-nominee lunges and bites onto Dad's hand. Your father roars a mix of shock and pain and, in reflex, punches his childhood hero in the mouth. Harrison Ford's jaw dislocates and a guttural gargle spews forth from his throat.

➢ Grab the Galil and go for the kneecap. Remember, Han shot first. Go to page 407
➢ Don't get cocky—let his security guys deal with it. Go to page 144

Hop-ons

The men commandeer a staircar, drive it up to an open jet bridge, and secure the long hallway that leads to the gate and the main terminal.

"All clear!" Corporal Gardner announces.

With a nod, you say, "Breach."

It's a standard push-bar door connecting the jetway to the building, and the men make their way inside using quick, practiced movements to check for hostiles. These guys have infiltration down to an art. While they check for fleshies, you take a moment to look around. The flight status screen above shows a whole board full of CANCELLED notifications. A few say DELAYED, and even fewer say ON TIME, apparently from when they stopped updating the system.

A loud, repetitive *thud* draws your attention over the rail towards the ground floor. The passenger drop-off area out front is completely flooded with the undead. They *slam* themselves against the glass walls, the barricaded entrance shuddering in response.

That's when you see the other figures milling about—*inside*. The ghouls found a way in from somewhere, and there are dozens looking up at you.

"Uhhh, Sarge?" Gardner asks, shaking your shoulder. "I said, 'What now?'"

"Gotta find the Ambassador, so..." you say through a dry swallow.

"Is this our egress route?" he asks, his thumb pointing towards the gate.

You nod, and the fireteam fans out, searching for the Ambassador. Though they move silently and communicate via hand-signals, they intermittently yell out for their target, and the growing horde on the first floor moans in excited hunger.

"Hello? We're over here!" a meek voice cries out from one of the shops in the terminal.

You jog over and see that the security gate has been rolled down; two dozen people are cowering within. *Smart place to hide,* you think, noting the snacks and foodstuffs in the concession shop.

"Ambassador Mays?" Corporal Gardner asks.

"Yes, that's us!" the slight man up in front announces. The crowd parts for a man in his mid-50s, with a politician's warm smile, his graying hair neatly combed and short-cropped. He wears a navy blue suit, the red power-tie beaming with authority.

"Thank god for the Marines," the Ambassador says.

"Get this gate up, quick. We have a way out, but we can't stay here long," you say.

Several tough-looking men in suits comply and raise the barrier. They all file out, and the Marines form a defensive perimeter around the crowd, like sheepdogs herding cattle.

The fleshies have found a way up, and they're flooding in from all sides. Your palms start to sweat; *it's time to go.*

"Keep moving!" you shout.

The horde is close on your heels, but it looks as though you'll just make it. The fireteam lets off clean, controlled bursts at the fastest of the undead, but it does little to stop the growing crowd. Finally, you arrive back at your gate.

"Sergeant Sims, the door lock is engaged," Corporal Gardner announces, a note of panic in his voice.

You step forward and take a look. *Damn!* You pushed your way into the terminal without realizing the door would lock behind you. Now there's a keypad and electronic lock blocking the way between your group and the way out.

"What do we do?" the corporal asks.

Shit, shit, shit! Think!

- ➤ There has to be an override or something. Order the Marines to cover you while you look! Go to page 53
- ➤ Turn back and fight our way through! We need to find an alternate way out! Go to page 382

Hosed

Despite Sam and Lily's insistence that this is not a good idea, you ready yourself for departure. Sam offers everything short of his rifle. "Want me to make you a shield? Forge a spear?"

"Nah, I'm faster when I'm not weighed down. Besides, I still got this pigstick," you say, showing off the baton.

"Goodbye, Ty," Lily says.

"See you later," you correct.

From the look on her face, you can see she's not convinced. With a sigh, you look out over the roof, and seeing the dry garden boxes, you get an idea. After a quick trip down into the belly store, you come back up with the longest length of hose the garden aisle had.

"Gesture of good faith," you say, screwing a spray nozzle to one end, handing it to Sam.

Sam helps you rappel over the roof's edge with the hose, then gives you more slack as you search for the alley water main. As luck would have it, there's an old spigot hookup compatible with the hose, so you screw it on and grab the ancient red handle to turn on the flow.

"Water the garden while I'm gone!" you shout. "I'll be back with my mom as soon as I can."

The couple waves to you before you turn to start jogging. Home can't be more than an hour away on foot, even if you do encounter undead on the way.

➢ *Knock on wood, then get going!* Go to page 223

Hospice

Skirting around the paraplegic nutter, you hoist yourself into the hospital window. It's just as you feared. The whole place is trashed, whether by riots or life-and-death struggle, you can't be sure. Probably both.

Prisons don't relish privacy, so the offices and exam rooms have windows large enough so that the rooms are essentially made of glass from waist-level up. Makes for an interesting view: undead skinheads roam the entire floor, many smearing dark gore across the nearest window.

As you move forward, hungry eyes lock onto you. They're coming from all directions, even from behind you. Continuing down the hall, you see a large cabinet of chemicals and medications, and can't help but notice the Flammable icon.

- ➢ Grab the fire extinguisher and smash the cabinet. The ensuing fire ought to buy you a bit of time. Go to page 39
- ➢ Keep going! Distractions really only apply to me, whereas nutters are singularly focused. Go to page 133

Huff and Puff

"Colt, come again?" the radio says. "I was telling you out of courtesy."

"And so am I. We won't open our doors for you."

There's a pause, then, "We'll open them ourselves. Delozier, out."

"Captain, that's not a good idea. Have your men stand down. Captain? Delozier!" Sam says, but the walkie-talkie returns only static. He dashes forward on the roof and hurls the radio while screaming, "FUCK!!!"

After a moment, Lily says, "You knew this would happen eventually."

Sam sighs, looking out towards the military barricades. "I just didn't think it would happen so soon. And I didn't think it would be Delozier…"

"Fifty-percent infected?" you ask Lily. She simply nods, so you continue, "It's time to blow those doors, Sam. Man didn't leave a choice."

He turns, his jawline set. "You're right, Ty. Head inside. I'll give you the detonator; I'm staying up here to reason with him."

"It's not automatic?" you say.

"More damage if you wait until there are a few of them inside."

"Sam…." Lily says, not more than a whisper.

He keeps his eyes on you. "I'll do everything I can, but if diplomacy fails?"

Sam goes for a storage tote on the roof and pulls the lid off, removes a brick of machinery and hands it over. Atop the circuitry is a standard light switch, like those inside any apartment.

"You'll know what to do."

"But…first you try to stop them? From up here?"

"That's right," he says.

With a nod, you take the device downstairs. It's relatively dark in the store, with the storefront windows barricaded. The metal doors look almost frail, knowing what you hold in your hands. Part of you hopes Sam will diffuse the situation and come down in a few minutes to tell you the coast is clear. But there's another, darker part of you that wants to flip that switch.

You hang back and settle in behind the "Expert Desk" used for customer service. You set the detonator on the counter, sit low in the stool, and wait.

Five minutes go by, then ten. Maybe they're not coming? You consider heading back up the stairs when you hear an engine out front. It's a loud, diesel chug. Sounds like a garbage truck…or a Humvee.

That's when the shouting starts. You recognize Sam's voice from the rooftop, but you can't quite make out his words. It's a heated argument, that much is certain.

Then there's a pounding on the door. Not *knock-knock* but more *slam-pound*, like a medieval battering ram. After a few more hits, the doors smash inward and sunlight streams in. Several figures come into the store, silhouetted against the light; you can't make out their particulars.

- Hit the button! Go to page 41
- Ahhh, I can't do it! Hide or call out for a truce or something! Go to page 38

Human Nature

It makes sense to stick close by, you figure. You've seen this area daily. You know the high ground, where to find food, water, shelter. Maybe heading back to the shooting range is a good start? There should still be running water, and more than enough in the armory to hunt for food and keep you safe.

A few miles into your hike, you pick up on engine sounds. Using your rifle's scope, you see a Humvee and three motorcycles on the horizon. Are they coming back from the shooting range? Your gut instinct: *Looters*.

"Get down!" you cry, pulling Jason towards an abandoned station wagon.

The caravan slows down at the traffic jam you're using for cover, and from your position against the pavement, you see several pairs of boots on the ground.

"We spotted you a ways back," a man says loudly. "Come on out, or I send a grenade under that car to clear you out for me."

Standing up, you position your rifle so it's a clear threat. There are five men in total, two in the Hummer and three on bikes. They've taken this whole "apocalypse" thing to heart, from the looks of it. They're dressed like they stepped out of Jason's *Borderlands* videogame.

The bikers hop off and form a semi-circle on the road, brandishing weapons and effectively surrounding you.

"People call me The Duke. What's your name, sweetie?"

"I'm...Rosie," you say. "My brother and I don't want any trouble."

"No trouble at all. Last Rosie I fucked was Rosie Palm and 'er five sisters. Shoot the kid, take the breeding stock."

For an instant you're frozen, unable to process what you just heard. Then one of the bikers shoots Jason and that's when furious instinct takes hold. You drop three of them right off the bat, but they've spread out enough that you take a shotgun blast from a biker on your flank.

With any luck, you'll bleed out. If not, the rest of your life won't be pleasant.

THE END

Hunger

Heading outside, you take a look at your motorcycle parked out front. Can't really pick up lunch in that. Well, you could, but the guys might not appreciate the pizza so much after a ride with the box tucked under your arm. No, you'll have to walk. Could be good to work out the kinks in your back injury anyway.

Pulling out your phone to check what's close, you're met with zero bars of service and no network. *Great.* You're definitely getting a refund on this month's billing cycle. How did people find a place to eat before cell-phones?

"Excuse me," you say to a man standing in front of a dry cleaning shop.

He looks up, glares, then backs inside the store, closes the door, slips the sign to "Closed" and shuts the blinds. You can hear the bolt slam home in the door. *Asshole, much?* Do you have something on your face or what?

Up ahead a crowd has gathered. If you're lucky, it's for a food truck. Pushing your way through, you see that a stretch limousine has crashed into a dentist's office. The wheels spin, as if the driver were trying to wedge the limo even further into the building. Guy must be passed out, with his foot on the accelerator.

"Anyone call 9-1-1?" you ask.

"Phones are down," someone says.

"The government took down the satellites. Just down the block, they're doing some operation. Part of a cover-up," another guy says.

"No, I got a call through. Ambulance inbound," a professor-type adds.

"Who's your provider? I can't get anything," a tween asks.

"Anybody check on the passengers?" you interrupt.

"You a doctor?" a woman says condescendingly, her eyes on your workshirt.

"I'm clearly a mechanic, bitch. But I know this much: if the guy doesn't ease up on the accelerator, he'll burn out the engine. Could catch on fire."

The crowd looks at the limo, then back to you.

➢ "Fuck it. Anybody know of a sandwich shop near here?" Go to page 238
➢ "Sigh. Fine, I'll do it. Buncha pussies." Go to page 209

Hunger for Home

As the day warms, the kendo armor grows stiflingly hot. You're thankful that the helmet's face-guard is open and allows a breeze, but thirst claws at your throat. About halfway to her house, Haley stumbles and falls off the road.

You rush to her side and pull the heavy armor off her small frame. Shockingly, the girl's underclothes are dry. They should be drenched in sweat. The fact that they're not means her dehydration is severe. Looking around, you see a large tree nearby.

"Nathanael, take her armor. We need to get Haley into the shade."

With no water, your only recourse is to fan cool air onto the girl's face, once you've carried her over to the tree. After a few minutes, her eyes flutter open, and then she vomits. This isn't good.

"Armor off, both of you. We need your full strength."

It takes the better part of an hour, but eventually Haley comes to and says she's strong enough to walk again. At your command, the students abandon their armor but keep their *shinai* as walking sticks. It's hot and slow-going, but you're now the only line of defense and are forced to take rest breaks at every shade tree along the way.

When you finally arrive, you see a pair of walking corpses out front. Haley's house has a raised porch, most likely to protect against flooding; the stairs are barricaded by an overturned BBQ, a porch swing, and a pair of couches. With this as the only entry point, the undead don't seem to be able to climb up to the front door. Even so, they don't give up, and paw through the slats of the porch railing like mindless automatons.

"Are they...?" you ask, removing your sword.

"No," Haley says, "I don't know them."

At the sound of human voices, the pair turn to face you. One is a police officer, or *was*, at least; her uniform is so filthy that you can only tell because of the badge pinned to her chest. The other is a prisoner in an orange jumpsuit. Their wrists are handcuffed together.

Two quick strokes behead the pair, just as a voice shouts, "Oh, my God!" and Haley's mother steps onto the upper balcony. "It's them!" she shouts.

Haley's father joins her out front, then Nathanael's mother, and Nolan's parents.

"Hang on! I'll grab the ladder and let you in," Nolan's father says.

Not much of a choice here:

➤ *Deliver the trio of students to their parents.* Go to page 117

Hush that Fuss

The ability to nap on the spot is perhaps the greatest asset of the overworked. You instinctively wake at each stop, quickly scanning to see if you've arrived, then nod back off for another forty winks.

This time you stir because something feels off; *wrong*. The bus has been stopped for too long. You sit up and look out the window. It's not just the bus that has stopped, you see now—it's the entire city block, frozen in place.

An accident? A parade? A protest? Whatever it is, you don't have time for this shit. You look to the front and see a police officer speaking to the bus driver. Outside, motorists abandon their cars, fleeing on foot from an unseen threat. Is it a terror attack? A crazed white guy starting another mass shooting?

"Everyone remain in your seats!" the cop up front shouts, a hand on his piece. Guy looks scared.

The homeless dude next to you stirs, looks at you with crazed eyes. No—bored eyes. Hungry eyes. He chomps his teeth together, then *moans*.

➢ Open the emergency exit and escape! Go to page 109
➢ I need to get away from this guy! Rush the front of the bus. Go to page 64

Inheritance

Jason hits priority one: refilling the water bottles, while you repack everything into two rucksacks. *Guess we don't need Dad's,* you think with morbid regret. Then you scour the house for anything useful you may've missed. The *coup de gras*, of course, is Dad's foot locker from his Marine days.

It's padlocked, but that doesn't stop the bolt cutters that you find in the garage tool chest. *Better take these along too, just in case,* you think as you open the lid to reveal a neatly organized collection of memorabilia. Photos with his USMC brothers. Medals for valor, as well as for his wounds. Commendations. That kind of thing.

Under the top layer of sentiment, you lug out a ballistic "bulletproof" vest and set it aside. Too heavy. Beneath the body armor sits a pair of Kevlar sleeves Dad used for welding in the motorpool machine shop. You slip these on your forearms and take the combat gloves beside them. There's a Ka-Bar combat knife, and you take that as well. Lastly, the chest holds his Marine-issue helmet.

"I'll take that, if you don't want it." Jason already wears Dad's ballistic vest and wobbles uncertainly beneath the added bulk.

"It's too much, Jay," you say, weighting the helmet in your hands. "I'll keep the sleeves, since it'll stop bites, but—" Your eyes grow wide with an idea and you practically shout "—we can use our paintball armor! Lightweight, stop a bite, and we can move quick."

"Good idea, but I'm still taking the body armor. There are enough trigger-happy coots out there on a good day."

"Suit yourself, lunkhead."

There's only one main road out of town and into the woods—and that tunnel to freedom is up ahead. A police barricade was set in place to prevent a mass exodus from town, but plenty of people ran the barricade, and so can you.

The only light comes from the sirens of abandoned patrol cruisers. You scan the area, but find no sign of the police officers. The Jeep's headlights suddenly glint off something on the road, and you slam on the brakes, but too late. The tires scream and hiss when they hit the spike strip, and you skid to the side, the Jeep threatening to flip. You hold your breath, turn into the skid, and close your eyes. The Jeep comes to a stop and after a moment, you head out to check the wheels.

They're fucked; you'll have to continue on foot.

"C'mon, Jay, load up. Take whatever you can carry, but not too much. You don't want to—"

"Yeah, I get it. I'm not a kid, you know."

Several figures wander on the road ahead and a low, breathy moan is terribly amplified by the tunnel to the rear. A whole chorus of the damned.

You raise your rifle, inspecting the weapon to make sure you've got a round chambered and realize you've only got the Ruger factory standard JX-1 ten round magazine loaded. Why didn't you put one of the larger ones in? *Damn.*

"I'm going to empty my mag, and then you cover me while I reload."

"*Rog*," Jason replies.

The two of you make short work of the gathered undead. With your brother to cover you, it's essentially a turkey shoot. Fifty Zulu, down just like that. You must've backpedaled to slow their approach, you realize, because even though you rushed forward, you ended up back at the Jeep.

"Restock ammo," you say.

"We're damn well-supplied here," Jason says. "Maybe we should stick around until first light?"

- ➢ No way. Keep moving, and eventually take guard shifts somewhere less hot. Go to page 316
- ➢ Great idea. Cab of a semi-truck should work well. High off the ground and roomy enough. Go to page 226

Inhospitable

"They..." she says, swallowing hard before continuing. "A lot of people are dead, Luke. It's bad. Really bad. The medical personnel are fighting, but we were losing techs by the hour. The administration didn't know how to handle an emergency like this. We were told not to leave, and most of the staff decided to barricade themselves in the cafeteria, but I know that wouldn't stop the attackers, and—"

"Hey, hey, slow down, Melissa. What attackers?"

"You wouldn't believe me. I...I had to get out of there. People are..." she trails off, adding in a whisper, "...*eating* each other."

"How can that be?" you say.

"Rabies?" Christian asks.

"It started in the morgue, Luke. The corpses...I don't know how else to explain it. The corpses came to life, or not life, I dunno. That's not my department, but when security managed to pin one down, the docs said no heartbeat, no blood flow, no pain, no emotion. Only hunger."

"*Imouto...*" you say. "Something happened, and you're in shock. Come, sit."

"See? I knew you wouldn't believe me. But there's no time—we have to leave, *now*. It's martial law. If we don't go now, they won't let us."

"Living corpses? Come on..."

"Yes, that's exactly what they are! You can stab one in the heart and it'll keep coming. The only way is to crush the skull," she says.

You close your eyes and think back to the homeless man. The way he didn't feel pain. His eyes—the only thing you saw in them—pure animal instinct. *Hunger.*

"Once bitten, it only takes someone six hours before they're a 'living corpse' themselves. We had our first patient three nights ago, but kept it under wraps. They were flying in a CDC team—but get this—the CDC cancelled because they had their own 'specimens' back home. I don't think the hospital will be there tomorrow, Luke. And we need to leave now before this barricade traps us all. Let's go!"

"Go? Go where?" You almost laugh at the sheer ridiculousness of it all.

"Haven't you been listening?! Away. Away from *people!*"

"Melissa, these kids' parents will come looking for them. We can't just—"

"Leave them here, then! Or put a note on the door. I don't care what you do, just come with me. Do you have any idea how dangerous it was for me to get here? The military is already setting up outside your front door!"

You can't just leave the kids here, you know that much.

- ➤ But maybe she's right? If you all gather and run for it while there's still time.... Go to page 29
- ➤ These are just kids! And you've got an old man with you. There's no way you can run. Go to page 136

Inked

The tattoo parlor boasts a large glass storefront, used to show off designs in-progress. Several comfortable-looking chairs and needle stations sit at the ready, and there's a motorcycle on display in the center. The hours-sign shows that it's a 24-hour joint, and a sticker on the door reads, "This door to remain unlocked during business hours."

Yep, it's unlocked.

"Hello?" you call out. "Anybody alive in here?"

No response. The place seems abandoned. You check the motorcycle, but it's for display only. No battery, and the fuel tank is probably empty. There's a back room with a private station, most likely for those getting tattoos on their private parts. Still, it looks like a nice place to rest, and it's big enough to lie on while someone paints your lower back.

You could lock the front door (sign be damned!) and take a load off in the back, or keep exploring the nearby buildings.

- ➤ Yeah, don't want to throw out the baby's bathwater. Time to get some sleep. Go to page 394
- ➤ The strip club. It's designed from the ground up to keep out unwanted flesh-hungry men. Go to page 361
- ➤ The liquor store. I could use a drink after these last couple of days, and the windows have bars. Go to page 234
- ➤ The payday loans building. With all the people they screw, they've gotta be ready for a mob invasion. Go to page 259

Inner Sanctum

The door opens with an exaggerated creaking, loud enough to make any horror fan's hair stand on end. The floors are filthy from invaders, though from the living or from walking corpses, you can't be sure.

"Sensei..." Nolan says. When you turn, he points to an empty dish on the entry table and adds, "Mom and dad's keys are gone."

"So's all the food in your kitchen," Haley says.

"Someone's coming," Nathanael says, his eyes glued on the doorway.

"Behind me, in the kitchen," you command.

A trio of walking corpses follow into the house, though the entry funnels them into a single-file line. With as much effort as you might spend trimming hedges, your sword chops the three of them down. When you rend their flesh, they don't bleed, and only once you've beheaded the ghouls do their limbs stop moving.

"They're not human right, master?" Nathanael says.

"Perhaps no longer," you say, cleaning your blade. "But it is important to remember that they once were. Now come..."

- ➤ "...we must continue on. It is not safe here." Go to page 52
- ➤ "...let us clear the house and wait for Nolan's parents to return." Go to page 405

Insider Information

You call out to Hefty, who comes to join you and Jose while Tyberius and Angelica stay with the new guy.

"What's going on here?" you ask. "Everything okay?"

"Sure. He's injured, so I wouldn't worry too much 'bout that. Bum shoulder, looks like."

"Think he's alone?"

"Yeah. Said his unit went down at the hospital."

"Makes sense. Seem like a good guy?"

"Well, he's Air Force. Can't say that gasmask of his gives me much comfort. Truth is, I think he knows more than he's lettin' on."

"How so?"

Hefty's eyebrow arches. "How so? He's government. You think some world-crushing virus came on without Big Brother knowing about it? No way. This ain't the flu, boss. Dollars to donuts, Uncle Sam created this thing. Maybe they fucked it up, but it stinks of The Man, know what I'm sayin'? And this Sims guy, he knows somethin', I can tell. You're asking me for advice? I'd say keep him close. Guy keeps talkin' about signalin' rescue. Not sure about you, but if there's an Area 52 where the President is ridin' this thing out, and I'd like to be somebody's plus-one on their invitation."

"Thanks," you say with a nod.

Maybe Hefty is right, and the new guy knows something. Maybe he's a survivalist. Either way, it's probably a good idea to keep him close. But first…you need to assert dominance. Or maybe get a second opinion from one of the others?

- Introduce yourself. Make sure he knows you're the boss. Go to page 383
- Take Angelica aside, ask her to shed some light. Go to page 148
- Take Tyberius aside, ask him for the low-down. Go to page 348

Internment

The walk down the street is very difficult for Master Hanzo, and by the time you arrive to the National Guard encampment he's wheezing from lack of breath and taken to the infirmary tent. He'll get more attention from the medical staff, you're assured.

"He's not sick," you tell the military leaders. "The man is in remarkable health for a centenarian, but time comes for us all."

They nod profusely, and gently lead the old man away. It's the last time you'll ever see him alive.

The children are taken to a nursery of sorts, where you're told they'll be reunited with their families as soon as possible. There's no visitation allowed between tents, so you have no way to know when (if at all) your students find their parents.

For you, it's one of the many general tents for "survivors." *What, exactly, have I survived?* you wonder.

Days pass. The daily cycle consists only of receiving food rations twice daily and being escorted periodically in groups to "hygiene tents." This incredible boredom is peppered only by the distant sounds of gunfire. A doctor visits with clockwork regularity, and after a brief exam, determines which of the "survivors" are taken to the sick tent. It's almost tempting to fake illness just to see your old master again.

No one answers any of your questions. Even with the aid of meditation, you can't help but worry over Hanzo and your pupils. *Was this the right choice?* That question is answered when breakfast simply doesn't come one day.

When you push your way through the tent flap and into the open, you learn that the National Guard has abandoned camp. That would explain all the engine sounds early that morning. The street is all but clear, though rubbish and the smell of death float on the breeze.

The other "survivors" flee from the tents. They all had loved ones they were kept from, and now move out to find them. Your thoughts drift to your sister.

Inspecting the camp, you find everything abandoned, save for the horror in the back alley. It's a dumping ground, and the corpses here aren't walking, that's for sure. Bodies lie piled up, all with massive head wounds, either from bludgeoning or bullet holes. The dead furthest back in the alley are burnt and charred beyond recognition. But they didn't have time for the ones up front, the recent dead.

The fresh bodies.

- ➤ *I must know*—look at the bodies. See if there is anyone you recognize. Go to page 203
- ➤ *Past is past.* Turn and get walking. Find some food; keep moving. Go to page 92

Interrupted

The children run through their warmup exercises, and it's nice just to be able to concentrate on the here and now; the moment. The outside world is not something you can control, but giving small corrections like *keep your attack at forty-five degrees, align fists with the center of the body,* or *do not clench your shoulders* allows you to re-center and realize that you don't need to control anything.

"Kendo, at its core, teaches you to adapt. You do not choose when or how your opponent attacks; you can only choose your defense. Remember this in all aspects of life. None of us chooses what happens to us, we can only choose how we react."

"Lucas, you must come!" Master Hanzo says from the office doorway. He never calls you by your first name unless you're alone. This must be urgent. You rush over, and the class follows. "Listen. This is on an unassigned AM station."

A gruff man's voice suddenly crackles in through the speakers, "…you're not alone…civilian camp…be humanity's…and all survivors…Route…ansmission-only…way communication."

"That doesn't sound like a normal broadcast," Haley says.

"It's not," Master Hanzo confirms. "This is certainly local, but our antenna is not strong enough to receive the transmission. Yet there is a way."

"Master…what are you saying? That someone is trying to talk to us?"

The old man nods. "During the war, the community put a large antenna on the roof and we listened to reports all the way from Japan. It is not difficult. If you bring the radio up top, you can use the antenna to boost the signal."

"I thought that was a cell phone tower up there?" you say, somewhat stunned.

"Proof that you don't know everything yet," he replies with a smile.

There are no stairs up to the roof, so you'll have to get on from outside. A dangerous prospect, especially with armed soldiers patrolling the streets.

- ➢ The captain mentioned there are other civilians in the hardware store across the street. Perhaps I can borrow a ladder? Go to page 20
- ➢ If Nathanael helps me, I can push the dumpster in the alley and boost myself up to the top. Go to page 55

Intravenous Intervention

You shoot the center man, and the NICU erupts in screams. You shoot at the ceiling to quiet the staff, then say, "Now there are two doctors, one for here and one who's coming with us. Who'll it be? Don't make me choose for you."

A few eyes flicker behind you. Jason stares blankly at your cold-blooded move with shock, not watching your back. When you turn, you see the nurse whom you took hostage holding a syringe, but too late. She plunges the needle into your neck and depresses 10 milliliters of air straight into your jugular. The effect is near-instant death by cardiac arrest.

THE END

I Ran

So…you pussed out, but why not? You're not in the goddamned infantry. This isn't what you signed up for. Besides, indiscretion is the better part of valor, right? You've done your job as an electrician. Now you'll let these combat operators do theirs, and soon it'll all be water under the fridge.

Not that you'd expect them to understand, so it's best to find somewhere to hide. There isn't much inside the C-17, which is kind of the point. It's a big, empty cargo container, and most of the space is filled by men, gear, or air.

Up, that's the only place to hide; you'll have to climb into the "rafters." You hoist yourself up and nestle amongst the wires and pipes in the ceiling, hoping the men will be too busy checking out their gear to notice you've disappeared.

Looking around for a decent spot to lie down, you're caught completely off-guard when you're suddenly brought down by your ankle. It's at least a ten-foot drop, and all the air leaves your lungs when you slam onto your back. Your joints crack and you wheeze for breath. It takes effort to sit up, cut short when a boot presses against your neck.

"The fuck do you think you're doing?" asks Lt. Dosa, the Marine Corps mission commander.

"Checking…electrical…?" you manage.

"Like hell. We both know you were hiding."

You say nothing. He takes his boot from your throat and offers you a hand. You take it and he brings you to your feet.

"Goddamn coward. We'll deal with you once we get stateside. In the meantime, stay here. I don't need you fucking up my operation."

The LT turns and walks away, leaving you with the entire combat unit starting at you with cold disdain. A Navy SEAL steps forward, and before you can react, cracks you in the jaw with a haymaker. After an explosion of white, everything goes black.

➤ *Go here to regain consciousness.* Go to page 120

Journeyman

The Ferris wheel isn't stopping, so you'll have to jump. You psych yourself up for it, but all you see in your mind's eye are images of your fat ass flopping out against the pavement, providing an all-you-can-eat Sims buffet for the trio of fleshies. Then a better idea flashes through your mind.

"Come on, grab my hand!" you shout.

She gets what you're saying and picks up her frantic pace. Amazing how hope of escape trumps general fear. She makes it to the steps leading to the Ferris wheel loading area, bounding up the stairs with hands raised, but you're just out of reach. You'll have to lunge forward and grab her.

Though your inner-action star is roaring to come out, you're aware of yourself enough to know that you can't pull her up on strength alone. When was the last time you did a pull-up? Instead, you jam your left wrist up between two bars, making a fist and anchoring yourself in the chair, then lean out to grab her with your right arm.

She grabs hold, her manicured nails clawing into your uniform. The extra weight pulls you from the chair, but your left arm pins you in place. It feels like you're being ripped apart.

"Climb...*up!*" you shout through gritted teeth.

Then the pain really starts. One of the ghouls grabs onto the woman's dangling leg, literally ripping your left arm from its socket. You scream out bloody murder, but somehow keep your fists clenched tight—the one keeping you in the chair, while the other is mutually locked on the woman in the middle.

She struggles to kick at the fiend as the wheel takes you up for another trip around. *Blinding motherfucking pain!* You always assumed that was a figure of speech, but no, it's true. Your vision goes pure white.

Finally, with a handful of torn panty-hose, the fleshie falls from the ride and hits the pavement like a water balloon with a crunchy shell. The woman climbs your body to get inside the carriage, then helps settle in. You struggle for breath, color returning to the world, while blazing pain ripples along your left arm. Wriggling your fingers, you still have motor control, but barely.

"You saved my life," the blonde says. Then she kisses your gasmask, leaving a perfect lipstick print on the plexiglass.

The Ferris wheel shifts momentum, and you remember the other two ghouls down below. You unsheathe Isabelle and mentally steady yourself, but as you come around, you see a pair of men run up. A black guy in tattered business casual holds a sledgehammer and a thin redneck-type holds a formidable length of lead pipe.

They hit the landing hard, dispatching the remaining undead with practiced moves. Slim approaches the Ferris wheel controls and stops the ride when your carriage reaches the bottom.

"Enjoyin' the view?" he asks in a thick Southern accent.

The big guy extends a hand to help the blonde off the ride; she gingerly accepts it.

"What the hell were you thinking, running off like that?" he says.

"I wanted to get the soldier's attention. Besides, he handled it."

They all look to you. "Yeah...no big deal," you say, stepping out of the carriage and playing it cool.

"Well, regular *Last Action Hero*," Slim says, before playfully slugging you in your injured shoulder. You roar in pain, and your vision goes white once more like a lightning strike. "That's what I thought. Brave, but fuckin' stupid."

"Well, I'm glad he did it," the blonde says with a glare.

"I'm sure you are!" the big guy says with a laugh. "I'm Tyberius, you just saved Angelica, and my man here is Hefty. So what's your deal, Darth Vader?"

"Sergeant Sims. US Air Force electrical maintenance specialist."

"Are you working with the guys doing all the roadblocks?"

"I don't…I don't think that's a thing anymore, but no."

"Then what *are* you doin'?" Hefty asks.

Your head swims. All you can think to say is, "I'm going to signal rescue, at all costs. So…"

"You should come meet our, well, our leader," Angelica says with a smile. "Fair warning, she can be a real bitch."

Your brain is still trying to process your shoulder injury, so you simply nod. These people seem nice enough and you're better off getting on their good side while you wait for rescue to arrive. Not much of a choice here:

➤ *Follow the group to meet their leader.* Go to page 122

Jumped

You sprint towards Craig, unable to keep the "*Sonofabitch!*" from escaping your lips. Still, you catch him by surprise, and he turns just as you clobber the man with the wrench. He's down for the count.

With a hard slap, you hit the reverse button on the garage door.

"It's closing!" a man shouts, just before gunfire erupts.

Several shots ping off the metal insides of the garage, and several more find homes in your flesh. You fall to the floor, body going numb as your lifeblood drains out.

"Goddammit!" the leader shouts. "I wanted her for breeding stock!"

With any luck, you'll bleed out. If not, the rest of your life won't be pleasant.

THE END

Jumpstart

As you slip the keys for the first car out of the plastic document protector, you eye the motorcycles in the corner. Just gotta get past this shift before you can get back out on the track again...

Best to keep busy, you remind yourself. A watched pot never boils, and a workday spent thinking about tomorrow never passes. You head out to the parking lot to find the silver Volvo from the after-hours lot, turn the engine over and bring it in.

The radio blares to life. A man is saying, "...it's all unsubstantiated right now, but I what I can say—what I know for sure—is that downtown is in a state of chaos. Steer clear of St. Mary's Hospital. There was some kind of incident—"

"It's waaaayyy too early for that kind of bullshit," you say aloud, flipping off the dial.

You bring the car into the garage, your back singing in pain as you step out. You stifle a groan of pain when you see Craig reviewing the files at his station.

"Hey, what's up, Kay?" Craig says.

"Another day, another terror attack."

"Oh shit, really?" Brian chimes in from the other side. "It isn't kids, is it? I hate when it's kids."

"Hospital, I think."

"What happened?" Stephen asks from the lobby doorway.

"Somebody shot up a buncha kids in a hospital," Craig says.

"Damn...."

"Brown and foreign? Or white and domestic?" Josh asks, coming from the bathroom.

They all look to you, and the Oxy still hasn't kicked in yet, so you say, "I only listened for a second. If you want to know what's up, turn on the goddamned radio yourself."

They all look away, and at length, Craig says, "Nah, that stuff's just depressing." The rest nod in agreement and you all get to work. The Volvo's writeup shows:

    OWNER: Mr. Tesshu, L.
    MAKE: Volvo
    MOD: S60
    MIL: 115,612
    NOTE(s): Regular service interval. Oil change. Check shocks.

Three cars up, three cars down, ticking the hours by. You go to look at who's next on the pile, but a glance to the clock shows it's already past noon. Better start thinking about lunch, but might as well call that last owner for pickup before you check with the boss.

When you pick up the receiver, the phone at your station is oddly silent. Almost as if the thing is unplugged, but a quick check shows it's connected just fine. Plus, it was working this morning. *That's weird*, you think, reaching over to give Josh's phone a try—same results.

Huh. Better let the boss know. When you open the door to the admin area, you find Owen watching the lobby TV. It's footage from the local news chopper, showing a big convoy of military vehicles going through town. Traffic is intense and it takes a while for everyone to pull over so the convoy can pass.

"You see this?" Owen asks. "Some kind of large-scale military exercise, they're saying."

"Boss, phones are dead."

Owen frowns, then turns back to the check-in desk to try the line there. From the look on his face, you can tell he's not even hearing static. Owen then takes out his cell phone and dials.

After a minute, he hangs up and says, "It's not just us. Something's wrong with the phone company."

"Great. I was about to ask if we should order some lunch, but sounds like we'll have to get carryout with the phone problems."

"I'll go," Josh offers.

You didn't even notice him in the doorway behind you.

➢ "No, I'll go." I could use some fresh air. Go to page 174
➢ "Yeah, okay. Just don't take too long, the guys are already getting hungry." Go to page 314

Just Ourselves and Immortality

Someone up ahead tries to use his Dodge Ram as a battering ram, but it's not happening. Traffic is gridlocked. Several figures wander up ahead, trying to assess the problem, but when one man raises his hand to block the light from all the headlights, you realize just how strange it is that the rest aren't. They're just wandering, like they're bored. That is, until the man with his hand raised calls out.

The group turns in unison on the man and brings him to the ground. You can't see what's happening, but you can hear the man's screams echo off the concrete walls. A palpable wave of panic flows through the tunnel, suffocating drivers until some snap and abandon their vehicles. It's total chaos as the dozen or so wanderers catch those trying to escape.

"Don't look," you tell Jason. But he doesn't shy away, and you don't force him. "We're safe in here, right, Dad?"

When you turn back, you find he's just looking out the window. His skin is pale and slick with sweat.

"Dad?" Slowly, tentatively, you reach back and put a hand on his shoulder, gently shaking him. In an unnaturally smooth and deliberate turn, his head comes around to look at your hand. His eyes rise up to meet your own. He opens his mouth. You pull back your hand—

—and the stranger reaches out and bites down on your forearm! You scream out in pain and try to pull away, but he's latched on like a pit bull. Jason shoves the man away, but all it does is help him rend and tear your flesh.

Finally, your brother manages to bring up his shotgun. Though it's an awkward move inside the Jeep, he swings the barrel round to point at the guy's face.

"Let her go!" he screams, blasting the ghoulish man with the 16-gauge.

For a moment, your ears ring with deafening silence. Adrenaline keeps the pain at bay until you look at the grotesque carving that was once your forearm and now is only so much meat.

"Tourniquet!" Jason cries.

But it doesn't really matter, does it?

You're INFECTED!

Keep Calm, Carry On

You're sweating like crazy, but you force your face into a mask of calm. Once the fighting is done, the soldiers' weapons find you as their focus. They're clearly panicked; either not trained for something like this, or freaking out, now that a drill has become reality.

When you look to the bodies of the attackers, your own sense of panic swells in your chest. Time crawls by, and an odd detail sticks out: the blood doesn't spread further than the size of the wounds. Nothing drips or spurts out.

"I just want to go home!" you shout, realizing the truth.

"This area is under strict quarantine," the leader calls, his shouts muffled by a gasmask.

"My mom, she—"

"It's shut up or die, get it?!" one of the younger soldiers shouts.

"Stow that, Private," the leader snaps. "Take this man to quarantine."

The man points down the street to a large, green canvas tent. It's situated in the parking lot of a grocery store surrounded by a hardware store, a pawn shop, and a shop labeled "Dojo." You swallow hard at the sight of the quarantine tent and you've got a death grip on the police baton, a fact not lost on the soldiers.

"Drop the weapon! Don't make us do this the hard way."

Not much of a choice here:

➢ *Looks like you're now property of the US Army.* Go to page 374

Keep on Turning

She continues hobbling towards you, screaming, begging for help, but you offer only cold indifference from behind the plexiglass visor of your gasmask. As she makes it to the steps leading to the Ferris wheel loading area, the trio of fleshies finally catch up with her and tackle the woman onto the landing.

One of the ghouls bumps against your carriage when you pass over the landing, and you tuck your feet inside to avoid it. Luckily, they're far too interested in the current feast, and her cries slowly die out as you make your way higher.

Soon, you'll come around for another pass, and you might have to deal with the fiends then. You unsheathe Isabelle and mentally steady yourself.

But as you come around, you see a pair of men run up. A black guy in tattered business casual holds a sledgehammer and a thin redneck-type holds a formidable length of lead pipe.

They hit the landing hard, dispatching the trio of undead with practiced moves. Slim approaches the Ferris wheel controls and stops the ride when your carriage reaches the bottom.

"Enjoyin' the view?" he asks in a thick Southern accent.

The big guy steps up and yanks you out of the carriage.

"Hey, listen!" you say, hands raised. "There was nothing I could do. Everybody has to take care of themselves these days, yeah? But you guys seem like survivors, like me, so…"

"What do you think, Hef?" the big guy says. "Are we like him?"

"I ain't one to leave a woman for dead."

"Me neither."

He shifts the weight of his sledgehammer, and you go for your knife. The man rushes forward and slams his enormous sledgehammer into your forehead.

THE END

Kicking Yourself

I think we've established that you're not a very big guy. Still, given enough motivation (like, say, flesh-hungry ghouls closing in while you're trapped outside after an all-night march, for example), the doors stand no chance.

You grab the locked door-bar for balance and kick the glass doors again and again. At first the glass holds, but you eventually smash through. It comes as a bit of a shock as your foot goes through, knee-deep in glass.

Bright red arterial blood sprays out on the glass and a stabbing pain shoots through you. When you pull your leg back through the glass, that only makes things worse. Your shoe quickly pools with blood, and you're still no closer to getting in.

"Hell was I thinkin'!?" you scream out in rage, before hobbling away from the mall.

Eventually, you lose so much blood that the exhaustion cannot be ignored. You sit "just for a minute" and lose consciousness. When you awake, it's because the nutters have found you.

THE END

Kick the Bucket

You help bucket-lady to her feet, and she rises in response to your touch so easily there's a twinge of regret when you push her into the path of the oncoming ghoul. Her cot tips over, and with it, the bucket of human *squick* that dumps out across the concrete floor of the tent.

The ghoulish woman takes your gift and bites into the sick lady, evidently unconcerned with spreading her own infection into an unhealthy host. Other people in the tent are awake now, and a few are screaming. You go back to your cot.

The screams bring in the guard from outside, and he stands with his rifle at the ready. "Another *Turned*," he says into a chest-radio. "Go for a transfer to aggressor tent."

Two more soldiers come in, looking interchangeable in their gasmasks. The guard says, "Don't let her bite you."

The pair grab the woman, one putting her in a headlock while the second binds her wrists together. They drag her from the tent.

One of the tent's occupants, a man whose brow is slick with sweat, stares at you. He knows. You stare back, cold, and the man turns away.

Doctor Abdous comes in the tent and looks with horror at the scene of blood and bile. She checks on bucket-lady's bite wound, which isn't even bleeding, then helps her lie down on her cot. The doctor looks to you.

"Was anyone else bitten?"

➤ "Shouldn't you strap her down? What if she rises in the night?" Go to page 33
➤ Try hitting on her. Something like, "You wouldn't want to spend the end of the world alone, right?" Go to page 320
➤ "No, ma'am. We're all ship-shape in here, obviously." Go to page 335

Kiddiewinks

Your tac-gear bounces heavily and the strain on your legs feels a bit like running through mud. You shout warnings, but this is a war zone. In-between the deafening volleys of rifle fire, your calls are drowned out by shouts of *"GET SOME!!!"*

Finally, you catch the Ranger's attention, but he can't make out what you're saying. He turns your way to see what you want—right as the kiddos arrive. They take him down, frenzied like a school of piranhas on meth. You raise your rifle, but firing at the hellions is impossible without shooting him as collateral damage. Your shouts are soon drowned out by the Ranger's guttural, blood-curdling screams.

"You saw that coming?!" a nearby SEAL shouts, hatred in his eyes.

Several of the other soldiers open fire into the crowd of kids, so you join them, avoiding the confrontation with the SEAL.

"Aim for the head, fucksticks! Am I the only one who's ever seen a goddamned zombie movie?" Lt. Dosa shouts in between shots at hostiles.

"Sir, we have reports of VIPs trapped in the terminal," a soldier says.

"Who?"

"The Ambassador and his staff. It was the diplomatic rendezvous point."

"Damn," Dosa growls. "They're mission-essential. We have to get him out."

- Don't make eye contact, and hang back towards the C-17. Go to page 135
- Volunteer to lead a force inside. Go to page 147

Kinda Ironic, No?

You run to the next entrance; the service department of the same big-box store. It's just a single door, but it's equally locked. Damn. Better keep going. You're starting to grow a tail, like a cosmic, flesh-eating comet; the nutters follow you from door to door.

Food court? Locked. Second department store? Locked. Employee entrance? Locked. Every single damn entrance is locked and with each pit stop, the growing crowd gets closer.

Seriously? You broke out of a prison but can't break into a shopping mall?

Eventually, you make it back where you started, only this time you've got nowhere to run. At least thirty zombies crowd in around you, ready to make you their first meal of the day.

THE END

The Last Supper

When the dinner call goes out, you're at the part in the novel where the girl hiding in the farmhouse basement manages to sneak outside and get to her cellphone from the Jeep. Her friends are being held hostage, but does she have enough battery to call 911?

You'll have to find out later. "Hang on, let me finish this chapter" is never an option in the slammer. The cell doors open and you proceed to the cafeteria in an orderly fashion. You arrive and prepare to take your seat in the usual segregated-by-race arrangement, when you're surprised to see a few inmates already seated.

One is your cellmate. Looks like they opened the SHU and dumped out the contents. Celly nods at you in recognition. The other inmate you recognize is simply known as Solitary. He's the guy everyone in here recognizes.

The man's been in solitary confinement for as long as you've been here, probably longer, and he always finds a way back into the SHU as soon as he's been released. A lifer who prefers solitary to the yard, they say. Even now, he wears wrist and ankle cuffs, the two shackled together so the man can't raise his hands over his head—the price of being a repeat violent offender.

You take your tray and find a seat, when someone starts screaming.

Jumping up, you move to the outside walls; removing yourself from the fight, lest you take an accidental shiv between the ribs or a blow from the guards. The cafeteria forms a ring around the fighters, just like high school. Only something is terribly different. It's not two men fighting, it's one man *biting* another.

"Shit, that's Don Vito," mutters a nearby skinhead.

"Get him off of me!" shouts the poor victim, but no one moves to help.

Vito D'lunga is the head of the largest mafia family in the state, and thus the *de facto* boss of the prison. If he wants to bite somebody, that's his business.

The guards rush in and pull the victim away, and Don Vito reels back to latch onto a new one. It's Bobby, the skinhead who beat you in foosball this afternoon. Bobby puts up his hands and the mob boss takes a bite. Looks like Bobby won't be playing foosball for the foreseeable future.

Realizing this isn't a traditional fight, the guards focus on Don Vito. Even in his frenzied state, the guards fear the man.

"Take it easy, Mr. D'lunga," one of the guards says, hands up almost as an apology.

Vito snaps his jaws and lunges at the guards, managing to catch one, who screams as Vito bites down. There's a blur of movement in your peripheral vision, and you flinch as Solitary darts past. Despite the shackles limiting his movement, the man moves like quicksilver.

Solitary sweeps the mob boss's legs out from beneath him, sending D'lunga to the ground. He then stomps on the prison boss's head, again and again, until D'lunga stops moving—save for the black blood that oozes from his fractured skull.

You hardly sleep a wink that night, tossing and turning with dreams of being bitten. You practically sleepwalk through breakfast the next morning, and you're still dragging major ass when the call comes for Sunday morning church.

Chapel is neutral ground. Despite their immoral proclivities, most inmates are religious men. Blame it on temptation, the devil made me do it, that kind of thing. That, coupled with the warden's higher punishments for any "malcreant behavior" on church grounds, makes for a quiet atmosphere every Sunday.

"When evening came, Jesus was reclining at the table with the Twelve," the preacher says. He has a Bible in his left hand, but it's closed; a prop. He has this part memorized. "And while they were eating, he said, 'Truly I tell you, one of you will betray me.'"

A terrible, hacking cough sounds out behind you so loud the preacher has to wait to continue. You look back and see one of the skinheads hacking into his wadded up t-shirt. He releases the shirt and leaves black, sticky phlegm across his chest, like he'd swallowed tar and coughed it back up.

The other neo-Nazis don't seem to care. They're all sweaty, paler than normal (which says a lot), with dark veins pressing up against the skin, and hollow eyes.

"They were very sad and began to say to him one after the other, 'Surely you don't mean me, Lord?'" the preacher says.

You lean over to the con next to you and whisper, "What's up with the KKK back there?"

"One of 'em ate his cell mate last night," the man says, in a thick Russian accent, his face blank. "Others are filling up the infirmary. Some kind of rabies, they think."

Shit, you think. *Prison outbreaks spread fast.* Then you remember Vito in the cafeteria last night and the skinhead he bit. "Was it Bobby? The guy who...."

The Russian simply shrugs. With a new sense of dread, you look back up to the preacher, who's saying, "…while they were eating, Jesus took bread, and when he had given thanks, he broke it and gave it to his disciples, saying, 'Take and eat; this is my body.'"

A terrible shrieking roars out, and it takes some effort not to lose your bowels right there. You duck forward and turn around to see one of the skinheads attack a guy you're pretty sure is Yakuza.

A guard takes an Asp from his belt and, with a snap of his wrist, expands the telescoping baton. That's when the rest of the skinheads shoot up, as if suddenly awakened, and surround the guard.

Solitary is here, in his shackles, and pulls the chains around one of the frenzied fiends' necks from behind, but there are far too many of the frenzied ghouls for him to take on alone. There was only one guard posted in the chapel, but with all the screaming, it won't be long until the others arrive. In fact, when you look over at the preacher, you see him trigger the silent alarm under his podium.

This is it. This is survival. So what're you gonna do?

➤ Run. Go to page 211
➤ Fight. Go to page 146
➤ Hide. Go to page 286

Latch/Key

The next morning, after breakfast, you watch from the glass doors as the National Guardsmen pack everything up. They move all the cars from the streets to make room for their exodus, and many walking corpses are drawn by the noise, but with all the soldiers out on duty, they make short work of the intruders. It's better to think of them as walking corpses, otherwise you're watching the military shoot civilians in the head.

Once the quarantine is officially disbanded, those held in the tents go every which way. You're considering rushing out to let them all know about Camp Salvation when a pair of familiar faces catch you from the crowd. A man and a woman, both haggard from exhaustion, make a beeline for the dojo.

"Mom! Dad!" Mason shouts, palms up against the glass in excitement.

He pulls the doors open and the trio shares a heartwarming reunion full of hugs and kisses. The other kids look on longingly, then past the family and into the street, hoping to find a glimpse of their own parents.

"You were in the quarantine?" you say.

"They barely let us out of our tents!" Mason's father says, then, putting a hand out for you to shake, says, "Seriously, thank you. If Mason would've been hurt...or...well, I don't know what we would've done."

Pushing the compliments aside, you tell them all about the radio broadcast and Salvation off Route 14.

"Well let's go!" the boy's mother says. "We can fit two more in our car. What are you driving?"

You shake your head. "I need to be here. With communication down, the other parents will be coming here, don't you think?"

"I suppose," she replies.

"You're a good man, Mr. Tesshu," the boy's father says.

"Be careful in your car," Master Hanzo adds. "Many people will be desperate even after only a few days. If you look like you have something worth taking, there are those who will try to take it."

The family nods and the class says goodbye to Mason, who assures his peers that he'll save them a spot at Salvation.

No one else comes that day, nor the day after. The remaining food has been stretched thin and the water in the bathroom sink finally stopped this morning. You'll have to head out soon for supplies. Though you've kept the door locked and shied away from the glass, there has been some excitement.

Many walking corpses have passed by, like silent spirits on a pilgrimage. Several military men came back through the streets, though you're thinking it's more likely they were men who stole military Humvees. Either way, when they started shooting their machine guns at the hardware store across the street, it was difficult to get the twins to stop crying.

It's even more difficult to tell the class that they'll have to go to bed without dinner. Tomorrow, you assure them, tomorrow you'll go find food.

There's a great pounding and thrashing at the doors in the middle of the night. A few of the walking corpses have stopped to slap against the glass, especially when you were still running drills, but once you kept away from the entry during the day, they mostly wandered away. This is more urgent. This is a distinctly human panic.

When you unlock the doors, Liam and Stella's parents tumble in. The twins rush to greet their family, but they barely even see their children.

"Lock the goddamned doors!" the father shouts.

As you do so, you see several hundred eyes glinting in the moonlight outside.

"How many are there?" you ask.

"Too many," the mother says, tears in her eyes.

That's when the group of undead smashes against the glass doors. It's unlike the strange curiosity the early attempts displayed. This is pure, rabid hunger. They know people are inside, and they burn with desire to join you. Some leave bloody smears on the glass as they break their fists on the doors.

"You have a back exit?" the man says, holding Stella while his wife picks up Liam.

Nathanael points the way and the family starts running. It's time to go, *now*.

"Master Hanzo!" you shout, pounding on the office door.

Haley screams and you flip around. The back door is open, the twins and their parents gone, and a stream of walking corpses flows from the alley and into the dojo in their place.

"Stand back!" you cry.

Then there's a crash as the glass doors explode under the force of a thousand dead bodies. They must feel no pain, because the ones up front continue towards you despite the glass tearing their flesh to ribbons.

Their greedy, hungry teeth come for you all. With only a wooden sword for defense, there's no way you'll make it out of this alive. But at least there won't be enough of you left to rise again.

THE END

Lawful Evil

Your eyes scan the bodies, starting with the smallest. There are some children in the piles, which is tragic, but none of them look familiar. Your heart soars, and that leaves you feeling guilty. They were each familiar to someone, after all.

Exhaling slowly, you turn to leave. That's when a shock of white hair catches your eye. You move closer, carefully rolling the body onto its back with your foot. But you already knew it was Master Hanzo, didn't you? He stares up at you with blank eyes and a third, red eye on the forehead.

A painful moan comes from your chest. This man was there for you, even after the death of your parents. He helped your family emigrate from Japan and is solely responsible for your station in life. And these people left him here like trash.

- Take him to the Dojo office. There is no earth to bury him in this concrete jungle, but you can't leave him in an alley to rot. Go to page 143
- Say your goodbyes now, usher his spirit to the next world, then leave his body and move on. Go to page 92

Lawful Good

After tucking Dad and Jason in for *the long sleep*, you load up the Jeep, grab the map and compass, and head out. It's hard to believe they're really gone. It feels like you're just driving out to meet friends, and you'll be back home soon, and so will they. Dad cleaning his guns and Jay tapping away at his smartphone.

But all that's gone now. There's nothing there for you now. And the memory of discharging your weapon into the skulls of your family will keep you from ever going back. There's only one main road out of town and into the woods—and that tunnel to freedom is up ahead. A police barricade was set in place to prevent a mass exodus from town, but plenty of people ran the barricade, and so can you.

The only light comes from the sirens of abandoned patrol cruisers. You scan the area, but find no sign of the police officers. The Jeep's headlights suddenly glint off something on the road, and you slam on the brakes, but too late. The tires scream and hiss when they hit the spike strip, and you skid to the side, the Jeep threatening to flip. You hold your breath, turn into the skid, and close your eyes. The Jeep comes to a stop and after a moment, you head out to check the wheels.

They're fucked; you'll have to continue on foot.

There are several figures wandering inside the tunnel already, but there's no other way out of town. The tunnel is jammed, in a literal sense, with cars crashed into one another. You keep your rifle at the ready and move forward.

A low, breathy moan is terribly amplified by the tunnel. But it's not just one—it's a whole chorus of the damned. You raise your rifle. The first figure growls and charges in at you—*crack!* He falls limp at the command of your 10/22.

Suddenly the whole tunnel is alive and frenzied. Your rifle is low-caliber, but in this confined space, it might as well be a dinner bell. Dozens of deadened eyes glint in the darkness and a whole crowd of crazed, hungry Zulus now stumble forward in anticipation.

Crack, crack, crack! You make each shot count, knowing the Ruger factory standard JX-1 ten-round magazine will soon run dry and you'll need to replace it. Why didn't you put one of the larger ones in? Damn.

You try to cut a lane through the cars, only shooting those who stand in your way. As you dart forward, light and nimble on the balls of your feet, a snarl catches your attention. From the cab of a semi-truck, the driver tumbles out on top of you. You slam against the pavement, your breath purged from your lungs. When you wheeze back in, you choke on the viscera streaming from the gaping maw of the man astride you.

Blinded, you put your hands up to block the attack, and the trucker bites down on your forearm.

You're INFECTED!

Lawful Neutral

The visitation room is predictably devoid of visitors—undead or otherwise. When you turn back, you're met by the correctional officer, who's uncomfortably close. Before you have time to react, the guard slaps a cuff around your wrist, then secures the other with one of the clasps on a meeting table.

"Hey!" you shout.

"It's safe here," the guard says. "We'll come back for you."

The doctor says nothing, averting his gaze. The men head out the front door, leaving you to stew in your anger. It's likely he meant it when he said they'd be back, but it never happens.

Did the two die? Were they infected? Was the prison evacuated, and you were forgotten? Probably some combination of these things, but it doesn't matter. You're left here to rot, given the choice between chewing off your hand or starvation, which is no choice at all.

THE END

Learn with a Purpose

Nathanael rises to a high kneel; his waist is straight and his thighs are extended in line with his torso, to add height. He puts his hands together in prayer pose and quotes, "Kendo is a way to discipline the human character through the application of the principles of the katana."

"Good. And what does *that* mean, Christian?"

"Hone strength and honor?" he says, as if it were a question.

"Correct, but what else? Haley."

"Improve the self, improve the community, nation and world," she recites.

"Is a katana a weapon? Nolan," you say, targeting one of the younger boys.

"No!" Mason shouts before clamping his hands over his mouth. "Sorry, sensei."

"Kendo is…defense," Nolan says, looking away. "Of others and myself."

"And who is the greatest enemy? Liam? Stella?"

"Myself," Liam says.

"Liam," Stella adds. The students all laugh.

"The *untrained* self," you correct. "Only through knowing oneself can you defend others. And the Kendo purpose? To mold…"

In unison, like reciting the Pledge of Allegiance, the youngsters all jump in:

"To mold the mind and body.

To cultivate a vigorous spirit,

And through correct and rigid training,

To strive for improvement in the art of Kendo.

To hold in esteem human courtesy and honor.

To associate with others with sincerity.

And to forever pursue the cultivation of oneself…"

They continue on. The younger students only know keywords, while Nathanael's voice is loudest and Christian and Haley's lips at least move throughout.

"Did you get all that, Salvator?"

The young boy, probably around 6 years old, looks to his mother for help. She sits off to the side, attention on her cellphone, and crosses one leg of her elaborately printed yoga pants over the other. Not finding the answer there, he turns back and simply nods.

"We have a fast learner! It's okay if you're feeling like this is a lot for one day; learning is a lifelong process. How about this…I'll learn from you, if you promise to learn from me. Deal?"

"Okay…" he says, almost a whisper.

"First lesson, answer, 'Yes, sensei' or 'Master Tesshu,' okay?"

"Sin…say?" he tries.

You nod, smile, then stand and say:

➤ *"Class, I'm going to show our new pupil around. Set up drill stations."* <u>Go to page 256</u>

Left Behind

The doctor takes your fire extinguisher and cleans the gore off while the guard cuffs your hands behind your back. Finally, they're ready to go.

"*Great*," the guard says, pointing towards the blaze with his baton.

It's true, the fire is spreading at such a rate that you can no longer reach the front door. The doctor steps out of the office and points to the ceiling tiles.

"Up and over?"

"He can't climb with his hands cuffed," the guard says. "We'll have to come back for you."

"No, no way!" you shout.

The pair of them drag the desk from the office to the hall, shut you in the office, then one-by-one hop on and pull each other into the ceiling.

You wait. At some point, the smoke from the flames curls under the door and into the office as the fire eats at the air and breathes smoke in return. You cough until you can't breathe, then you pass out, never to wake again.

THE END

Let the Wrong One In

Owen unlocks the door with some hesitancy, but promising food and safety, the five men come in. "You made the right choice," the leader says. "Problem is, we've got enough fat white guys. Take the breeding stock and shoot the men."

What did he just say? You're so stunned you can barely think, but the flurry of gunshots that follows snaps you out of it. You grab the closest thing—a torque wrench—and swing it at the nearest man.

He flinches, so you miss his head, but he screams out as you hit his shoulder. The leader rushes in and knocks the wrench away with a machete, then he punches you in the gut. As his men bind your wrists behind your back with zip-ties, he says, "I like the feisty ones. Boys, I formally call dibs. This one goes to my personal breeding stockade."

Then they blindfold you.

➤ *Go limp, but plan an escape as soon as you can.* Go to page 56

Like a Wrecking Ball

You push your way through the ring of people and over to the driver's door. Swinging it open, you practically fall back at the grisly sight within. The front windshield is coated from blood-spray and one of the driver's pale hands is still clamped over the arterial wound in his neck.

Reaching past him, you turn off the limo, but you're afraid to move the guy. You heard that somewhere. "Never move someone who's had an accident if you don't have to." That's what the paramedics are for. Still, better check the back.

From this angle, you can see the partition, which is also coated in blood and gore and…has some hair caught in it, has been raised. The driver's hair is short-cropped, and this is long, feminine hair. Complete with waves and highlights.

"So fucked up…" you mutter, stepping back into the light. The gathered crowd watches intently, but none offer to help. "Yeah, I got it, thanks!"

Then you open the back door. The interior of the limo is in total disarray, even more than you might expect from a crash. The TVs, once mounted, are cracked off the walls, with parts strewn about. The glasses and champagne bottles are only so many shards now. And the three women inside are in various states of ruin. Like they've had parts of their body burned away by acid. Or eaten.

It looks like one woman is still breathing.

You lean in to get a better look, and a fourth woman latches onto you. She has wild, manic eyes and a tongue that waggles out of her chipped-tooth grin.

"Miley…Cyrus?" you say, baffled at seeing the celebrity in this state.

She chomps off her own tongue trying to bite you, and you fall out onto the pavement, dragging the 95-pound waif out with you. You elbow Miley in the mouth, and her tongue bounces on the pavement right by your face. Switching tactics, you roll over, pin her down, and slam her head on the concrete over and over again.

Eventually, she grows still and the world is a better place. But as you check yourself for wounds, you realize—she bit you.

You're INFECTED!

Limited Resources

The motorpool is essentially an enormous garage-style warehouse. You've never been in here before, but everyone has seen the outside of the building. It's where the bus drops you off on in-processing day.

Parked inside is that same prison bus and three patrol cruisers. Along the side walls are several stations for washing, maintenance, refueling, tire rotation, that kind of thing. And a singular, obvious-to-spot board with all the keys. They're helpfully labeled too! All you have to do is hit the button to open the gigantic, rolling garage door, claim your vehicle, and you're free!

Celly and his closest *hermanos* dig through the lockers and find a few spare police uniforms. They pass them out and change out of their prison jumpsuits. One of the biggest *cholos* takes the vehicle keys from the wall.

"Hey, what about me?" you say.

Celly turns and says, "You? Why, you get to drive the bus, man. You got the most important job of all, Hefty! You're breaking that gate down. Once you do that, we're even."

"Even?"

"You had a pretty cozy stay here, *amigo, porque* nobody fucks with my cellmate. But we're not cellmates any longer, we're free men!" This last part he shouts, then squeezes you on the shoulder.

➤ Remind Celly who helped get him out of his cell in the first place. Demand a cruiser and tell him one of his cronies can have bus duty. Go to page 325

➤ Whatever. Somebody's gotta be the battering ram, and you can take bus out of here as easily as a car. Go to page 137

Lockdown

Normally, rabbiting out of a situation is your worst choice in prison, because there's nowhere to run. At best, you're going from one end of the cage to the other. At worst, you're looking like a coward to the other inmates and pissing off the guards.

But somehow, you know, "normally" has gone out the window. These nutters are eating each other, and you need to get as far away as possible. You run for the doors, but they're locked from the outside. Just in case the preacher puts the guard to sleep, no sneaking out. *Damn.*

Wild-eyed and frantic, you look for another way out, though it's hard to look away from the carnage. If only there were some sign, some key to salvation! Searching for help, your eyes fall upon the arm's-spread, stained-glass visage of Jesus.

Of course! The stained glass is a work of art, not like the reinforced, mesh-inlaid safety glass found elsewhere in the prison. Fueled by sheer terror, you pick up the metallic baptism bowl and hurl it at the window. You pick up a candlestick to clear a larger hole in the broken glass, but a growling moan draws your attention to the other side of the chapel.

The nutters, all six, stare at you with dead, hungry eyes. The shattering drew them in, and now you're a much bigger target than the other inmates who cower, whimpering, in the wings. No time to waste. You run at the window, jump, and plant a foot on the jagged edge of the window, the thick rubber sole of your shoe protecting your foot as you leap to the other side.

Those crazy bastards push through the window right after you, the glass ripping their flesh, but they don't care. One catches an edge in the stomach and keeps on going, even as the shards pull his intestines out.

You stare in shocked disbelief a moment longer, then turn and dart out into the yard. A warning shot rings out, the grass exploding by your feet. You drop to your knees, hands over your head. This is guard-speak for, "If you keep running, the next one won't miss."

Rolling over, you look back and see the nutters keep on coming. A red blossom appears in the lead man's shoulder, and the *crack* registers a split second later, but even this doesn't stop them. You close your eyes and curl into a ball as the nutters surround you.

When you open your eyes, you see the gang of six on the ground, their black brain fluid staining the green lawn of the yard. Turning back, you see three prison guards in riot gear, rifles smoking. If they went to the armory, you can be sure it's worse than just the church, but you've never been so happy to see the cavalry arrive.

"Lockdown," one says, "Get back to your cell."

You nod furiously, feeling yourself for wounds, but you're miraculously unscathed.

Lockdown, in prison terms, means no leaving your cell. Food is brought to you, showers consist of rubbing your body with handfuls of water from the sink, and people go stir-crazy. Celly grows more aggravated by the minute.

Just to calm your nerves, you scratch half of your remaining lotto tickets, but all three were a bust. Only three more remain, and it's hard to space them out. The boredom is broken up by occasional bedlam. Shrill screams come from other cells.

People beat against the bars like apes at the zoo. Some even fling excrement at the guards.

Rumors fly down the cell blocks: *Sick bay is overrun. The guards are getting sick. There's no warden anymore. The whole city is gone, one of the guards told me, and soon they'll abandon us too. Not just the city, man. The country. Those nutters? They're not just crazy. They're the walking dead. Fucking zombies, man.*

At dinnertime, the rioting starts up again.

"Hey, what's goin' on?" Celly asks the neighbors.

You come close and listen in as the man replies, "The CO delivering food. Says it's the last meal 'for a while.' He promises they'll be back with help from the army, but this is it, we're fuckin' dead meat!"

"No, no, no," you find yourself saying. "Not like this. I gotta get outta here. Not like this!"

"Get a grip, *amigo*! I got us covered," Celly says.

You turn and look at him, and he peels up the corner of his mattress to reveal a large, industrial hand-file about the size of your forearm. He quickly sets the mattress down as the guard delivers dinner.

➤ Celly, for the win! Take your dinner and get to work breaking out.
  Go to page 293
➤ Screw that! Try to bribe the guard with your remaining lotto tickets.
  Go to page 404

Locked and Overloaded

You expect some kind of protest from the crew, but for the most part, they act like that was the plan all along, and Airman Belliveau gives a quick tutorial on how to use the system. There's a carabiner you can hook into your combat vest, then, with both gloved hands on the rope, you put one arm behind your back to control your descent. He'll stay up top to operate the pulleys, while you go out with the other five Airmen.

The men fast-rope out of each side while the pilot hovers close to the hospital. You watch as the rescue team fans out to find the military brass among the crowds of soldiers, and direct the evacuees your way.

Taking a deep breath, you drop out of the helicopter and, miraculously, make it down without busting your ass. Several of the key personnel are already wounded and have to be hooked into the ropes and raised mechanically.

But the helicopter draws more attention than the crew would like—both from the shambling dead and the frenetic living. You might as well be dropping yourself as a baited hook into chummed waters.

Hundreds of groping hands reach out and grab hold, and you scream to be raised up. Airman Belliveau tries to recall the ropes, but the motors whine under the weight. As you go up a few feet, more of the crowd latches on. It's like hell's version of a barrel-of-monkeys.

And every single rope system is under the same pressure.

The combined weight of thousands of bodies all scrambling, either for rescue or to eat the flesh of the living, proves too much. You can't see under the mobbing crowd, but Belliveau clearly wasn't able to cut you loose.

Death comes mercifully quickly when the helicopter turns on its side and comes crashing down on top of you, like the world's biggest lawn-edging tool.

THE END

Locked In

Fueled by sheer terror, you pick up the metallic baptism bowl and hurl it at the window. You pick up a candlestick to clear a larger hole in the broken glass, but a growling moan draws your attention to the other side of the chapel.

The nutters, all six, stare at you with dead, hungry eyes. The shattering drew them in, and now you're a much bigger target than the other inmates who cower, whimpering, in the wings. No time to waste. You run at the window, jump, and plant a foot on the jagged edge of the window, the thick rubber sole of your shoe protecting your foot as you leap to the other side.

Those crazy bastards push through the window right after you, the glass ripping their flesh, but they don't care. One catches an edge in the stomach and keeps on going, even as the shards pull his intestines out.

You stare in shocked disbelief a moment longer, then turn and dart out into the yard. A warning shot rings out, the grass exploding by your feet. You drop to your knees, hands over your head. This is guard-speak for, "If you keep running, the next one won't miss."

Rolling over, you look back and see the nutters keep on coming. A red blossom appears in the lead man's shoulder, and the *crack* registers a split second later, but even this doesn't stop them. You close your eyes and curl into a ball as the nutters surround you.

When you open your eyes, you see the gang of six on the ground, their black brain fluid staining the green lawn of the yard. Turning back, you see three prison guards in riot gear, rifles smoking. If they went to the armory, you can be sure it's worse than just the church, but you've never been so happy to see the cavalry arrive.

"Lockdown," one says, "Get back to your cell."

You nod furiously, feeling yourself for wounds, but you're miraculously unscathed.

Lockdown, in prison terms, means no leaving your cell. Food is brought to you, showers consist of rubbing your body with handfuls of water from the sink, and people go stir-crazy. Celly grows more aggravated by the minute.

At dinnertime, the rioting starts up again.

"Hey, what's goin' on?" Celly asks the neighbors.

You come close and listen in as the man replies, "The CO delivering food. Says it's the last meal 'for a while.' He promises they'll be back with help from the army, but this is it, we're fuckin' dead meat!"

"If only I had my fucking file, *aarrrrgh!*" Celly cries in dismay.

The guard moves quickly, delivering dinner as fast as he can.

"Wait!" you shout, briefly catching his attention.

➢ Threaten the bastard. Try to get him to come in and teach you a lesson! Go to page 108
➢ Offer the man…sexual favors. Go to page 108

Locked Up

Fueled by sheer terror, you pick up the metallic baptism bowl and hurl it at the window. You pick up a candlestick to clear a larger hole in the broken glass, but a growling moan draws your attention to the other side of the chapel.

The nutters, all six, stare at you with dead, hungry eyes. The shattering drew them in, and now you're a much bigger target than the other inmates who cower, whimpering, in the wings. No time to waste. You run at the window, jump, and plant a foot on the jagged edge of the window, the thick rubber sole of your shoe protecting your foot as you leap to the other side.

Those crazy bastards push through the window right after you, the glass ripping their flesh, but they don't care. One catches an edge in the stomach and keeps on going, even as the shards pull his intestines out.

You stare in shocked disbelief a moment longer, then turn and dart out into the yard. A warning shot rings out, the grass exploding by your feet. You drop to your knees, hands over your head. This is guard-speak for, "If you keep running, the next one won't miss."

Rolling over, you look back and see the nutters keep on coming. A red blossom appears in the lead man's shoulder, and the *crack* registers a split second later, but even this doesn't stop them. You close your eyes and curl into a ball as the nutters surround you.

When you open your eyes, you see the gang of six on the ground, their black brain fluid staining the green lawn of the yard. Turning back, you see three prison guards in riot gear, rifles smoking. If they went to the armory, you can be sure it's worse than just the church, but you've never been so happy to see the cavalry arrive.

"Lockdown," one says, "Get back to your cell."

You nod furiously, feeling yourself for wounds, but you're miraculously unscathed.

Lockdown, in prison terms, means no leaving your cell. Food is brought to you, showers consist of rubbing your body with handfuls of water from the sink, and people go stir-crazy. Celly grows more aggravated by the minute.

Just to calm your nerves, you scratch half of your remaining lotto tickets, but all three were a bust. Only three more remain, and it's hard to space them out. The boredom is broken up by occasional bedlam. Shrill screams come from other cells. People beat against the bars like apes at the zoo. Some even fling excrement at the guards.

Rumors fly down the cell blocks: *Sick bay is overrun. The guards are getting sick. There's no warden anymore. The whole city is gone, one of the guards told me, and soon they'll abandon us too. Not just the city, man. The country. Those nutters? They're not just crazy. They're the walking dead. Fucking zombies, man.*

At dinnertime, the rioting starts up again.

"Hey, what's goin' on?" Celly asks the neighbors.

You come close and listen in as the man replies, "The CO delivering food. Says it's the last meal 'for a while.' He promises they'll be back with help from the army, but this is it, we're fuckin' dead meat!"

"No, no, no," you find yourself saying. "Not like this. I gotta get outta here. Not like this!"

"If only I had my fucking file, *aarrrgh!*" Celly cries in dismay.
The guard moves quickly, delivering dinner as fast as he can.
"Wait!" you shout, briefly catching his attention.

➢ Threaten the bastard. Try to get him to come in and teach you a lesson! Go to page 108
➢ Try to bribe the guard with your remaining lotto tickets. Go to page 404
➢ Offer the man…sexual favors. Go to page 108

Logic Prevails

"I don't think so," the guard says.

But the doctor steps forward. "It's true. We need his help as much he needs ours," the doc says. "I'll go on record as such, once this riot is over."

You can't help but laugh. "Paperwork? C'mon Doc, look around. The dead is risin'."

The doctor bobbles his head uncertainly. "Technically, the patients' hearts *have* stopped beating, but it isn't until true brain death—as you've seen—that I would qualify the infected as 'dead.'"

"We're all dead if we don't get moving," the guard says.

"Ain't that many, we can just push on through," you say, adding, "If we work together."

The doctor's Adam's apple bobs up and down with a hard swallow, but he doesn't protest. The guard heads out, and you're right there with him. You hit one of the undead bastards with the fire extinguisher on the way, sending his teeth onto the carpet.

While you and the guard defend the doorway, the doctor gets the door open by using his keycard. Your heart soars when you hear the chirp that means the door is unlocked and open. He pulls the door open, and you're in position to go first.

➢ This is your chance to escape! Time to be a treacherous bastard....
  Go to page 70
➢ Keep the extinguisher raised, check for zombies, sweep the room.
  Go to page 205

Long Range

You're not really close to your younger brothers. They never really knew dad during the "glory days," and so his current form doesn't affect them as much. Besides, they're all two states away, which might as well be two lifetimes, given the conditions out there.

After saying half-hearted "see-ya-later"'s, you take your bike out onto the open road. Things are bad out there, *really* bad. There must've been some kind of cover-up until it got so big that "they" couldn't hide it anymore. Until today.

You drive past an ambulance with the back doors open. The inside is painted with gore and a figure in the center eats something. The person is so encrusted in viscera that you can't tell if it's a man or a woman, but it looks up to you with hungry eyes and you drive on.

Outside of your apartment building, a police cruiser is crashed into a fire hydrant, spraying a geyser of water into the air. A woman runs from the building in her nightgown and a man chases after her with a baseball bat. A shotgun blast echoes from somewhere inside the building.

Best leave your knickknacks where they lie and hit the dusty trail. It's tempting to stop at the local gas station, but there are fistfights at the pump. You're at about half a tank, which should get you to a station further from chaos.

On the way out of town, you see an ad for a local gun range. That'll definitely move you to the front of future fuel-pump lines. So you park at "OPEN FIRE," and head inside in search of firearms. The front door is locked, but as dad used to say, locks only stop honest thieves.

Once you've broken in, you see that you weren't the only one with this idea. The front has flecks of drying blood on the counter, but the gun lockers sit open. There are still plenty of weapons and ammo, though the shelves for 16-gauge shells, .22 caliber rifle shots, and 9mm bullets sit empty. You're about to take a Colt 1911 .45 and Mossberg 12-gauge when you hear the door behind you creak open.

A quick glance over your shoulder reveals five men. They're decked-out in paramilitary gear and leather. Clean-cut types with hard arms and soft bellies. Each holds at least a handgun on his person. You also notice several large knives. One has a belt of grenades...are those real?

"Great minds..." one of the men says.

"Plenty for everyone; help yourself. I was just leaving," you say.

"Didn't you hear? We're supposed to stick together. I think we're lucky to have found each other," the man in the center says.

"Yeah, real *lucky*," another says.

"Well, not that lucky. We did follow you from the garage, after all," the center man says.

He takes a step forward. The others follow.

- ➤ I don't want any trouble. Say, "Take what you want; I'll look somewhere else." Go to page 281
- ➤ Take the Colt and show 'em just how lucky they are. Go to page 243

Looters

Food, water, weapons, blankets, medicine. With your powers combined, *I am surviving the apocalypse!* That's the best you can come up with, on short notice anyway. Owen said he had to stay with the garage just in case anyone came by to pick up their cars. That left five categories and five employees, so you're out looking for medicine. More Oxycodone, specifically.

There's a pharmacy at the shopping center where you normally fuel up and grab your daily Big Gulp of Mountain Dew. It's a Walgreens-style mini-mart where you can get just about anything. Lawn chairs and hammocks are in the "stock up for spring" section, but you're just looking for a few bags to fill with pills.

There are plenty of other people here, of course, but it's more of a mad-grab than it is a territorial claim. *Grab what you can! The cops don't care! They've got enough to worry about!* These are the battle cries of the looters.

You find that sweet, sweet Oxy, then snag as many other medications as you can, checking labels and ingredients for a wide variety. Antibiotics and painkillers is the name of the game. Acetaminophen, that's a fever and pain reducer, right? Niacin? What's that for?

"Ladies and gentlemen, if I can have your attention, please!" a man shouts.

A quick glance over your shoulder reveals five men. They're decked-out in paramilitary gear and leather. Clean-cut types with hard arms and soft bellies. Each holds at least a handgun on his person. You also notice several large knives. One has a belt of grenades…are those real?

"This here is a citizen's arrest. Ya'll are taking valuable property that does not belong to you. Turn it in to my deputies in an orderly fashion."

They fan out across the store and one points over towards you. "Found the mechanic chick," he says. The center man looks to you and grins.

➢ Make a run for it. Go to page 317
➢ I don't want any trouble. Say, "Take what you want; I'll look somewhere else." Go to page 281

Lucky Day

Scratch, scratch. The metallic film comes off the lotto ticket, collecting under your thumbnail. Two apples, a pair of skulls in concert with two sets of crossbones, and—one more apple! That makes you the big winner. You turn the scratch ticket over to see how much three apples are worth. Drum-roll, please…

Twenty bucks. Well, at least it'll pay for this week's supply.

You hide the rest of the cards under your mattress for later. Scratching one per day gives you something to look forward to in this place.

What now? Do a couple of pushups, maybe take a dump. Not much else to do. With a sigh, you look around for a way to kill time before the dinner call. After today's incident, your cellmate is currently in the SHU (AKA "the shoe," AKA solitary confinement) and his new bedding sits neatly folded atop the bare mattress. You pick up the paperback novel on his nightstand—*Calm Before the Storm*.

You're about to sit and read, but your gaze stays on the folded bedding. His contraband's in there. You could always take a peek?

➢ Nah, I'll just read this paperback and wait for dinner. My Celly's a huge, scary guy, so it's not worth the risk. Go to page 199

➢ Who am I kidding?—I'm going to look. If I don't, I'll never be able to stop thinking about it. Go to page 305

Mad Dash

Before leaving, you open the back and strap on a pack, then hand another to Jason. You look at the other two packs in the back, but you know your father and this stranger will have a hard enough time just walking. Jason helps Dad from his seat. He starts deliriously wandering towards the front of the tunnel.

"I'll catch up, stay with Dad!" you shout, hurrying to help the other man out.

As soon as you open the door, he lunges for you, snarling, snapping his jaws and taking you firmly in his grasp. He pulls you in, but you break the hold. Dad taught you that one after your first kindergarten experience with a bully, and you've been practicing breaking grapples with Jason for as long as you can remember.

The seat belt holds the crazed man firmly in place and you leave him there, jogging to catch up with your family.

"The other guy's lost it," you say.

"I think…" Jason starts, but trails off when he catches sight of a dozen figures wandering through the headlights.

"Hey, what's going on?!" one man shouts.

All the others suddenly turn in unison and descend upon the hapless man. Not wanting to be next, you push forward, weaving between the cars and dragging your father along by the arm. *He's strong, he'll be okay. He has to be okay.*

Some of the drivers start to panic and blare on their horns. Others actually try to ram their way out of the traffic jam. The wanderers quickly lose interest in the man and you rush past two cars just as one slams forward—with you caught in-between.

With excruciating pain, you know your hip is shattered. It's not long before your cries of anguish bring the wanderers your way. Jason does his best to defend you, but there are too many and he has to reload before they're done with you.

This won't be pleasant.

THE END

Mad Props

Jason sighs, but doesn't argue. He positions himself in a flanking position so that you can fire at a crisscross pattern, maximizing damage while minimizing friendly fire. While he gets set up, you look for something to distract the gang. Though the mall is full of gunfire, you'll be shooting very close to the biker gang, and it's a fair bet that they won't appreciate it.

You're near one of those skater/goth/naughty-party-gifts stores and the pleather-clad mannequin out front gives you an idea. Moving quickly, you lift the lifesize plastic doll onto a skateboard from the display rack, then go for the lighters. The one with the USMC skull and crossed rifles should work nicely. "U.S. Marines: Mess With The Best—Die Like The Rest!"

There are several bottles of lighter fluid on sale, so you douse the mannequin, light it up, and send it boarding into the center of the chaos. The gang members immediately wheel around to face this new threat, and you open fire, using a photo booth as cover.

The Zulu don't evade, so it's a turkey shoot.

The gang members, however, think you're trying to kill them. They go for defensive positions, and return fire. You fall back behind the photo booth and wait for a break in the action.

With their attention on you, several gang members scream out as they receive bites from the last remaining Zulu, then finish your job for you and drop the ghouls with small arms fire.

"Cease fire!" you scream. "Lower your weapons and we can all go our separate ways."

"Over my dead body!" one of the bikers shouts, just before he unloads on the photo booth.

"If you say so!" Jason shouts.

Your brother's sixteen-gauge sends buckshot into the man, and you use the opportunity to swing back around and draw down on the rest of the gang.

"Weapons down, now!"

The nearest biker brings up a shiny, nickel-plated pistol and you put one into his shooting arm at the shoulder. He drops the weapon involuntarily and the other bikers do so by their own accord.

"Disrespect the dead again, and you'll join 'em. We're going to back out real slow, and so long as there's no sudden movements from this corral, we all live happily ever after, get me?"

The bikers nod. More undead flow in from the recesses of the mall, announced by an echoing *moan*. Best hurry.

➤ *Get going while you still can.* Go to page 237

Mama's Boy

You jog through the open streets, following the bus route, which is cleared of cars in preparation for the National Guard departure to support the hospital.

Moving down the middle of Main Street keeps you clear of the wandering infected that come from the alleys and side streets. They moan and claw at the open air and some of the "healthy" ghouls come at you in a stumble-run, but it's uncoordinated and you're faster than they are.

It's only twelve miles from work to home, and your bus stalled a few miles before the bank, so it should be ten or less miles that you're forced to run. Still, you spend your days at a teller counter, not training for marathons, so you have to walk for stretches. When you slow down, the tail of undead behind you grows, which is motivation enough to keep your rest breaks short.

When you turn onto your street, you're almost shocked to see your apartment building. Part of you worried it would somehow be gone. Or at least crumbling; maybe engulfed in flames. But there it is, same as always. The garden your mama was working on this morning sits complete, waiting to grow.

Inside, the lobby is a mess. Letters and bills are strewn about just below the wall of mailboxes, one of which sits open. Some of the floor tiles are speckled red. You head up to your apartment, with the police baton at the ready. The stairs squeak when you walk up them, as if they're already unaccustomed to use. As you pass Ms. Alaina's place, your nearest neighbor, you hear moaning from within. The outside door handle is smeared with blood.

With a deep breath, you return home.

"Mama?" you say, after opening the door.

A figure comes rushing in at you, and you instinctively raise the police baton, but too late. She slams against you, knocking your breath out and squeezing you tight with an animal-like embrace.

"Tyberius!" she cries. "Don't you ever scare mama like that, boy!"

"Oh, mama..." you say, melting in her arms like a child.

She's alive! *Thank you, God.* Your eyes swell with tears of joy.

"You wouldn't believe how people actin' a fool in here. Sit, sit. What's it like out there? You okay? Sweatin' like a beast, ain't you?"

She leads you to the kitchen table and sets you in a chair, then brings water. After you drink, you say, "It's bad, mama. People—people are saying... *zombies.*"

She laughs and waves the word away. "*Zombies.* Ha! Back when I was a girl, in Africa, *Nzambi* was the name of a god. You sayin' we have gods walkin' around now? Ha!"

"I don't know what it is, mama. But I think that doctor on TV and his 'eternal life' drug has something to do with it, so maybe 'gods' ain't too far off! Gods, devils...end of days."

She doesn't answer right away, but you can tell that hits her. At length, she says, "Let me make you some breakfast, boy."

When she turns and opens the refrigerator, you see spotting on her blouse; at the shoulder. It's dark, almost crimson and you barely notice—but it's there.

"Mama, what happened?" you say. When she doesn't answer, you get up. "Mama! You're hurt, what happened?"

"Sit back down now. I'm makin' breakfast."

Instead, you rush over and pull at her shirt. She cries out in protest and swats your hand, but not before you see it. The wide collar of her blouse stretches to reveal two rows of teeth marks—upper and lower—swollen and puffy.

She's been bitten.

You fall back like you've just been struck. "Mama…what happened? Please…"

She's starts crying, but wipes it away. "Ms. Alaina, she was wailin'. I want to see if she okay, but she is not. Not all, son. She attacked me and…I tried to call the police, but no one is answerin'! I got out, though. I got out."

"When was this?" you hear yourself say, but the words feel hollow.

"She woke me up this morning. Crying and crying. Goin' on an' all."

Now you're crying. You can't help it, it just comes out.

"Tyberius! Stop that now! Can't we…I wanna make you breakfast, okay?"

"Okay, mama," you say, trying to compose yourself.

She turns back and starts beating the eggs. At length, you sit back down, but you can't stop your shoulders from shuddering. You can't push out the pain, no matter how hard you try. It lives in your chest now, a part of you.

Mama must hear the weeping, because she starts humming to herself as she cooks. You force yourself to watch her cook, not letting another goddamn thought in your head. You just watch, living in this moment alone. Mama making you breakfast. Humming to herself.

She delivers the plate with a forced smile and it reminds you of the morning after your brother Julian died. For her sake, you eat the food, just like that day, giving *mmm*'s of pleasure.

"Do…" she says, in almost a croak. It sits there in the air for a moment, then she clears her throat. "Want…juice?"

"Sure, mama."

She goes back to the fridge and you eat. Truth be told, it's good, and you're starving. She left you a full plate and you wolf it down. You've got a mouthful of eggs when there's a loud crash. The sound takes your eyes to the kitchen floor, where there's porcelain from a broken mug mixed in with orange juice.

Looking up, you see your mama just watching her hand, which sits open, numb. Her mouth is open too, moving, like she's trying to talk but can't. Like she's having a stroke. The refrigerator kicks on to a louder setting as the open door makes the appliance think the temperature is too high.

"Mama?"

Her head snaps towards you, a look in her eyes you've never seen before. Her breath comes out husky, as if she's still trying to speak. She takes an uncertain step towards you.

"Mama, *no no no*. Please, God, no…."

Now she's practically growling and raises both arms towards you, clawing at the air with her one hand.

➢ Try and hold her. She's your mama, she'll snap out of it. Go to page 227
➢ Fight her off. You can't let her scratch or bite you. Go to page 79

Misery Loves Company

"I'm not in any misery, I promise!" Brian shouts.

"You can't just kill a man because he's wounded," Stephen says.

"He's not wounded," you counter. "He's *infected*."

"We don't know how this works yet," Craig says.

Owen steps forward. "It's true, Kay. Maybe he'll recover? We just don't know."

"Fine. If you all lack the sack to do it, I will. But I will not be the next link in a chain of victims," you say, taking the wrench and walking over to Brian.

Brian scuttles backwards on his rear, cradling his ruined arm. Genuine fear in his eyes. No one wants to die, but the alternative to a quick death is rotting in the trunk of a Honda right now. You raise the wrench, but a sucker punch hits you in the back of the head.

"Crazy, murderous bitch!" Stephen yells.

It takes you by complete surprise, and you fall to the floor before Brian. The frightened man looks to you, to the wrench, then up to Stephen. Grabbing the wrench, you turn and hit Stephen in the shin. He screams out in pain and stumbles back while you gain your footing. Craig pulls out a multi-tool survival knife from a pouch on his belt and brandishes the blade, trying to look threatening.

"You better be prepared to kill me, Craig," you growl.

"That's enough!" Owen shouts.

You send an icy glare towards your boss, holding the wrench ready, like a cornered animal.

"Give me the knife," Stephen says.

"Stay out of it!" you scream. "I'm doing him a mercy. I'd do it for each and every one of you."

Wrong thing to say. Craig reaches out to hand the knife to Stephen, so you rush forward with a barbarian's battle cry, hoping to cut him off. Stephen reaches out to take the knife and you swing the wrench at his arms.

He turns with the knife, just in time to intercept you, plunging the knife deep into your gut. Everything freezes for a moment, like the group needs a minute to process what's happened. You push away from Stephen, the knife sliding cleanly from the wound.

You fall to the floor, dark blood and bile pouring from the stomach wound.

"God *damn* it! Look what you made me do!" Stephen says.

With any luck, you'll bleed out before Brian rises again. Gut wounds are a slow death, and you've got six hours on the clock.

THE END

Monster Truck

You take everything from the Jeep and abandon the vehicle, in favor of sleeping in the semi-truck tonight. The tunnel is full of slain Zulu, but you've seen enough horror movies not to walk too close to the corpses.

Jason steps up, opens the passenger door to the truck, and a snarl catches your attention. From the cab of the semi-truck, the driver tumbles out on top of you. You slam against the pavement, but your paintball armor absorbs most of the blow. Even better, the viscera streaming from the gaping maw of the man hits your plexiglass mask and not your face.

You put your hands up to block the attack, and the trucker bites down on your forearm. Jason blasts the truck driver's head clean off with his sixteen-gauge and you get to your feet. Checking the bite wound, you see that the Kevlar sleeve just saved your life. It hurt like a bitch, but you're left unscathed.

The rest of the truck is empty, and fairly clean, for having housed a living-dead driver. The door is a little gross from where the ghoul tried to claw his way out, but you can avoid that side. Safely inside, you clean your helmet and body armor with some wet-naps from the glovebox.

"Where should we go tomorrow?" you ask.

Jason doesn't reply. Instead, he hands you the map and compass. You unfold the map, take note of the tunnel, and see what's nearby. The map gets a little "fuzzy" outside of town; that is to say, everything surrounding civilization is marked by a unified green blotch.

- ➢ Stay close to home. Your shooting range isn't far off, and it's better to stick close than to head off into unfamiliar territory. Go to page 173
- ➢ Into the woods. We can find supplies and a more detailed terrain map at a Ranger Station—Helpful, knowledgeable, friendly! Go to page 26

A Mother's Love

You stand and wrap your arms around your mother, crying as you do. For a moment, she just stands there in your embrace, allowing herself to be hugged. *It's all going to be all right.* Then she bites you, right in the chest, and pain forces you to push her away.

She comes for you again, and you grab her by the wrist, swinging the small woman around and taking her under the chin with your other arm. The bear hug works, and though she struggles mightily, you have her immobilized.

The blood from your chest stains through your clothes and into her blouse, but eventually stops. You can't be sure how long you hold her, but eventually she stops too. Hesitant, you release her, and she steps away. When she finally turns around, she looks right through you. Whatever courses through your blood has done its damage, enough that she no longer sees you as prey. She sees you as an equal.

And with that, you'll be together forever.

You're INFECTED!

Motorin'

The motorpool is essentially an enormous garage-style warehouse. You've never been in here before, but everyone has seen the outside of the building. It's where the bus drops you off on in-processing day.

Parked inside is that same prison bus and three patrol cruisers. Along the side walls are several stations for washing, maintenance, refueling, tire rotation, that kind of thing. And a singular, obvious-to-spot board with all the keys. They're helpfully labeled too! All you have to do is hit the button to open the gigantic, rolling garage door, claim your vehicle, and you're free!

There's a big, red, plunger-style button by the garage door. You slap the button, and the motor kicks on, painfully loud. Guards and nutters alike will surely heed the call. Time to head out.

- Take a cruiser. Go to page 291
- Take the bus. Go to page 236

Must be True

Everyone gathers in the lobby, where the TV currently plays a racing DVD. When you flip the input to cable TV the screen shows a handsome man in a lab coat giving a press conference, smiling brightly against the flash of cameras. The headline reads, "Will YOU Live Forever?"

You turn the channel, where Jennifer Lawrence appears on the set of Colbert, but something feels off. Neither are moving or speaking. Finally, he just *wheezes* and his eyes glaze over. It looks like the man had a tiny, almost imperceptible stroke.

"Stephen?" Jennifer says. The camera pulls back and Colbert turns to face his guest, and both motions occur eerily at the same speed.

"Are you—" she says, putting a hand on his.

Suddenly he's got her wrist and is pulling, hard. At the same time, he lunges over the desk, trying to get to her. She screams and punches the TV host with her free hand. She's got a mean left hook, but it doesn't even register, and Colbert claws at the starlet with his own free hand.

You turn the channel, this time to the local blonde eye-candy newswoman. Alison Argyle, oddly calm, reads from the teleprompter, "In an ironic twist, it seems many of those killed are users of the new longevity wonder drug Gilgazyme®. It's still unknown if there is a connection between the drug and the homicide sweep hitting major urban centers across the country. No spokesperson for the creators of Gilgazyme® has agreed to comment as of this broadcast…"

"Go back to the other one," Brian says.

But you can't. The television is suddenly taken into local control and your community Sheriff appears on the screen. You change the channel instinctively, but it's all the same. You're not sure, but it seems that something like this hasn't happened in decades. With so many channels…

"The Governor has declared a state of emergency," the Sheriff announces. "But we are as of yet unprepared for any sort of mass evacuation. We're working as hard as we can to set up aid stations and sanctuaries. In the meantime, work with friends and neighbors. Find a group. Nobody can beat this thing alone. And… we need all the help we can get."

The image switches to a stationary, soundless PLEASE STAND BY message. There you have it. You're on your own, but so is everyone else.

"So…it's not just the phone company," Stephen says dryly.

"From the look of the TV, it's the whole country," Brian says.

"But it'll pass, right?" you ask. "I mean, it's going to be bad, sure. But it'll pass."

"Maybe," Owen replies. "How long has this *Gilgazyme®* thing been on the market? Couple of weeks, right?"

"The apocalypse," Craig says, reverence in his voice.

"Bullshit," you say. "It'll pass. We just need to…

- ➢ …Head home; wait this thing out with family." Go to page 218
- ➢ …Lock the garage down tight. Right here, right now." Go to page 368
- ➢ …Get supplies. Split up and meet back here." Go to page 219

Nature's Path

After promising to see the families again soon at Camp Salvation, you leave at dawn. Now you enjoy the cool of the morning as you hike along the marshes. With daylight to guide your trail, you're able to stick to the higher ground and avoid the thickest parts of the swamps.

Even so, your exposed armor quickly swells with moisture, and you're left feeling like a hiker with soggy socks. You'll have to make sure to air them out tonight. Swamp water warmed by body heat and left to simmer in a dark, dank sock is the exact formula for fungal growth.

Putting your mind elsewhere, the glades seem almost *too* serene, compared to the chaos of the city. It reminds you of a poster from Master Hanzo's office that reads, "When it seems the country is in ruins, remember there are still mountains and rivers."

Sage advice when the people of the city are eating one another.

It's still early, perhaps not even yet noon, when you arrive at the setting of Liam and Stella's neighborhood. With the twins under Master Hanzo's care, they're safe for now, but if you can't find their parents, what will you do? Could children so young hike from the inner city with you to Salvation? Could Master Hanzo? The man is strong of spirit, but he barely walks a hundred steps in any given day.

The peaceful birdsongs are replaced by screeching home alarms, the clean air by rot and excrement. A thick black cloud hovers over the neighborhood, an ominous sign of smoldering house fires. How is it that even a neighborhood on the outskirts of town has already fallen to the scourge? Perhaps the quarantine was not the start of it all, but a last effort to stall the inevitable?

That's when you arrive. Their house has scratch-marks on the door and boarded windows, and a message spray-painted across the door and siding, "SICK INSIDE."

- I must see for myself. I've come so far; I can at least put the twins' parents to rest. Go to page 296
- I will heed this warning. Time to focus on the living: Master Hanzo and the twins need me. Go to page 295

Neo-Nazi Zombies!

You round the corner of the laundry building, hot on Solitary's heels. He runs hard, but so do you, desperate to get away from the trigger-happy guards back in the armory. The sweeping searchlights can't reach you from the shadows of the cafeteria, but it looks like Solitary is heading towards the prison hospital.

Bad idea, you think. If these nutters are sick, that'll be ground zero for patient zero, and you'll have zero chance in there. You're just about to say as much when Solitary makes a hard turn towards the entrance to the machine shop. It sits on the back side of the laundry building, and you immediately get it—no weapons from the armory? What's next best thing?

Solitary does the key-dance, trying to move quickly, but it's dark out and that's a *big* ring of keys. A hungry moan draws your attention from the base of the hospital where a skinhead corpse, missing its lower half, claws towards you. What's worse, his moaning draws in more of the fiends.

Suddenly the busted-out infirmary windows pulse with life as every goddamned white supremacist in the prison pours out like worms from a rotten apple. Some fall from the top windows, three stories up, but the sickening slap of their bodies against the pavement does little to slow them.

Just as the KKK horde reaches the machine shop, someone grabs you. As you scream and spin around, you see that Solitary has the door open, and it's he who pulls you in.

You slam the door, glad to have a building between you and the army of nutters, but the machine shop's large windows are a concern, even if they are reinforced by mesh wire. Solitary moves quickly, claiming a nail gun and some loose two-by-fours, and works to board up the windows.

➢ Great idea! Help him secure the machine shop. Go to page 371
➢ That'll only slow the bastards down—look for a back way out. Go to page 377

Neutral Evil

"What for?" the doctor says.

Do you really have to explain why being among a cast of troublemakers sounds better than staying with the infirm and infected? Not in a way you can articulate, so you just shove her away and flip over your cot. You kick the sick woman's bucket away, spraying the far side of the tent with the worst fluids to come out of a person.

"Get the goddamned guard!" you roar.

The doctor takes the hint and rushes out the front flap of the tent. A moment later, a gasmask-clad soldier returns, his rifle at the ready as if he's clearing a house in Fallujah.

"You want me to end you, Troublemaker?"

"Take me to aggressor tent!"

"Shut the fuck up and sit down!"

"Get me out of here! I belong in aggressor tent!"

To demonstrate your explosive rage, you throw more equipment around the tent. You scream and roar. Two other guards rush in to see what's going on and give a look at the first man.

"You *really* don't want aggressor tent. I'm doing you a favor here. Calm. The fuck. Down."

Instead, you charge the men. You only want them to take you seriously, so you don't put your full effort into it, but it's enough that they stop trying to help you out and switch to beating you with their rifles.

The three men drag you out of the tent and through the military compound, back to an alley where two other guards let you pass. Once you make it through, you find yourself among dozens of bodies—some charred and burned, but most freshly dead.

"There is no aggressor tent, asshole. That's just something we tell the med-heads so they don't give us shit for terminating their patients once they *turn*."

"Wait…"

"You shoulda listened."

The men open fire.

THE END

Neutral Good

You pull out your police baton from the waistband of your work slacks, ready to fight. In a lightning-fast move, the wooden sword swoops in and cracks against the joint where your thumb meets your wrist—forcing you to drop the weapon. Then the sword is up and at the ready again.

The man stares at you, a dull, almost uninterested expression on his face.

You bring your fists up as a distraction, then reach out with your foot to kick the baton back towards yourself, but the staff lashes out again, this time connecting to your ankle. You roar with pain and your nerves scream out in concert.

Blind with rage, you bum-rush the guy, but his sword is already up and waiting. The man dashes to the side, windmills the wooden sword around, and slaps you in the back—sending you reeling. You hit the floor chest first. It's a padded practice mat, but still your ribs crack from the impact.

When you get up and turn around, the man stands calmly, sword raised. His eyes dart to the side, and you follow his gaze to a rack full of practice swords. Is that a challenge? *Accepted!*

You grab one of the swords two-handed, like a baseball bat, and attack with brash haste. What you lack in skill you'll make up in ferocity. You swing the wooden sword like mad and the guy effortlessly parries the blows. The fact that it's so easy for him makes you all the more enraged.

You bring the sword up over your head and he plunges his own into your abdomen. Coughing, you offer one more wild swing. The man slides out of the way and slaps the end of his sword against your elbow. Your whole arm goes numb and, in reflex, you drop the weapon.

That's when you see that the National Guard soldiers have arrived, rifles raised.

"He is all yours, gentlemen," the Japanese man says.

You're too exhausted for any other choice:

➤ *Hands up, go quietly.* Go to page 374

Never Sicker

Flashlight on and wits about you, it's time for a drink. The door is unlocked and lets out an electronic *ding!* when you push it open. Damn thing must be battery-operated. After a moment, nothing appears to stir, so you take a look around.

Looks like the owner just abandoned the place. Several bottles lie broken on the floor, most likely from looters, but the store was well-stocked and they didn't clear the place out.

Tequila? Seems like an occasion for tequila. Ooh, wait, there's that Top Shelf cabinet up front. The one with the three-digit prices for each display bottle. A quick crack with Mitch the M4's butt and the case is open. You grab the most expensive one, lift your mask, and take a swig. Then another. Annnnnd a third. But that's it—gotta keep your wits about you.

It's almost an instant buzz, but the sounds of scratching somewhere in the back kills it. You pull the gasmask back down and get ready. Flashlight and M4 pointed as one, you sweep back towards the sound, keeping as quiet as you can. Your heartbeat practically echoes in the silence.

When you make it to the back, you see that the rear of the liquor store has been broken open. It's the loading doors where the supply truck drops off the week's shipment, and from the thick black tracks left burnt on the pavement, you can tell the delivery guy left in a hurry. The truck's ramp was probably still attached and ripped the rolling gate right off its hinges.

"Damn...."

At that exact moment, a pair of zombies burst forward from the periphery of the supply area, and you stumble back, knocking over a whole shelf of wine bottles. You aim and shoot; one down! The other is already on top of you and grabs hold of Mitch the M4. You pull hard and discharge a round into the thing's gut, but it won't let go. Ever heard of a "death grip?" Yeah, they don't compare it to a vise for nothing.

One of the bottles catches underfoot and you fall back—hard. The ghoul comes on top of you, still gripping the rifle with one hand, and now claws at the gasmask's faceplate with the other. Dropping the rifle, you wrestle with the creature with one hand and search for an advantage with the other.

BOOM! Right through the head with your sidearm and you're free. *Thanks, Deb!*

After a moment to right yourself and check for others, you open the bottle for another drink and to clean up a bit. Something thick and black oozes from both infected brain cavities. It's difficult not to vomit and you're ready to leave. With the back of the store wide open, can't sleep here anyway. Where next?

- ➤ The tattoo parlor. With its tough-guy design scheme, nobody will mess with me there. Go to page 180
- ➤ The strip club. It's designed from the ground up to keep out unwanted flesh-hungry men. Go to page 361
- ➤ The payday loans building. With all the people they screw, they've gotta be ready for a mob invasion. Go to page 259

New Exhibit

God, you haven't slept that good in days. Exhaustion has a way of doing that, but fear has a way of keeping you awake too. Maybe that was the difference? In the garage, you never knew if someone was going to turn and try to bite you. In the horse stall, well, a worse fate loomed. It's strange, because you barely know Jose and Angelica, but you felt like…like you could trust them to watch your back.

When you check your watch, you see that it's nearly noon. You slept through the whole morning? Apparently the canopy in this exhibit is dense enough to block out direct sunlight, and you still feel like you could sleep longer. So what woke you up?

That's when another peanut shell hits you.

"Looks like one of 'em's finally up," a man says in a thick Southern accent.

You shoot to your feet, grabbing the wrench, but the pair of men are on the other side of the bars. One of them is a tall, well-built black man wearing tattered business casual and wielding a sledgehammer. The other is a thin-as-a-rail redneck-type with a plain white tee and jeans, who holds a lead pipe.

"Mornin', sunshine," the redneck says. He tosses another peanut and adds, "I know the sign says don't feed the animals, but ya'll just look sooooo cute in there."

"Who are they?" Angelica whispers, awake now.

"C'mon, Hef. You're freakin' her out. Can't you see she scared?" the big man says.

"Ha. A ragged pair like you hardly scares me," you say, shaking your head. "Just leave us now, peacefully. I don't want to have to hurt you."

"It ain't like that," the big guy says. "I'm Tyberius. My thin friend here is Hefty. Why don't you come on out and we'll all grab something to eat, real civil like?"

"I'm Angelica. That's Jose." When you don't reply, Angelica adds, "Her majesty is called Cooper."

"Angelica, stop talking. Leave the negotiations to me," you say in a low voice.

"Doesn't look like they have guns," Angelica whispers. "And I'm hungry."

"Didn't ask for your opinion," you growl.

You look to your Chef companion, who shrugs and says, "*No entiendo.*"

The thin guy shakes his head and says, "We in this together. The living, that is. What, you wanna get eaten?"

"Is that an offer?" you say, eyebrow raised. Attempting to disarm them.

Thin guy flushes, and the big guy laughs. Gives you a handsome smile and says, "Listen, we're just looking for some food. It's okay with you if we get some lunch, huh?"

- ➢ "Sure, you go your way, we'll go ours." Go to page 27
- ➢ "Fine, but don't think that makes us together." Go to page 106

Night Ranger

The modified school bus chugs to life when you turn the engine. *I think I can (escape), I think I can (escape)...* You put the bus in gear and drive out of the motorpool, turning towards the front gates. *Shit! The gates.* Usually, someone manually opens those things so vehicles can pass through the inner and outer fences going to and from the motorpool. In your rear-view mirror, you see the guards from the armory heading your way. They set up and take aim. *Damn!*

Looks like you're going to have to ram the gates. Do you have room to gain speed in this behemoth? Probably not. Unless you make room! You keep the bus in reverse and head towards the guards.

They dart out of the way and, once you've backed up almost to the yard, it's time to plow your way through. As you floor the gas pedal and head back towards freedom, the guards come back and open fire. The bus windshield is reinforced, so the bullets only paint spiderwebs across your field of view.

One of the guards has a weapon that catches your eye. It kind of looks like...a grenade launcher. It's stocky and black with a thick, rotating chamber of tube-fed ammo. He takes aim and fires as you pass, and a shattering somewhere behind you signals a clean hit. You wince and brace yourself for an explosion, but it never comes.

It takes a while for the bus to build up steam, but you're soon up to ramming speed. By the time you make it to the inner gate, the barrier doesn't stand a chance. You have to correct an involuntary fish-tail, but it barely slows you.

The second fence, the outermost barrier, is more formidable. Eyes stinging and breath growing short, you smash through the second fence. It catches something under the bus, and your side mirrors show a shower of sparks in your wake.

When you look in the main rear-view mirror, you see a cloud of smoke—inside the bus. Are you on fire? Now you turn back for a better look. There's a canister rolling around on the floor, angrily spewing smoke. That's the source.

As you start to cough, a burning sensation burrowing in your throat, you realize it's tear gas. That bastard guard! The cloud grows thicker and your vision watery. Soon it's impossible to see. Hacking, wheezing, you miss a bend in the road and slam into a ditch. Unable to think of anything other than breathing, you scramble for the door mechanism and free yourself, stumbling out into the night air.

Off to your side is a police cruiser; the guards have chased you down. Now they open fire and you do a lead dance before you fall into the field, dead.

THE END

No Fairytale Ending

Only yesterday, a shopping spree at the mall would've been your greatest fantasy, but tonight it leaves you feeling hollow. If you could have rounded up your friends and had the mall to yourself? That would have been amazing! Then your thoughts turn sour. Friends that you'll probably never see again. Friends that, in all likelihood, will soon be dead or infected, if they're not already.

No more sleepovers, no more birthday parties, no makeup or dresses. You won't even have a prom.

"Sarah, are you okay?" Jason asks.

You realize you're crying; mourning for a lost childhood, but when you look at Jason, the tears flow in earnest. He's only fourteen, and the world has come to this?

"No prom, Jay. No more going to the movies. No homecoming football games. No college. No jobs. No future."

"Doesn't sound all bad to me. No cleaning my room. No more dirty dishes. No school!"

A laugh escapes through the sobs. Then a sobering look washes across Jason's face.

"I just realized...I'm going to be wearing braces for the rest of my life," he says.

Despite everything, the mall was a welcome escape from the reality waiting for you back home. But as you pull into the driveway, you're filled with hesitation. What if Dad's condition is worse? Should Jason see that? What about the guy in your bedroom?

"Ready?" Jason asks.

"Yeah, just...don't tell Dad I cried, okay?"

Jason shrugs. "Whatever."

Now then, back to business. You say:

➢ "Let's check on the stranger first." Go to page 406
➢ "Let's see if Dad has a plan." Go to page 378

Not Having It

The tween chuckles and says, "There's a *Subway* down the street, but that's about it."

Most of the others just stare, aghast, as you shrug and walk away. Most go back to watching the freak show that is the limo wreckage, but you can still feel some of their eyes burning into your back. But so what? It's not like they're doing anything to help, right?

So you continue on, hoping the eponymous sandwich shop can make one of those giant six-foot-long party subs (and, of course, deliver it), but it's not meant to be. There's a sign on the door that says, "Closed due to illness."

➢ Screw that. A sign like that just means it's free sandwich day. Go to page 351
➢ Damn it. Walk back. Go to page 385

Notice Me, Senpai!

Nathanael moves with his *shinai* just like you taught him: Bare feet shuffle along the mat in quick, controlled steps. Then he shouts, building up energy in his *ki* before executing textbook *kote-men*: first slapping down the hobo's arms at the wrists, then following up with a blow centered on the forehead.

There's a loud *crack*, but the man doesn't even register the blow. *Drugs,* you think, rushing in to take over for your pupil. Christian strikes against the man's back, wanting to pile-onto the defense, but your shouts send both of them away.

The man's focus has switched from the screaming mother to your students, so you step in to divert that attention to yourself. With a hand out, you take the *shinai* from Nathanael, then plant a sharp jab into the bum's sternum. His lungs make a loud moan of exhalation and he staggers back.

Shuffling your feet, you crack the wooden sword against the man's hands, knocking them askew. You've probably just broke the man's knuckles, but not his attack. He comes for you relentlessly, and you use that to your advantage.

"Doors!" you shout.

Mason and Nolan each open a door to the dojo, and you step around to bring the madman lunging towards the outside air. You duck out of his path, then kick as he passes to send him reeling over the sidewalk and into the rows of stalled vehicles. The children cheer as you re-enter the dojo, close and lock the doors.

"Defense comes from re-directing your opponent's energy," you say, not missing a chance for instruction. "In real life or in Kendo, it is the same."

"He's insane, he tried to bite me!" Sal's mother shouts. "We need to call the police!"

Clearing his throat to make his presence known, Master Hanzo says, "All circuits are busy."

"911 is busy? That's impossible!" she shouts again, hysterical.

"Bad man's getting up," Liam says.

The children all rush to the glass doors to watch. Traffic in the streets is at a standstill, you realize. Gridlocked. Someone passes by on a bicycle with most unfortunate timing—the bum is up, and lunges, tackling the cyclist. Several motorists come out to help, and end up getting bitten for their trouble.

A booming gunshot cracks in the morning air and the homeless man's back opens with a hole clear through to the front, but it doesn't stop him.

"Children! Look away from there!" you shout.

"Army men!" Stella shouts.

Getting a closer look, you see that she's right. On the far distant edge of the street, several canvas-covered trucks unload men and supplies. They're setting up a barricade.

"Come on, Sal," his mother says. "Let's get some help."

- ➤ "Tell them I have children here. Good luck." Go to page 273
- ➤ "No! Do not take the boy, he is safer here." Go to page 271

The (Not So) Fun House

You follow Sims into the funhouse, where the double-doors open automatically with a hiss. Artificial smoke pours out while a strobe-light gives off a lightning effect from inside and a pre-recorded "Witch Cackle" echoes throughout. Guess there are a few downsides to the park still having electricity. The doors will slide open for the undead just as easily, so you'd better get going.

As you rush inside, you see a tall, thin man dart out from the smoke and shadows wearing his own combat fatigues and gasmask. In a panic, Sims swings his oversized knife and the man lashes out to block. It's a hard connection, and the blow lands with a painful *crack!*

In response, the world around you shatters. It was just a fun house mirror, obscured by the low light and fog machine. Now that Sims is cursed with seven years' bad luck, you take a moment to look around. To the right is a small doorway with an official EMPLOYEES ONLY sign pinned above. *Perfect,* you think. That way you don't have to deal with more trickery and bullshit.

The double doors slide open once more, with the other survivors rushing in behind you, bringing in sounds of moaning and chomping teeth at their heels. Time to move! The narrow doorway doesn't open up to a room, but instead to an equally narrow hallway. The corridor is illuminated by red lights, which feels like an odd choice, given that no customers should normally pass through here.

You stumble over boxes of costume masks, spare fog generators, and myriad plastic detritus: false chains, bones. You can hear the zombies on your heels, tripping over the same hazards, but still gaining on you.

The next turn in the hall is only an alcove. There's the inside of a clown costume, hollowed out so an employee could insert his or her hands inside the clown gloves, like hell's version of an infectious disease isolation glove box. That explains the red lights; they're so the employees can keep their night vision.

You pass several other such "scare stations," barely pausing to see if each is a way out. Finally, you make it to another doorway at the end of the hall—it's your way out! You sprint past the werewolf-dressed mannequin and through the door. The room is dark, so you feel for a light switch, finding the panel on the left side.

When power comes on in the room you see…it's a bathroom. The goal may be to scare the shit out of the guests, but the employees are the only ones with access to a pooper.

Turning back, you see what you already knew—the hallway is thick with the undead. Shoulder-to-shoulder, trampling over each other, all to get to you. The gang is looking to you, but they can see it on your face. You've failed them.

THE END

Not So Fast

You rush towards the rack of *shinai*, barely slowing down as you pull a wooden sword and windmill it about to ready position. The homeless man stays focused on the terrified mother as your students shrink away from the crazed attacker.

He grabs hold of her and his mouth opens wide, like a python dislocating its jaws before feeding, before the man goes for a bite. It's sloppy form to take full, sprinting strides in Kendo, and after a lifetime of short, controlled steps it feels alien to lunge at the man.

You jab at the man with a non-traditional leaping strike to the forehead, hoping to knock him back before he can sink his teeth into the woman. But the spray of red that erupts from her neck screams of failure. The children shriek in response.

"Doors!" you shout.

Mason and Nolan each open a door to the dojo, and you step around to bring the madman lunging towards the outside air. You duck out of his path, then kick as he passes to send him reeling over the sidewalk and into the rows of stalled vehicles.

Returning, you lock the doors behind you, then pull off the cloth belt around your *gi* and wrap it around the sobbing woman's neck. It's a terrible spot to be wounded, because you can't tie the tourniquet too tightly, lest you suffocate her.

Clearing his throat to make his presence known, Master Hanzo says, "All circuits are busy."

"No ambulance?" you say.

He simply shakes his head.

"Bad man's getting up," Liam says.

The children all rush to the glass doors to watch. Traffic in the streets is at a standstill, you realize. Gridlocked. Someone passes by on a bicycle with most unfortunate timing—the bum is up, and lunges, tackling the cyclist. Several motorists come out to help, and end up getting bitten for their trouble.

A booming gunshot cracks in the morning air and the homeless man's back opens with a hole clear through to the front, but it doesn't stop him.

"Children! Look away from there!" you shout.

"Army men!" Stella shouts.

Getting a closer look, you see that she's right. On the far distant edge of the street, several canvas-covered trucks unload men and supplies. They're setting up a barricade.

"Come on, Sal," his mother croaks. "Let's get some help."

➤ "No! Do not take the boy, he is safer here." Go to page 271
➤ "Tell them I have children here. Good luck." Go to page 273

Not the Answer

You hit the cop square in the jaw. It's a sucker-punch, and the man takes another step before he falls like a sack of potatoes. Still, you manage to catch him and help lower the guy to the concrete. He'll wake up with a helluva headache, but at least he's no longer one for you.

Crouched over the cop, your hand hesitates over his holster. That pistol…if it really is a terrorist attack or whatever, this could be a major asset.

Then the shadows of several soldiers fall over you.

"We got an infected here!" a man shouts from behind.

"Shoot 'em both; it's the only way to be sure," says another.

You hesitate a moment longer. Should you threaten with a show of force? Or put your hands up? Too late. In the next instant, the group opens fire with their rifles, taking you and the cop down in an indiscriminate shower of gunfire. Whatever's going on here, these guys aren't taking any chances.

THE END

Not without a Fight

Their eyes open wide with the speed at which you claim the handgun and draw down on the men. They start to raise their hands, but already blew that chance. The apocalyptic wasteland will be a better place with a few less assholes in it.

Click.

Your own eyes grow wide at the realization. The Colt isn't loaded. What, you thought a gun-safety nut leaves his gun-locker loaded? That's what the one on the owner's hip is for. In fact, if it weren't a state of emergency, you would've needed a welding torch just to open the supply.

"Fuck," you say.

"Exactly," the center man replies.

Then he punches you in the gut. As his men bind your wrists behind your back with zip-ties, he says, "I like the feisty ones. Boys, I formally call dibs. This one goes to my personal breeding stockade."

Then they blindfold you.

➢ *Go limp, but plan an escape as soon as you can.* Go to page 56

Not Yet

You shake your head. You're not one to disobey your father, but this is just wrong. Jason, on the other hand, doesn't share your reservations. He marches right on over to the door and before you can finish, "Jay, wait!" it's open and the panicked man stumbles into your living room, falling to the floor in a bloody heap. His attacker rushes in right behind him, snarling and reaching out with frenzied arms. Whatever instinct possesses the man sends him straight toward Jason.

Suddenly, a red mist sprays out of the far side of the lunatic's head and he collapses, dead. You realize you've shouldered your rifle and the gunshot was yours. You don't even remember moving, you just remember one thought entered your head as the crazed attacker moved toward your brother. One word, really: *No*.

A quick glance to the other man shows that he is unconscious on the ground. The tension gone from the moment, you lower your rifle. *Oh, God,* you think. That was as easy as one of Jay's paintball games, easier even.

"I just killed a man," you say, but it sounds disconnected. Like someone else is speaking.

"You killed the enemy," Dad says. "Charlie."

"It was a z—zom…" Jason can't bring himself to say it.

"Zulu…the enemy," you say.

"Right," Dad confirms. "It was either him or Jay."

- ➤ Check on the unconscious man. Go to page 266
- ➤ Drag the dead body outside and lock up. Go to page 357

No Warning

You rush out into the yard, but it's already dark out and you're offered little in the way of information. Still, the lights of the cell block shine brightly, so you can orient yourself. The searchlights from the guard towers sweep across the prison grounds.

Something makes a *squick* underfoot, like the yard after a heavy rain, but it's not mud—you can smell that much. You bend down to get a better look, and when the searchlight sweeps across, you see you're standing on top of something that was once some*one*. As the light continues, you see several more horribly dismembered and gutted corpses splayed out across the yard.

You stumble away from the body, trying not to vomit. The searchlight turns back, following you, and when it comes across your body, a *crack* sings out from the guard tower and a terrible pain slices through your right thigh.

You howl, limping back towards shelter. If they're shooting on-site, the prison must be in a terrible state. Another *crack* rings out—and this time the marksman doesn't miss. Headshot.

THE END

The Nun Also Rises

With Jason's help, you get your father to his feet.

"Dad? Daddy, can you hear me? I'm...I'm trying to say goodbye." The man looks over at you with glossy eyes and a slack jaw. "You've been bit. It's bad. So we're gonna wrap—we're gonna help you so you can rest, okay, Daddy?"

A flicker of understanding lights behind his eyes and he gives the slightest nod. The group of ushers waits by the altar with a white sheet. As your father walks into it, they encircle him, swaddling the man in several layers of cloth. They tie ropes at his ankles, knees, chest, and neck. He's secured into the devil's cocoon—where he'll metamorphose into *Zulu*.

Father Thomas says a blessing, and then your father is laid to rest on the third pew from the front. Several other identical shapes fill your vision. In fact, all of these pews are filled by wrapped, immobilized bodies.

"Tell the sisters we need more sheets," Father Thomas instructs his altar boy.

Jason pokes at the bundle next to Dad, and the person trapped within wriggles violently, falling to the floor, groaning. Jason backs away, startled. Other wrapped parishioners take up the call and thrash about in their bindings, adding their own disturbing moans to the chorus.

"Jay, I think we should—" you start, cut short by a scream.

It's the altar boy, mobbed by the dozen sisters from the annex. They're a fiendish coven now; fully-turned *Zulu* on the hunt.

"*The power of Christ compels you!*" a woman screams, rushing forward.

"Angelica, no!" Father Thomas cries. "We must bind them. Come, men, help me!"

"*The power of Christ compels you!*" she screams again, holding out her rosary crucifix towards the nuns. Before you can react, Jason runs after the crazed woman, and throws her to the side to prevent her meeting the same fate as the altar boy. One of the nuns—Sister Mary—grabs your brother's arm.

> ➤ Nooo!!!! Time to exorcise some demons using the gospel of Ruger. Go to page 248
> ➤ Sprint over and shoulder-tackle the woman. There are more living than undead in this cathedral, and you can overwhelm them by force. Go to page 247

Nun-chucked

Sister Mary sprawls out when you bash into her, freeing your brother and attracting the attention of the other sisters. Now you enact the revenge fantasy of every troublemaker whose ruler-slapped wrists wanted to strike out and backhand those who scolded their back-talk. You punch, kick, and strike the nuns with righteous indignation while the ushers claim sheets to wrap the sisterhood.

When it's done, you sit down on the pew, breathing heavily and sweating from the exertion. You've got blood on your hands—literally—and a quick examination of your forearms tells you some of it is your own. During the struggle you were bitten several times. The adrenaline rush must have been enough to block the pain, but it doesn't matter....

You're INFECTED.

Nundead

With a firecracker *pop*, you send a .22 into Sister Mary's habit and it transubstantiates into red mist out the other side. Jason frees himself from her grasp and backpedals from the rest, unslings his 16-gauge, and blows the face off the nearest Bride of Christ.

"No!" Angelica screams, grabbing your brother from behind.

Several other Zulu nuns come for Jason, and he's vulnerable, while he has to grapple with the crazed housewife at his back. Not wasting a beat, you attack the woman with the butt of your rifle, landing the blow directly into her perfectly coifed blonde tresses. As she falls to the ground, you shoot the nearest nun.

"Stop!" Father Thomas cries, stepping between you and the sisters. "We must bind them!"

You back away with Jason while the ushers help Father Thomas subdue the rest of the rabid women; most of them give bites to their would-be saviors as thanks.

Pulling Jason away, you say, "This place is hotter than a pair of mice screwing in a wool sock in front of the fireplace. Let's go."

"Not so fast," a man says from the cathedral entryway.

It's not one man, but five. They're decked-out in paramilitary gear and leather. Clean-cut types with hard arms and soft bellies. Each holds at least a handgun on his person. You also notice several large knives. One has a belt of grenades…are those real?

The blond housewife Angelica rushes towards them, clutching a candlestick from the altar.

"Thank you, Jesus, please, take me with you," she pleads.

"Certainly," the lead man says. "Any woman who ain't been bit can come with us."

His eyes come to land on you.

"No, thanks," you say. "But *they* could use your help."

"Ain't interested. Drop your weapons, missy. Boys, grab the breeding stock, take care of the rest."

Jason fires his shotgun at the nearest man, but at that range, the guy just gets peppered with shot and lets out a pained scream. The other men open fire, and you do as well. You take three of them down, but they give a lead funeral to both you and your brother.

THE END

Nut Shot

You lunge forward and butt-smash the paintball rifle into Jason's groin as hard as you can, which is pretty hard. Your brother collapses, coughing from pain, hands cupped around his injured fourteen-year-old's manhood.

"Not funny," you say, standing and removing your own mask. "CEOs and company presidents are eating one another, and that's not a joke, Jay."

Jason simply wheezes.

"Anyway, hope you enjoyed your Saturday pick. Next time we're seeing a chick-flick, *muahahaha*."

You turn and start out of the paintball arena. "C'mon, I'm late for my shift at the range."

➢ *Get driving before dad calls.* Go to page 167

Oathbreaker

Master Hanzo's death weighs heavily on your conscience. You gave the man your word that you'd return, and you failed. You helped the children find their way to their parents, and that is something to be proud of, to be sure. But you'd be nothing without that man. He didn't just teach you martial arts, he taught you courage, respect, and a willingness to help those in need.

"I'll have to save others," you say aloud. "As many as I can. I will bring them to Salvation and together we will survive."

Better get walking. The old reformatory is deep in the woods, and you'll have to cross the city once more before heading into the wilds.

Go to page 160

Occupied

Suddenly your legs kick to life, and you find yourself hurdling the barrier. You couldn't see it before, but you fly over the bodies of several other would-be line breakers. Some have blood-encrusted mouths.

You practically fly down the street on adrenaline-boosted strides. Still frantic, at the next intersection you stop and look around. What you see is another city block, cordoned-off, and your heart sinks. This area is a downtown strip mall, the road filled by another block of commuters held hostage in their sedans. Your mouth dries up and you get a vertigo feeling. Just how big is this quarantine zone?

Several National Guard soldiers look your way, one of whom clutches a radio with one hand and signals towards you with the other. Best get out of sight.

You duck behind a newsstand. The place has already been attacked, from the looks of it, what with tabloids covering "Celebrity Cannibals" smattered in fresh gore and newspapers with headlines on the new *Gilgazyme*® wonder drug torn, tattered, and strewn about.

The countertop drink cooler sits open, a few water bottles left inside. Without hesitation, you reach for a bottle, twist off the cap and chug.

"Hey, that's not for sale!" a man hisses.

You spit out half of the water, raising your baton in fear. The man—the newsstand owner, from the looks of it—looks over your shoulder, and nods, then shrinks back into his hiding spot behind the counter.

The whole cooler suddenly explodes, not two inches from your head, with a deafening boom. You duck and spin around, looking for the source. Off to your left, there's some kind of Karate dojo where a man tries to pull young and curious eyes away from the storefront. To the right, there's a hardware store with a man and woman up on the roof. The guy points and you turn to see a pawnshop directly behind you. Leaning out of a barred window is a redneck holding a bolt-action hunting rifle, a Duck Dynasty cap on his head.

"Act like a thug, die like a thug!" the man shouts.

He slides back the bolt-action, reloading the weapon.

- ➢ Go for the Dojo! Who's going to shoot at a bunch of kids? Go to page 97
- ➢ Go for the hardware store! The man must've warned you for a reason. Go to page 158
- ➢ Go for the pawn shop! He's close—charge the shop owner before he can reload. Go to page 47

Offered Up

With barely a moment to think, you hurdle the pew benches and run up on stage. There's a large altar where communion sits prepared, ready to wash away your sin with grape juice and *Jeezits* instead of wine and bread. This is a prison; a prison on a budget.

The preacher already cowers behind the altar and puts his hands up, expecting you to bite him. When you don't, he points away with desperation, but you shake your head.

"Go! I was here first!" he says, as firmly as a whisper will allow.

"What do you think this is, hide-'n-seek? Sorry, father."

His eyes turn to your rear, and when you look back, you see the gang of nutters has found you. Suddenly, the preacher shoves you into the crowd before running off. The last words to escape your lips are the Lord's name in vain.

THE END

Off the Rails

Maybe the aircraft's movements are merely due to final approach? It didn't feel like you slept that long, but that would explain it. Just a traffic pattern before landing. Maybe. Time to find out for sure. Unlike a commercial airliner, the cockpit isn't sealed off like a quarantine zone, so it's easy to interact with the Air Force crew.

"Any idea how much longer 'til we're home?" you ask the loadmaster near the front.

"Ahhh, change of plans. I'm…not sure it's my place to say more."

Great. You push past the loadmaster and head into the cockpit, and the man doesn't try to stop you. Before you can ask what-the-hell's-going-on, you look up and see a face full of airplane, flying only mere feet ahead. The C-17 is being refueled! But you didn't need mid-air refueling on the way to the mission, so why on the way back?

"What the hell's going on?" you ask.

The pilots ignore you.

Once the refueling is complete and the planes detach and separate to a safer distance, the copilot finally turns to address you. "We've been re-routed, Sergeant. There was a sister-op last week in Venezuela that didn't end as well. Or maybe went too well, depending on how you look at it."

"What does that mean?"

"It means *Viva fucking Chavez*," the pilot says. "And *Viva* the whole goddamn country."

"What does *that* mean?" you repeat, voice frayed.

"Venezuela is lost. We're heading into Manaus to evacuate US personnel out of the region before the rest of the continent goes too," the co-pilot says. "You guys'll be providing security once we touch down."

You get that sinking feeling again, only this time the plane's not turning. Time to…

- ➢ Find somewhere to hide. You're an electrician! And you don't want to lose your seat to some refugee. Go to page 186
- ➢ Find your weapons and battle-rattle. Get ready to shoot some undead commies! Go to page 73

Off the Streets

"Quickly!" you say, rushing towards the nearest house.

Adrenaline pumping, you don't stop to see if it's unlocked. Instead, you kick the door in, only to find a walking corpse right on the other side. Your sword moves before you even have time to think, and you split the ghoul in half from neck to navel. The thing falls to the floor, but continues to thrash about even after being disemboweled.

"Out the back, let's go," you say.

The back patio leads to a freshly mowed, fenced-in back yard. Quintessential suburbia. The Humvee and motorcycles are loud enough that you can hear the men in the streets behind you, and you're thinking of hopping the fence and continuing on, when you see a large garden shed and change your mind. If these men are looters, they're looking for food and medicine, not lawnmowers.

Ushering the three children inside, you close yourself in the shed.

"Sensei, how do you know they're dangerous?" Nathanael asks.

"All men are dangerous, depending on the situation, young one."

"But they could help us!" Haley protests.

"It's true, they could. But whether or not they *would* is a different matter. This is a distraction on the path, not the path itself. We have an old saying in Japan, 'If you try to catch two rabbits, you will catch neither.' We are not out looking for friends, we are out looking for your families."

"Yes, sensei," they all say in unison.

"Good. Those men didn't need our help, and we don't need theirs. Once they're gone, we'll head to Haley's."

Haley's house might be "on the way" to Nathanael's, but it's certainly not close. It's in a newer development, one that backs up against the marshes, so you follow the long road away from suburbia and into swamp-front property marketed as "Gladedale Estates."

Stomachs rumbling, you hope that whether or not you find Haley's parents, there will at least be something to eat. There's a greasy spoon restaurant just off the road and you watch as each of your students lock onto the diner, their heads moving in unison. Your own salivary glands tingle at the prospect.

- ➢ Keep moving. Her house is out of the way, but only a few hours of walking remain. Go to page 175
- ➢ It's worth a quick detour. Someone passing out from hunger would be a longer delay. Go to page 300

Of Low Caliber

"Light 'em up, Jay!" you cry.

Your brother blasts his 16-gauge at the man's center-mass, while you pop off shots from your 10/22 at the guy's face. But here's the thing—Dad recommended these weapons because they're light, relatively quiet, and you can carry lots of ammo. They're ideal for fighting against Zulu, not a man in full body armor.

The shotgun sends its flak true, which happens to be exactly what the flak jacket is for. The man wouldn't even feel the pellets. Meanwhile, your .22 caliber rifle shots get deflected by the man's facemask. If you had something with a little more punch, your shots would've gone right through, but instead, the man sprays at you both with his sub-machine gun.

And his shots go through your clothes with ease.

THE END

The Old Man and the Tea

The children scurry to their positions and you wave Salvator to your side.

"Hey, is this a dead zone?" his mother asks, waving her cell phone. "No service at all. Do you have Wi-Fi?"

Resisting the urge to sigh, you say, "You're welcome to try your luck outside."

"Thanks," she says, stuffing her phone into her purse and taking your advice.

"Now then, Salvator-*san*."

"It's just Sal," the boy says, matter-of-factly.

Offering a smile, you nod, then lead him over towards your tournament armor. "This is my armor; what do you think? Would you like armor of your own some day?"

The boy nods and you continue, "Kendo is a full-contact, vigorous sport, so we wear armor to protect ourselves. At first you will learn movements, but eventually, you will face opponents much larger than yourself who will attack with all their strength."

He looks up with full eyes and says, "With a samurai sword?"

"With *shinai*," you say, pulling one of the wooden practice swords from a rack on the wall. You touch the tip to the helmet on your armor and add, "They may be only bamboo, but a strike here, to your *men*, can still be painful, and that can be scary. But you must choose: Will you learn to fear pain and run? Or will you learn to stand your ground and defend against the strike? You cannot learn both."

The boy nods, though you know you're only sowing the seeds. He won't understand these lessons for a long time yet, but repetition is key. Repetition is key.

"I want to introduce you to someone very special, so follow me."

At the rear of the dojo, there is a hallway with a door that leads straight out into the back alley, a bathroom to the left, and an office to the right. It is the latter where you lead your pupil.

Inside, resting on a large sitting pillow is Master Hanzo, an old man with white hair. He holds an equally ancient pipe in his lips, though it remains unlit. His large, bushy eyebrows, which flare out like cat-eye glasses, indicate a gaze down into a novel.

"Master Hanzo," you say, knocking on the open door. "Our new pupil is here."

Hanzo closes the book, *Sociality Abounds: A Novel by Jacques Deleon*. There's a sticker canted sideways on the cover, "Nobel Prize Winner." *Always the philosopher*, you think as he looks up. Young Salvator hesitates.

"Go on, don't be afraid. Sensei Hanzo trained me when I was around your age. Many of the students come to call him 'Grandfather Hanzo,' you know."

"And I like that very much," the old man says.

"Master Hanzo owns the dojo, though he has passed on the responsibility of teaching to me, your sensei. As the newest student in the class, your responsibility will be to bring Master Hanzo tea before we begin each session. This is a great honor."

The boy looks from you to Hanzo and back again, unsure how to respond.

"Come now, I will show you how to make the tea. In Japan, tea preparation is its own art form and people gather to watch the ceremony, much like going to see actors perform at the theaters here in—"

A violent, urgent scream sounds from the dojo entry. It strikes you down to the bone, but the instinct to protect your students propels you forward.

"Stay with Hanzo!" you shout, running forward to see what's happened.

It's Salvator's mother screaming as a homeless man rushes into the dojo after her. The children hold *shinai*, clearly terrified, but they're much closer to the entry than you. You'll have to act fast.

- ➤ Tell Nathanael to fight the man off while you get the younger kids out of the way. Go to page 239
- ➤ Grab a *shinai* and rush in—no time for talk. Go to page 241

One against All

Angelica looks at you with disdain, but that's okay, because when the other men from Duke's gang arrive at the stables, they won't find you here. Instead, you head out into the night, using darkness for cover as you try to find a way out. There's gotta be a spare motorcycle or an old car you can hotwire to make your escape.

Though it's a dark night, many of the former farm's structures are illuminated, and you can use their glow to see. It's a noisy community, that's for sure. Laughing, yelling, even gunshots as they fight off the dead. A strong smell too; someone's BBQing. Maybe everyone gets a steak dinner?

Hounds bay, much like during a prison break. Which, in a sense, it is. Powerful flashlight beams sweep the fields and one comes to rest on you.

"Here she is!" a man shouts.

If you run now, you might get lucky and they'll shoot you. If not, you'll be returned to the stables, only with much tighter security this time. And probably many more "visitors."

Not much of a choice, is it?

THE END

On Loan

The building is locked, but through the glass door you can see the lobby is undisturbed. Most likely, the owners just didn't come to work today. A quick crack with Mitch's butt and the glass near the lock breaks open. You reach in, release the deadbolt, and let yourself in. One nice thing about the power going out—no alarms. That's why you *always* get a battery backup.

A sweep of the building shows a large lobby and a counter with four computer stations, with an office in the back for a manager, and an employee bathroom. There's only the front door and a fire door in the back, so it's defensible.

Granted, you broke in fairly easily, but—despite needing to shoot them in the head—the fleshies seem pretty brain-dead. You should be able to lock up and make a quick getaway out back if you hear their dead hands pawing for a way in.

That couch looks inviting, or you could take a look at the other buildings in the area.

- You're not one to kick a gift horse in the mouth. Lock the door and get some sleep. Go to page 277
- The liquor store. I could use a drink after these last couple of days and the windows have bars. Go to page 234
- The tattoo parlor. With its tough-guy design scheme, nobody will mess with me there. Go to page 180
- The strip club. It's designed from the ground up to keep out unwanted flesh-hungry men. Go to page 361

Open Season

When the buzzer sounds and the doors of the cell block open in unison, it's instant chaos. Whatever is infecting people and turning them into flesh-hungry nutters, more than a few of these inmates have it. Men begin biting, stabbing, punching, and throwing each other over the rails. It's a full-scale riot within seconds.

There were occasional riots in the past, more than the average taxpayer would believe, but you played it safe. Every riot would end up with at least one death, and a dozen or more sent to the infirmary. Meanwhile, you sat in your cell like a model citizen and waited out the violence while other inmates had their temper tantrum.

What'll it be this time?

- ➤ The safest place in a stampede is in the herd. Stay with the flood of inmates and rush the yard outside. Go to page 166
- ➤ Never change a winning strategy—wait out the initial rush from my cell, then follow the path of destruction. Go to page 392

Operation

"Doc! Doc!" you scream.

Now the *Turned* in the room grow restless. Frenzied. That's when the main tent flap opens. There's some light from outside, so you can see the silhouette of a gasmask-clad soldier. He brings menace with him, and it's genuinely terrifying here in the dark. You want to keep screaming, but you've lost your voice.

The room erupts with the brightness of a lightning strike; it's the muzzle of the soldier's rifle as he shoots the first infected in the head.

"*DOC!!!*" You thrash and scream and kick and bite at the air in the darkness—just like all the other infected around you. A moment later, the crack of gunfire shakes the tent and illuminates the scene once more at the next cot over. He's going person-to-person, one bullet for each. "No…please…." you sob.

BANG! There's a bright flash, just like the others, but this one doesn't go out. Is this what dying is like? Heading in "towards the light" for good?

"What the hell do you think you're doing?!" cries Dr. Abdous. Without her surgical mask and goggles, she's stunning. Like an angel, if this was heaven. But, no, the lights are on in the tent, you realize. The soldier stands only one cot away from yours, three dead patients in his wake.

"Stand back, doctor. We're falling back to the hospital and I'm acting on orders."

"Corporal Amos…you're killing people."

"They're not people," he says, cold.

"I'm people!" you scream.

"These are my patients, under my direct care," she says, circling back towards you. "And you need my permission to…well, you can't just fucking *terminate* them!"

He laughs and shakes his head. "What do you think is happening here, ma'am? My orders come straight from Captain Delozier, and he specifically told me to carry them out whether or not you object."

She pulls out a small pair of shears and cuts through your binds. Must be the same kind of scissors they use to cut people out of their clothes in the ER.

"Ma'am! You do not have the authority to—"

"Want to shoot me too, Amos? Did Delozier give you *that* authority? Get up, Tyberius. Stay behind me." She uses herself as a human shield, leading you out to the front flap. Seeing the rest of her "patients" chomping their teeth like mad, she adds, "Do what you will with them."

"Ma'am, you can't."

"I just did." She turns and hands you the police baton that was taken from you when you arrived. Her eyes are full of tears, but she's holding them back. "Go, now. Hurry!"

You nod your thanks, then turn and run. It's hard to believe she really stuck her neck out for you like that. You only know one woman that strong, and you're going to go help her if it's the last thing you do.

> *Go home, before it's too late.* Go to page 223

Optimism

You hunch next to one of the military Humvees, Angelica by your side, doing your best to stay below the line of fire. The soldiers know enough to aim for head-level, so you know to stay low. The helicopter hovers above and a man rappels down into the crowd.

The effect is like dipping your finger in honey before poking an anthill. The crowd of dead latch on, so much weight, in fact, that they threaten to take the helicopter off its flight path. There's just so many of them!

They continue their slow, patient onslaught of the hospital, and the only fatigue you see is in the soldier's weapons. There are far more undead in the city than these men have bullets for. A realization that comes too little, too late. You look around; they have you surrounded.

I'm going to die here, you think.

The good news is that you won't just take a single bite—there won't be enough left of you to rise again.

THE END

Orders and Chaos

Though you know it's the right move to leave the civilians holed up in the cafeteria, you feel sick at leaving those kids in there. In anger and frustration, you plow your shoulder into the chest of the nearest SWAT-thing, knocking the ghoul onto its back. A foot on its chest, you stick your rifle under the faceplate and offer a point-blank shot.

The front entrance is barricaded as well, and the rest of the evac team heads an emergency exit, so you waste no time doing the same. Immediately, you're forced to put down two fleshies as the six Airmen shoot their own way through the crowds.

The hospital parking lot looks even worse from the ground than it did from the air. It looks like the SWAT team was defeated, and a dozen police vehicles sit abandoned. So are several National Guard Humvees, which leads you to one conclusion—this operation has failed.

Throngs of undead continue to stream in from all around. A construction worker grabs your arm, and you're barely able to put him down with his being so close. One shot, one kill.

"Where's the target?" you ask.

"I don't know! We lost radio contact!" Airman Belliveau yells over the commotion.

"So what the hell's the plan?"

"Keep looking!"

The rescue team burrows deeper into the crowd, but you hesitate a moment. The odds are overwhelming. It's tempting to abandon ship.

➤ Stay with the rescue team. Maybe they can call in the helicopter? Go to page 96
➤ There's a sandwich shop across the street. Get dinner, don't become it. Go to page 81

Oregon Donor

After skipping breakfast, the cold cut sub might as well be manna from heaven. Especially after the morning you've had. You eat up, then lick the sauces off your fingers. The sandwich didn't go far, though, and you're still hungry.

You watch as the rest of the sandwich is passed around and unceremoniously devoured. All that remains is the extra piece from bucket-lady. As the minutes tick by, you consider asking if she's going to eat it. From the looks of it, she's sleeping now. Maybe you should just take it?

"Excuse me…" you start, then cut yourself short when you hear someone moaning in pain.

In the far corner of the tent, a woman with skin like a marble statue falls off her cot. Someone nearby asks if she's okay, then screams out. Did she just bite that guy?

The screams bring in the guard from outside, and he stands with his rifle at the ready. "Another *Turned*," he says into a chest-radio. "Go for a transfer to aggressor tent."

Two more soldiers come in, looking interchangeable in their gasmasks. The guard says, "Don't let her bite you."

The pair grab the woman, one putting her in a headlock while the second binds her wrists together. They drag her from the tent.

You wake up, not even realizing that you'd dozed off. *Hope that doesn't make the concussion or whatever worse.* Your stomach grumbles and you stand up. You take a step towards the sandwich on the cot across the aisle, then turn and grab the bucket. The contents of your stomach shoot out into the bucket before you even know what's happening.

There's a shimmy in your bowels and you feel them loosen, but your colon catches the flow. Just barely.

"That's not good," Doctor so-and-so says. "Grab the bucket, c'mon."

Following her out of the tent, you come to see the guard.

"Bucket needs emptying."

The man sighs so loudly you can hear it through his gasmask. He bids you to follow, then points to the gutter and a sewer drain. "Toss it in, then we'll bleach it."

"Wait!" the doctor shouts. "You're throwing biohazardous waste into *the sewer*? Do you have any idea how irresponsible that is? This man has dysentery! Do you want to contaminate the whole city?"

"Who gives a shit? There's something much worse infecting people already."

"Hold up…I have dysentery?" you say.

She sighs. "Most people recover from dysentery in the modern world, but I'm not sure how many IV bags we have and…"

Your head swirls. Dysentery is something that used to kill people. At least in *Oregon Trail*. At best, you're going to be seriously incapacitated, and that's bad enough when people are eating each other.

You're INFECTED…with dysentery!

Outback

"There is a back exit. Go now and I will do my best to slow the soldiers."

"Thanks," you say before rushing from the dojo and into the alley in the back.

It's a thin road, the kind that's perpetually wet and cold from a lack of sunlight and natural drainage, built to house each of the business's dumpsters. If you were to run to the left, it would lead you back to your stalled-out bus.

No-brainer here, you're heading right.

The alley opens into another street full of shops: a tattoo parlor, a payday loans building, a strip club, and a liquor store. You recognize the area. One of these "establishments" has sucked out a large chunk of your paycheck in the past, and you'd relish the opportunity to get revenge.

Unfortunately, this block is under National Guard quarantine as well. Worse still, it appears as if you've made the trouble-maker list, because a group of them spot you and move in.

- How big is the National Guard unit here? Keep running. Go to page 112
- They're just doing a job, right? Hands up, and hope they keep you safe. Go to page 374

Out Cold

You move toward the injured man, who's basically snoring in a pool of his own blood. Well, at least he's still breathing. You lurch back after you hear a grunt, but you realize it's just Jason dragging the dead man toward the front door. You open the door for him, then stand at the ready with your rifle. After a moment, Jason returns safely.

"I think there's more of them out there," he says, locking the deadbolt.

You're shaking, on the verge of crying. You look at the red carpet entrance, following the blood trail, and come to a spatter of brain against the wall. The picture of Grandpa from WWII has miraculously stayed clean, but the black-and-white photo of Eisenhower chewing out his generals is filthy.

"That needs to be us," Dad says. "They had no clue the horrors they were getting into, they just knew there was an evil that needed to be stopped. And that's what we're faced with now. See this?" he points to the framed art on the other side, the print of *Rosie the Riveter*.

She stares at you with her stern determination, rolling her sleeve with fist pumped in the air, flecks of blood against the glass frame adorning her uniform in an apropos symbol of your own call to action. She proudly proclaims, *"We Can Do It!"*

"I need you to be like Rosie, Sport," your father says, the same look of determination on his face.

Do you have it in you? *Rosie the Riveter* was a symbol. A leader of those who grew up thinking they were helpless; that other people were in charge of the world. She inspired a generation to stand up and do their part. How can you be like Rosie?

Not much of a choice here:

➢ *Mask your uncertainty. Stand tall, shoulders back, and say, "What do I need to do?"*
Go to page 352

Overpriced

With so many windows, the moonlight makes it possible to search the gift shop. It's abandoned, though many of the park's paying customers seem to have swiped a t-shirt and a snow-globe on their way out. Still, you get to feast on a dinner of chocolate designed to look like rocks. Worth it? Maybe for the calories, but you'll be sleeping on an irritated stomach—and a pile of stuffed dogs with stiff leashes attached, meant to look like they're being walked.

The next morning, you regroup at the front.

"Okay, I'm thinking we'll split the park right down the center, east and west, north and south, as viewed from the Ferris wheel," you say. "Report back for lunch. We're looking for flashlights, food, anything useful."

"Haven't you ever seen a horror movie?" Angelica asks.

You cross your arms across your chest. After a terrible night's sleep on the stiff, cold floor, it's too early for this crap. "Yeah, I have. And in case you didn't notice, it's broad daylight outside. There's no full moon. No thunderstorm. No goddamned eclipse. And you're no virgin in peril, lady."

"I'm putting up with your 'leadership' so I don't have to be alone," she says, firmly.

Tyberius and Hefty avoid eye contact, waiting to see what you'll say. After a moment, you go with:

➢ *"You're putting up with it because you'd be dead without me. We're splitting up. You three go together, I'll take Jose. Meet back here."* Go to page 336

Painting the Office

"Open the goddamn door!" you shout, but the ranger only backs away.

It's locked, and you can't blast through with your 10/22. But Jason gets it, and puts his 16-gauge up against the door handle. With a *BOOM,* the door is open.

"Where's your first aid kit?" you demand.

The Ranger huddles in the back corner of the office, wide-eyed and clutching at some kind of canister.

"Are you bit?" Jason asks.

She shows off a bite-wound on her collarbone and your brother raises his shotgun. *BOOM*—he puts her out of her misery. You set to looking for a first aid kit.

"Sarah, stop," he says.

When you turn back, you see he's torn away his trousers to get a better look at the wound. There are clear, undeniable teeth-marks in his flesh.

"I don't want to end up like Dad. You gotta shoot me, sis. I'm ready."

You swallow hard, then take a deep breath. He's right, and you know it.

"I love you, Jay."

"I know," he says with a half-hearted smile. "You have to survive. Dad always said mom lived on inside our hearts. I always thought it was cheesy, but… Just survive, okay? Take us with you."

Then he closes his eyes. You raise the rifle, hands shaking.

➢ Do it, shoot him and survive. Once bitten, soon biting. Go to page 312
➢ No, you can't. He's your brother! Lock him up here and leave. Go to page 19

Paint It Black

The children nod solemnly, and no doubt Nathanael shares your fears—if the door is open, it's possible you'll find only sorrow inside Nolan's house. The entry carpet is stained with clumsy trackmarks too numerous to count. The black smudge by the door blooms into the intruders' tracks, spiraling out like petals on a deadly flower.

The kitchen is straight ahead, and all the cabinets are open. Like a plague of locusts came through—not a single food item was spared. Maybe his parents packed up and left? Or maybe someone came and pillaged the home.

"Hello? Is anyone here? It's Lucas Tessh—"

"Master Tesshu!" Nathanael shouts from outside.

You turn and run, sword at your side practically leaping from its scabbard and out into open air as you rush from the house.

Three walking corpses have encircled the children. Two women and one man; little doubt as to their intentions when they grope and snarl for your pupils.

"Back!" you command.

In Kendo, rarely do you engage more than one opponent at a time, so you quickly prioritize the attackers. The man is nearly a foot taller and at least thirty pounds heavier than his companions, so he's the biggest threat. But one of the two women is closer to the children.

In a split second, the decision is made, and you put down the trio of attackers with three clean swipes. That was too close. If you had been further inside the house, you might not have made it back in time.

"Where's my mom and dad?" Nolan asks.

"Not home," you say. Adding,

- ➢ "We'll stay the night, just in case they're out looking for you." Go to page 405
- ➢ "Let's continue on to Haley's and Nathanael's, then we'll try back here on the return trip." Go to page 52

Parenting Done Right

His form distorts through streaming tears but you wipe your eyes, hold your breath, still your aim, and squeeze off a shot. A single red hole, no wider than pencil-thick, appears on the Zulu's forehead and just like that, the man collapses.

You fall to your knees, eyes burning and heart in your throat. Jason tries to comfort you, to tell you that you did the right thing, but you can barely hear him. Instead, you hold your brother tight until his sobs break through and you rock him in your arms like you did when he was a baby.

After a time—five minutes, five hours, who knows—the tears stop and you compose yourself.

- ➢ Things are likely to get worse from here. Take one more look around for supplies before we go. Go to page 177
- ➢ I can't spend another minute here. Take the Jeep and get as far away from here as you can. Go to page 114

Parenting Expert

"The roads are blocked, and you're in no shape to go anywhere," you say, putting your back against the door to the outside.

"I know…what's best for my son," she practically growls.

"Not if you're thinking about taking him out there! A man was just shot!"

"Now you're holding us hostage?"

"If I have to save you from yourself, so be it."

"Tesshu-*san*, enough! Let them go," Hanzo says, bringing the boy to his mother.

"But master…"

"The code, yes, yes, I know—the code. Bushido says to help others, not to bend them to your will."

He's right, and you know it. Only one choice here:

> *Tell her, "Good luck. When you find the authorities, tell them I am here, watching over the other children."* Go to page 273

Parish the Thought

Father Thomas, along with an altar boy and several other men, hold and bind the flailing stranger in a white sheet. Your father reclines against the altar, drifting in and out of consciousness. You get a distinct feeling—he's next.

"What are you doing?" you demand.

Father Thomas stands and steps toward you. "He has the possession, your father?"

"What. Are. You. *Doing?*" you say more firmly, both hands on your rifle.

"This is the devil's work, this mass possession. If we stop them from spreading evil, the Lord will shine his light upon them, rebuke the devil inside, and the faithful shall be healed. Let us keep your father here, child, he'll be safe in the House of God."

They're wrapping and immobilizing the infected like mummies. For what? Exorcism? Faith healing? Jason looks to you. What do you think?

- Well, it's more merciful than shooting the infected, right? Maybe it's worth holding onto hope. Go to page 246
- They can keep the stranger, but you and Jason are taking Dad and leaving this place. Go to page 113

Parting Ways

She assures you that Sal will be fine; that they're headed straight for the army. Still, you're left with a sinking feeling in the pit of your stomach. Who fired that shot out there? If it was the army, that means they're firing on unarmed civilians, which is insane, even if the guy *was* insane. And if it wasn't the army...that means there's a vigilante lunatic who's taken the law into his own hands.

"Sensei..." Mason says, pulling you from your thoughts. When you look back to your students you see full, almost cartoonishly frightened eyes, like in the anime of your childhood.

"The music, let's listen," you say. "Remember, achieve peace within...?"

"Achieve peace without," the students chant in unison.

"Allow me," Master Hanzo says.

But when the old man makes it to the boom box, it isn't the tranquility CD that he plays, but the radio—which is tuned to an emergency broadcast. The newsman speaks with the cadence of a disc jockey, clearly uncomfortable with the weighty position he finds himself in.

"We're getting, ahh, reports of neighborhood closures? Is that right?" there's a pause, then he comes back, "Can't say for sure how many, it's all unsubstantiated right now, but I what I can say—what I know for sure—is that downtown is in a state of chaos. Steer clear of St. Mary's Hospital. There was some kind of incident, and based on the images of gasmasked troops we've seen, for my money, it's a terrorist attack. Okay...my producer says I shouldn't say that, but the conclusion is the same: Stay indoors, people. Traffic is stopped and there are National Guard barricades cropping up all over downtown, so it's not like you're going anywhere anyway, right? We'll get you more info as we get it, so stay tuned, but in the meantime—*smooooth Jazz*.

"Here to take you away, it's Art Blakey and the Jazz Messengers with *Moanin'*," the DJ signs off and a saxophone takes over.

"Master Hanzo, why don't you bring the radio into your office? Christian, help him with that. Then grandfather can tell us if he learns anything new. Maybe try to call some of the parents, okay?" you say, taking the radio and handing it to your pupil.

"They'll come get us?" Haley asks.

"Of course your parents will come."

The door *dings* and you turn. "Luke?" the woman says.

"Who are you?" Nolan asks.

"Class, this is my *Imouto*—my sister. Meet Melissa Tesshu."

But this is no time for a formal introduction, you can see that much from her appearance. She wears her St. Mary's hospital administrator badge and lanyard with blouse untucked and pants ripped on the left knee. Her hair is disheveled and makeup runny from tears or sweat, or both.

"How did you...?" you start. Then, after collecting your thoughts, you say:

➢ "What is it like at the hospital?" Go to page 179
➢ "What is it like outside?" Go to page 22

Passover

"No way, Celly. I'd never touch your shit. Don't I remember catchin' *you* looking through my mail for nakey pics? Those blankets came as-is. If somthin's missin', take it up with laundry crew."

Deny, deny, counter-accuse, deny—the most effective way to lie.

"Okay, okay, keep your shirt on, *amigo*. I was just looking forward to doing some carving when I got out, *comprende*?"

Trying to swallow down the dread when you hear *carving*, you give your best sympathetic nod.

Chapel is neutral ground. Despite their immoral proclivities, most inmates are religious men. Blame it on temptation, the devil made me do it, that kind of thing. That, coupled with the warden's higher punishments for any "malcreant behavior" on church grounds, makes for a quiet atmosphere every Sunday.

"When evening came, Jesus was reclining at the table with the Twelve," the preacher says. He has a Bible in his left hand, but it's closed; a prop. He has this part memorized. "And while they were eating, he said, 'Truly I tell you, one of you will betray me.'"

A terrible, hacking cough sounds out behind you so loud the preacher has to wait to continue. You look back and see one of the skinheads hacking into his wadded up t-shirt. He releases the shirt and leaves black, sticky phlegm across his chest, like he'd swallowed tar and coughed it back up.

With a new sense of dread, you look back up to the preacher, who's saying, "...while they were eating, Jesus took bread, and when he had given thanks, he broke it and gave it to his disciples, saying, 'Take and eat; this is my body.'"

A terrible shrieking roars out, and it takes some effort not to lose your bowels right there. A guard takes an Asp from his belt and, with a snap of his wrist, expands the telescoping baton. That's when six inmates shoot up, as if suddenly awakened, and surround the guard.

This is it. This is survival. So what're you gonna do?

➢ Fight. Go to page 146
➢ Hide. Go to page 252
➢ Run. Go to page 215

Pave Hawk Down

The helicopter sets down on top of the hospital and the six Airmen leap out to secure the rooftop. You check your M4; only fourteen rounds left. Better make 'em count. The pilot gives you a thumbs-up and you disembark.

The grit of the rooftop crunches under your boots, though it's more something you feel than hear. There's no sound but the helicopter. The rescue team opens the roof access door and floods inside.

You follow behind, and as soon as the exit door closes behind you, you're greeted with stunned silence. The six of them stand in rows of three against each wall, weapons lowered, as a former doctor and two undead nurses approach.

"Stop where you are!" Airman Belliveau commands with a hand extended, palm flat.

Not wasting another second, you put the three down. In adrenaline-fueled panic, your second shot goes wide, so it takes four rounds. The twice-dead ghouls fall to the floor and the rescue crew turns to you, weapons raised.

"Nobody told you guys what's going on?" you ask.

"Rabies," Belliveau says.

"Some kind of biological weapon," the operator next to him says.

"Terrorist attack," another Airman adds.

You shake your head. "It's that *Gilga*-shit. Supposed to make people live forever, but instead makes them living dead."

"We're supposed to minimize casualties to the infected," Airman Belliveau says.

"Yeah, well, that's the flying ointment, isn't it? You get bit, you're infected. The only way to stop the infection from spreading is a headshot, so...."

The team nods in understanding and moves down the hall. With the blackout, the hospital is on emergency power and the corridors are sparsely lit by a battery-powered flood-light, one per hall.

An orderly staggers out, his position given away by the shadow he casts, and you put him down with one between the eyes. Without these emergency lights, you wouldn't stand a chance.

The halls crowd with more fleshies after every shot fired, so you do your best to conserve ammo and steer clear. Still, you have to fire three more precious rounds just to make it towards the exit signs. The elevators are down, so you'll have to take the stairs. Six sweaty, mask-fogging flights down.

On the main floor, several police SWAT members mill about, listless. Until they see you. Then the hunger rises from behind their riot helmets and their arms rise to greet you. You steady yourself and aim at the nearest—*crack!*

His head snaps back from the shot, but then rights himself. There's a spider-web pattern on the mask in front of his right eye. Bulletproof. And six of the armored bastards stand between you and the front entrance to the hospital.

At the far end of the hall is an unexpected sight. The hallway is cordoned off with waiting-room couches and coffee tables, secretaries' desks and filing cabinets. There must be a couple thousand pounds of office furniture between you and the next area of the hospital: the cafeteria.

And more shocking still, there're people on the other side. Living people. You can see their blood-stained faces looking at you with terror through the glass portholes in the double doors beyond the barricade. They look to you with pleading eyes. Men, women, and children. It hits you like a punch to the gut—they think you're here to rescue *them*.

"We can't. We have our orders," Airman Belliveau says, noting your stare.

The soldiers continue on and more ghouls come in from the eaves. It's getting crowded in here. But can you just leave all those people?

- ➤ They're safer than I am—avoid eye contact and keep moving with the extraction team. Go to page 263
- ➤ What's the point of being on a rescue team if not to rescue people? Help them out! Go to page 340

Payback

It's hard enough to sleep when every creak or rustle of wind grates on your nerves, but with a gasmask on, it's impossible. But you figure this place didn't get hit by the plague, and you're alone, so you can take the thing off for a night.

Once you do, you fall into a deep sleep on the lobby couch. Which is interrupted at some point in the night by a kick to your shin. When your eyes shoot open, you're looking down the barrel of a shotgun.

"Guess I'm debt-free now, asshole," the man holding it says. "Payback's a bitch."

Wait, what? Your mind scrambles. Debt? Payback? Holy shit, the guy thinks you own the place!

"No!" you shout, reaching up to stop him.

Too late. *BOOM!*

THE END

Perfect Gentleman

"Mind your own goddamned business, we're just talking," the soldier says.

"No, we're done here," Lily says.

You stand your ground while she walks away. The man stares at you with hatred in his eyes. You're not sure how much time passes, but it feels like you've been standing here staring each other down your whole life.

"Mother—" the man says, stepping towards you.

His curse is cut short when you smack him over the head with the police baton. You don't even remember telling your hand to pull it from your waistband, but somehow it knew to be ready. He collapses, screaming, and his hands go to his head.

"What's going on here?" Captain Delozier demands, stepping out from the stairwell.

The other soldiers come running, rifles raised at you. Lily comes to your side, placing herself in front of the rifles.

"What. The fuck. Is going on?" Delozier reiterates.

"Bastard just hit me," the soldier complains, coming to stand. "Crazy motherfucker."

"You had it coming," Lily says.

"Hey!" Captain Delozier cries. "We need to get along here!"

"Then this troublemaker needs to go," the man says, showing off the red spot on his forehead.

"So do you," Lily adds.

"Lily…" Sam says, low.

"I'll go," you say, surprised to hear yourself say it. "But you watch this man, Sam."

"Ty, no!" Lily says.

"I don't belong here."

"You do," Sam protests.

"Bring back your mom, okay?" Lily says. "We'll wait for you."

I hope you're still here, you think, but you just nod.

➤ *Go home, before it's too late.* <u>Go to page 223</u>

Pessimism

The dragon rumbles towards the survivors, and the wall of dead turn to greet you. They're mainly hospital staff and patients, so you see lots of surgical scrubs and hospital robes on the ghouls.

Now they're going under *your* knife.

The machine chews through the group with disgusting efficiency, and soon you're able to slice a hole in the barrier for the survivors to escape. Yet, as soon as you do, they start piling up barricades again.

"What the hell are you doing?" you cry over the diesel. "We've got to get out of here!"

"It's not safe!" a woman in front yells in response.

"No shit, but it's only getting worse. Come on!"

Though they still hold sad, hopeless looks on their faces, none move. One at a time, they start to shake their heads, "no."

"Help will come for us!" another woman shouts.

You're about to reply when a young boy points behind you. Looking back, you see more ravenous dead have converged on the rear. Angelica readies the claw, but your heart sinks when you see the dead approach. Instead of hospital goers, this gang is made up of SWAT police and hardened soldiers—all having failed their rescue mission—all on a new mission from hell to tear the flesh from your bones.

You should have known better. There will be no cavalry to save you.

"Clear us an exit with that claw!" you cry.

Angelica smashes through the wall and then you back around to angle the dragon through. Once out into the night air, the swelling crowd of dead comes for you. There are just so many!

Taking the vehicle up and over the curb, you head into a nearby park. Many of the dead are attracted by the hospital battle, but your construction vehicle draws a large crowd of followers as well. The dead don't move fast, but neither does your mighty steed. It's a terrifying chase of desire versus diesel.

A park bench bolted to the ground groans as you grind it into the earth. The undead also fall beneath your tread with sickening crunches. Ahead, the other side of the park is buttressed by a large concrete wall; easily ten feet high, if not more.

"Angelica, we're getting off up there! Stretch out that claw, make us a ladder."

She gets the idea and does her job as you position the vehicle. You turn off the engine, hop up, and scramble the length of the claw, pushing Angelica up and over the wall. The dead follow on your heels, but scaling the claw requires a level of dexterity too difficult for their singular minds.

Angelica rolls out of the way and you smack against the pavement on the other side with a painful drop. The sting shoots through your ankles and up into your back, blinding you with a white flash of pain.

"Cooper, look out!" Angelica cries.

A pair of undead—*zookeepers?* Yep, tan short-shorts and everything—come for you from the side. You strain to stand up and position your wrench, but residual pain from the fall slows your movements. Angelica cowers behind you, waiting for you to make the first move. You curse and prepare to fight, but out of nowhere, a man in kitchen whites appears. He hits the ghoul with his frying pan so hard it falls off its feet. Then he finishes it off with a butcher's meat cleaver.

"Nice swing, Jose Conseco! Where the hell'd you come from?"

"He followed us from the hospital," Angelica says.

"*Hola, mucho gusto,*" the man says.

"I don't speak Spanish, do you, Cooper?"

You shake your head. The man points to you and says, "Cooper?"

"Yeah, Cooper. Thanks for the help, okay?"

You turn and walk away, with Angelica and the man following you. Feeling far too tired for this shit, you stop and turn to the Hispanic chef. "Listen. Thanks, okay? *Gracias.* But I don't know you and you don't know me. Let's go our separate ways, okay? *Ciao. Auf Wiedersehen.*"

"*Adios,*" Angelica says.

"That's right," you say. "*Adios,* Jose."

He shakes his head and says, "*No, yo voy contigo. Yo he estado escondiendo en ese hospital demasiado tiempo sin esperanza, y de repente llegas de la nada. Nunca he visto tal fuerza. Eres un luchador y yo quiero luchar contigo. Mi nombre es Guillermo y si usted me acepte, seré su humilde y respetuoso servidor.*"

It's a long, impassioned speech, of which you get nothing. In a low voice, you turn to Angelica and say, "Catch any of that?"

"I don't think we're getting rid of him," she replies.

"Jesus. Well, whatever. At least he has a good swing. Okay, let's go, Jose."

"*Mordido?*" he asks, champing his teeth twice.

"Hungry?" you ask.

"I think he's asking if we've been bitten."

"Oh, no," you say, then mime biting Angelica, shake your head, and add, "Nooo. No *bite-o's.*"

He nods and follows you. When you look to your watch and activate the glow, you see it's nearly four in the morning. You're beyond exhausted and sure that your two followers are too. Time to find a place to sleep.

➤ It's a zoo—maybe you can find a temporarily closed exhibit and lock yourself in the cage. Go to page 235
➤ There's bound to be a staff office or something. All you need is a door that you can sleep against. Go to page 373

Phrasing

"Oh, don't worry about that," the center man says with a leering grin. "We'll take what we want. It's the dawn of a new world, sweetie. Play your cards right and you might just end up somebody's wife."

Your jaw clenches and you want nothing more than to knock this asshole in the jaw. After a lifetime of "get in the kitchen and make me a sandwich" jokes, you have no sympathy for pigs like him.

They come for you, but you won't give them the satisfaction. You don't scream, you don't kick and punch. Cold and stone-faced. There will be a time to fight, but it's not now. Five against one aren't great odds.

They bind your hands behind your back with zip-ties, then blindfold you.

➢ *Sit quietly until your moment to strike.* Go to page 56

Pilgrimage

After breakfast, the National Guard unit starts to break down their encampment. You steel yourself to tell the class they're heading out into the fray, but at least they'll be headed home. Eventually. They're gathered around you now.

"*Ki*...?" you ask.

"Spirit!" the class answers.

"*Ken?*"

"Sword!"

"*Tai?*"

"Body!"

"Good," you say. "These are the three pillars of kendo. None of you believed me on your first day when I told you I was only going to teach you three things, but perhaps now you see it is true. And today is the culmination of your training. Today, each of us must become *ki-ken-tai-icchi*—full synchronization of spirit, sword, and body."

"Master Tesshu, what is today?" Nolan asks.

"Today we leave the dojo. We go find your families."

"Isn't that...dangerous?" Haley asks.

You nod. "Yes. There are walking corpses out there, ghoulish fiends who will try to bite and eat you. But we will wear our kendo armor to keep their teeth away and bring *shinai* to protect ourselves. Together, we will protect one another."

"Sensei, a word?" Master Hanzo asks from the office door.

"Everyone—gear up! Be ready to go in ten minutes," you say, then head towards the office.

"Mom! Dad!" Mason shouts, palms up against the glass in excitement.

He pulls the doors open and the trio shares a heartwarming reunion full of hugs and kisses. The other kids look on longingly, then past the family and into the street, hoping to find a glimpse of their own parents.

Mason's father says, "Seriously, thank you. If Mason would've been hurt...or...well, I don't know what we would've done."

Pushing the compliments aside, you tell them all about the radio broadcast and Salvation off Route 14. "That's where you should go now. I will try to reunite my other students with their families, and then we will see you there."

The family nods and the class says goodbye to Mason, who assures his peers that he'll save them a spot at Salvation.

"Ten minutes," you say, before going back to speak with Master Hanzo.

"Please, shut the door," he says. Adding, "You need to leave me here."

"W—what?"

"I am an old man, with a bad heart. I will slow you down and endanger you all. But if you leave me here, I will tell any other parents to go home and wait for you there. And the twins. They're too young for this. Find their parents, and tell them to come claim their children."

"Master Hanzo, I can't just—"

"I know why you're afraid," he says, before fishing out a box from the shelves behind the office desk. "It's dangerous to go alone! Take this."

Inside the box is a full-sized, curved samurai katana and a smaller, matching *wakizashi*—short sword. They're sheathed in ornate scabbards, and you lift the larger sword to inspect the design. Carved into the wood is a detailed mural of a dragon fighting a tiger. Unsheathing the weapon, you see that it's flawless.

"Your father gave me this set as payment for training you in the kendo arts. When I die, it was supposed to go to you, along with this dojo. But the time for sentiment is over. This is yours now."

"Master Hanzo, this set is wonderful, but I don't know if I could use it. I've never used a real sword. I don't know…that I could kill," you say, head bowed.

"The sword is the soul of the samurai!" he yells. "This is *katsujinken*—the sword that brings life. You must protect your pupils, and remember that you cannot kill a *walking corpse*. If you strike down a fiend that hopes to attack the children, you are bringing life. Take it, you must. And you must go on this mission alone."

You close your eyes, feeling the sword—Life-bringer—in your hands and letting the new responsibility sink in. At length, you say, "I will come back for you and the twins—I swear it."

As you don your custom-fit kendo armor, you take the time to mourn for the uncertainty of it all. Will you ever know what happened to Sal? To Christian? Will you really meet up with Mason again? With your sister? Will Master Hanzo and the twins be safe here? And—perhaps most pressing—will the other students still find their families alive and well? It's just Nathanael, Haley, and Nolan now.

After saying farewell and journeying outside the dojo, you push all those thoughts from your mind. You will only survive this if you remain mindful of the present.

Across the street, on the rooftop of the hardware store, you see two silhouettes in the morning light. One is of a man holding a rifle, and the other—a woman—waves in greeting. You wave back and continue on.

"Where's your car?" Nolan asks.

"As fate would have it, it is being serviced today. Perhaps this is a blessing in disguise? I fear the roads are more easily navigated on foot. Look around."

Each city block that you pass has an abandoned military containment section. Yours was the epicenter, with the grocery store parking lot allowing room for tents, while the store itself must have provided your daily meal rations. The grocery store is completely cleaned out.

The day threatens to be a warm one, made warmer still by all the hiking. You'll want to check convenience stores for water bottles along the way. The new sword fits perfect along your side, but the weight is different. Much heavier than the *shinai* the children carry. Much like your burden. *Focus,* you tell yourself. That doesn't matter now.

All that matters are the half-dozen people who stumble forward. Seeing them up close, all your skepticism of the concept of the living dead vanishes. One man has seven bullet holes in his chest, yet stumbles and gropes at you all the same. There's a woman whose lower jaw is missing; completely ripped off. Her tongue lolls out of her exposed throat, like a dog on a hot day. Each walking corpse has injuries that don't bleed and skin so pale, it could glow.

"Ready yourself! Strike and move, just like practice. This is no different."

The sword sings out with a metallic *shing!* as you unsheathe the blade. It glimmers in the early light, ready to serve your will. In movements so practiced they're nearly unconscious, you rush forward and bring the sword down on lucky Mr. Seven's forehead, splitting it open like a melon. The sword may be a family heirloom, but if was crafted by a master and kept battle-ready by Hanzo.

It's a shock to the system how easy it was to dispatch a human man. You stare at the corpse as his bifurcated brain pools out onto the pavement; no longer living in any sense of the word. Only when your students scream does your attention return to the present.

They shout, just like you taught them, to enliven their spirit when they attack. With small, controlled steps, they engage the remaining ghouls. Striking, parrying, and evading the groping hands, they make your own spirit soar. Moving in concert with their rhythms, you dispatch the walking corpses in turn as the students batter them away with the wooden *shinai*.

In only a few short moments, the battle is won.

"I couldn't be more proud," you say, wiping your blade clean before sliding it into the scabbard.

Nathanael, Haley, and Nolan grin, unafraid.

"What now, sensei?" Nolan asks.

- ➢ "I'm going to take you home, youngest to oldest." Go to page 74
- ➢ "I'm going to take you home, based on who lives closest." Go to page 74

Pill Popping

"C'mon, let's snag some antibiotics or something," you say.

A woman in scrubs runs past you, down the other hall. Her latex gloves are coated in gore, along with the front of her scrubs, surgical mask, and plastic operating glasses.

"I need to get me one of those masks," Jason remarks.

Would be nice if you'd brought your paintball mask, wouldn't it? You round the corner to the Pharmacy waiting room, where you're met by a violent display in-progress. A scraggly blond man throws a chair at the customer window, but it bounces off the security glass.

"Open the goddamned doors!" the man screams, now brandishing a nickel-plated hand cannon.

A woman cowers behind him with greasy, matted brown hair and grungy clothing. She holds her hands over her elbows, hugging herself, and sways back and forth.

"Junkies?" Jason whispers.

The blond man reels on you, waving his pistol wildly. "You fucking cops?"

Jason looks to you, fear deep on his face. This guy really must be strung out if he thinks a couple of kids are cops. What now?

➢ Explain that, no, you're not cops. In fact, you want to help him break into the pharmacy. Go to page 88
➢ Engage. He clearly has no idea what he's doing with that piece, and that makes him a liability. Go to page 347

Pray for Mercy

You slip down to the floor, pull out the kneeling bench, and slide under the next pew. You're almost completely hidden by the profile of the narrow bench. Sometimes it pays to be skinny.

While violence erupts all around, you stay as still as you can, hands up over your face to muffle your adrenaline-fueled heavy breathing, as well as to stop the smell from reaching you.

Viscera slaps against the linoleum floor. Bright red human innards and dark brown excrement. The piss of a hundred terrified prisoners runs down their legs and onto the floor. You close your eyes, not wanting to see, but you can still hear the terrible screams. The anguish and pain. You were caught up in a prison riot once, but that was anger that deafened your ears back then. Now it's pure terror.

Then you hear an inhuman growl and feel someone claw against your flesh. Your eyes shoot open and you see a dead man, a living corpse with his throat ripped open and one eye gouged out. The vocal chords in his ruined throat still sing out, and you can see them, sticky and wet.

Then the man bites into you.

You're INFECTED!

Pray Tell

The main sanctuary is dimly lit, with the overhead lights turned down low enough to highlight the stained-glass window murals and the glow of candles on the altar. *Probably should blow those out while there's still power*, you think. *Might need them later.*

As your eyes adjust, you realize there are upwards of thirty people gathered here. There's a low murmur of prayer, Hail Marys, and those speaking quietly to one another. At least half the congregation wears blood-spattered clothing or makeshift bandages.

"I think we might have had better luck at the hospital," Jason says.

"No," a meek voice offers from behind.

You turn to see a blonde woman in her fifties. She's well-dressed in white pants and a floral blouse, bedazzled in gold jewelry. After a second look, you notice the material is blood-flecked. Her face is painted in makeup by a practiced hand; it's beautiful, really, and you feel a twinge of jealousy. It's stupid, you know, but it makes you realize you'll never have to worry about finding a date for the prom.

"I'm Angelica. I think I've seen you two in here a few times. Normally I'd say you shouldn't have those…things…in here," she says, indicating your weapons, "but this isn't *normally*, is it?"

"Have you been to the hospital, Ms. Angelica?" you ask.

She clutches at her rosary crucifix. "Prayer is all that can save us. Modern medicine is failing all around us, but here, here we have hope in our Lord."

"Yeah, well, you can hope in one hand and shit in the other—see which one holds more."

"Jason!" you scold.

Your brother shrugs. "Let's check on Dad."

➢ "She's right, Jay. We need hope, now more than ever. Let's see how Dad's holding up." Go to page 272
➢ "I want to check out the donated supplies in the annex before we go." Go to page 23

Predatory

The gate leading to the base is usually manned by two or three Security Forces cops, but they're nowhere to be seen. Either abandoned their post or dead. *Not sure which is worse,* you think.

The gate itself is destroyed. The onrush of people seeking safety on the base left the ID-check lanes clogged by smashed cars and trucks. Can't take your Camry with you, so it's time to chug as much water as you can before abandoning ship.

With Bob on your back, Isabelle at your side, and your M4 (let's call him Mitch, as long as we're naming gear) in your hands, you head out into town on foot. Might as well name the revolver you've got holstered too. She seems like a Deb. Where should you take your little family?

The businesses right outside the base are the kind you always cautioned young Airmen to avoid. The kind looking for a quick score from eighteen-year-olds flush with their first big payday. Now, these stores might be your best hope for safety. *Is that irony? It seems like irony,* you think.

It's already dark out and getting darker fast. Suddenly you're hit with a chill, and a wave of fear washes over you. As you look for the source, you see the street lights shut down block-by-block. All the lights in the surrounding buildings go dark in a rolling blackout. Last to go are the neon signs, which flicker, and finally die.

Thinking quickly, you duct-tape a flashlight to Mitch's barrel. Duct-tape was the first thing you put in Bob, so it takes a minute to dig it out. In that minute, an undead trio stumbles onto your path, and you finish wrapping the flashlight as fast as you can. With only seconds to spare, you put the three of them down. Eleven shots left inside Mitch. Time to get inside for the night.

Where to?

➢ The tattoo parlor. With its tough-guy design scheme, nobody will mess with me in there. Go to page 180
➢ The payday loans building. With all the people they screw, they've gotta be ready for a mob invasion. Go to page 259
➢ The strip club. It's designed from the ground up to keep out unwanted flesh-hungry men. Go to page 361
➢ The liquor store. I could use a drink after these last couple of days, and the windows have bars. Go to page 234

Preparing for Life

"*H*ooah," he says, then peels back his collar to show the Latin phrase tattooed around his collarbones. "Haven't heard much from the King since they took the compound. Got any news?"

"You mean the Duke?"

"Shit, you really were there! No offense, but I didn't see him letting bedmates out to drive his wheels."

"I'd have been his Duchess…if things went right. I'm sad to report that the compound has been overrun."

"Damn. Nothing left?"

"Anyone still there is sick, I can promise you that. In fact…if you can call in an airstrike, that'd be a mercy."

"You're here to initiate Plan X-ray?"

"Ummm…?"

"Sorry, you probably weren't told the codename. In the event of a total loss, Duke set it up that the compound would be firebombed."

"Yes. That's exactly why I'm here. Call it in."

The soldier nods solemnly. "We're evacuating from the hospital. Turn right and follow the soldiers. I'll see that you get a seat on one of the birds."

You nod, then turn, rolling up your window as you go.

"That was some quick thinking," Angelica says.

You shrug. "I work at an auto shop. I'm used to bullshitting the customers."

The road is narrow from all the barricades; wide enough to drive down, but not enough to turn around. One way only—ahead. You're funneled down the street and eventually come to St Mary's Hospital.

But when you pull up, you're greeted with a full-scale battle. Men stand atop military-grade Humvees, firing massive machine guns. One guy tosses a grenade into a crowd of undead, and after the deafening explosion, none are left walking. Now they're crawling. The damage is disgusting, but still they come.

And there are *a lot* of them. It's like the whole city is converging here. You've never seen so many people in one place, even on television. Still, there's some hope. You see a military helicopter in the sky and another one that has landed on the rooftop. Time to take your bludgeoning weapons from the back and go. Where to?

➢ Stay here. Use the soldiers for cover and await extraction. Go to page 262
➢ Head in. There must be someone inside who can fly you out in that chopper. Go to page 82

Present Reality

"I was just out here," you say, "And—"

But words fail you when you see the homeless guy wearing a doctor's white robe and surgical scrubs. You can tell he's not a real doctor because of the filth on the clothes and the scraggly red beard that hangs down to his chest.

Wait, no, that's not a beard. His face is skinned, peeled and sagging—which gives it the shape of a red, fleshy beard. The homeless/doctor/thing gurgles a growling moan, then stumbles towards you. As a crowd, you back away, but there's something fascinating about the way he moves. And doesn't bleed.

A gunshot roars through the silent moment, taking the thing by the shoulder, but that doesn't even bother the fiend. Another round bursts through his chest, but still, nothing. Then his head explodes into pulp and the man falls to the ground, still.

"Get the fuck back inside!" a man's voice roars.

It's a SWAT van with a sniper on the roof. He smacks the side of the van and the black behemoth peels out and speeds away.

"Has the whole world gone loco?" Stephen asks.

"We need to know how big this thing is," Owen says.

With a knowing nod, the group follows the manager inside to the lobby TV. After adjusting the input from DVD to cable, he flips on the TV. Alison Argyle, oddly calm, reads from the teleprompter, "In an ironic twist, it seems many of those killed are users of the new longevity wonder drug Gilgazyme®. It's still unknown if there is a connection between the drug and the homicide sweep hitting major urban centers across the country. No spokesperson for the creators of Gilgazyme® has agreed to comment as of this broadcast…"

The television is suddenly taken into local control and your community Sheriff appears on the screen.

"The Governor has declared a state of emergency," the Sheriff announces. "But we are as of yet unprepared for any sort of mass evacuation. We're working as hard as we can to set up aid stations and sanctuaries. In the meantime, work with friends and neighbors. Find a group. Nobody can beat this thing alone. And…we need all the help we can get."

The image switches to a stationary, soundless PLEASE STAND BY message. There you have it. You're on your own, but so is everyone else.

The room is silent, each man taking the news at his own pace. You know enough to realize that action is required in a crisis. After a moment, you clear your throat and say, "It'll pass. We just need to…

- ➤ …Get supplies. Split up and meet back here." Go to page 219
- ➤ …Head home; wait this thing out with family." Go to page 218
- ➤ …Lock the garage down tight. Right here, right now." Go to page 368

Price for Flight

The cruiser comes to life with a satisfactory growl. You put the car in gear and drive out of the motorpool, turning towards the front gates. *Shit! The gates.* Usually, someone manually opens those things so vehicles can pass through the inner and outer fences going to and from the motorpool. In your rear-view mirror, you see the guards from the armory heading your way. They set up and take aim. *Damn!*

Looks like you're going to have to ram the gates. You floor the gas pedal and briefly fishtail as you peel out and accelerate towards freedom. The guards open fire and you duck down, keeping your eyes just above the gap in the steering wheel.

In about six seconds, you're already up to sixty mph by the time you reach the first fence. The cruiser smashes through the metal with ease, but the airbags deploy, punching you in the face. In reflex, you wrench the steering wheel and flip the car.

When you come to, you're back in the SHU. You're wearing a neck brace, and everything hurts. You groan as you try to sit up. Really, you should probably be in the infirmary. The fact that you're not is bad news for the prison, and worse news for you.

You can't be sure what happens out there, but you can guess. No one comes back for you, not even at mealtimes. It's an agonizing four days before you finally expire from lack of water.

THE END

Pride before the Fall

You turn and sprint away, knowing full well that you don't need to be the fastest, you just don't want to be the slowest. Tyberius outpaces you easily and Hefty is right on your heels, but Jose and Angelica don't have a chance.

You look back, watching the lion close in on them, and turn away just as Jose raises his cleaver to defend himself. You can't watch.

When you turn your attention forward, four lionesses charge in from the sides. One takes out Tyberius while two more go for Hefty and one for you. Perhaps if you had read the signs at the zoo, you'd know that the females do the primary hunting. And they just brought your group down together.

THE END

Prison Break

The industrial-strength file chews up the bars and spits out curled iron shavings, decorating the cell floor like a Greek god's bathroom after some mighty manscaping. Celly leans into the task, adding his weight to the force against the bar.

When he offers the file to you for a turn, the rod is hot from friction. Looking closely, you see that the textured edge of the file has grown dull from the labor. Doesn't matter, you really only need one bar, and without any guards to stop you, you'll have one pried off in only half an hour. After his second turn, Celly yanks the bar back and forth, breaking the last bits through brute strength.

"Good luck, Hefty," Celly offers, keeping the loose bar for himself.

One doesn't earn an ironic nickname like "Hefty" by being sort-of skinny. It has to be you. Hell, you'd have to file through two more bars to get Celly out. Instead, it's up to you to head down to the control room and open the cell doors.

After a nod, you squeeze through the hole. As you walk past all the other inmates, the men howl at you in a mix of jealousy and pride. You're out! And soon they will be too. More than a few of the men have blood crusted around their mouths, staining the front of their jumpsuits. These don't howl; they *moan*. You walk on the far edge of the catwalk to keep free of their grasping arms.

The control room waits at the end of the cell block. It's a small room, connecting Cell Blocks A and B, and holding the controls for both. Once inside, you're greeted with a control panel and several security footage screens. Here you learn there are still a few guards left in the prison enclosure, fighting off the infected nutters from sick bay. They don't have any reinforcements from the local police like they normally would in a riot. No National Guard, nothing.

Most of the inmates are still in their cells from lockdown, and with a push of a button, you can free them all. Or, it might be easier to slip out of the prison unnoticed, alone.

- ➢ Open the other cells. With an army of cons tearing down the walls, you'll be out in no time. Go to page 260
- ➢ Leave the other guys locked up. Less chaos if I go it alone. Go to page 322

Problem with Authority

The guy's looking salty; he's the kind of man who would relish the opportunity to thump you over the head. You raise your hands, hoping to placate the police officer.

"Sir, that homeless guy on the bus is trying to…I dunno. Eat people? Ask your buddy."

Now he looks concerned and takes a step back, hand going for his firearm. "You were exposed?"

"What? No, wait…exposed to what?"

"If you're potentially infected, I need to hand you over to the soldiers, son. If you do not cooperate, I will be forced to shoot you."

"Hey, I'm cooperating, man! Sir!"

He nods. "Then let's go."

The barrier up ahead is controlled by National Guard soldiers; men in uniformed cammo wearing gasmasks and wielding rifles. These weapons scan the crowd for potential threats and as you approach, some rise to train on you. Suddenly, you're feeling very vulnerable.

"This one was exposed to one of the infected," the cop tells the soldiers.

"Okay, sir. Remain calm and everything will be fine. We're going to take you into a quarantine camp down the street. If you resist—" a soldier says, his words suddenly cut short. Gunfire erupts and you freeze in place, eyes closed in reflex like a frightened child. It's the screaming that follows that gets you to open your eyes again.

Two men in nurse's scrubs have flanked the soldiers with an arms-out, mouth-opened, animalistic attack. Several dark roses bloom on their chests where they've been shot, but it doesn't appear to bother the men in the least.

One of the crazed nurses slams into the cop, taking the man to the ground. His police baton falls at your feet. You pick up the weapon, maybe thinking you'll help, but the barrage of gunfire keeps you away from the action. You look back, afraid there might be more crazies behind you.

Instead, you find frightened men, women, and children fleeing from vehicles—perhaps motivated by the attack—and hear authorities shouting for peace from behind barriers and bullhorns.

➤ Stay calm, keep out of the way, and don't move. Wait the firefight out. Go to page 193
➤ Screw this. Use the distraction and get the hell out of here. Go to page 251

Promise Keeper

It's almost unfathomable to head away from Salvation and into the city once more, much less downtown and into the epicenter of chaos. Still, it helps to have the skills of a samurai. It might take hours to traverse the city on foot when that same trek would be minutes in a car, but the roads are either impassable or patrolled by roving gangs.

On three occasions, you're forced to run through buildings and out the rear to escape human assault. Once, a wall explodes just inches from your head; either from a warning shot or a miss by an unskilled sniper. You don't wait to find out which.

Finally, you turn the corner to the street that houses your dojo. The hardware store across the street is riddled with high-caliber bullet holes and the storefront is demolished from an explosion. When you turn to the dojo, your heart sinks when you see the glass entry demolished.

The practice area is full of meandering figures—time to clear the place.

You turn to a nearby parked car; tires flat and windows broken. Reaching in, you press the horn over and over again, sending a high wail echoing through the city. That does the trick. The wandering dead growl and moan in frenzied hunger and turn your way. Some of the "healthier" corpses even stumble-run after you.

Cutting the fastest ghouls down, you wait for the crowd to leave the dojo. Then you run around to the alley and the back way in. The door sits propped open by a twice-dead corpse and you quickly see that the place is abandoned.

Yet the door to the office remains closed.

You can't help but hope...and when you open the door, there he is. He lies on one of his reclining pillows, his chest softly rising and falling. Sleeping, but *alive!*

"Master Hanzo!" you cry, closing the door before embracing him in a bear hug.

"Easy, easy Lucas-san," he laughs. "I feared I'd never see you again. The twins, their parents came, but they brought the dead with them. I hope they made it home safely."

You nod knowingly. "And now you and I will go to Salvation and meet my *Imouto*. I won't leave you, Master. Not again."

He shakes his head. "It is I who will be leaving you, my friend. I haven't had my pills in days now. My heart won't take the burden much longer."

"I—we'll get your medicine. You can—"

"Stop! Listen. You will let me go in peace. With dignity! I am happy with this. Not one man in a thousand has such a luxury. Remember, a samurai knows when to fight...and when to die," he says.

The old man lies back down and closes his eyes, breathing heavily. Deep down, you know he can't hike through the wilderness and fight off living corpses or gangs of raiders. At least there is some solace knowing that he'll likely die in his sleep. You don't want to be without him, but it's a selfish desire. Bushido is to be selfless. Remember, samurai means to serve. You saved your pupils, now save yourself. Go. Find this Salvation, and your own.

Go to page 160

Proof Positive

The front door is locked; no surprise there. With the windows boarded up as well, it won't be easy to get in. The garage has a keypad, but with no power, the door would be useless even if you knew the code. You walk around to the back, where there's a sliding glass door with couches and a bookcase backed up against it from inside. You could probably get in this way, but it'd take just as long as prying open the boards.

Looking up, you see the second-story windows are clear. A support beam runs from the patio up to the rooftop; you should be able to scale it. The attached gutter creaks as you use the anchor pins for toe-holds, but you make it up.

The first window you try, as luck would have it, is unlocked. You head inside what must be the master bedroom and bring your sword to hand just as something lunges at you from the shadows.

A quick parry of the attack and you're barely able to stop your counter-attack in time. Your sword hovers inches over a man's brow, his eyes gorgonized from fear and focused on the steel. It's the twins' father, and he holds half a wooden baseball bat, sheared from when you deflected his swing.

"Master Tesshu?" he says, dumbfounded.

"I'm sorry," you say, bringing the sword down into its scabbard, "but with the sign on your door, I assumed…"

The man nods and says, "It's a bluff—to deter looters."

"So no one is actually bitten?"

He shakes his head, then turns and shouts, "It's okay, honey. It's just Master Tesshu."

His wife comes in, the trembling forms of Liam and Stella at either side.

"How…?"

"I'm sorry," she says. "We were able to make it to your dojo not long after you left, but…those *things* followed us."

"Master Hanzo?" you ask.

The man shakes his head. "We barely made it out ourselves."

"Did you see it?"

"We didn't stick around, but he was an old man. I'm sorry, there's no way he…." The man says, leaving the inevitable conclusion unspoken. You nod, then close your eyes and accept the darkness welling up within. He continues, "The kids told us about that camp. Is that where you'll go now? How do you know it's not a trap?"

"Salvation…something about the man's voice. I'm not sure, but my instincts say he's a good man."

"Well, I wish you the best of luck, but I think we're safer here for the time being."

You nod again.

- ➤ "I have a promise to keep. I will go say goodbye to my old master."
  Go to page 295
- ➤ "Likewise. For now, I will head to Salvation in hopes of finding my sister."
  Go to page 250

Puppet Master

"Not bad, but if we're going to run this place, we'll need some changes," you say, taking his wine glass and pacing the room.

"*We?* Hang on now, let me tell you something about the Duke—"

"We. Long live the queen. Your men only work for you now because they think you can give them what they want. Food, shelter, women, power. But that's a fleeting illusion. Men will die for their queen. Will your men die for you?"

"I think so, yes."

"I'm not sure you know your men as well as you think you do. I've heard grumblings, even in my short time here. Men often talk…after, and word gets around the stalls. Hell, Bud thinks he could fill your shoes, that's plain to see. But the way he was hitting on me the whole way here? That's the kind of disrespect that could ruin an organization like yours."

Duke's face crumbles into a frown. So many new ideas, and all of them negative, it's almost too much for an egomaniac to process. Which means you'd better keep it going.

"Take Bud, for instance. Do you think he's the best choice to run a brothel?"

"Brothel?"

"What do you think you have in those stalls? You have a brothel, but not a madam. You need your women to be strong and healthy, and part of that is making them understand their place. Not a job for a man and his belt leather, but making them understand as only a woman can."

"You…you want to be in charge of the women?"

"Who else? If you want me to trust you, that has to go both ways. If you want my love, you need to earn it," you say, putting your hand out expectantly.

"Bud!" Duke cries. The man rushes in and Duke adds, "Give me your key to the stockade." Bud does so and Duke hands the keys over to you.

"Boss, what's going on?"

"See?" you say. "See how he questions you?"

Duke's face crumples again, like a toddler being told no. "Bud…do you…do you want to fuck her?"

Bud's eyes open wide and his mouth drops open. "I…well," he stutters, then laughs. "Boss?"

"See?" you say again. "He doesn't take you seriously."

"Now hang on!" Bud says.

"Answer me honestly, Bud."

"Boss, c'mon. What do you want me to say?"

"Get your men in order, Duke. I'm going to go do the same with my women," you say. He nods as you turn and leave, his attention focused on Bud.

You've done it, though it's hard to say for how long. He's under your spell, but it's bound to wear off sooner or later. As you close the door on your way out, you see Bud staring at you with a murderous glare. Time to go.

- ➢ Straight out into the woods, right now. A dress isn't best, but time is of the essence. Go to page 370
- ➢ Back to the stalls. Take Bud's key and get back in your riding clothes before you go. Go to page 397

297

Push Come to Shove

The guard slaps you in the shoulder with the Asp baton, then shoves you against the office desk, cuffing your arms behind your back. The doctor just stays out of the way. You scream and curse at the correctional officer, but this is what he's paid to do. You're an unruly inmate, and in his mind, he's restoring order.

"We'll be back," he says.

They leave the office, locking you inside. You watch as they run down the hall to the secure door at the end. The guard does his best to keep the ghouls at bay, but one Asp is no match against a hungry crowd of the things. He screams out just as the doctor gets the door open, and they barely manage to leave before they're overtaken.

It's likely he meant it when he said they'd be back, but it never happens. Or, that is to say, it doesn't happen before the horde comes for you. The office glass is reinforced, but those nutters don't feel pain. They bash their fists to pulp until eventually, the door gives way.

With your hands cuffed behind your back, you've got no chance. You're eaten alive.

THE END

Quarantined

She shakes her head. "Don't you watch the news? I don't mean to lecture, but it's amazing to me how many people don't know what's going on. Haven't you heard anything? Read a paper or seen what's happening on the Internet? Follow social media? The city is under martial law. The Governor has declared a state of emergency, but he's the fourteenth state official to do so. People who should be dead are…well, they're *leaving* the morgue, get it? This quarantine was set up to make sure they don't go too far."

She examines your head wound while she talks, and it kind of reminds you of the way the guy behind the chair tends to use the barbershop as his soapbox. *Captive audience*, as they say.

"What do you mean 'should be dead'?"

"Just that. It's some sort of infection that paralyzes the body's pain-response centers and rewires the central nervous system for aggression. The infected patients take a turn for the worse, and that's what we call the event. *The Turn*. That's when people with bullet wounds just keep on coming. I've never seen someone shot in the head for an illness before, but I can't say I blame that response now that we've gotten to this point."

"How bad is it?"

She sighs. "It's bad. Containment—it—I'm not sure it'll even work."

"I see gasmasks. Since I don't have one, am I already 'infected' or whatever?"

"You're not showing symptoms, and you weren't bitten, right? That's the leading theory for disease vector right now. There's no evidence to support the idea that the plague is airborne, but we'll know in six hours either way, won't we?"

"We will?" you say. "Is there like a blood test?"

"There's an extremely short incubation period."

➤ "So will I be free to go in six hours, then? Assuming I don't *Turn*?" Go to page 334

➤ "What about the other people in here with me? Who's showing symptoms or bitten?" Go to page 379

Quick Bite

The diner is devoid of people, either living or dead. Unfortunately, most of the "easy pickings" are gone too. The glass pie case has been raided. So has the cash register, by some fool that doesn't understand how an apocalypse works. When you try the lights, you learn the electricity is gone too. But there is a gas stovetop that should still work without power.

"How about pancakes?" you say. The children all nod eagerly, and you add, "Find what you can and bring it here. I'll light the stove."

The electric lighting mechanism is worthless, but gas pours out when you test the knob. Just need to find a match. A great clang of falling pots echoes from the back and Nathanael lets out a terrified scream.

When you make it back, you see Haley and Nolan beating a man in kitchen whites with their *shinai*, but the walking corpse doesn't even seem to notice as he tears into Nathanael's prone form. The ghoul's skin is deep blue from time spent inside the freezer.

Not wanting a bloody death for the sake of the student beneath the corpse, you insert the sword in the dead man's ear, then kick the twice-dead corpse off your eldest student. Something black pools out from the head wound.

"Have you been bitten?" you ask, your sister's warning echoing in your head.

Nathanael nods with tears flowing down his face. He touches himself on the shoulder, just to the side of his uniform's collarbone pads. "Do it quickly, master."

Instead, you lower your sword. The thick cloth of his kendo armor is unbroken, with no sign of blood. Kneeling, you unfasten his uniform to get a better look. Several dark, purple teeth-marks flush beneath his skin, though it's just bruising. A pinch, not a bite.

"The world is running short of second chances, but today you're a very lucky young man!"

Nathanael reaches up and hugs you, laughter mixing with his sobs.

"Do we still get pancakes?" Nolan asks.

The hike to Haley's house helps digest the enormous meal you share. Fortunately, you had plenty of water to wash it down because it's sweltering outside. The humidity by this marsh-side neighborhood is almost unbearable.

Haley's house has a raised porch, most likely to protect against flooding; the stairs are barricaded by an overturned BBQ, a porch swing, and a pair of couches. With this as the only entry point, the undead don't seem to have been able to climb up to the front door.

"Clever," you say. "See how—"

Just as a voice shouts, "Oh, my God!" and Haley's mother steps onto the upper balcony. "It's them!" she shouts.

Haley's father joins her, then Nathanael's mother, and Nolan's parents.

"Hang on! I'll grab the ladder and let you in," Nolan's father says.

Not much of a choice here:

➢ *Deliver the trio of students to their parents.* Go to page 117

Quit Early

The double doors are unlocked. The main thing this tells you is that the employees left before the end of the day and didn't bother to lock up. Or, perhaps, they didn't leave at all. They could be inside, infected and waiting.

"Hello!?" you yell. "I'm coming in!"

The store lights are on, but the area is quiet. Looks like somebody raided the jewelry counter already, though the store is largely untouched. No one tends to steal a Sunday dress at the end of the world. The distinct lack of moaning is comforting, but that is tempered by a new, unsettling thought: to law enforcement or security, you would look very much like the looter that you are.

"Not here to cause trouble," you say, almost as an afterthought.

You turn back and see several figures in the far distance, stumbling your way. The infected may not be smart, but you have to hand it to them, they're persistent. Better lock the doors.

Heading into the main mall, the place is truly abandoned. Locking the exterior entrances as you go, you see that quite a bit has been stolen from the various stores, though a few rolled down their security gates to protect their wares. Your stomach leads you to the food court, which has plenty in reserve with which to sate your hunger. Sandwich shop? Cold cuts should be easy. Or maybe you're feeling industrious and want to fire up those pizza ovens.

After dinner and a second lap around the mall, the power suddenly dies—total blackout. Better stop by the overpriced candle shop.

Though you're sleeping in the mattress store next door, you're woken in the middle of the night by a wailing alarm. They're breaking through the double-doors of the department store! You rush over and see the entrance bathed in moonlight.

Aiming for a better look, you stay in the shadows, hoping that the ghouls can't miraculously see better than when they were alive, and move around to get a good angle on the doors. But it's not the infected horde like you've feared—it's a man in a convict-orange jumpsuit.

He smashes the outer set of doors with a large pipe, letting himself in. It's muffled, but you can hear his curses when he finds the second set of doors locked. Several wandering dead come into the entrance way behind him.

Should you help him out? He's clearly an escaped prisoner, but you've seen your brother Julian wearing that same color. What would mama want you to do?

> ➤ She'd want me to survive. Push some furniture in front of the door and keep out the crowds. Go to page 375
> ➤ She'd want me to help. Let the man in and fight off the infected together. Go to page 98

Radio Somewhere

As a class, you huddle in the back office to listen. Truth be told, the twins couldn't care less what the radio says, and Nolan and Mason are just old enough to realize that you find the boom box important, though they're not quite able to grasp *why*.

Master Hanzo turns the radio on and Jazz music comes through the speakers. You all wait in silence, hoping the DJ will soon interrupt with some news.

"Change the station," you say.

"It's the same song," Haley says.

"What?" Nathanael asks.

"From yesterday. That's the same song or whatever from when the DJ talked about closing school."

"She's right," Hanzo says. "Shhh, listen."

The song finishes up with a flurry of piano keys and brass notes, fades out, then starts up again from the beginning. The exact same song.

"It's on loop?" Nathanael asks.

"So what?" Mason says. "They love that song or something? That's dumb. I wouldn't do a radio station with just one song."

"No one would, dummy. That means there's, like, no one at the controls or whatever," Haley says.

You nod, "Master Hanzo, try an AM station. Talk radio."

He flips the dial and a woman with a reporter's voice is saying, "—but it's a bit odd, don't you think? He's just sitting there?"

A man then says, "We received word from Dr. Richard Phoenix himself, this kind of thing is normal. It's quite a shock to the system to accept that you're going to live forever."

"Uh-huh, well I suppose it would be," the woman replies. "If you're just joining us, this is AM with Amy and I'm here with presidential hopeful Mitt Zombie, ahh, Zomney—*Romney*—whew! Really sorry about that, folks. Rough couple of days in the studio. And his press secretary, Saul Andreas, who was just explaining why Mr. Romney will be resurrecting his campaign for the next election cycle. Would you say, with the help of *Gilgazyme®* that Mr. Romney is just going to 'wait out' the competition?"

"I'd say that he's able to play the long-game unlike any other candidate in history. Part of why America and China have such a hard time seeing-eye-to eye is because we tend to think it terms of election cycles, while China thinks in terms of *centuries*. They've been around since the dawn of history, and see themselves in a secure position on the globe."

"And now your guy sees things the same way, is that it? But what about those already worried about elitism in Washington? Doesn't immortality create a new class of…umm, what's he doing now? Please stay seated, Mr. Romney. If you have something to say, there's a mic right—hey! What the hell? *Aghhhhhhh!!!!!*"

The live broadcast becomes a stridency of blood-curdling screams and Master Hanzo hurries to turn the dial. The new channel is mostly static and the old man leaves it there, catching his breath from the excitement.

A gruff man's voice suddenly crackles in through the speakers, "…you're not alone…civilian camp…."

"What is that?" you say, "Re-tune it, see if you can get a better signal."

"…be humanity's…and all survivors…Route…ansmission-only…way communication."

"That doesn't sound like a normal broadcast," Haley says.

"It's not," Master Hanzo confirms. "This is certainly local, but our antenna is not strong enough to receive the transmission. Yet there is a way."

"Master…what are you saying? That someone is trying to talk to us?"

The old man nods. "During the war, the community put a large antenna on the roof and we listened to reports all the way from Japan. It is not difficult. If you bring the radio up top, you can use the antenna to boost the signal."

"I thought that was a cell phone tower up there?" you say, somewhat stunned.

"Proof that you don't know everything yet," he replies with a smile.

There are no stairs up to the roof, so you'll have to get on from outside. A dangerous prospect, especially with armed soldiers patrolling the streets.

➤ If Nathanael helps me, I can push the dumpster in the alley and boost myself up to the top. Go to page 55
➤ The captain mentioned there are other civilians in the hardware store across the street. Perhaps I can borrow a ladder? Go to page 20

Raise the Roof

By sunset, you've put in five hours of solid work. In a strange way, this might be the closest you've ever felt with your mother, despite the fact that she's half a city away, with an ocean of quarantine in between. Growing up, you never really got why she'd want to work so hard for something you could walk down the street and buy for no effort at all.

Your back aches, but it feels good to have accomplished something. In the glimmering twilight, you look out over the rooftop garden. Half a dozen raised-beds constructed from storeroom palates stand gravid with seeds, soil, and potential. Plenty of room to walk between them and harvest their crop: carrots, potatoes, radishes, squash, cabbage, and watermelon.

The only thing missing is water. Sure, several drums are stored on the roof, but that's for drinking. As Sam said, it's for, "When downstairs dies and we have to rise up top."

Now he says, "Hot damn, Ty! You've been busy."

You turn back to see Sam and Lily come from the stairwell, Lily holding a trio of Styrofoam to-go meal containers while Sam brandishes a bottle of Kentucky bourbon and three metal camping mugs.

"Found this in the manager's desk," Sam says, breaking the seal and pouring. "I figure a nip at the end of a long day might help us sleep a bit."

"And I've got dinner courtesy of the National Guard," Lily adds.

You take the cup with a nod of thanks, then sip while your eyes go to the horizon. The whiskey warms your chest as you drink and pain in your muscles slowly numbs. But a different sort of pain comes flooding in.

Mama. You can't help but think of her out there, alone. Worried sick about you, no doubt. And maybe…sick…herself. Downing the rest of the cup, you try to drown the thoughts.

You clear your throat, then say:

- ➢ "Once it's dark, I'm out of here. I have to find my mom. I'll come back with her, if I can." Go to page 87
- ➢ "I could use a refill, Sam. This shit ain't gonna get easier, is it?" Go to page 153

Rank and File

Slowly unfolding the blankets, you look over your shoulder. You can't help it. Obviously, no one's there, but it's a reflex of being sneaky. It's not like you're *good* at being a criminal. You're in jail, after all.

Oh…shit.

Inside the gray wool blanket is a large industrial-looking file. Like, the size of your forearm. The kind of thing that could produce shanks on a mass scale. This is *bad* news. Why? It's almost as bad as smuggling in a weapon. Worse, in some ways. Your Celly smuggled in a goddamned *weapons factory*.

Here's the kicker: Right now, this is your cell and yours alone. If the guards decide to do a cell toss, it's your ass on the line. Something like this could put you in the SHU for a week and add another year to your sentence.

For-profit prisons are always looking for an excuse to add time.

- ➤ Toss the thing out the window. You can always feign ignorance when your cellmate wonders why it never arrived, but ignorance won't work on the guards. Go to page 93
- ➤ Put it back. Celly's a huge guy, remember? If he wants to make shanks, you don't want to get on his bad side. Go to page 199

Ratlines

The three of you separate from the rest of the group without a word, and in the chaos, the C-17 closes up without you. Most likely, you're presumed dead. With the crowd of zombies growing larger by the second, there's no time for the LT to be sure.

"C'mon!" cries Agent Bertram. "Our only chance is to follow that C-17."

They lead you to a small, ratty-looking hanger where a local pilot waits with an antique private plane. You know enough military history to notice the *Luftwaffe* emblems painted on the hull and wings. The pilot gives a thumbs-up and clears the chocks while the agents board.

"Hold on, we're taking a fucking *Nazi plane*?"

The agents pause and Danly says, "It's a seaplane. So far as I've seen, those things out there don't swim."

"But it's gotta be almost a hundred years old!" you protest. "How do we even know it can fly all the way to America? The range can't be that far, can it?"

Bertram grins. "How do you think it got all the way from Germany in the first place?"

"She's in great shape. Constant maintenance, recent restoration. There are airshows every year," the pilot says.

"Sims, this is Garcia. Garcia, Sims," Agent Bertram says.

"Hi, *mucho bueno* to meet you," you say, still eyeing the plane.

"You know I don't speak Spanish, right?" the pilot asks.

"That's okay, neither do I."

The C-17 rumbles loudly and you look back to the runway. There are still hundreds of civilians scrambling to board with their families and thousands of undead following their lead.

"Now or never," Agent Danly says.

- ➤ "Go without me, I'm not flying in that rust bucket." Go to page 350
- ➤ "Man, I sure hope you guys know what you're doing…." Go to page 331

Realism

The dead don't move quickly, but they move faster than the plodding pace of your behemoth. If you're going to avoid the crowd of undead doctors and nurses at the cafeteria, you'll have to do it on foot.

When you dismount and turn down the opposite hall, you're greeted with an even more terrifying sight. Instead of hospital goers, this gang is made up of SWAT police and hardened soldiers—all having failed their rescue mission—all on a new mission from hell to tear the flesh from your bones.

You should have known better. There will be no cavalry to save you.

Though you can try to fight your way through, their armor is meant to protect against rioters. For example: protection against a wrench-wielding madwoman. And now the dead from the cafeteria entrance are behind you, cutting off escape.

Don't worry, there won't be enough of you left to rise again.

THE END

Red Rover

You sprint towards the National Guard barrier, but the men stand stock-still. With their faceless gasmasks on, it's almost like they're mannequins set in place for a Potemkin defense, and as you get closer to the line, their rifles rise to meet you.

They wouldn't shoot an unarmed man, would they?

Not stopping to find out, you hurdle the saw-horse style barrier and the men open fire. You're shot a dozen times, and with the last bits of life draining, you land atop several other would-be line breakers. Some have blood-encrusted mouths.

THE END

Repeat Offender

You round the corner of the laundry building, hot on Solitary's heels. The sweeping searchlights can't reach you from the shadows of the cafeteria, but it looks like Solitary is heading towards the prison hospital.

Bad idea, you think. You're just about to say as much when Solitary makes a hard turn towards the entrance to the machine shop. It sits on the back side of the laundry building, and you immediately get it—no weapons from the armory? What's the next best thing?

You round the corner after him, but the man was waiting for you. He lashes out with a guard's telescoping Asp baton, cracking you hard in the shoulder. You cry out, but just as quickly, he hits you again.

"Fucking psycho!" you scream, nursing your arm.

He then lands a blow on your knee, and when you fall to the ground, he hits you with a kick to the rib cage.

"Why?" you groan. He ignores you, going for the locked machine shop door.

A hungry moan draws your attention from the base of the hospital where a skinhead corpse, missing its lower half, claws towards you. What's worse, his moaning draws in more of the fiends.

Suddenly the busted-out infirmary windows pulse with life as every goddamned white supremacist in the prison pours out like worms from a rotten apple.

You try to get up, but it feels like Solitary probably broke a rib. Wincing with pain, you climb to your feet just as the bastard makes it into the machine shop and closes the door.

Stumbling, you realize he's ruined your knee as well. The horde of KKK zombies rushes towards you, and you're left with nowhere to run and no way to defend yourself.

THE END

Restless

With a sigh of relief, the big guy says, "I'm Tyberius. My thin friend here is Hefty. We've met Jose and Angelica."

"*Mi nombre es Guillermo*," Jose says.

When you don't reply, Angelica says, "Her majesty is called Cooper."

"How did you guys find us?" you ask.

"Was on our way to the cafeteria when Angie called out to us," Tyberius says.

Damn her! She's going to get you killed. She agreed to your "what I say goes" terms, but technically, you didn't say anything about calling out to random people.

"Don't ever do that again," you say, eyes narrowed. That leaves an uncomfortable silence, so you lead the group outside. Louder, you say, "I've got three goals: water, food, shelter. These two are along for the ride, and I said they could tag along, so long as what I say goes. Same rules apply if you guys—"

"Seriously?" Hefty says. "The dead're eating the living, and you're worried 'bout the damn pecking order? Lady, you're lucky we found you. We'll keep you safe if *you* tag along with *us*."

Something in his tone strikes you as painfully reminiscent of the self-righteous bastards you just left in the dust. Angelica would have you trade one group of masters for another, and just the thought boils you up with anger. You raise the rifle and fire—sending the dart past Hefty and into an undead wanderer.

You all turn and watch the ghoul, though she still stumbles forward. The dart did nothing. In frustration, you rush in and beat her with the stock of the rifle, which sends teeth and flesh flying, but doesn't crack the skull. Instead, you sweep her legs and use the barrel of the weapon to crack her head against the pavement until she stops moving.

"Worthless piece of shit," you say, tossing the rifle.

"They don't sleep," Tyberius says.

"Got it, thanks," you say. Then, to Angelica, "Try your Taser on the next one."

"Won't work," Hefty says.

But Angelica nods, and it doesn't take long to find a suitable candidate. She fires, ironically, on one of the zoo's security staffers. The undead man seizes for an instant, but the shock isn't continuous and he continues unaffected.

Angelica drops the Taser and Jose finishes it off with his cleaver.

"Tried to warn ya," Hefty says. "Non-lethals don't work. Gotta brain 'em."

"Just tell me now. Are you gonna be a problem?"

The thin guy shakes his head and says, "We in this together. The living, that is. What, you wanna get eaten?"

"Is that an offer?" you say, eyebrow raised. Attempting to disarm them.

Thin guy flushes, and the big guy laughs. Gives you a handsome smile and says, "Listen, we're all a little hungry. It's okay with you if we get some lunch, huh?"

- ➤ "Fine, but don't think that makes us together." Go to page 106
- ➤ "Sure, you go your way, we'll go ours." Go to page 27

Retail Therapy

The road is clogged by wrecks and traffic, but you've spent more than enough Friday nights at the mall to find a detour using the Jeep's 4x4. The parking lot is overflowing and gunfire peppers the night air. Looting is in full force.

"What are we doing here again?" Jason asks. "We have food and water at home. Ammo too. What else do we need?"

"Let's assume you're about to be stuck at home for months on end, what would you grab?"

Jason shrugs. "Videogames?"

"Let's assume no power."

"Boardgames?"

"Jay, we just won a shopping spree! Remember that bomber jacket Dad said we couldn't afford? It's on a 100% off sale! This is your last night out. Ice cream? C'mon, I'm buying whatever you want."

Now he's on board and you rush inside. There are whole armies of looters waging territorial gang wars but as a pair of small kids, you're not even a blip on the radar. It probably doesn't hurt that you're better armed to boot. Staying unseen as best you can, you go for essentials: Top-shelf perfume for a future without regular showers, boxes and boxes of tampons for—

"Ah, we can use those as bandages, right? Good idea, let's stock up," Jason says.

You nod, trying not to blush.

Jason gets his bomber jacket and a pair of mirrored aviator sunglasses. Next, you swing by the shoe store together, looking for the newest, most expensive styles. That's when things get really chaotic.

Zulu are in the mall, you realize. Several men hold down a dead, pale-skinned woman and pull off her necklace and rings while she snaps her jaws in frustrated hunger. Another man uses a sledgehammer to bash away an attacker, whom he sends crashing through a Tipi cultural display.

Several wandering corpses seem to be fighting a biker gang, but instead of taking it seriously, the bikers spray the dead with soda water. Then they start throwing pies into the faces of the ravenous Zulu like it's all some joke.

"That has got to be the dumbest thing I have ever seen," Jason says.

In truth, it makes you feel kind of bad for the infected. They may be Zulu, but isn't this a little disrespectful of the dead? These were people, once upon a time.

- ➢ "I gotta put these Zulu down. Watch my six." Go to page 222
- ➢ "Let's get out of here before these morons get everyone killed." Go to page 237

Riveting

You shake with fried nerves while your vision grays and narrows. Instantly sweaty, cold and clammy, with light-headed nausea and chest pains. It's hard to breathe. Blood is everywhere, and you don't even remember the last few minutes. You're suffering from shock, you know from your lifeguard course.

Closing the door to the office, you slump against it. You want to sob, to let it all out, but something feels dead inside of you. And why not? Dad is dead, Jason is dead...Sarah is dead? It would be so much easier if that were true. If you could be together, as a family. With mom even. *With mom.*

You think to what Jason said, about mom and dad living on. And now Jason too. Then you think about dad in the living room, pointing at the World War II pictures. Rosie the Riveter. *We can do it!*

Maybe...maybe they're all dead. Maybe Sarah died with them. But if you act like Rosie, *become* Rosie—tough and motivated—maybe they'll all live on inside of you.

"We can do it!" you say aloud. *We.* Mom, Dad, Jason, Sarah. Together, all your best qualities combined into Rosie.

Rolling up your metaphorical sleeve, you stand up, wipe your tears away, and scan the office for anything useful. A radio control panel catches your eye, so you start there. When you flick it on a deep, gravelly voice comes through. He's saying, "—it won't be our last, God willing. Any and all survivors are—"

"Hello? Hello???" you say, clutching the CB-style transmitter and depressing the talk switch.

"—smission-only message, we are not currently capable of two-way communication," the voice continues when you release the switch. So it's only a recording? You slowly lower the radio mic, but listen, hopeful the message will repeat itself or that someone might respond. The radio crackles.

"If anyone is out there, know that you're not alone. This is Colonel Arthur Gray of the civilian camp, Salvation, broadcasting in the blind. We have food and shelter and weapons. This may be humanity's greatest threat, but it won't be our last, God willing. Any and all survivors are welcome to join us at the old reformatory off Route 14. I repeat, this is a transmission-only message, we are not currently capable of two-way communication."

Salvation. Your heart flutters. A civilian outfit, but paramilitary run—by a *Colonel*, no less! *Hot damn!* Heading back out away from the gore, you take a more detailed terrain map from the office. Good news: the reformatory is on your map. Bad news: it's not close; a couple weeks' hike, at least. You'd have to essentially skirt the whole town. Maybe a month in the woods.

But you'll have Dad's skills, Jason's sense of humor, Mom's compassion, and Sarah's grit. You'll survive, help anyone you can, but shoot anyone who's bit. And if you have to help someone who's bit, you'll take a part of them with you. That's how it works now. Why? Because *we can do it!*

Go to page 160

Roadside Rest in Peace

Though the dead are slow, they are persistent. And just like you, they appear to have no choice but to congregate. On the way here, you saw one of the dead shuffling with a terribly mangled leg. Knowing she couldn't possibly catch up, you let her be. Big mistake.

The *moaning* when they see the living—that's what calls in others. So now you know. You can't let a single be. You have to kill them all, or more will come, and the ones they call will call in more, until it snowballs out of control.

Which is why you scan for the dead while waiting for Tyberius to finish his pit stop. The block doesn't look like much. There's a pawnshop where a man sitting in the window lies dead, shot. There are plenty of twice-dead ghouls on the ground too. Lots of bullet casings. Ty focuses on a hardware store where the entrance is caved in like it was shot by a tank. It's possible; the rest of the building is coated with huge gunshot pockmarks that must've been caused by something military-grade.

"A man and woman was here," he says. "Across the street at the karate place—a full class of kids was hiding too."

You look over to the dojo he points out, but there are no signs of people anywhere.

"Whole National Guard barricade here but now…so many people—do you think they made it out?"

You don't say anything, and Angelica simply looks away. Jose continues to wait patiently, but Hefty tries to comfort his friend.

"Sure, man. Some of 'em, anyway. They had to, right? Mathematically…."

Tyberius nods, but doesn't look convinced.

"We ready to go?" you ask.

He simply turns and starts walking.

➤ *Head to the amusement park.* Go to page 86

Runner

While waiting for Josh to go get lunch, you get to work on another car. *Annnnnnd* finish the job. What the hell is taking him so long? Might as well park it and bring the next one in.

Except the lot out back is full; no spaces to park the car. Frustrated, you open the side gate so you can drive around and park the car in the front lot. When was the last time the back lot filled up? You can't remember it ever happening, but it makes sense if phones are down and you can't tell anyone their ride is ready for pick-up.

After parking, you get out just as a young man comes sprinting up. He's probably a recent high-school grad, or rather, a dropout, from the looks of it. He's got all the tell-tale signs of a meth-head. Wild eyes, disheveled greasy hair, and blood spotting his torn t-shirt.

"Gimme a ride, lady!" he shouts.

"*No*," you say, in as low a register as your voice will allow.

"C'mon, please—"

"Step off, junkie, before I have to hurt you," you growl. He just stares, more bewildered than anything, then looks over his shoulder. "Kid, I don't want to have to call the cops."

He laughs like someone who can't believe their ears and continues running. You watch until he turns the corner, then walk back through the side gate, closing it before heading into the garage.

"Is lunch here yet?" Craig asks.

Ignoring the question, you say to the group, "Everybody take a minute to call all your completed jobs. Try your cells."

"Mine stopped working a while ago," Stephen says.

Craig pulls out his cellphone, taps the screen a few times, then holds it up. Several tones go off, then a pre-recorded message says, "We're sorry, all circuits are busy now. Please try your call again later."

"The hell?" Brian says.

When you look up, you see Josh in the lobby, heaving for breath, hands on his knees. Owen pats him on the shoulder. Without a word, the four of you in the garage rush over to join them.

"Just calm down," Owen says.

"*They're fucking eating each other!*" Josh screams, more manic than you've ever seen the man. He stumbles, then slumps onto the couch.

"Get him some water!" Owen shouts.

"They…shot…guy was…crazy…" Josh wheezes, completely out of breath. The guy's a chain smoker, and probably hasn't run in years, but something has him spooked.

➢ The TV. Check the news. See what's going on out there. Go to page 229
➢ Go outside, see for yourself what he's running from. Go to page 290

Rush Hour

Sobbing, throat tied in a knot; you focus on driving as best you can. There's only one main road out of town and into the woods—and that tunnel to freedom is up ahead. A police barricade was set in place to prevent a mass exodus from town, but plenty of people ran the barricade, and so can you.

It's fully dark out now, and there's no sign of the police officers. You look into the rear-view mirror to see if they're behind you, shocked when you catch sight of yourself: Face almost as red as your hair, and streaked from sobbing. The Jeep's headlights suddenly glint off something on the road, then everything becomes a blur as the Jeep flips.

You finally open your eyes, looking at the world from an inverted angle. You can't be sure how many times the Jeep rolled, but it ended with the roll-bars against the pavement. Several figures wander the road ahead and a low, breathy moan is terribly amplified by the tunnel to the rear. A whole chorus of the damned.

You reach for your rifle—just beyond your grasp. The first figure to come clear in the headlights is a man in a business suit, his necktie pulled so tight that his eyes literally bulge from his head. The white oxford shirt he wears is smattered in gore up to his nose.

More follow. Mothers, fathers, children. Truck drivers, cops, commuters. They all come for you.

THE END

The Sandman's Daughter

You end up sleeping in a cemetery. The infected aren't dead bodies rising from the grave, they're living souls turned into undead fiends. Which means there shouldn't be much in the way of Zulu here. Plus, the wrought-iron fencing should keep you safe for the night. Jason takes first watch and you fall fast asleep.

In the dream, you're standing amidst a sea of uniform white crosses marking the graves of all those who served this country and paid the ultimate price. Despite the lack of inscriptions, you know the gravestone before you is Dad's. Jason lies nearby, curled in the fetal position, weeping.

All at once, the crosses start sinking into the earth, just like quicksand, all save your father's. Jason sinks into the ground and you go to save him, but Dad climbs out of the earth, the green grass oozing away like swamp water.

"Let's be together, Sport. *Forever.*" He grabs you and brings you down into the muck.

You scream out, and just like that, you're awake. With a Zulu right on top of you.

The undead construction worker holds you down, chewing on your right forearm. With incredible pain, you can actually hear the ghoul's teeth *crack* and *crunch* against your bones.

Jason shoots awake at the sound of your screams, then, with a deafening *KA-BOOM!* he blasts the man point-blank in the face with his shotgun. You push the corpse off and feel your forearm for the bite. Miraculously, the Kevlar sleeves kept his teeth at bay. You'll have bruises from the pressure, but that's it. Didn't break the skin.

"Asshole!" you cry.

"I fell asleep..."

"You get tired, you wake me up, understand?"

"I'm sorry—"

"No! No goddamn apologies, Jay. When you're on watch, you're on watch. It just doesn't happen again, got it?"

Your brother nods, his eyes welling with equal parts terror and tears. You want to comfort him, but you swallow the words. He has to learn. After a beat, you say, "I bet that guy followed us from the tunnel. Must've missed him, somehow, but that means this place ain't secure. We gotta keep moving. There's prolly more, definitely on their way after that shotgun blast."

Jason doesn't reply. Instead, he hands you the map and compass. You unfold the map, take note of the tunnel, and see what's nearby. The map gets a little "fuzzy" outside of town; that is to say, everything surrounding civilization is marked by a unified green blotch.

- ➢ Into the woods. We can find supplies and a more detailed terrain map at a Ranger Station—Helpful, knowledgeable, friendly! Go to page 26
- ➢ Stay close to home. Your shooting range isn't far off, and it's better to stick close than to head off into unfamiliar territory. Go to page 173

Scooter

You grab an umbrella from the patio furniture display and take it like a lance, jousting your way through the crowd. Aiming for the guy who pointed you out, you charge towards the door. *Why you?* your head swims. *Who are these guys?*

The man goes for his handgun and you slide the action on the umbrella, sending the canvas open and locking the umbrella in the open position. A gunshot *cracks* and a hole appears in the umbrella tarp, the bullet missing you by inches.

The tip is padded to avoid children accidentally skewering each other, so you don't damage the guy when you smash into him, but you do manage to knock him into the lawn chair display and splay him out on the floor.

Then you make it outside. Your motorcycle is right where you left it, and you turn the key and shift into first gear. That's when the gunshots fire in earnest. Several hit you in the torso, knocking you off the bike.

"Goddammit!" the leader shouts. "I wanted her for breeding stock!"

With any luck, you'll bleed out. If not, the rest of your life won't be pleasant.

THE END

Screwed

The inside of the club is exactly how you pictured it. Horseshoe stage set before pleather seats; dark and seedy. You share dinner with the strippers while telling about your recent mission—leaving out the bit about the US being at fault for the plague that's tearing the world apart and eating it. The women listen with rapt attention, clearly impressed by your heroics.

After dinner, they lead you to a back room with a VIP tag on the door. Inside, there's an honest-to-goodness rotating bed. And a bottle of champagne on ice.

"Is this…?" you ask.

The women disrobe without a word, then move to help you with your clothes. Let's be honest, Sims, you're a red-blooded, weak-willed, American male. You could die tomorrow, why not live tonight?

After the best night of your life, you awaken with a growling stomach and a full bladder. Stretching, you get up for a racehorse of a piss and find you're alone. The place is empty, and the women are gone.

With a note of panic, you check your gear. Both firearms are gone, along with the rest of your food and water. They left your mostly-empty pack, your gas-mask, and your knife, Isabelle.

Those bitches, they took your stuff and just left you here. You feel so…*used*. Then you shrug.

"Totally worth it," you say, chuckling to yourself.

Well, no food, no water. Can't stay here.

➢ *Time to go scavenge.* Go to page 327

Security

"Guy can't take a fuckin' hint," Brian says.

"I think it's a bad idea not to take their help," Craig says.

"Noted. I'll make sure I leave space for your dissenting opinion in my captain's log," Owen replies.

You watch out the front window as the men talk amongst themselves. After a moment, they notice you watching. Slowly, they each turn to face you, and grin.

"Boss, we need to secure these windows," you say.

"Truth be told, we're better off sealing ourselves in the garage," Craig says. "The front office is mostly glass and—aside from the bathroom—isn't worth much, strategically speaking."

"There's a second shitter in the garage anyway," Stephen points out.

"Okay, let's grab anything that looks useful and take it in the garage," Owen replies.

You nod, then after one last look at the group outside, add, "And let's weld the fuckin' door shut."

Josh isn't much help, but when five other grease monkeys who spend all day fixing cars put all that effort into securing a garage, it becomes a veritable fortress. The downside is that you don't have much in the way of food. Your inventory consists of: a mostly-empty box of donuts containing the stale, jelly-filled flavors that no one wanted, a bin of popcorn kernels and powdered butter taken from the lobby, a dish of mints kept at the register, and Owen's Costco-sized can of coffee "crystals."

Craig informs the group that you'll want to add a scoop of the crystals to each cup of water; it's not much, but it is a source of calories. You inform him that he can go fuck himself if he thinks you're drinking that sludge.

Presently, the group waits on the popcorn maker for dinner while Josh groans in pain from the break couch. He's covered in blankets that're soaked through with the man's sweat.

"He's ice-cold," Owen says. "Do we have anything to use as a space-heater?"

Josh makes a noise like a tire going flat, and suddenly his chest becomes still.

"Is he…is he dead?" Stephen asks.

"If his wound was infected, it's possible," Craig shrugs. "We should isolate him, or we might all get sick."

"Where? We barricaded this whole place tight," Brian says.

"We can still open one of the roller doors," Craig suggests.

➤ "No. Put him in one of the car trunks." Go to page 337
➤ "Open it, quick. We need to keep the air clean in here." Go to page 164

Seeking a Friend (with Benefits?)

The doctor blushes, and the edges of her mouth turn up in a smile. "Guess there's not much time to be coy these days, is there?"

She finishes checking on the other patients in the tent, then leaves. You're left to simmer in self-doubt, wondering if you'd read the situation wrong, when the tent flap opens. Doctor Abdous consults a clipboard, then speaks with confident professionalism.

"Patient…Tyberius? If you could come with me, please."

You stand up and follow her out the tent, past the guard, and into the main compound. It's a strip mall parking lot filled with other tents. With the sun setting, nearly everyone is inside. As you pass the main area, she takes off her surgical mask, goggles, and gloves. Despite no makeup and her hair done up in a messy bun, she's stunning. Even worked to the bone and running on no sleep.

"The guards change shift in ten minutes," she explains as you continue on. "Meaning those who saw us leave won't be around to ask questions. This is me."

She stops in front of a navy blue Ford hatchback crossover. She finds the keys, unlocks the car and opens the door.

"Are we going somewhere?"

She leans in for a whisper. "The seats fold down."

"Oh," you say, thinking, *Smooth, Ty. Real smooth.*

You make up for the moment by leaning in and kissing her. It sets off a spark and she shoves you inside the car, ripping off your clothes and fogging the windows in only a matter of moments.

"I've never done this before," she says.

And you'll probably never do it again, you think, then say, "It's the end of the world."

Somehow it doesn't come off cheesy, probably because it's true. She takes you inside herself then, and rides you with an intense passion. All those frustrations, all the people she couldn't save, all the thoughts that humanity is dying—they all come out in a liberating, anger-driven fuck. Sure, it leaves you feeling used, but you're not one to complain.

You spend the rest of the night just talking; getting to know Morena Abdous. Learning about her life and family. You tell her about your mother and the loss of your brother. Then you make love once more, gently this time. Focused on pleasing each other and taking your time to explore.

It's morning now and there's a pounding on the car window. One of the National Guard soldiers. Morena covers up with your dress shirt and cracks open the door.

"Sorry to…*interrupt*…ma'am, but we're clearing the streets."

"What? Why?"

"Orders. The quarantine is officially Can-X, and all remaining personnel are reassigned to assist the hospital. Yourself included."

"Okay, give me five."

"Yes, ma'am," the soldier says before moving on to the next car.

"What's Can-X?"

She starts dressing and says, "Military-speak for cancelled. It means things are worse at the hospital than we'd feared. Here, I think this is yours."

She reaches under the passenger seat and produces the police baton you carried before you were brought here.

"Don't go," you say.

"The soldiers will be busy packing up. I suggest you sneak out now, while there's an open window."

"The hospital…just don't, Morena."

"What would you have me do, Ty? I'm a doctor. This is what I signed up for. Go find your mother, she needs you. Maybe…." She says, trailing off and thinking better of it. She leans in and kisses you, then says, "I won't forget you."

Unsure what to say, you just nod.

"Get going," she says, forcing a smile.

"I'll tell my mom about you."

"Oh, geez…" she says with a laugh. "Go."

She's right and deep down, you know it. This is your best chance to get back home. Not much of a choice here:

Go home, before it's too late. Go to page 223

Self-interest

"Sorry, fellas," you mutter to the cell block security footage.

Unfortunately, these screens don't give you any information on the world outside the prison. If the guards aren't getting local reinforcements, things are probably worse outside than they appear in here. You've got to find a way out, and fast. Escaping from prison is nearly impossible, but with a massive distraction (like, oh, say, inmates and guards eating each other, just as an example), you've got a chance.

There are two ways out. First is the public entrance, where visitors come to see their friends and family. Unfortunately, you'll have to go through the infirmary to go that way. The other option is the service entrance by the motorpool, but that particular building is in the most secure wing of the prison, located behind the SHU and the armory.

Where to?

➢ Head out into the Yard to get a better look at the state of things. You need to know the big picture before you plan your next move. Go to page 245
➢ Stay quiet, stay out of sight, and go for the motorpool. With any luck, the guards won't have taken all the cars yet. Go to page 129
➢ The front way out is the closest. The infirmary won't be easy, but you'll be careful. Go to page 387

Semi-shelter

"The truck'll do! Bring everything you can."

Loaded up to the gills, you waddle your way to the 18-wheeler. With the tunnel clear of Zulu, you're free to take on some extra weight.

Jason steps up, opens the passenger door to the truck, and a snarl catches your attention. From the cab of the semi-truck, the driver tumbles out on top of you. You slam against the pavement, your breath purged from your lungs. When you wheeze back in, you choke on the viscera streaming from the gaping maw of the man astride you.

Blinded, you put your hands up to block the attack, and the trucker bites down on your forearm.

You're INFECTED!

Service (with a Smile)

The service entrance is locked; the handle remains stiff when you give it a turn. But when you pull, the door swings wide. There in the door crack is a small, pink Zippo lighter, waiting so someone could let themselves back in. *Bless the smokers,* you think with a grin before realizing that if the person didn't come back for it, they're most likely dead.

You turn back and see several figures in the far distance, stumbling your way. The infected may not be smart, but you have to hand it to them, they're persistent. Better lock the doors.

Heading into the store, you find no one on duty. Must have fled in a hurry. There's a reception desk and behind that lie several offices, the entrance to the warehouse, and a security hutch. Without hesitation, you go for the security nook.

Nothing for you to use, unfortunately. No pepper spray or Tasers, though you're not sure those would even do much against the undead. The good news? The security feeds are still hot. You look at the various closed-circuit TV screens, scanning for signs of life…or death. No movement.

After a few more minutes, you satisfy yourself that the mall is indeed abandoned. Time for a look around. Your stomach leads you to the food court, which has plenty in reserve with which to sate your hunger. Smoothie stand? If nothing else, you can eat the fruit and down the overpriced almond milk. Or maybe you're feeling industrious and want to fire up those chicken fryers.

After dinner and a second lap around the mall, the power suddenly dies—total blackout. Better stop by the hipster/goth paradise and crack some glowsticks.

Though you're sleeping in the mattress store next door, you're woken in the middle of the night by a wailing alarm. They're breaking through the double-doors of the department store! You rush over and see the entrance bathed in moonlight.

Aiming for a better look, you stay in the shadows, hoping that the ghouls can't miraculously see better than when they were alive, and move around to get a good angle on the doors. But it's not the infected horde like you've feared—it's a man in a convict-orange jumpsuit.

He smashes the outer set of doors with a large pipe, letting himself in. It's muffled, but you can hear his curses when he finds the second set of doors locked. Several wandering dead come into the entrance way behind him.

Should you help him out? He's clearly an escaped prisoner, but you've seen your brother Julian wearing that same color. What would mama want you to do?

- ➢ She'd want me to help. Let the man in and fight off the infected together. Go to page 98
- ➢ She'd want me to survive. Push some furniture in front of the door and keep out the crowds. Go to page 375

Shaws*hanked*

"This one's got a big mouth, no?" one of the *cholos* says.

"Hefty, Hefty," Celly says, shaking his head. "If I have one of *mi hermanos* drive the bus, what use do I have of you?"

From behind, a sharp pain digs in, right at your kidney. You stumble forward, grab onto Celly and hold tight as something warm flows down your backside. You try to talk, but the pain chokes off whatever words you might have. Celly pushes you away, and you fall to the ground.

"Sorry, but I said you're no longer in my protection. Shoulda took the deal. *Vaya con Dios.*"

THE END

Shift Change

If there's one place you're guaranteed to find a doctor, it's the ER, right? And—even better—these guys have probably been working on bite wounds all night. Maybe they know how to treat the infected? Maybe they can stop this plague?

When you make it to the ER, the whole place is a madhouse. Orderlies push hospital beds through the halls, narrowly avoiding collisions with nurses. The laminate floors are streaked with blood. Patients wail and scream from all around. One man who's strapped to a gurney snaps his jaws at everyone who passes. In short, the ER makes the roads you took to get here look like a carousel ride.

"Excuse me. Sir? Ma'am? Hello? Can you help me?"

No one answers; it's like you're invisible. They're all frantically trying to meet the overwhelming demand for triage. It's like a WWII clinic. Soon they'll start marking foreheads to prioritize treatments based on survival chances.

You tap a nurse on the shoulder, and she flips around, eyes wild. Seeing you're not trying to bite her, she shouts, "You need to check in at the front desk!" and turns back down the hall.

The front desk, however, is empty. You scan the ER for an easy target; after all, this is a kidnapping mission. Ahh, there! A young, female, Indian doctor steps out from one of the operating rooms. She slips off bloodied gloves and pulls down her surgical mask to let out an exaggerated sigh. She looks exhausted.

You wave Jason over and follow her down the hall and into the break room. On break? Perfect! Cornering her, you say, "We need your help."

She puts up her palms in mock surrender. "I'm sorry, but—"

"Not a request, ma'am," you say, raising the rifle.

Now her arms shoot all the way up in genuine surrender. A disgusting bite mark on her wrist draws your eye. You lower the rifle.

"You're bit?" Jason asks the obvious, then adds, "Can you treat it?"

"Not that we know of. We're trying, but it's only an average of six hours before the infection fully takes hold. At that point the patient's heart stops, and the hunger instinct starts. It's fascinating, really. It's an animated stasis; a medical contradiction."

Six hours? That's it? When did Harrison Ford bite Dad? It must be getting close. And that guy at the house already had a bite when you found him....

- ➢ Better head home. If nothing else…to say goodbye. Go to page 83
- ➢ Pharmacy. You have to try! Get some antibiotics or something. Go to page 285
- ➢ How about a second opinion? To the cafeteria. Maybe you can catch another doctor on break? Go to page 149
- ➢ To the morgue. If these things really are coming back from the dead, the guys down there should know, for sure. Go to page 150

Shit Creek

A gasmask is only so useful, and as the mid-day's heat pounds onto your combat uniform, the visor starts to fog up with drips of perspiration. Out in the open you should be okay, right? You really only need the thing for engaging fleshies. You'd only be wearing down the filter with 24/7 usage.

So you lift the mask up on top of your head, letting the breeze wick off the sweat. The city smells of death. Rotting corpses, excrement, blood, bile, and all the other bodily fluids. It's almost enough to put the mask back on.

Several undead mill about the streets, but none have spotted you yet. It'll require extreme caution not to frenzy the group again. Yeah, it both sucks and blows to be without any firearms, but you're still alive, and that's more than most can say. Still, you can't knife-to-re-death all the fleshies in the city, so priority one needs to be: Signal rescue.

It's impossible not to dwell on the fact that the government was partly responsible for the plague, but they'll have some kind of backup plan. We wouldn't attempt an operation like this without contingencies, right?

All you have to do is find a way to contact whatever remains of the government, and rescue will surely come. You're still in the Air Force; they'll happily pick you up and you can join the fight where you were always meant to be—safely far, far behind the front lines.

That quarterly computer-based-training on survival and anti-terrorism sure would come in handy right about now, but you always pencil-whipped the Air Force ancillary courses, figuring you mostly had to survive life behind a desk.

But a few lessons stayed with you. For one, you know you should steer clear of downtown. There will be marauding bands of looters to contend with, and with your military uniform, even the good people will mob you like the lone lifeboat afloat after a cruise ship capsized; all passengers scrambling to get aboard the overwhelmed dinghy.

So where to, if not the heart of the city?

- ➤ Head to central park. I can start a signal-fire, and it's probably the best open-space to set up helicopter extraction. Go to page 51
- ➤ That mega theme-park is fairly close. Odds are, not many people will head there during crisis, so I should be free to forage and use whatever crisis-center they have. Go to page 411

SHOOT ALL THE THINGS!!!

Burst firing into the prepubescent crowd, you blast the children into oblivion. You're like the Oprah of gunfighters: *You get a bullet! You get a bullet! And you get a bullet! Everybody gets a bullet!* When the kiddos you didn't score a headshot on keep coming towards the Ranger, he turns to face them and you switch to single-fire and take them out one by one, with his help.

"Thanks," he huffs, offering the first smile you've seen from these men. "How'd you know they were infected?"

The uncertainty must show on your face, because the man's smile falters. With a curt nod, he turns back and helps a man in bloodied business casual and his wife or girlfriend get onto the plane.

"Aim for the head, fucksticks! Am I the only one who's ever seen a goddamned zombie movie?" Lt. Dosa shouts in between shots at hostiles.

"Sir, we have reports of VIPs trapped in the terminal," a soldier says.

"Who?"

"The Ambassador and his staff. It was the diplomatic rendezvous point."

"Damn," Dosa growls. "They're mission-essential. We have to get him out."

➢ Volunteer to lead a force inside. Go to page 147
➢ Don't make eye contact, and hang back towards the C-17. Go to page 135

Sick Call

"Well," she says, dabbing your head with something that stings. "This is the sick tent. So…once you're no longer sick…I assume they'll move you somewhere else."

"Other tents?"

She nods. "The main tent is for voluntary quarantine, but since the men have taken to calling you 'Troublemaker,' I'm guessing that might be a hard one to get transferred into. Although I suppose you've got a better chance moving there than you do of a field commission into the command tent with Captain Delozier."

Unable to nod, you grunt in understanding.

"Tell you what, though, I'd consider yourself lucky. There's also aggressor tent, where they put the *real* troublemakers."

"What about the whole quarantine zone or whatever? When can we go home?"

You can feel her tense up, and it's like the tent grows a bit colder. For a long moment, she just works at bandaging your head. At length, she says, "It really isn't my place to say."

"So you're not part of the army?"

"Well, no, I'm actually a naval reservist, but they didn't ask me here for my tactical advice."

The bitter tone of her words hangs in the air, scattered only when the nearby woman starts vomiting in her bucket. The lady groans and her stomach makes an equally pained noise, then she sets the bucket down next to her cot—and starts to unbutton her pants.

"I'll come by later to check your bandages…and to change her bucket," Doctor Abdous says at length, her tone changing to professional once more.

- ➤ "Wait! I volunteer to be here. Put me in the main tent, please. My head wound isn't that bad." Go to page 334
- ➤ "I'm sorry." Take the doctor hostage and get out of here. It worked once, it'll work again. Go to page 355
- ➤ "Go get the guards." Time to get transferred to aggressor tent. Go to page 232

Sideline Chat

Bubba or whoever comes back, and you remind him that you do not consent to being property. If the guy in charge wants to see you in a dress, it'll have to be as a corpse. You don't specify if it's you that'll be the corpse or this "Duke" character. Doesn't matter, he fumes, threatens violence, but ultimately balks and leaves you be.

A few minutes later, a familiar face arrives.

"Craig? What the hell are you doing here?"

The man sighs, then lifts his pant leg to reveal a tattoo: *Ad Vitam Paramus*.

"I didn't know it'd be like this, Kay. Believe me. When he posted online about 'breeding stock,' I honest to God thought he was talking about rounding up literal livestock."

"And now that you know…?" you say.

He looks away.

"You're just as guilty, then."

"No," he says. "My family will be safe here. I won't…just listen. I came to tell you that you can make something for yourself here. Duke really likes you. If you forget about the start, you could end up as the First Lady around here."

"I bet that'd make you feel a lot better, wouldn't it? I mean, if I married some redneck, you'd have a much better time sleeping at night than—oh, say—if he's raping me while you try to sleep, trying to forget that you sold me into slavery."

He's beet red now. "It would make me feel better, Kay. Because it's the best offer I can give."

➢ Fine, I'll put it on. No friends to keep close, but you can keep these enemies closer. Go to page 89
➢ Tell Craig he can wear the dress. You're nobody's bitch. Go to page 54

Sims the Slayer

The old Nazi seaplane idles, engines at the ready, drawing attention from the crowds, but not nearly so much as the C-17. Despite obvious evidence to the contrary, people and undead alike hold out for a miracle to allow them to board. The C-17 rolls right over them in a sickening display.

The powerful engines send the crowd flying as the giant military plane carves a path through the crowd. Garcia taxis out behind the C-17 while you look from the window with fear. A few people sprint towards the plane and many, many more fleshies stumble-run after you.

Something slams against one of the wings, and you jump in response. Then, a moment later, the plane rises into the air. The crowd below continues to scramble in seeming chaos, an angry ant-hill against the shrinking landscape.

The small plane nearly falls out of the sky from the powerful wake turbulence the C-17 gives off, but somehow you stay aloft.

The old Nazi-bastard plane is slow but ironclad. Still, you might as well be rafting on a lifeboat from Brazil to the US. It took the better part of a day to fly out to Russia in the C-17, and it's taken the better part of *a week* to go from Brazil to Mercury City in this bucket of bolts. You even had to take shifts flying to allow sleep rotations.

"Takeoff and landing are the hard part," Garcia had said. "Just keep the altitude gauge where it's at, and keep the wings steady. Basically autopilot, no?"

In fact, this godforsaken journey took so long, you had to land in the North Atlantic so the pilot could refuel. Yep, you actually set down on the sea, and watched the infinite blue horizon while Garcia dug out some fuel cans from the cargo. So, yeah, by the time Mercury City finally comes into view, you're ready to swear off flying for good.

Brendan Droakam's warehouse is down by the docks in the shipping district, meaning you don't have to go far on land. This would be great news, except the wooden gangplanks are crawling with the undead.

"*Amigos*, grab the machine-guns," Garcia says.

I thought he said he didn't speak Spanish? you think.

"These work?" Bertram asks with disbelief.

"What? You guys don't use live ammo in your airshows? That is *maluco*."

The agents fight over control of the forward gun, while you take the aft. Garcia makes two passes along the dock, and you obliterate the ghouls below, making them dance *Thriller* as you riddle them with large-caliber bullets.

"We have a few bombs," Garcia says, posing the statement as a question.

"No," the agents say in unison.

Garcia shrugs. "Save them for later, then."

"You guys made it!" shouts a man in a red, white, and blue camouflage military uniform. He has the same nondescript military/G-man appearance as the pair of agents.

"Hey, Captain America, what the fuck are you wearing?" Danly says.

"Supersoldier uniform prototype. I've got a lot more toys for you boys inside."

"Uhhh, did you say 'supersoldier'?" you ask.

"Droakam, this is Sergeant Sims," Agent Bertram introduces. "He helped get us out of the hotzone. He's good under pressure and has a gift with technology."

"Air Force, huh? Well, I'm happy to have you on-board as our test-pilot. I'll explain inside."

The warehouse lab is vast and open, modular, with equipment crates too numerous to count. Though mothballed, dusty, and coated in a layer of guano, you can tell this used to be a formidable, *Men in Black*-style test site.

Droakam continues, "I'm with the FBI's Supersoldier Unit, and suffice it to say we've got every major technological breakthrough in the last 60years, most of which was too expensive or complex to put into production."

"I'm *actually* a pilot," Garcia says, raising his hand like a kid in class.

"Great, I think we have some drones tucked in here. But first, let's get Sims suited up. After that fireworks display you guys set off, it's a good bet we're gonna have some living-dead company real soon."

Droakam walks over to a crate stenciled with DINOSKIN MARK IV. He opens the lid to reveal a mannequin wearing an olive-green bodysuit, scaled and reptilian.

"The newest and best in body armor," Droakam explains. "Lightweight, breathable, and incredibly durable. The scaling provides multilayer protection against gunshots or knife attack, which makes it an ideal first line of defense against bites and scratches. Hell, a pit bull couldn't break the surface. Try it on."

The group focuses on other crates while you change. You're concerned the suit might not fit, but the fabric sort of "molds" to your body, hugging your gut like a more comfortable version of a corset. When you rejoin the group, you see Droakam opening another crate labeled, EKИƎ EXOSKELETON LOADER.

"What's that?" you ask.

The front of the crate opens to reveal another mannequin, much like the one you found wearing your DinoSkin suit. This plastic man, however, is almost entirely naked—save for an odd line of metal tubing that runs along the arms, legs, and spine.

"Step out," Droakam says and the mannequin walks out of the crate. "Release." The metal portion collapses onto the floor, which sends the mannequin tumbling over. "Go ahead, Sims," the man prods.

You step onto the "feet" and the suit climbs up and over your body, attaching itself to the Dino-Skin with snakelike movements. The process is eerily lifelike. You lift your arms to inspect the add-on, and almost punch yourself in the face. Each movement is effortless, like floating through a cloud in a dream.

Suddenly inspired and energized, you lift one of the larger crates and it comes off the floor as easy as a helium-filled balloon. You toss it into the air, sprint over to its trajectory with ease, and catch the crate once more.

Laughing with glee, you bound through the warehouse like gravity has suddenly weakened. Like you're playing on the moon. The fun is cut short, however, when several pawing, pounding ghouls find the warehouse. The moan is unmistakable. There are a *lot* of the fiends outside.

"What about guns?" you ask.

"Even better," Droakam says, stepping to a slender, rifle-sized crate.

This one is labeled BUZZKILL and the agent opens it to reveal an enormous broadsword; something that looks like it fell off the pages of a Japanese Manga. Droakam hefts the weapon out of its case, letting its considerable weight rest on the concrete floor.

"Some of the egg-heads at DARPA figured body-armor might get to a point where guns would soon be obsolete, so they came up with this bad boy. Go ahead, take it."

Though it was an obvious effort for the man, the blade is weightless, with the help of your exoskeleton. The metallic surface is complex, like it's been laser-etched with a circuitry pattern. You find a large thumb-switch on the grip just below the hilt, and the sword lets out a soft hum when you switch it on. Touching the tip of the blade against the concrete, it melts through the floor like butter.

"*Buzz-Kill*. I get it, even if it's kind of a lame name."

"Beats calling it *The Vibrator of Death*," Droakam says. "Care to take it on a test run against our uninvited guests out there?"

You nod, and agents Bertram and Danly head to the doors, ready to slide the porthole open and allow you to charge through. As a final step, you pull out a gasmask from your rucksack and pull the black, rubbery thing down over your face. What a sight you must make! Like some kind of comic book hero. A masked-man in green-scaled tights with some future snake-thingy against your sides and wielding a fantasy sword, Sims...*The Slayer!*

The agents barely manage to get the doors open before your super-strides bring you out into the crowd of fleshies beyond. Your sword technique is lacking, so you swing the thing like a baseball bat, but even so, the effect is devastating.

It's just like in the movies when someone swings a sword and nothing appears to happen until the other guy just slides into two pieces. The zombies fall in half, their innards pouring out like a bucket of nightcrawlers. You wade through the muck, slicing the ghouls with near-effortlessness. A pinch on your leg draws attention to half of an undead man gnawing on the Dino-Skin on your calf.

You pick up the torso and fling it several hundred yards away. This is like fighting a gang of preschoolers. Preschoolers made of play-dough. In a few quick moves you've dispatched dozens of zombies. And you're not even out of breath. Normally, you get out of breath chugging a beer.

This. Is. Amazing! You turn back to applause from the three agents and the pilot. Looking over the hundreds of crates, you can't help but swell with hope.

"I knew there'd be some kind of government rescue in an event like this, I just never thought I'd be part of it," you say. "We're going to save the goddamned world, so..."

[Go to page 104](#)

Single Payer

"I'm sorry, but I don't think it works that way," the doctor says with a laugh, though you can tell she knew your question was serious. "Don't worry, the National Guard has everything under control. You're safe here. Try to get some rest."

And with that, she's gone.

Even though you're exhausted, you're pretty sure you're not supposed to sleep with a head injury. Where did you hear that? From the boys on the football field, maybe. The doc did say to rest, but probably just meant to take it easy.

There's not much here in the way of entertainment. Somebody has a paperback called *Reapers*, but that seems a bit morbid, given the situation. You try your cellphone, but the screen is shattered. Looks like the phone's final act of defiance was to protect your thigh against a police baton.

When you look up, you see people passing around a huge subway sandwich, tearing off pieces in a literal act of breaking bread. The woman with the bucket takes a piece, but evidently she can't stomach it right now, so she leaves it on her cot opposite the bucket.

Then she passes the sandwich to you.

➤ Eat up, best to keep your strength. Go to page 264
➤ Wave it off and lie down for a bit. Go to page 393

Sinking

Two hours later, the scene repeats itself. This time, it's the man whose cot was next to the last ghoul. Luckily, he was nice enough to bite into the guy with the leg cast instead of you. The guards come, take the *Turned* man, and day folds into night as you wait for whoever's up next.

At some point, as boredom sinks in and adrenaline sails off, you fall asleep. You really weren't planning on sleeping tonight, but despite your best efforts, sleep comes. Exhaustion has a way of doing that.

You have a nightmare that you're sinking through the inky-black depths of the sea, falling away from the night. When you fall off your cot, you wake up. Only…you didn't fall. You were pulled off. It's Bucket Girl and Castman, both *Turned*. Both tear into you.

A scream bubbles up, but the infected woman tears out your throat before it can manifest. Now that you can't breathe, it's easy for the pair to eat you alive.

THE END

The Sixth Man

Jose follows you, well, because he can't speak English and that's the man's *modus operandi*. You head towards the signs for *Squeeeensland*, the amusement park's very own waterpark district. Thinking aloud, you say, "If Hefty figures out the food situation, we'll need water. Lots of tanks down here. Just need to figure out at what point the chlorine is added and stop the process."

Jose nods, a blank look on his face.

"You're a good man, know that, Jose?"

Same reaction.

Gulls and other birds have returned to the park, and you can hear them squawking overhead. As you continue into the waterpark, you're surprised to hear the gurgling of water and spray of rides, though the groaning equipment seems stressed. A bloated corpse floats in the entrance fountain, which sprays a rosy-pink fondue of viscera.

Catching yourself from retching, you see that most of the waterpark is clogged with bodies and clothing. If there is fresh water, it'd better be upstream from this cesspool.

The main attraction in *Squeeeensland* is a wave pool, where several ghouls flail about, unable to escape the tide. Zombies don't swim, it seems, and the current is stronger than their will. For now.

"Let's go," you say. "We'll have to do a full cleanup once we know the park is secure."

Jose nods, a blank look on his face.

Back at the front, you're forced to wait for the group. They're late. Which either means they got into some kind of trouble, or they're simply undisciplined. As it turns out, they've found another survivor.

Tyberius, Hefty, and Angelica approach with a military man in battle uniform and a black gasmask over his face. He's covered top to bottom with tactical gear and reminds you a lot of the survivalists at Duke's compound. You already don't like him.

Still, they don't look like they're being held hostage, and the man doesn't even appear to be armed, save for an oversized knife. But there might be others. Might be a sniper watching you right now. Better find out for sure.

- Take Tyberius aside, ask him for the low-down. Go to page 348
- Take Hefty aside, ask him for the skinny. Go to page 182
- Take Angelica aside, ask her to shed some light. Go to page 148

Skeletons in the Closet (and Trunk)

"Jesus, Kay," Craig says.

"No, she's right," Owen says. "Brian, you and Stephen pick him up. It's not the best place, I know, but we'll bury the man proper when this is all over."

You open the trunk to the Honda sedan sitting on the automotive raising-platform, readying it for the guys. Brian nods and Stephen simply gets to it, but when they grab Josh, his corpse suddenly moves.

"He's not dead!" you shout without thinking.

Realizing your error, you clamp your hands over your mouth. Too late. Both men look to you, and in that instant Josh grabs hold of Brian's arm and bites into it with a ferocity the man never had in life.

Brian screams bloody murder; high-pitched like a child. Owen grapples with Josh, but it's like trying to wrestle a speed-freak. You run to the nearest tool bin and grab a wrench. From behind, you put the wrench in Josh's mouth length-wise, like you might do with someone having a seizure. He keeps biting with such force that he cracks his teeth on the wrench, and enamel splinters off in a disgusting display.

"In the trunk!" you shout, angling towards the car.

It takes considerable effort, but the three of you get Josh off of Brian and into the trunk. After slamming the door shut, you use the pneumatic lift to raise the car on the platform. Josh continues thrashing inside the trunk, moaning and wailing.

"Shut him up!" Craig shouts. "There's more out here...they, they *hear* him...they're coming!!!"

You look out one of the porthole windows on the garage door and see that he's right. Already, there are a dozen shambling figures. Heads lolling about on uneven shoulders, arms outstretched, moaning with flesh-eating greed.

"The moaning is drawing them in," you say with realization. "Bring the car back down. We have to finish this." The men looked panicked, but none protest. Owen lowers the car. Everyone looks to you, and you realize you're still holding the wrench. "Pussies," you say. "Open it."

As they do, Josh lurches out, crazed as ever. You take both hands and baseball-swing the wrench at his face; his head spurts flesh and *cracks* under the impact. He bounces off the trunk lid, but still is in a frenzy. You hit him again and again, until the force of the blow smashes his skull open against the trunk lid.

"How long ago was Josh bit?" you ask.

Owen looks to the clock. "Six hours, roughly."

"So Brian has until midnight, give or take," you say.

"Until what?" Brian says, panic on his face.

"What're you saying?" Stephen asks, with eyes narrowed.

- ➤ "We need to put Brian out of his misery, now, before this spreads any further."
  Go to page 225
- ➤ "We should tie him up or something. You saw what happened to Josh."
  Go to page 44

Skinned-Heads

Running with the Aryan Brotherhood has equated with "doing what you gotta do to survive" since long before you came here. In fact, you'd wager that less than ten percent in the gang are genuine fascists, just those looking for protection from the Latino and the black gangs.

While running, you ask the con who invited you along if he knows about the plan.

"They got a lot of ours in the sick bay," he says. "We break 'em out, then push forward to the front gates. Hot-wire some cars, and G-T-F-O*h yeah*, know what I'm sayin'?"

You nod, excited right down to your core by the prospect of freedom.

However, once you make it inside the hospital, you immediately realize something is terribly wrong. The place is trashed. Dark fluids are spattered like a horror-themed wallpaper.

"Billy Ray, let's go!" the con shouts to a man who stumbles towards him, arms open and moaning.

"You can't talk to these nutters," you say. "Best—"

Before you can finish, a scream bubbles up from inside as you're bitten in the back of the head. The bastard is actually going for your brain, just like in a B-movie. Instead, his teeth tear at your scalp. The skinhead gang pulls the man off of you, but the damage is done.

You're INFECTED!

Smash and Grab

You shoot a nail through the man's forearm, and he cries out in pain, dropping his weapon. To his credit, he recovers quickly with a helluva left hook. He's much bigger than you (who isn't?), and the blow sends you reeling.

Not wanting to lose the upper hand, you swing your pipe at his legs. He jumps back, but not fast enough, and you connect with his left shin. His bone sings out in a terrible crunch and the man roars in response.

You swing the pipe back for another blow and he actually leaps at you. He takes a hit from the pipe, but his momentum holds, and he tackles you onto the glass by the entrance. Landing on top of you, he pushes the pipe away.

Finally, you get a good look at the guy. He's a young black man, sweat beading off his brow and anger in his strikingly intelligent eyes. He wears a businessman's shirt and you bring the nail gun up to his chest, letting out nail after nail as fast as you can.

Still, the guy's clearly a born athlete, and he pushes the nail gun aside with his wounded arm and wails on you with that left hook. Your vision explodes with starlight over and over as he pummels you. After a dozen pounding cracks to your skull, you lose consciousness, never to wake again.

THE END

Some Rescue

No time to argue, you charge forward, darting around the SWAT-things, past the entrance and over to the cafeteria barricade. You're not the most agile or athletic, but the fleshies have even less coordination. Still, what they lack in finesse they make up in passion. The undead stumble-run your way.

"Clear these barriers!" you yell.

The terrified crowd looks at you with stunned expressions, but none move. One man yells something that might be "It's not safe!"–and suddenly they're all pointing behind you.

When you turn, you see that the SWAT zombies are nearly on top of you. Behind them, an-ever-crowing crowd of undead hospital workers. Your rifle is useless against their body armor, but you fire anyway. What else can you do?

The riot-gear ghouls pull you to the floor and snap their jaws behind their face-masks, mashing the shields against your flesh in an effort to bite. If it were only the six of them, this would be a wrestling match from hell. But as it stands, they brought company, and those in hospital gowns prove more deadly.

There won't be enough of you left to rise again.

THE END

Sorry, We're Closed

You motion for the children to stand back, putting yourself between the door and the group. Master Hanzo hands you a wooden *shinai*, just in case. The moaning cries quickly turn to bloodcurdling screams, and then a pair of gunshots ring out.

"Open the karate gym doors!" a voice rings out, clear as day.

When you look out, you find Captain Delozier with a handheld megaphone. Opening the door, a few of his men stand nearby a body and a wounded man stumbles inside and falls to the floor.

"Dad!" Christian yells, running to the man's side.

Despite his writhing in pain, you recognize the man as the boy's father. He cradles his own hands, which appear to have bite wounds on them.

"What the hell happened here?" Captain Delozier asks, lowering the megaphone.

"In truth, I do not know," you say. "I kept the doors closed and locked until you arrived."

"Good call."

Christian looks up at the army captain, then at you. Tears stream down his face. "Why didn't you let him in? I hate you!"

He lunges at you, and you simply take it, as the teen beats his fists into your chest, coming eventually to lean against you in a sobbing hug. You wrap your arms around Christian and allow him his grief. *Six hours,* your sister's voice says in your head. *Then a walking corpse.*

"What will happen to this boy's father?" you ask.

"We've got a doctor back at the camp. She'll see to him."

"I'm coming too," Christian says, breaking free from your hold and wiping his eyes.

"Christian-*san*..."

"The boy should have time with his father," Master Hanzo agrees.

Captain Delozier nods, then motions for his soldiers to come grab the man.

"You'll keep the boy safe?"

"Of course," the captain replies, though he doesn't meet your gaze. With that, they're all gone.

"Back to sleep," you tell your students. They obviously want to talk about what just happened, about what *is happening,* and so do you, but what would you say? There is an old saying your father used to say when people were hasty to judge: *A frog in a well does not know the great sea.*

Lying awake in the dark, you simply listen to the children breathing around you. Salvator is gone, and now Christian. For the better? Who can say? Eventually, you come to the conclusion:

➤ My responsibility is to the tadpoles in the well with me. Hard as it may be, I must push the others from my mind and live in the here and now. Go to page 342

➤ I will ask about the other boys tomorrow. Captain Delozier should be reminded of his responsibilities, too. Go to page 388

Sounds of Silence

The next morning, you're up early with Master Hanzo. The two of you share a pot of tea in silence, both knowing full well that the rest of the day will likely bring chaos. The morning sun slowly overtakes the hardware store across the street, and in turn, the peaceful dawn is overtaken by the sounds of children waking, when daylight penetrates the glass doors.

"Morning meditations," you say, hoping to extend the early peace.

Class is still sitting in relative silence, stretching if not meditating, when a few soldiers show up to deliver breakfast. Captain Delozier is not amongst them. They're doing "grunt work," if you understand the parlance correctly.

After thanking the men, you instruct Nolan and Mason to pass out the meals, which are miraculously enjoyed in silence. At length, Master Hanzo rises and excuses himself. "Local news begins soon," he says. "Time to monitor the radio."

"Can we listen?" Haley asks.

"Hmmm," you intone, thinking, *Is it better to shelter the students from the state of the world, or is knowledge power, in this case?*

- ➢ "No. Grandfather Hanzo will tell us if there is an important announcement. It's time for class. Consider yourself lucky—you will all be ready to test for your next *kyu*-rank after a few days stuck in here!" Go to page 184
- ➢ "Yes, we should all listen. Strong body, strong mind. It is all one. To be able to defend ourselves, we must be fully aware of the surrounding world." Go to page 302

Spared No Expense

As far as electrical tasks go, starting up the tram is a breeze. The park still has power, so either the rolling blackouts haven't affected this part of the city's grid, or the park is on its own supply. You'll want to find that out sooner or later, but for now—it's time for a tour.

The tram itself is ten cars long, and each car is designed to be unique from the others—like a carrousel, where you get a handful of eclectic choices to fit your personality. One car is a dragon, one is an Old West covered wagon; that sort of thing. You pick the third tram car, the one that looks like a spaceship, because it's the only one fully enclosed.

Sure, the voice actor narrating your tour is Carrot Top, and that alone makes you envious of the dead, but this is the best way to hit the highlights of the park. A few wandering fleshies grow curious from the noise and movement, and, save for the one that slaps against your window and bounces off, they stumble slower than the tram moves so you're safe.

First up is the entrance to *The Bramble,* a man-made wrought-iron "hedge-maze" that offers free prizes for anyone who can make their way through in under an hour. In order to keep the solution top-secret, the maze is covered so it can't be seen from the famous Ferris wheel.

And the coasters happen to be the next part of the tour. Swooping tracks arc high into the air and one, suspended upside-down, still has passengers trapped aboard. You jump up to the window, squinting to get a better view. As the tram car rolls under the coaster, you see that the whole group are undead, stretching and moaning. The darker parts of your imagination picture the group turning one-by-one, passing the infection six hours at a time over the course of a week, like hell's version of the telephone game.

Next, you're shown the *Forever Young* district, where the kiddie rides reside, as well as an enormous Fun House that during the Halloween season is redecorated as a haunted house "for big kids only," alongside the park's petting zoo and pony ride stations. The irony that *everyone* infected by *Gilgazyme*® is now forever young is somewhat overshadowed by the sight of several pint-sized walking corpses. And now the electronic, pre-recorded children's laughter that fills the tram car feels like gallows humor.

Trying not to think about it, you crane your neck to see the next part of the tour—passing over a lazy-river moat to a castle-themed hotel on-site; a full resort with swimming pool, restaurants, and a mini-golf course free for patrons. Might be a pretty nice place to hang your gasmask for the night, especially with the power still running.

As the tram rounds the northeast corner of the park, you see something on the tracks up ahead. It's one of those infirm-and-obese carts, this one long enough to carry about a dozen mobility-challenged passengers. The cart sits tipped over, crashed right in the middle of the track.

➢ Buckle up and brace for impact! Go to page 372
➢ Jump out of the tram before it derails! Go to page 95

Special Delivery

The contraband mail-route is simple enough. The guys in the laundry room pre-pack the bedding with this week's goods, so all you have to do is push the cart and distribute the neatly-folded stacks one-by-one along the cell blocks.

Like most things in prison, it's fairly dull work. The contraband sits tucked deep inside the blankets, so you don't even get to spy on your fellow prisoners to see what lurid items they paid to have imported. That particular job is a dangerous one, and not fit for someone with goals of one day getting released.

Most of the blankets crinkle when you pass the stack through the bars, hinting at the porno mags inside. Other than that, the most prevalent sound is the shaking of pill bottles. The inmates accept their goods with a nod, then wait for you to pass to the next cell before greedily inspecting their laundry for the good stuff. One cell after another, just the same as the one before.

Which makes it all the more shocking when mafia boss Vito D'lunga rips into his bedding like a kid on Christmas. You can't help but linger behind. What's got the Don so excited?

He giggles—yes, the hardened mafia boss actually *giggles*—when finds what he's looking for. He holds it up for inspection, allowing you a good look. The object is small, no bigger than the palm of his hand, but when he positions it between his thumb and forefingers to the light, the gunmetal blue and silver loops shimmer. It's a Gilgazyme® inhaler, just like on TV. Looking past the contraband, the Don catches your gaze. *Time to get out of here.*

"Know what this is?" D'lunga asks.

"I ain't a rat," you say, swallowing hard.

The mob boss lets out a belly-laugh. "Relax. Take a look. It's probably the closest you'll ever get to one of these things. Makes you live forever, know that?"

"So they say…."

"Costs a fortune, but it'll be worth it. Know why I smuggled it in?"

You shake your head, wiping sweaty palms against your jumpsuit. To have a private audience with Don Vito is usually bad news for someone outside *The Family*.

"I'm in for a hundred-eighty-year sentence, know that? A hundred and eighty years, if you believe that shit. That's really a death sentence, 'cept handed out by pussies. But the joke's on them, my friend. I'm going to be the first convict with the book thrown at him to catch the damn thing and add it to my private library. Hundred-eighty-years ain't nothin' to a man who'll live forever."

You swallow again, throat practically cracking with dryness, but he's waiting for a response. All you can think to say is, "Not worried 'bout the celebrity murders? The…uhhh…cannibals?"

He smiles. "When you'se a god, only natural to get a little drunk with power."

And with that, he turns away from the bars and into his cell. Looks like your cue to continue the route, and with shivers running down your spine, you speed through the rest of the deliveries.

➢ *Finish up and head to your own cell.* Go to page 220

Spoils

You help Sam Colt with the creaky metal doors and wait as Captain Delozier comes inside. The officer enters with a nod to Sam, and then a dozen soldiers file in behind him. Though many of the men wear gasmasks, most take them off when they enter the store. They openly take stock of the store...and of Lily.

"What's the situation, Captain?" Sam asks.

"FUBAR. These lunatics keep popping up everywhere, with the hospital as ground zero. They're marching us in there like lemmings."

"Then what're you doing here?" Lily asks.

Sam gives her a look, which she ignores. The Captain, however, looks furious.

"My duty is to my men," he says.

"We're happy to have you here, Captain." Sam says. "Please make yourself at home."

"Goddamn right we will," one of the soldiers grumbles.

"Cool it," Delozier snaps, and the man shuts up. "Sam, give me a tour, will you?"

Sam nods. "Lily, help the guys get settled in."

Captain Delozier follows Sam towards the stairs and you can hear Sam saying something about the rooftop garden just before they disappear behind the stairwell door. The soldiers look around the store and you just hang back. Not long ago, these guys saw you as a threat.

Lily clears her throat. "Food is what you brought with you, water is in the buckets by the stairs or up on the roof. I guess we'll have to figure out sleeping arrangements sooner or later. Bathrooms are in the back."

"Can you show me?" one of the guys asks, with a grin you don't quite like.

"The bathroom? They're back there."

"C'mon...show me."

Lily shrugs, then walks towards the back. Some of the men shake their heads, but they do so with smiles. You step forward, watching, on edge.

"First stop, men's room!" she says, with an exaggerated "ta-da" of her arms.

"What's inside?" he asks.

"Probably a toilet," she says.

"You sure? Show me." She laughs, like the guy is putting her on. "Go on, I can tell you want to."

"Uhh, you can fuck off now."

"I won't tell the mister if you don't. Help me get 'settled in'...I don't bite."

➢ Okay, enough is enough. Remind the guy that the lady said he can fuck off. Go to page 278

➢ Stay put. She can handle herself. Go to page 156

Squad Goals

Your pupils come to seated attention; resting atop their ankles with palms flat on their thighs. You turn to Haley and nod. She shrugs and giggles, her blue eyes and braces twinkling in unison.

"No room to improve? What about stride length? Or your tendency to bounce before an attack, thus telegraphing intent to your opponent?"

"Yes, sensei," she says, looking down.

"Nathanael?"

"Um, to like, focus my *Ki*. Be more vocal, I guess."

You nod, then turn to Christian, who says, "I wanna find out if I'm ready for the next level *kyu* test."

A small laugh escapes before you can help it. "If you have to ask if you're ready, then you are not."

"Awww," he says, bouncing and rocking back on his heels.

"Do not 'awww.' I asked for goals for *today*. Kendo exists only in the now. When you speak of next year, the spirits laugh."

He looks down and shrugs. "Well, just get better, then. Faster."

"Stronger!" Mason shouts. Everyone chuckles, and you give a smiling nod.

Nolan clears his throat. "My dad says to practice my grip."

"Very wise."

"I want to win," Liam says, eyes narrowed like he's offering sage wisdom.

"Me too," Stella says.

"Losing is a better teacher than winning," you say. "And to count wins is to measure the length of your acorns; time is better spent gathering, just as with experience. Now then—what about our new student. Salvator?"

The young boy, probably around 6 years old, looks to his mother for help. She sits off to the side, attention on her cellphone, and crosses one leg of her elaborately printed yoga pants over the other. Not finding the answer there, he turns back and simply shakes his head.

"For a first day, I'd recommend your goal be: to be able to tell your mother three new things about Kendo when time comes to go home."

"Okay…" he says, almost a whisper.

"First lesson, answer, 'Yes, sensei' or 'Master Tesshu,' okay?"

"Sin…say?" he tries.

"That's right."

You stand and say:

➢ *"Class, I'm going to show our new pupil around. Set up drill stations."* Go to page 256

Start a Riot

The junkie isn't holding his weapon like he's ready to fire, so you know you can get the drop on him. Even better, if he's either high or going through withdrawals, his hand-to-eye coordination won't be up to par. Still, you know better than to engage without cover.

The trash can off to your left should work perfectly. In a practiced paintball move, you dive to the side, roll into a somersault, and pop up just behind the waste bin. With your rifle barrel resting against the top, you *pop* three shots in quick succession—two to the chest; one to the head.

The junkie is down before he knows what hit him. You look to Jason—your brother has taken cover back against the hallway wall. The woman screams and rushes to her companion's side. You step up to the pharmacy window and tap on the glass.

"You're welcome," you say. "Now I need something for my dad. He's been bitten, what can you give me?"

The old man behind the glass slowly shakes his head.

"Are you freaking kidding me? Can't I get some antibiotics or—?"

"I'd help you if I could. I don't know how to treat your father, but if you find a doctor, someone who could prescribe the right medication...."

You give a groaning sigh and turn from the window. Your eyes grow wide at the sight of a man in full riot gear, aiming his submachine gun your way. You see a stern expression etched onto the hardened man behind his faceplate, and a USMC globe, eagle, and anchor tattoo on his neck.

➢ Yell "Semper Fi!" and drop your weapon. Go to page 21
➢ Screw it, shoot this guy too. Go to page 255

Street Smarts

You call out to Tyberius, who comes to join you and Jose while Hefty and Angelica stay with the new guy.

"What's going on here?" you ask. "Everything okay?"

"Yeah, it's cool, Coop. Dude actually messed his shoulder up pretty good while trying to save Angie."

"Hero type?"

"Eh, let's just say it's a good thing Hef and I heard the screams and came running."

"Hmm. Do you trust him?"

Tyberius purses his lips, then bobbles his head slowly, thinking it over. "I mean, I guess. Enough, anyway. I had a few run-ins with the National Guard when they was still up and running. Can't say I trust they had my best interests at heart, if you know what I mean, but this Sims dude assures me he's no longer operating under orders. That's not to say he won't be in the future. Keeps talking about signaling rescue. I see it like this: he comes from a pack of wolves, and I'm not gonna lie that scares me, but now that he's out and alone, he could be adopted to become our guard dog."

"Thanks," you say with a nod.

Maybe Tyberius is right and the new guy could be helpful. Maybe he is a sheep in wolf's clothing. Or maybe he is a junkyard dog who just needs training. Either way, it's probably a good idea to keep him close. But first…you need to assert dominance. Or maybe get a second opinion from one of the others?

- ➢ Introduce yourself. Make sure he knows you're the boss. Go to page 383
- ➢ Take Angelica aside, ask her to shed some light. Go to page 148
- ➢ Take Hefty aside, ask him for the skinny. Go to page 182

Strength in Numbers

You rush the trio of nutters, slamming the butt of the fire extinguisher as hard as you can into the skull of the nearest one.

"Come on!" you shout.

The office door swings open and the guard smashes into one of the ghouls with his Asp baton. The doctor cowers behind the correctional officer, so you and the guard finish off the third flesh-eating bastard together.

Once their undead bodies stop twitching, the guard looks you over. He removes a pair of handcuffs and you raise your hands, shaking your head and back away.

"I'll get the two of you out of here," the cop says. "But we can't have inmates running amok. If the warden sees us…"

Say:

- "Fuck you, and fuck the warden. You ain't cuffin' me." Go to page 298
- "You need me much as I need you. Let's go." Go to page 217

Stuck in the Middle

The C-17 booms down the runway, cutting a hole in the crowd. Garcia and the agents follow in its wake, using the cleared path to take off just behind the larger plane. They wax and wane under the strong currents left by the behemoth C-17, but they make it out.

Turning your focus back to *terra firma*, you're greeted by twenty-thousand hungry eyes. It's only about one-percent of the ghouls swarming the airport, but that's more than enough. The pilot was able to stay here in quiet solitude, but once they taxied out, this hangar drew quite a bit of interest.

Instinctively, you back into the hangar, then turn to run for an alternate entrance. As a matter of security, there's no back door. There's a big storage cabinet in the back and—reverting to child-like fear—you open the doors, hop inside, and hide, with your eyes closed.

The growling moans and shuffle of feet grow louder, and finally there's a clawing on the cabinet doors before the ghouls manage to pry the cabinet open.

Peek-a-boo, we see you!

THE END

Subway: Eat Flesh!

Out front, there's a fake plant potted in real soil, which you use to break the glass door and let yourself in. An alarm wails in response, but it blends in with the drone of sirens on the ambulances headed to the limo crash scene. Fun fact: Did you know that your best chance of getting away with robbery is during a disaster? The police are too busy actually *helping people* to come check out a bank in distress.

Still, you'd better make this fast food. They'll come by to check it out eventually. The alarm is wailing like a banshee, but luckily you have a pair of earplugs in the front pocket of your shirt to wear during loud jobs in the garage. They'll work here too.

For easy pickin's, you've got the rows of single-serve chip bags and the cookie display. But the sandwiches are made "fresh to order," so you're kind of out of luck there. Handfuls of meat and cheese? Maybe the bagged apple slices and bottles of chocolate milk in the fridge?

You hop over the counter in search of a to-go bag and see bloody footprints on the linoleum behind the sandwich bar. Your gaze follows the tracks to a breakroom and two pair of feet—lying down, one on top of the other.

Morbid curiosity draws you closer and you see a teenage employee with acne hunched over her middle-aged manager, scooping handfuls of his mid-section into her hungry maw. You must've gasped at the sight, because the ghoulish teen's head suddenly snaps towards you, eyes dead but staring intently.

Then she rises, unnaturally, like a snake floating out of a basket under a charmer's spell. With equally fluid, almost drunken, movements she comes for you.

"No! Stay back!" you shout.

You slam back against the counter and the cash register pops out in response. You turn to vault over the counter, but the teen grabs onto your mechanic's shirt and opens her mouth. Your arms shoot up in response, taking the girl by the throat. As someone who twists wrenches for a living, you have a tough grip, but the strangulation doesn't slow her in the least.

In fact, she's not even breathing.

Frantic, you look for a weapon. There's a small sandwich knife with a green handle that'll have to do. As you reach out with your right arm for the knife, the fiend lunges closer. You're strong, but there's something almost supernatural about her pull. Like she's at 100% strength and unable to dial down. Maybe drugs?

You stab her in the chest with the knife, plunging it down to the handle. Nothing, no response. No spurting blood, either. At the last possible second, you get the knife free and stick it under her chin, shoving her mouth closed and pushing the blade inside. All the way, until your palm is flat against her neck and the knife sinks inside her head.

She collapses, dead. What. The. Fuck? No real choice here:

➤ *Now that you've added murder to B&E, better get out of here.* Go to page 385

Survive!

"I'll call an ambulance, you and Jay get this guy into your bed for now," Dad says.

"But, Dad!" Jason protests.

"No. We don't know how this whole thing works yet, so we do what we can for our fellow man. Got it?" he says. You can't help but think of Dad's own bite wound.

Jason nods and the pair of you go about the task without another word. When you lay the man down in your room, you see a mark on his left palm. It looks like a bite, only without blood or signs of infection. Like it's old and dried-out. Still, the man seems to be at peace; resting with ease.

Back in the living room, Dad looks at his cell phone with concern. "911 is busy..." he says.

Then, in a fit of vertigo, he stumbles backward and falls on the couch, his head diving into his hands with a massive migraine. Composing himself, he says, "I just need to lie down a bit."

You're about to follow your father to his room, but Jason intercepts you with a compass and terrain map. "Let's plot the shortest route from home to the woods, you know, in case we have to get outta Dodge."

"Jay, I'm really worried about Dad," you say, voice thick with emotion.

"That's why we need to do the planning, right? 'Be like Rosie,' remember?"

You look away, unsure of yourself for the first time since you tried out for the track team. "You were never cut out to be a shot-putter," Coach said. But you overcame that, and you can overcome this too. You'll just have to think realistically, just like coach showed you. *That's* how you won the 800-meter.

Could running now be the best course of action? The world out there is a crazy place, and getting worse by the minute. You barely made it home from the range in all that traffic. Even so, you're not only thinking of yourself. How can you hope to drag a sick man out of town with only your kid brother for help?

"TV," you say with a nod towards the screen. "There should be reports of road closures, and we can mark those on the map."

Jason smiles, happy to have you back on board. He flips on the TV, where Alison Argyle, oddly calm, reads from the teleprompter, "In an ironic twist, it seems many of those killed are users of the new longevity wonder drug Gilgazyme®. It's still unknown if there is a connection between the drug and the homicide sweep hitting major urban centers across the country. No spokesperson for the creators of Gilgazyme® has agreed to comment as of this broadcast..."

The television is suddenly taken into local control and your community Sheriff appears on the screen.

"The Governor has declared a state of emergency," the Sheriff announces. "But we are as of yet unprepared for any sort of mass evacuation. We're working as hard as we can to set up aid stations and sanctuaries. In the meantime, work with friends and neighbors. Find a group. Nobody can beat this thing alone. And...we need all the help we can get."

The image switches to a stationary, soundless PLEASE STAND BY message. There you have it. You're on your own, but so is everyone else. Maybe it's time to find some help?

- The church. Take Dad and the wounded man in the Jeep. They wouldn't turn you away and wasn't there just a canned food drive? Go to page 354
- Skip town. Even though it'll be dangerous traveling with a bitten man, you're not ready to abandon Dad. Go to page 410
- The hospital. 911 isn't answering, so you'll have to take a doctor hostage and force him to help the wounded in your home. Go to page 100
- Let Dad rest a bit, head to the mall to pick up a few essentials. By the time you get back, he should know what to do. Go to page 311

Take Me to Church

The sun shines brightly, the last hurrah before dusk settles in, and there's an odd stillness in the air. No sirens, though smoke still columns on the horizon. If you weren't carrying weapons and two wounded men, it would be just like the drive you make most Sundays.

Driving quickly, using people's front lawns as your personal 4x4 detour route, it's not long before the stark spires of the gothic cathedral come into view. You park the Jeep and head up the walkway to the entry.

This is *your* church. You were baptized here. Confirmed here. Attended mass here. Dad didn't take you every Sunday, but he was no Christmas Catholic either. Whenever he got the itch for church, you knew it was because he missed mom more than usual that week. Now, God willing, this cathedral will be a sanctuary when you need it most.

"Are you wounded? Bitten?" the priest asks, stepping out from behind thick wooden doors and onto the stone steps of the entry.

You recognize the man—Father Thomas. He eyes your weapons, but you're not sure if it's nerves or relief on his face. He's hunched, grips the door with white knuckles, and speaks in an urgent whisper. His white collar is starting to turn brown from sweat.

"No, but we have two men in the car who are. Dad and some guy. Can you help?"

Father Thomas ushers you inside with open arms. "Of course, my children. Come in. The sisters are sorting donations in the annex and many parishioners are already in the main hall. Take your time, look around, see where you might help us while we help you. Give me a few minutes and I'll have some of the men bring in your wounded."

You nod, turn to Jason and say:

➢ "Donations? I suppose we should see what they've got in terms of food and medical supplies." Go to page 23
➢ "I want to do a headcount on who's here, and what state they're in. Let's check the main hall." Go to page 287
➢ "All that can wait. Dad's in pretty rough shape; we should probably stay with him." Go to page 272

Taken

"Sorry? For what?" she says, then her eyes grow wide when you reach out for her.

The doctor struggles, but you're a big man and it's easy to maneuver her around. A guilty feeling rises up, but you push it back down. She'll be fine; she's just your ticket out of here.

When you push through the entry flap of the tent, you see one gas-masked guard at the ready, while two more play checkers nearby.

"One of the *Turned* is attacking the doc!" the on-duty guard shouts.

"Damn, I liked her too," one of the others says.

They ready their weapons and without so much as a second thought: shoot. You want to scream that you're not infected, that this is in fact a hostage situation, but there's no time. These guys were as ready as a firing squad.

THE END

Take the Bait

"Guard!" you yell.

Arms folded, you wait. Still the fiend shuffles towards you. What the hell is taking so long?

"Hey, *GUARD!!!*"

You look to the front flap of the tent while you holler, but still nothing. Figures. Cops only show up when you've done something wrong. When you turn back, the fiend lunges at you and you put up your hands to block her. As she takes the fingers of your left hand into her mouth, you let out a blood-curdling scream.

The screams finally bring in the guard from outside, and he stands with his rifle at the ready. "Another two *Turned*," he says into a chest-radio. "Go for a transfer to aggressor tent."

With a quick kick, you knock the woman off. She brings one of your fingers with her.

"Goddamn! Take your fucking time, why don't you?! Just look at this!" you shout at the guard.

Indeed, just look at that hand.

You're INFECTED!

Taking Out the Trash

Jason holds the door open, careful to step out of the way while you stain the carpet red and drag the corpse by the ankles through the doorway.

The cool of evening settles in on the neighborhood, but not the peaceful chitters of suburbia you've grown up with. You leave the corpse curbside (ready for pickup!) and turn towards a new noise. A man backpedals, staying just out of reach of a woman who shambles after him on a broken ankle. Her jagged fingernails swat at the air between them.

"Please stop!" the man sobs. "What's the matter with you? Stop, Honey…"

Part of you wants to end it, to shoot her. Hell, part of you wants to shoot them both. But you move back into the house, shaking, on the verge of crying. You look at the red carpet entrance, following the blood trail, and come to a spatter of brain against the wall. The picture of Grandpa from WWII has miraculously stayed clean, but the black-and-white photo of Eisenhower chewing out his generals is filthy.

"That needs to be us," Dad says. "They had no clue the horrors they were getting into, they just knew there was an evil that needed to be stopped. And that's what we're faced with now. See this?" he points to the framed art on the other side, the print of *Rosie the Riveter*.

She stares at you with her stern determination, rolling her sleeve with fist pumped in the air, flecks of blood against the glass frame adorning her uniform in an apropos symbol of your own call to action. She proudly proclaims, *"We Can Do It!"*

"I need you to be like Rosie, Sport," your father says, the same look of determination on his face.

Do you have it in you? *Rosie the Riveter* was a symbol. A leader of those who grew up thinking they were helpless; that other people were in charge of the world. She inspired a generation to stand up and do their part. How can you be like Rosie?

Not much of a choice here:

➢ *Mask your uncertainty. Stand tall, shoulders back, and say, "What do I need to do?"*
  <u>Go to page 352</u>

Talking Heads

"*This*," Sam says, spreading his arms wide. "Everywhere."

"But what was wrong with that lady?"

"That 'lady' is one of the infected," Lily says.

"Infected?" you parrot back.

"This is it, Ty. The end of the world. The dead are rising," Sam says. You just stare at him, so he continues, "I've seen it. Lily too. Someone gets bitten, maybe it kills you or maybe you just get real sick, but then you become one."

"It's always the same, every time," Lily adds.

"From what I've seen, it only takes a few hours to spread," Sam says.

"If they're infected—like a sickness—it can be treated, right?"

"Sure, there's a cure," Lily says, showing off her handgun. "Bullet to the brain; no more infection."

"How? How'd this...?"

"Does it matter?" Sam says, getting angry. "This is it, man. You're not a banker anymore. The city is lost, Ty. You need to accept it, sooner than later."

"Let's head back inside," Lily says, eyes still on the carnage at the horizon.

As you head back down, you try to let everything sink in. The end of the world? The apocalypse? The living dead? The city...lost? That's when it hits you.

"*Mama*—I need to get home!" you say.

"I don't think that's happening anytime soon, Ty," Sam answers.

Before you can reply, there's a heavy pounding on the metal doors from outside. It's definitely a "cop knock" and it sends a chill down your spine.

"I'll handle it," Sam says. He steps over to the doors and slides open an eye-level panel. "Captain Delozier, what can I do you for?"

"We're here for the runner, Sam," a man says. The voice is stern, even muffled by the National Guardsman's gasmask.

"I'll take responsibility for him. You have bigger problems, I'm sure."

There's a tense moment and Lily shifts, taking the pistol in both hands.

After what feels like ages, the Captain says, "How's Daisy? Need anything? Water?"

"*Lily* is fine, thanks. We're good here, Captain."

➢ Stay quiet, but try to call home as soon as they leave. Go to page 409
➢ Wait! Tell the Captain he has to let you go. You need to get home and protect your mother. Go to page 91

Talk is Cheap

"I'm sorry to hear about your father, but there's nothing we can do. We've seen a 100% mortality rate in those bitten, and they usually only last a matter of hours before…" the doctor says, letting the unspoken conclusion hang in the air.

"We need to focus on those who've not been infected," the second doctor adds. "We may not be able to save those like your father, but there are many others here who need our help."

Dammit, you know they're right. What're you going to do, shoot them if they don't come home? And only a matter of hours…it's already *been* a matter of hours. With a sigh, you shoulder your weapon and turn away.

The nurse you took hostage stands behind you with a syringe full of air, but lowers the needle and backs away, wide-eyed. What was she up to?

"Let's go, Jay," you say, giving the nurse the stink-eye.

Where to?

- ➤ How about a second opinion? To the ER! They'll have a better idea what to do in an emergency. Go to page 326
- ➤ Pharmacy. You have to try! Get some antibiotics or something. Go to page 285
- ➤ Better head home. If nothing else…to say goodbye. Go to page 83
- ➤ To the morgue. If these things really are coming back from the dead, the guys down there should know for sure. Go to page 150

Tango Down

Time to dispense with the pleasantries: Dad taught you early how to clear a room, in case of intruders in the dead of night, but the training proves unnecessary here. No one's hiding behind the door, hoping to get the drop on you.

Instead, as soon as you step in and flip on the light, the man rises from the bed. His jaw hangs slack and his eyes shine with hunger. He's no longer limp and delirious, he's focused—*on you*. In his frenzy to get out of the bed, he gets tripped up by the covers and falls to the floor. Growling like an animal, he thrashes to get free.

"Stay where you are!"

The man gains his footing and you fire a round into the bed as a warning shot, but that only excites him further. Okay, no denying it—this guy's *Zulu*. One shot in the chest, but it doesn't even slow him. Not with a 22-calibre rifle. But the two-shot burst into his forehead drops the man like a sack of flour.

You stare at the kill, crimson fluid pouring out of him so dark it's almost black, and your thoughts turn towards Dad. When you look back, Jason is gone. You turn and sprint back towards the master bedroom, but skid to a stop in the living room. Dad walks towards you—aided by Jason, who has the old man's arm slung over his shoulder.

"He's...?" you ask.

"Still with us," Jason replies. "Barely."

"Daddy, what do we do?"

His eyes blink open and with renewed clarity, he hisses, "*Leave!*"

"No! I won't. I won't leave you."

"Once bitten...soon biting...."

"You won't turn. I'll stop it, somehow."

Jason wipes his eyes, "If you want to stop it, you'll have to shoot him in the head like that guy."

"Jay, no!"

Dad stumbles forward, then gathers himself. With extreme effort, he says, "If you live...we live...with you..."

He enters a coughing fit and falls to the floor, wheezing. Then he stops breathing altogether.

"Dad? C'mon, Daddy. Wake up!" you shout.

And miraculously, he does. Though when he rises from the floor, there's nothing you recognize of your father in those pale, bloodless eyes.

"Oh, shit..." Jason says.

Dad's head snaps towards your brother and a low, guttural growl comes from his throat. The metal of your rifle is cold in your sweat-drenched palms. *Oh, God. This isn't happening!* You're frozen, paralyzed. Time creeps by, each second lasting a decade. *He can't be dead, he can't. He can't be one of those things!*

"No...!" Jason cries as Dad's hands rise up to embrace his son.

➢ You can't do it—you know you can't. Scream for Jason to run! Go to page 115
➢ That's not your Daddy. It's Zulu. Put him down. Go to page 270

T & Assets

No windows, nothing to loot, and no way in. Perfect. The large, sturdy door should provide protection against the undead and the living, if you can get the damned thing open. They meant business when they installed a slab with four locks on it.

There's what looks like a fire door out back, but it's nothing more than a door-shaped seam against the alley wall. No handle, nothing. You go back around to the front and try the entrance once more. Sighing in frustration, you turn to leave, but then the door opens.

Rifle up, you spin around. It's a bleached-blonde, orange-tan, fake-tittied stripper wearing a see-through lace robe and not much beneath it. You lower the rifle and swallow, hard.

"Don't go, mister," she says through pouty lips.

"Are you alone?" you ask.

She opens the door further to show a brunette with thickly applied eye-shadow and mascara wearing an oversized men's business shirt. She shifts her weight on her toned, bare legs and smiles meekly.

"It's just us," the blonde says. "And we don't bite."

"I...I don't have much. Coupla' MREs, but I'll share what I've got in exchange for a place to sleep, so...."

"We like to share," the brunette says with a wicked grin.

Despite the blood rushing away from your head, you take a moment to think. Is this where you want to bed down for the night? Or should you tell them you're gonna look around a bit first?

- ➤ What kind of nutless wonder would leave these helpless hotties all alone? Head on in! Go to page 318
- ➤ The liquor store. I could use a drink after these last couple of days and the windows have bars. Go to page 234
- ➤ The tattoo parlor. With its tough-guy design scheme, nobody will mess with me there. Go to page 180
- ➤ The payday loans building. With all the people they screw, they've gotta be ready for a mob invasion. Go to page 259

Three's a Crowd

"Couldn't sleep? Us neither. C'mon in," Tyberius says.

This is the biggest suite in the hotel, consisting of a master bedroom off to one side and another bedroom with a pair of queen-sized beds across the way. In the common area there's a pair of couches, a fireplace, and an entertainment center.

Tyberius drinks champagne straight from the bottle and you're about to ask where Hefty is when the sliding door to the balcony opens. The redneck steps through and doesn't see you at first. From the glazed look of their eyes, the duo has a few bottles' head start on you. Maybe they raided room service?

"Always wanted to piss off the top of a hotel…awww, shit! Mr. Wizard! What's up, man?"

"Mr. Wizard?" you ask.

"Yeah. That was some magical shit getting the power back on."

"Ahhh, it didn't actually go out here. All I had to do was reset the hotel breakers. Must not be on the same grid as downtown, so…." you shrug.

"Lemme axe you a question," Tyberius says. "If you really in the Army, why don't you have any guns? I'd have a fuckin' tank, man."

"Air Force, but you're right…a good soldier wouldn't be caught red without his firearm. Truth is, well, I lost mine a ways back. I'm kinda inside myself about the whole thing."

"I feel ya. Had a nail gun, lost it in a fight," Hefty says, plopping down on the couch.

You're feeling a bit ashamed, so you don't enlighten them on how you lost your gear. Instead, you offer, "As soon as I can signal rescue, I'll be re-armed. Shouldn't be too hard, so…."

Hefty leaps up off the couch. "See? I fuckin' knew they knew what was up. Government planned this whole thing. They's just waitin' to let the population drop while the *Chosen* sit in their bunkers. A population cull, man. Then they swoop in, establish a goddamned *stratocracy* and act like they doin' us a fuckin' favor. Tell him, Sims."

You swallow, hard. From what you learned on the C-17, the government did indeed know "what was up." But can you admit that? Will they trust you if you do?

Tyberius flips a decorative metal bowl from the coffee table, spilling the potpourri from inside, then places it on Hefty's head.

"It's not tin-foil, but it'll have to do, you crazy motherfucker!" Tyberius says with a laugh.

Hefty throws it off, then leaps onto Tyberius and the two men enter into a drunken wrestling match. You back away as they grunt and slam into the furniture.

"Uhhh, I'm pretty tired," you say. "Probably have a long day tomorrow, so…"

- ➢ Go check on Jose. Go to page 127
- ➢ Go check on Angelica. Go to page 165
- ➢ Go check on Cooper. Go to page 75
- ➢ Head back to your room and get some sleep. Go to page 396

Thrown Away

"Sure," Slim says, stepping forward. "That corner, there?"

You reflexively look where he points, and that's when he lunges for you. He swings the pipe to knock your rifle askew, but you're faster. The CO2 cartridge sends a dart from the rifle into the man's chest and he hits the floor before he can take another step.

His friend drops to his side and tries to shake the tranquilized man awake. Nope. "Hef?" he says, feeling for a pulse. "He's not breathing!"

You look to the rifle, thinking, *what was the dose was for, an elephant?*

When you look up, you see the big man rise from the floor, screaming for vengeance and swinging his hammer. You jump back, but his reach is better and he hits you in the rib cage. The whole event is narrated by Angelica's shrieking.

You actually hear the crunch of your bones breaking, but you don't feel a thing. Somehow you're on the floor too, thrown across the room from the blow. You taste blood, and as your vision fades, you see him rising up for another swing of his hammer.

Then Jose hits him in the back of the head with the frying pan and Mr. *Hammer Time* falls in a heap next to you. Jose tries to help you up, but when you move, there's a burst of pain. You cough blood and it's hard to get your breath. Seems like your own ribs impaled your lungs, and the pain proves more than your body can handle.

Everything goes dark, never to shine again.

THE END

Thug Life

The gangs tear through the yard, destroying everything in their path, rushing towards the other buildings in the prison. The giant chainlink fences are no match for hundreds of men pressed against them. Roughly half the group breaks off towards the armory, while the rest continue on to the motorpool. Both options have their appeal, but there are sure to be more inmates than there are either weapons or vehicles.

What's your priority?

- ➢ I'm rushing the armory with the violent offenders. Let the others crash the gates, I'll walk out behind with a shotgun in hand. *Boom boom,* Mutha Fucka! Go to page 78
- ➢ I gotta get me some wheels! Looks like Celly has the same idea too. Hurry on to the motorpool to get one of the few cars. Go to page 210

Tight to the Chest

"How might I help you, sir?" you ask, keeping mum about your earlier excursion.

"Listen, there's no way to put this, no easy way or what have you...." Captain Delozier says, practically rambling. Even in the low evening light, you can see beads of sweat condensing inside his gasmask faceplate.

"Once spilt, you can't pour *sake* back into the cup. Come out with it, whatever it is."

"Right, okay. We're leaving tomorrow. My superiors are pulling us out. We're evacuating to the hospital and trying for a fallback point—" he abruptly stops himself. Does he know of the 'Salvation' camp? He studies your face, perhaps wondering if he gave up too much. "The point is: Tomorrow you'll be free to go. There are some women in the camp, some with kids. Maybe they'll take your students?"

You shake your head. "Sir, I have a duty to their parents."

"Their parents are probably dead," he says, unblinking.

"Perhaps. In which case, my duties increase. You don't know much about my dojo or even kendo, but we practice more than swordplay. In ancient Japan, the word for 'Samurai' came from the words for 'to protect and serve.' A life without honor is no life at all."

He shakes his head. "You want to get yourself killed, that's up to you. And tomorrow, it's *solely* up to you."

"It is true courage to live when it is right to live, and to die only when it is right to die."

"Sure. See you in the morning."

One last supper, one last breakfast. Then what?

- ➢ Head out once the barricades are lifted and take your pupils home. Go to page 282
- ➢ Stay in the dojo and wait for the parents to come. Go to page 201
- ➢ Go straight for this "Salvation." He's right; the parents are probably dead. Go to page 126

Timesuck

You log onto your workstation computer and pull up the Internet browser. It's one of those generic search-engine homepages with news, gossip, and cat memes. Up top, there's a photo of Lady Gaga in her "meat suit" accompanying a headline for her latest PR stunt: "Celebrity turns Cannibal, Police Claim Helplessness."

Fame Monster, Celebrity Cannibal, blah blah blah. There's another article about Joaquin Phoenix walking through his neighborhood naked, but your growing disgust for more Hollywood BS has you skip down to the next section.

PETA was protesting the use of rodent testing for *Gilgazyme*® at the Human Infinite Technologies lab and evidently chose to show their animalistic anger by biting each other bloody. The next feel-good story tells how several Wall Street CEOs have broken international law, intentionally it would seem, but are planning on living in Brazil until the statute of limitations wears off. Thanks to the new longevity wonder drug, they'll still be in their prime upon return to—

"Morning, Kay," Craig says, setting his stuff down on his work station. "What's new?"

"Oh, not much. Murder and corruption."

"I said 'what's new?'" he replies with a chuckle.

"Yeah. Nothing, I guess."

"Same shit, different day," Brian says from the other side.

Stephen comes in from the lobby, a full mug of shit coffee and a grin to match it. "You guys hear about Warren Buffett? They're calling his latest billionaire get-together 'The Warren *Buffet.*' The other hedge-funders fuckin' ate the guy."

"Gross. If I was gonna go cannibal, I wouldn't eat some old dude, know what I'm sayin'?" Josh asks, coming from the bathroom.

"First it was Eastern religions and healing crystals, then it was that Scientology crap, now they're getting their kicks seeing if they can get away with murder," Stephen says.

"Is cannibalism a belief system?" Brian asks. "Or more of a diet thing, like Paleo? Genuinely curious."

"Let's get some work done, huh?" you say. "Big day ahead of us."

You're elbow-deep in a spark-plug replacement, feeling around for the little bastards on the inside of a Ford pickup. It takes full concentration, so it takes you by surprise when Craig snaps his fingers right by your ear. In instinct, you reach up and grab his hand in your own grimy fist and *twist.*

"Agh! Hey, watch it!" he cries.

"Don't do that."

"Jesus, Kay. You were off in la-la land. I said, 'Are we taking lunch breaks or ordering in?'"

"Sorry, Craig. Let me go check with Owen."

Wiping your hands on a rag, you head towards the lobby and front office. Now that you think about it, you are fairly hungry. What time is it? The clock shows 12:20, but could it already be that late?

Josh is in the lobby talking with Owen when you open the door. Owen's saying, "It's not just a problem on our end. I tried calling the phone company from my cell and they've got that dead 'deet-deet-deet' sound, like a phone of the hook."

"Man, I haven't heard that tone in decades," Josh says, then noticing you, adds, "Our landlines are dead. Some kind of problem with the phone company."

"Great. I was about to ask if we should order some lunch, but sounds like we'll have to get carryout with the phone problems."

"I'll go," Josh offers.

- "Yeah, okay. Just don't take too long, the guys are already getting hungry." Go to page 314
- "No, I'll go." I could use some fresh air. Go to page 174

Togetherness

"Right," Owen says. "Okay, lock the gates and turn off any lights we don't need. Pull down the garage rollers and lock the doors. I think we all have a pretty good idea what's coming, so let's get ready for rioters, looters, and…"

"…others," Stephen finishes.

"Good start, but then we need to inventory food and use the bathroom sink to fill up whatever clean containers we have. We don't know how long the water will stay on," Craig says. Then, almost sheepishly, "I spend a lot of time on prepper message boards. This was kind of my hobby. I've got a generator and powdered goods back home."

Brian's eyebrows go up and he shakes his head, but doesn't say anything.

"Well…that's good. Then what do you think our priorities should be?" Owen says.

"Just as I said. Rule of threes, boss. The average person can only survive three minutes without air, three hours without shelter, three days without water, and three weeks without food."

"And three seconds while being eaten alive," Stephen says.

Craig ignores him and goes on. "Water, that'll be our first chokepoint. There are six of us in here and we need a half gallon per day each just for bare-bones survival. That's…over sixty gallons of water if we hope to make it long enough to even need to worry about starvation."

"Brian and Stephen, you guys clean out those fifty-gallon drums. Kay, why don't you and Josh—"

"Where is Josh?" you ask.

The guys look around, like he might be tucked away. Just a misplaced tool. The toilet flushes and Josh comes out of the bathroom, wiping his mouth on his sleeve.

"Looking a little green around the gills, champ," Craig says.

"When I was outside, that guy…." He pushes up his sleeve to show a grisly bite wound just above the wrist. The skin is as pale as porcelain and the veins beneath appear almost black.

"Christ, man," Stephen says, just as someone pounds on the garage door. A second later the service buzzer goes off.

"I'm here to pick up the Hummer!" a man cries from outside.

You look through the window to catch a glimpse. It's not one man, but five. They're decked-out in paramilitary gear and leather. Clean-cut types with hard arms and soft bellies. Each holds at least a handgun on his person. You also notice several large knives. One has a belt of grenades…are those real?

"Let him in," Craig says. "Can't leave people without a set of wheels."

"Just toss him the keys. We finished that job hours ago; it's parked out front," Brian says.

"He's still gotta pay. Maybe he'll give us something useful?" Craig says.

"Like the barter system; not bad," Stephen agrees.

Owen looks conflicted. Most likely, he'll listen to you.

➤ "Keep the doors closed, boss. Pass his keys through the mail slot."
  Go to page 12
➤ "We don't have much in the way of food; let's open up and broker a trade."
  Go to page 208

Tone Deaf

"C'mon, you bastards!" you scream, picking up an enormous monkey wrench from the garage tools. Owen gets the idea and takes a four-prong tire-iron. Stephen grabs a large pipe nearby.

You put Josh out of his misery with one quick stroke, trapping your former coworker's head between the wrench and the pavement and leaving nothing in-between but skull fragments and pulp.

"Craig! Look after Brian," Owen barks.

That's when you see face-to-bloody-face what you're dealing with. These really are corpses, animated and given life once more. Their flesh hangs in ribbons and many have gunshot or stab wounds somewhere on their body. Wounds that don't bleed.

Owen smacks one of the fiends with a backhand from the tire iron, but it just staggers away, head bobbing from the impact. A blow like that to a living man would've put somebody in the hospital, but this ghoul just keeps coming.

"Back into the garage!" you shout.

The group falls back and Craig smashes the controls to send the rolling gate back down. The fiends keep coming though, even as you batter them back. You can see something deep red, almost black, come oozing from the hairline fractures on their skulls, but that doesn't even seem to register.

The door groans as one of the undead—a small boy—is caught in the track of the rolling gate. The heavy gate crushes the boy, but that doesn't matter. Not to the group, anyway. You're backed into a room you've sealed off and the growing horde of undead is at the only entrance.

Their moans bring others to the feast. This won't end well.

THE END

Too Attractive

The night air cuts right through the dress, sending a chill deep into your core. The good news is that the dress is sheer black. Those roving patrols shouldn't be able to see you, with any luck. To be honest, you have no idea where you're going, but the Hummer didn't drive *that* long. You'll be able to make it to safety if you just keep walking. And if you find a road? Well, maybe the dress will come in handy, trying to hitchhike with anyone who might pass by.

As you reach the woodline on the outskirts of the camp, you can still hear everyone behind you with shocking clarity. Laughing, yelling, even gunshots as they fight off the dead. Casting a glance back, you see the former farm glowing with off-the-grid power. It must be visible from miles away. You smell it too; someone's BBQing. Maybe everyone gets a steak dinner?

Then you smell something, much, much worse. When you turn back around, you slam into one of the dead. She grabs at you, but you shove her away; her fingers rake against your bare arms and curl back ribbons of skin.

You howl in pain and a group of them *moans* back. They're all headed straight for the compound, you realize, because it's the only beacon of civilization for miles on end. But it's something you realize too late. Death before you and torture at your back; this won't be pleasant.

THE END

Tooth and Nails

You grab an electric saw, plug the thing in, and carve perfectly-sized planks from the pile of lumber. Solitary catches each as you toss the finished product his way, then uses the nail gun to bolt the wood across the windows.

For a few glorious minutes, all you have are the sounds of the saw and the nail gun, but as more and more of the nutters gather outside, their collective moans and growls drown out the power tools. Has it really been long enough to infect that much of the prison population?

There's a shattering sound, and the groans are suddenly much louder. One of the window boards breaks loose and a pale, bloodless hand paws its way inside. Solitary grabs the man's forearm and nails the dead hand against the other boards, using the fiend himself as a barrier.

No fluid comes from the flailing dead hand. It would seem no pain, either. The animated corpse just keeps pulling until flesh and bone part and the hand is free once more. Another board pops out and a skinhead bites through, for which Solitary rewards the undead man with a nail through the forehead.

You take one of the other windows with your saw, and when an arm breaks through, you attack it with the blade. The whirring teeth send crimson-and-black plasma spraying across the workshop, and the arm twitches for a moment even after you sever the limb.

Then the door breaks open and the Nazi bastards flood into the workshop. You drop the saw and go for a pickaxe. Solitary uses the nail gun until it finally dry-fires empty. It's a valiant effort, but the noise of your machinery and the frenzy of the crowd has drawn in every infected nutter in the whole prison and you're quickly overwhelmed.

THE END

Trainwreck

A scream brings you back. It's a woman, her scream perfectly evolved to pierce the cave-man part of your brain into action. When you open your eyes and look around, you see the battered train car, and slowly the memory of the wreck comes back. The train is on its side and you're lying atop shattered glass and concrete against what used to be one of the windows.

You push yourself up and the woman screams again. No, wait, that time it was you. Your left arm is inflamed and incredible pain unlike anything you've ever experienced shoots through you. Wriggling your fingers, you still have motor control, but barely. Broken? You don't think so. Dislocated, maybe.

The woman screams again (for real this time) and when you stumble out of the tram car, you see a blonde running from a pack of three crazed admirers. She locks eyes with you and heads your way. You unsheathe Isabelle and mentally steady yourself.

With your left arm all but useless, it's not going to be easy. The tried and true tactic of grabbing the ghoul to stay your aim as you slam Isabelle into their skulls won't work with one arm. You'll have to improvise.

Luckily, the blonde isn't totally useless. She wields a gaudy candlestick and together, the two of you take out the three fleshies. It's difficult, and sloppy, but somehow you both make it through unscathed.

"You saved my life," the blonde says. Then she kisses your gasmask, leaving a perfect lipstick print on the plexiglass.

"Brave, but fuckin' stupid," a man says with a thick Southern accent.

When you turn, you see a black guy in tattered business casual with a sledgehammer and a thin redneck-type with a formidable length of lead pipe.

"Well, I'm glad he did it," the blonde says with a glare.

"I'm sure you are!" the big guy says with a laugh. "I'm Tyberius, you just saved Angelica, and my man here is Hefty. So what's your deal, Darth Vader?"

"Sergeant Sims. US Air Force electrical maintenance specialist."

"Are you working with the guys doing all the roadblocks?"

"I don't…I don't think that's a thing anymore, but no."

"Then what *are* you doin'?" Hefty asks.

Your head swims. All you can think to say is, "I'm going to signal rescue, at all costs. So…"

"You should come meet our, well, our leader," Angelica says with a smile. "Fair warning, she can be a real bitch."

Your brain is still trying to process your shoulder injury, so you simply nod. These people seem nice enough and you're better off getting on their good side while you wait for rescue to arrive. Not much of a choice here:

➤ *Follow the group to meet their leader.* Go to page 122

Tranquility

It takes a bit of time, but you find a building that fits the bill for the night in the form of the zoo's security offices. Angelica claims a Taser, but with limited charging stations on the move, you're certain she'll be carrying nothing more than a brick in a day or two. Jose turns his nose up at the pepper spray, but you? You've now got your very own tranquilizer gun.

With its long, slender barrel and calming green stock cradled in your arms, you fell into a deep sleep. In a windowless room, the sun doesn't wake you. Instead, it's men's voices. The real world blends back from dreams of a return to the survivalist compound.

You jump up in a cold sweat, take the rifle, and rush out. There waiting are Jose and Angelica, along with two others. Jose stands with his back to the corner, the cast-iron frying pan in one hand and his butcher's cleaver in the other.

Angelica, however, seems completely at ease. The men do too. They have the look of men who think they own the world. One of them is a tall, well-built black man wearing tattered business casual and wielding a sledgehammer. The other is a thin-as-a-rail redneck-type with a plain white tee and jeans, who holds a lead pipe.

"The fuck?" you say.

"Whoa, lady!" the big guy says, raising his hands at sight of the rifle.

"She ain't gonna shoot us, she's just scared," the redneck says.

So you point the rifle at him.

"Let's all just calm the fuck down," his friend says.

"We're just talking," Angelica adds.

"Did I say you could talk?" you say, not looking over to her.

"You the leader of this group?" the big guy asks.

"That's right."

"Ain't nobody the leader of nothin' no more," the thin guy says.

"I'm in charge of this rifle, and if you don't want me to prove it, I suggest you shut the fuck up."

That does the trick, for a bit. "You won't waste a shot on the living," he says at length.

"Won't I?"

"Lady, I think we all just real tired and probably hungry. It's been a long couple of days, yeah?" the big guy says, repositioning his sledgehammer.

- ➤ Lower the rifle and say, "You're right. I think we got off on the wrong foot." Go to page 310
- ➤ Say, "Throw your weapons in the corner by Jose, then we talk." Go to page 363

Trouble

The National Guard soldiers take you, and they're rough about it. It's hard to tell if it's out of anger or fear, but those emotions are really two sides of the same coin, so take your pick. It all happens so fast that it's hard to remember the order of things. Your skull is throbbing. They struck you, to be sure; multiple times, from the way your body feels after.

There will be no cell phone video of police-state brutality. No, there's something far worse "going viral" right now, so the other citizens on the street turn a blind eye as you're clubbed and dragged away.

Presently, you find yourself inside a tent, something wet and sticky coating the back of your head. The memories are like flashes. A rifle butt lashing out. The look of the pavement as you're dragged down the street. The cold, emotionless gasmasks that stare at you.

Now you're seated on a cot, trying to get your bearings. The police baton you carried is gone, but other than that, you're in one piece. The surrounding tent is large, constructed out of olive-green canvas—straight out of an old rerun of *M.A.S.H.* that mama watches. The flaps are reinforced by metal grates like the ones that keep crowds corralled at a concert. The thick canvas has no window holes, so it could be day or night and you'd have no idea. A large set of fluorescent lights hangs from the center and a thick, industrial extension cord runs out and under the flaps.

The tent is packed with other refugees, from the nearest guy, with a splinted and raised leg, to the green-pallored woman on the other side who clutches a vomit bucket. The whole tent is filled by a dozen ragged, tired people held against their will.

And then there's the nurse walking between the cots, making her way towards you. She wears jeans and a long-sleeved men's workshirt, latex gloves, surgical mask, and the kind of protective eye-goggles people wear in shop class.

"Let me take a look at that head wound," she says, pulling your hand away from the spot in question.

"Nurse, I—"

"It's Doctor, actually. Doctor Abdous. And you are?"

"Tyberius."

Despite the mask and goggles, you can see the smile in her eyes and hear it in her voice when she says, "What a nice name. Pleased to meet you, Tyberius. I'm going to wrap your head now, okay?"

- ➢ "How long do I have to stay here?" Go to page 329
- ➢ "Doc, what's going on? Why's the army here?" Go to page 299

True Neutral

The convict smashes open the glass to the inner doors and is already reaching through to get to the lock when you arrive and smash his knuckles with the police baton. He screams, but backs away from the doors in reflex. It gives you just enough time to slide the heavy, multilayered table of "sales and specials" sitting at the entrance in front of the doors. When the man pushes again, he finds the doors don't budge against the barricade.

"Fuck you, motherfucker!" he screams.

"I'll put it on your tombstone, asshole."

Then his screams become incomprehensible as the infected finally catch up.

Using his death as a distraction, you go out the service entrance with your new clothes and give mama that funeral.

It's a strange feeling to dress up a dead body, which is probably why most people pay a mortician to do it. The feeling is even worse when it's the body of your mother. But she dressed you at the start of your life, so it's almost fitting that you do it at the end of hers.

Once she's lying peacefully on her bed in a dress she could have never afforded in life, you shower and put on your suit. You know she'd gush at how handsome you look. You know she'd be proud.

For the ceremony itself, you try to think of a Bible verse, but your mind is blank at the sight of her. You want to sing *Amazing Grace*, but your throat is a knot of pain and emotion. At length, you kiss your forefingers, then touch them to your mama's lips.

"Bye, mama."

The extension cord behind the entertainment stand should work well enough for your own sendoff. Wrapping it tightly around your neck, strangling yourself before lying down on your own bed. After only half a minute, every fiber of your being screams out for air and you claw at the cord, but you did too good of a job with the knot. You struggle for a minute more before you pass out.

It's all finally over. *See you in the next life, mama.*

THE END

Trust Issues

"Fucking *pendejo!*" Celly screams, pacing about the cell with hands out, like he's strangling your invisible effigy. His muscles are tight and veins bulging. Then, all at once, he calms down. "You think I had that to—man, *cabrón,* I was just gonna carve some crosses up for Easter, man. For *mi madre.*"

The hulking man sighs, and turns to face the barred doorway. Then he turns around, looks you in the eye with hatred, and goes for your mattress. He takes the lotto tickets from your usual hiding spot.

"Celly, no!" you try, but too late. He rips the tickets to shreds.

"There, happy? Nobody gets contraband this week."

You hardly sleep a wink that night, tossing and turning with dreams of being bitten. You practically sleepwalk through breakfast the next morning, and you're still dragging major ass when the call comes for Sunday morning church.

"When evening came, Jesus was reclining at the table with the Twelve," the preacher says. He has a Bible in his left hand, but it's closed; a prop. He has this part memorized. "And while they were eating, he said, 'Truly I tell you, one of you will betray me.'"

A terrible, hacking cough sounds out behind you so loud the preacher has to wait to continue. You look back and see one of the skinheads hacking into his wadded up t-shirt. He releases the shirt and leaves black, sticky phlegm across his chest, like he'd swallowed tar and coughed it back up.

With a new sense of dread, you look back up to the preacher, who's saying, "…while they were eating, Jesus took bread, and when he had given thanks, he broke it and gave it to his disciples, saying, 'Take and eat; this is my body.'"

A terrible shrieking roars out, and it takes some effort not to lose your bowels right there. A guard takes an Asp from his belt and, with a snap of his wrist, expands the telescoping baton. That's when six inmates shoot up, as if suddenly awakened, and surround the guard.

This is it. This is survival. So what're you gonna do?

- ➢ Hide. Go to page 72
- ➢ Fight. Go to page 146
- ➢ Run. Go to page 214

Tunnel: Your Way Out

Solitary gives you an angry glare as he's boarding up the windows, but you keep looking for an escape. The air vents are too small, even for you. The only windows are those up front, the one's presently being boarded up. And there's no back door.

You're about to give up, when you notice an odd patch in the side wall. It's about the size of a door, but blocked up with a poorly-constructed brick-and-mortar barrier. What the hell? You scratch your head at this odd space, but then it hits you—the laundry is on the other side. There must have been a connecting door, but the staff sealed it off to prevent tools from the machine shop going missing in the laundry. But with shoddy workmanship such as this....

The nutter bastards are starting to break through! With renewed vigor, you claim a sledgehammer from the tools and go to work on the wall. On your fourth blow to the brick, you see a crack run through the mortar.

Solitary wrenches the hammer from your grip and goes to work on the wall himself. He's a much larger man, and in only two massive swings a huge chuck of the wall goes down. The pair of you shove and clear your way through as the undead Nazis do the same at the window.

Inside the laundry, Solitary goes for one of the massive washing machines and you help him shove it on its side—creating a barrier to cover the way through. You look around for another way out, but already human figures stagger outside the windows here too.

Solitary pries open a sewer grate, then pulls a tiny Maglite flashlight from his utility belt. He shines it into the pipe below, then indicates you should go inside. The pipe is tiny, but you just might be able to squeeze through. It'd be an extremely tight fit—no way you could even bring the utility belt—and impossible for Solitary to fit inside.

"No way, we in this together!" you say.

A furious pounding starts against the washing machine barrier with a dozen haunting growls to accompany. The nutters won't be kept out for long.

"Go," he says, the command more of a croak than a word.

You look at the tunnel, then to the barrier, then back to Solitary.

He gets in your face, screaming now. "*GO!!!*"

Without looking back, he rushes to face the horde, smashing limbs with the sledgehammer as they try to gain purchase on the washing machine and shove their way through. Knowing you've got no other option, you drop the bulky utility belt, take the flashlight in your mouth, and slip into the pipe.

It's so snug, it's like the damned thing was designed with you in mind, and you're just barely able to shimmy your way through. Slimy water slops against your chest and neck, and the light shows no end to the tunnel. If this doesn't lead out, you're screwed.

Just as panic sets in, you come to another grate. With every last ounce of strength you have, you push through to open air. You dump out into a muddy drainage pool, stand up, and turn to face the prison.

Funny, the damage doesn't look so bad from here.

➢   *Take one last look, then start walking towards the city, a free man.* Go to page 138

Turn for the Worse

You reach out to knock, but Dad's door must not have been shut all the way, because it cracks open when you rap your knuckles against it.

"Dad?" you say into the darkness, pushing the door open slowly. Maybe he's still resting? The creaking door gives way to a rasping wheeze. "Daddy?"

"...don't turn on the light..." a voice says. It's so faint and breathy, you can't even be sure it's him.

"Jay, wait out here."

"But, Sarah—"

"Jason, get some water or something. Check outside for looters. Make yourself useful!"

He looks down, scolded, then turns and leaves. With mental images of those things in the mall flashing through your mind, you ready yourself for what Dad might look like now. Finally, you step forward into the room. Eyes struggling to adjust, scanning frantically for the outline of your father, who's nowhere to be seen. Your heart is pounding.

"...don't—" he starts again, cut short when a concussive *BOOM!* rocks the other side of the house. *Jason!*

You're already running back in the direction of your bedroom when your brother screams and a second shotgun blast goes off. In practiced moves, you unsling your rifle and shoulder the weapon. When you come around the corner, all you see is red. The stranger you'd been keeping in your room now lies on the floor with a gaping hole in his chest. Thick, black blood radiates into the carpet; a Jackson Pollock of devil wings. The second shot took his face.

Jason slumps against your bed, clutching at his left bicep. Bright red arterial blood pulses out from between his fingers and runs down his forearm. Your once-white bedsheets are now a nightmare of red.

"He bit me! Fucker *bit* me! Cut it off!" your brother cries.

➤ Tourniquet, then assess the situation. Go to page 84
➤ No time to waste...*TAKE THE ARM!!!* Go to page 161

Twice Shy

The doctor looks away, debating.

"C'mon, who am I gonna tell?" you press.

She shakes her head, then sits down on the cot next to you. She points at a woman in the corner, her gray face barely visible under a heap of blankets. "That one's up first. Bitten…maybe five hours ago? If you were to look at her left forearm, you'd see the telltale blackened bite wound. The flesh becomes necrotic as it fights off the infection before the body gives up and it reverts to 'healthy' skin. The shivering and sweating is normal, then the fever will break and it looks almost like recovery. Until she starts attacking."

"Why not put her away from us? If this is a quarantine and all…."

The doctor looks at you with sad eyes and practically deflates. "Tyberius…you all are separated from *us*. This other one probably has dysentery, but it's hard to tell. The rest of them? Bite wounds and scratch wounds. Everyone is showing some sign of infection."

Let *that* sink in for a minute.

"I need to get out of here," you say, your voice somehow managing a calm whisper.

"The guard outside the tent might not think that's the best idea," the doctor says. "Stay calm, don't make any trouble, and you'll be okay. The guards take the infected to aggressor tent once they *Turn*. I'll come back to check on you."

- ➤ "I'm sorry." Take the doctor hostage and get out of here. It worked once, it'll work again. Go to page 355
- ➤ Take the proactive approach: Kill everyone else in the tent once the doctor leaves. Go to page 40
- ➤ Doctor's orders: Stay alert, stay out of the way, stay alive. Go to page 393

Unbelievable

Head swimming, you rush back to the garage. There are others out on the street in similar states of panic, and they stumble after one another. Sirens fill the air, peppered by gunshots. Just what the hell is happening?

When you make it back to the garage, you notice the shared look of shock on Josh's face. The others are gathered around him in the lobby. "I saw…I saw…" he mutters.

"Kay, you're back," Owen says. "What's going on out there? Josh's smoke break…well, we can't get three whole words out of him."

"Everybody's…." you say, unsure how to explain it.

"Christ, her too?" Brian asks.

- ➢ "Come outside, see for yourself." Go to page 290
- ➢ "There must be something on TV. Check the news." Go to page 229

Under Cover of Darkness

Though the parents try to convince you not to go out alone (at night!), your calm demeanor convinces them not to belabor the point. You promise you'll see them at camp Salvation after you've completed your obligations, and ask if they'll look for your sister and tell her you're on your way.

Where the day was sweltering, you're grateful for the thick padding of the kendo armor at night. A few vehicles pass in the dark, and you choose to hide from their lights. The kendo armor is dark; black in some places and blue in others, making you practically invisible when you choose to hide.

Once back in the city, you're forced to flee from the walking corpses. They have no problem "seeing" you, even from behind cover. Somehow they just *know*. It makes for a hard night, constantly looking over your shoulder, altering your route several times to avoid the ones that cluster together in groups. Your sword may give you an advantage, but you can't take on an army of the undead.

It's already daylight by the time you escape the city and almost noon by the time you make it to the twins' neighborhood. The air smells of rot and excrement. A thick black cloud hovers over the neighborhood, an ominous sign of smoldering house fires. How is it that even a neighborhood on the outskirts of town has already fallen to the scourge? Perhaps the quarantine was not the start of it all, but a last effort to stall the inevitable?

That's when you arrive. Their house has scratch-marks on the door and boarded windows, and a message spray-painted across the door and siding, "SICK INSIDE."

➢ I will heed this warning. Time to focus on the living: Master Hanzo and the twins need me. Go to page 295
➢ I must see for myself. I've come so far; I can at least put the twins' parents to rest. Go to page 296

Upstream

Several of the men in suits use small-arm fire to keep the throngs of undead away from the Ambassador, but their pistols will only go so far. One of the staffers—the meek man who originally called for help—screams out as a zombie clamps down on his arm. The suited men ignore him; their priority is the Ambassador.

With a shot from your M4, you free him, but the damage is done. Whatever this *Gilgazyme®* shit is, it spreads through bites. Should you shoot him too? Best to leave it to a medic once you're out on the tarmac. For now, you need to conserve ammo and focus on pushing directly into the crowd of ghouls.

"Christ, I feel like a salmon swimming upstream," a suited man with a beard says.

"Yeah, and there's an overpopulation of bears," another replies.

Another staffer screams out as a ghoul with a pan-flute hanging from around his neck attacks.

"Corporal Gardner! Make a hole!" you shout, pointing at one of the barricades with a chop of your hand.

A hollow *thunk* announces the shot, and a moment later, there's a satisfying *KA-BOOOOOM!!!* and a gigantic hole where their barrier once stood. The resultant shock knocks over several fleshies; this is the best chance you'll get at escape.

"Push through!" you shout.

With some effort, the crowd of survivors makes it through the crowd of undead and out into the open. You lost three more staffers along the way, but the Ambassador makes it out unscathed.

"Damn, that was fucked," Corporal Gardner says, relief in his voice.

It's true. You got the Ambassador out, but barely. Not the smoothest operation.

➢ *Tell a medic about the wounded, then help get everyone back on the C-17.* Go to page 135

Useful

"A new face," you say, extending a hand as you approach the man. "I'm sure they told you that I'm the leader of this merry band of misfits."

"Sergeant Sims. US Air Force electrical maintenance specialist."

"A pleasure. This here is Jose, man doesn't *habla mucho*, but he's good in a fight. I'm Cooper, and I guess you can think of me as your new commanding officer."

Even behind the gasmask faceplate you can see the shock in his eyes. He takes your hand and says, "I'm going to signal rescue, at all costs. So…"

"Yeah, sure. Whatever. In the meantime, any chance you can get the power back on in the hotel? There's a restaurant on-site, and it'd be nice to have a real meal, don't you think?"

"Listen, Cooper, you seem…nice, but I'm not one to take orders from random strangers, so…."

You sigh and say, "I was trying to be civil. Truth is, I think you could be useful, Sims. I really do, but I don't take chances. I protect my friends and my friends protect me, but if we're going to travel together, I need to know I can trust that you'll do what I say."

After having shaken his hand, you're able to pick out which shoulder is the one giving him trouble. Now you grab that arm and *twist*.

Sims screams out in pain, but no one moves to help him. You bring him down to the ground by the arm, and he's all too willing to follow your lead when it comes to this.

"So what's it going to be, *cuntfuck*? Are we going to be friends or not?"

"*YES!!!*" he screams.

"And what I say goes?"

"Yes, yes! *Goddammit*, yes!"

After that, Sims is like putty in your hands. And the others get a reminder not to fuck with you. When you turn back, Jose is smiling.

Sims got the power back to the hotel in less time than it took for Jose to make a gourmet meal for the group. Just like at the zoo, most of the food was rotten due to a lack in refrigeration, but there were still some nonperishables and the man proves a miracle worker with rice and beans. You're bringing people together, Kay. It's really working. Now you just need to set up the park for the long term.

Which is why you're sitting at the breakfast table the next morning plotting out that very idea. "Hefty, you mentioned supplies. Most everything here has expired. What are our other options?"

"We got tunnels. That's how we use'ta get around when I worked here. Miles of tunnels, connecting ride'ta ride, shop'ta shop."

"Underground access tunnels?" Sims asks.

"Oh damn," Tyberius says, brightening. "That's where they store food and shit, right?"

"Bingo," Hefty says, "shooting" the man with gun-fingers.

"Sounds like a plan," you say.

Hefty leads the way to the nearest subterranean tunnel entrance—a set of large-double doors at the base of the gigantic Ferris wheel. Tyberius and Jose tug at the doors, but they're locked. There's a keypad next to the doors and Hefty tries his old employee code, but it's long since expired. Sims pulls out his knife to pry open the access panel for a hot-wire, but Angelica stops him.

"Why don't we use this?" she says, pointing to an EMERGENCY MANUAL OVERRIDE sign posted just above a pump handle.

"Yeah, well, even a blind squirrel is right twice a day," Sims says with a grin.

You nod and pump the override handle. There's a deep, bass-filled *thud* as the pump disengages the lock mechanism and the guys at the doors go for another try at opening the tunnels. They look like standard metal doors from the outside, but there's obvious extra mass inside and it takes concerted effort to lug the heavy doors open.

"Shoulda remembered the override," Hefty says. "Tunnels were the emergency evacuation route after all."

"Wait, what?" you say, with a sinking feeling.

Tyberius looks your way, then you see it on his face too. In unison, you shout, "*DON'T!!!*" but it's too late.

The groaning doors give way to a massive cacophony of moans. *That's why this park was so empty!* The tunnel doors were too thick for the noise to escape (or for the undead to escape, for that matter), but as the first undead stumble out of the darkness, you know you're in trouble.

Tyberius and Jose hold tight to the doors, trying desperately to stop their massive momentum and push them closed, but there's no time. Even if they do manage to reverse the swing, there are thousands of those things now pushing back.

In fact, tens of thousands of zombies now pour out from the tunnels. An entire day's worth of tourists and families, park workers, plus anyone they called to join them at their subterranean sanctuary. After a week underground, every last man, woman, and child is an infected, ravenous monstrosity.

And they're all headed your way.

The horde flows out from beneath the Ferris wheel, sending your group reeling back from snapping jaws and groping hands. The healthier, fresher corpses stumble-run after you, and you're forced to run in the opposite direction from which you came. The other survivors flee for their lives and you desperately look for an escape route.

Bad news: the park layout and frenetic fiends at your heels leave no choice but two terrible escape routes. Split-second decision, where to?

➢ The gigantic maze. The ghouls lack critical thinking, and I'll quickly lose them in the steel bramble. Go to page 14
➢ The haunted fun-house up ahead. Ghouls with LED eyes don't scare me nearly so much as flesh-and-blood undead. Go to page 240

Vestigial Law

By the time you make it back to the scene of the limo accident, an ambulance has arrived. In addition to a pair of paramedics, there are also two armed security personnel. Not exactly police; perhaps security from the hospital. Do ambulances normally travel with armed guards?

The paramedics are treating the limo driver, who's laid out on a stretcher. He's anemic, and crimson radiates from a wound on his neck. Something black lies under the skin, as if the veins have been filled with ink.

"I want Tasers on full charge," one of the paramedics says to the guards.

The paramedics move to the back of the limo, open the doors and reach in to pull out a young woman. Or at least what's left of her. It looks like she's had her skin burned away by acid. Or eaten.

Then someone from inside the limo grabs one of the paramedics and pulls him in. A woman shrieks from inside the vehicle, or maybe that's the paramedic. Hard to tell, especially once the scream switches to blood-gurgling. The paramedic's hands cling to the door frame.

One of the guards pulls out his handgun and points it at the limo.

The second paramedic rushes in to grab his co-worker's hands. The other guard hurries in with his Taser and starts shocking something inside.

"Work her back!" the guard cries.

"Shoot her!" the second paramedic screams. "Shooooot *her!*"

But the guard with the handgun is gorgonized by fear.

➤ Do it yourself. Rush in, take the handgun. Go to page 386
➤ Something is seriously wrong. Get back to the garage and warn your co-workers. Go to page 380

Vigilant Vigilante

Taking the handgun from the shell-shocked guard is easy; he's all too happy to be free from the responsibility of the weapon. You aim at the limo, looking for the source of the attack. The fiendish woman continues attacking the paramedic until he breathes his last. Then, once his heart has stopped squirting blood all over the other men, the young woman is done with him.

The others stumble back as she stumbles out at them. She has wild, manic eyes and a tongue that waggles out of her chipped-tooth grin.

"Miley…Cyrus?" you say, baffled at seeing the celebrity in this state.

As if in recognition, she turns towards you. But you're not looking for an autograph. You pull the trigger and a third eye blooms on her forehead, all life leaving from the other two eyes. She falls on the ground in a heap, and you turn to give the handgun back to the guard. A few people have cell phones raised, capturing video. Good thing they don't have any service, otherwise you'd be a YouTube star.

"You're all welcome," you say.

➢ *Head back to the garage.* Go to page 380

Visitation Rights

It's pitch-black out, which is a strange feeling, because you've never been outside of your cell after dark. Still, the lights of the cell block shine brightly, so you can orient yourself. The searchlights from the guard towers sweep across the prison grounds.

Avoiding the lights, you hurry past the cell block, duck behind the chapel, then continue towards the administration complex. You'll have to go through the hospital in order to make it to the visitor entrance.

A hungry moan draws your attention from the base of the hospital where a skinhead corpse, missing its lower half, claws towards you. What's worse, his moaning draws in more of the fiends.

As more of the racist zombies drop from the hospital windows, it occurs to you that this might not be a bad thing. If you can pull more away, it'll make passing through that much easier.

- Make a ruckus, and draw more of the nutters out into the open. Go to page 402
- Stay quiet. Old legless is doing enough on his own. Hurry into the infirmary. Go to page 171

Voicing Concerns

The next morning you spend alone, meditating, steeling yourself for possible confrontation. Finally, a few soldiers show up to deliver breakfast. Captain Delozier is not amongst them.

"Good morning. May I inquire on the whereabouts of Captain Delozier?"

The soldier you ask makes a huff that fogs up his gasmask, and you're unable to tell if it's a laugh of impertinence at your expense or at the thought of his superior.

"I'm sure he's doing something important," a second soldier replies.

"Will you radio him, please? I have some concerns I'd like to bring up."

They say they will, then continue on their route. While you're waiting, you tell the children to eat. No sense in having them worry, much less eat cold food. At length, Captain Delozier arrives.

"Mr. Miagi, what can I do you for?" he asks.

Ignoring the jibe, you go straight into it. "I would like to know about my students, the young Salvator and the boy Christian you took last night. The health of their parents, too."

"Listen, they're fine. They'll continue to be fine for as long as I'm posted here, okay? Don't bother me again with this kind of minutia. Anything, you know, *important?*"

"I'd...I'd like to come visit the children, I think."

The captain sighs, and his intonation grows impatient as he says, "I get that you're concerned, but that really isn't feasible. You'll have to trust me on this one. I mean, this is why I'm here, get me? The safety of the public is my number one concern."

"I'm afraid I must insist, sir. Only a short visit."

"Are you deaf? Or just willfully ignorant? Don't forget that I'm allowing you to stay here as a favor, but I can't have you as a thorn in my side. You're interrupting operations with this nonsense."

His voice gets louder and harsher with each word. The children have stopped eating, instead focused on the conversation. Master Hanzo suddenly appears beside you and says, "Please sir, continue on your business. I will talk with my friend here."

Delozier shakes his head. "Get it together, okay? Same team." Then he's gone.

"Master Hanzo..." you say.

"Quiet. You are too young to remember, but the last time the government thought our people were a threat, they put us into camps. Right here, they took us from our homes. And the ones who didn't go along quietly? The ones who caused trouble? We never saw them again. You'll say it's different now, but remember, the son of a frog is also a frog. If you push these men, if they see you as a troublemaker, it will end poorly. And not just for you. Think of your pupils. Now, sit, eat."

You eat in silence, avoiding the glances of those around you, and try to think about the words of Master Hanzo. It's true, they could have easily forced you into their quarantine tents. How far can you push them? But, by the same token, how far should you let them push you?

At length, Master Hanzo rises and excuses himself. "Local news begins soon," he says. "Time to monitor the radio."

"Can we listen?" Haley asks.

"Hmmm," you intone, thinking, *Is it better to shelter the students from the state of the world, or is knowledge power, in this case?*

- ➤ "Yes, we should all listen. Strong body, strong mind. It is all one. To be able to defend ourselves, we must be fully aware of the surrounding world."
Go to page 302
- ➤ "No. Grandfather Hanzo will tell us if there is an important announcement. It's time for class. Consider yourself lucky—you will all be ready to test for your next *kyu*-rank after a few days stuck in here!" Go to page 184

Voyeur

You watch, hovering close against the peephole. The man's pounding and hollering continues, and you flinch with each baritone *thud* against the door. Then you see what he was running from. Another man, crazed and hungry, tackles him right against the frame. For a moment, the peephole goes black. When light once again shines through, it's against a wet, red filter.

The crazed man is *biting* the other man.

You step away, hands clasped tight against your mouth, speaking only with the horrified look on your face. Your brother and father know what's happening too; they can hear it through the door. The guy shrieks in horror, wrestling for his life.

"Things are worse than they're telling us on the news," Jason says.

"Put the bastard down—open the door and shoot the attacker," your father says, his words making your hair stand on end.

"Wh-what?" you protest.

"I need to see you do it, Sport."

"But he's unarmed..."

"So? He's killing the other dude—just listen!" Jason says.

Your father nods.

➤ Pick up your rifle. Guy doesn't deserve to be a ghoul-scout cookie. Go to page 141

➤ Refuse. That's murder! I can't just shoot the guy.... Go to page 244

Vultures

His eyes narrow and he says, "Sweet ride. Where'd you find it?"

"Abandoned. Only had a flat, so I guess somebody left in a hurry. I can swap out a spare pretty quick, though," you say, tugging at your mechanic's shirt for emphasis.

He steps back, looks to the rear of the car, then says, "Spare's still on the back."

"Uhhh, yeah, I got another one from my garage. Can't be too careful these days."

"No, ma'am, you cannot. I'm going to divert you to a FEMA camp we have set up nearby. Great place to ride out the storm. Turn left here and follow the line of soldiers."

You nod, then turn, rolling up your window as you go.

"That was some quick thinking," Angelica says.

You shrug. "I work at an auto shop. I'm used to bullshitting the customers."

The road is narrow from all the barricades; wide enough to drive down, but not enough to turn around. One way only—ahead. You're funneled down the street and eventually come to a fence. A huge forklift pulls up behind you. It's holding a concrete barrier on the lift.

A pair of soldiers open the fence ahead, and you see a large open area full of people. You pull forward, but realize quickly that something is off.

"Cooper..." Angelica says, realizing the same.

The way they move, it's almost a shuffling. Collectively, the group turns to you and *moans*.

"Fuck!" you shout.

Slamming on the brakes, you shift into reverse—just as the forklift slams into your bumper and pushes forward. Tires squeal, burning rubber, but the forklift is stronger. The Hummer is shoved inside and the concrete set behind you, then the forklift backs up and the fence is closed.

The dead surround the Hummer, and you're left with no way out. But you're not going down without a fight. You slam on the accelerator, blasting through corpses with the cattleguard. They fall before you like hell's version of dominoes, and soon you're no longer driving on pavement.

The 4x4 keeps the wheels spinning, sending sheets of gore out behind. Eventually, though, the hundreds of corpses prove too much and viscera gums up the engine, killing the Hummer.

Your last decision will be to die of hunger in the car, or head out into the arms of the dead for a quicker death.

THE END

Waiter

From the safety of your bunk, you watch the carnage in silence. Old grudges end in shankings from people without a high school diploma who naively assume this is just another day in the slammer. Those without an axe to grind fight off the nutters, throwing punches at the undead bastards in a lethal game of bloody knuckles.

Finally, the inmates start to thin out as most of the men rush the yard outside. Those left behind are the corpses of the unfortunate and the animated corpses who feed on them.

You get up to go and the cheap mattress groans with creaky springs. Dozens of hungry eyes turn your way. For a moment, you hesitate, hoping they'll focus back on their meals, but it looks like the nutters prefer fresh food.

Sensing that you're on the menu, you make a break for it, but a veritable wall of undead stumbles towards you; this is a game of Red Rover for keeps. Planting your shoulder, you go for a break through the lines, but the nearest ghouls catch your baggy prison jumpsuit with gnarled fingers.

You can hear an audible *snap* from broken and dislocated fingers, but they don't care. They don't call it a *death grip* for nothing.

With you as the lone healthy, uninfected man in the cell block, the fiends converge on you and eat you alive.

THE END

Waiting Room

You wait patiently, but not for long. Most everyone in the tent is asleep, when the woman in the corner rises. *Turned.* The thick woolen blanket she wore falls off, revealing slate-gray skin and a bite wound that sits on her forearm as placidly as a butterfly on the trunk of a tree.

She scans the tent with dull, uninterested eyes, her gaze eventually coming to rest on you. Why? Because no one else is awake? You seem the most *alive*, perhaps? Or maybe the infected instinctively know to ignore others with a tainted bloodstream?

Doesn't matter, really. Whatever the reason, she staggers your way. Leaning back on your cot, you feel the metal crossbeam shift under your thighs.

- Take the beam, kill the bitch. Go to page 32
- Shove bucket-lady in her path. Go to page 196
- Call for the guard, but stay put. Go to page 356

Wake the Dead

It's hard enough to sleep when every creak or rustle of wind grates on your nerves, but with a gasmask on, it's impossible. But you figure this place didn't get hit by the plague, and you're alone, so you can take the thing off for a night.

Problem is, you snore. A lot. Like, planning on disability pay for sleep apnea levels of snoring.

You shoot awake when you hear a crash. Mitch the M4 jumps to your shoulder. That's when you register the growling, the moaning, and the crunch of glass under clumsy feet.

When you look out into the main area, you see about thirty zombies rushing in. And they see you. Remember how many shots you've got left? Definitely not thirty. Not that you'd have time for thirty shots anyhow.

You spring back to the rear fire-exit and shove at the push-bar. Damn thing is jammed! You put your shoulder into it and use adrenaline to slam against the door. It flies open and you sprawl out into the rear alley.

Another twenty ghouls are there to meet you. Your snoring is so loud that you've had hotel complaints. Now? It got you killed. They surrounded the building while you were snoring logs, and there's no escape from the mob.

Luckily, there won't be enough left of you to rise again.

THE END

Walked Right into It

"Somebody's gotta teach you some manners, missy. Duke'll appreciate it. Hope that dress goes well with black and blue," he says, fishing out the key to your stall.

He unlocks the door but it doesn't budge, thanks to the wedged broomhead.

"The hell?" Bud says, "What'd you do?"

"Some tough guy. Can't even get the door open."

"I'm gonna enjoy this," he says, slamming his shoulder against the door.

"I highly doubt that."

Two more shoulder-slams and the broomhead falls out, the door swings open, and Bud comes rushing in. You swing out the spear, plant the dull end under the toe of your boot, and aim the business end at Bud's neck.

He never even saw it coming but it hits low—impaling the man in the chest. He falls to the floor, coughing up blood. Slower death, but it'll do. You scoop up his key to the stalls and head out. Turning to Angelica's stall, you pass it through.

"Here, take it." you say, "I'm going to find a bike and get out of here while it's still dark. I'd recommend you get going too."

"I'm coming with you."

"No, no way."

"And we need to let the others out."

"Go ahead, I'm out of here."

"Cooper, please...."

Her eyes shimmer somewhere between hopelessness and despair.

- ➤ Tell her, "Good luck," and make your escape while she's busy freeing the others. Go to page 258
- ➤ Help her release the others. Tell her, "You can follow me out of here, but it's on you to keep up." Go to page 61

A Walk in the Park

The next morning's meet-up starts over cereal and ultra-pasteurized milk. Cooper scours a park map while Angelica disinterestedly picks at a few dry coco-puffs. Guillermo gulps his food, then sits stoically, awaiting the group's next move. Tyberius and Hefty look hung over.

Your left shoulder still aches, but in a dull, numb, dead-limb kind of way. Seems like you'll have to survive this thing with one arm tied behind your back. The good news is that you won't have to do it alone.

They're a rag-tag bunch, to be sure, but you know everyone here has the same motivation: Survival. And that knowledge brings a sort of trust. You can lean on them now, while wounded, then just think how happy they'll be, once you're able to signal rescue!

Soon enough, you'll end this nightmare once and for all.

Go to page 160

Wearing the Pants

"What happened?" Angelica asks when you return to the stables alone. "Where's Bud?"

"I wouldn't worry about him, or Duke," you say. "But there are a lot of patrols out there. The dead are coming in earnest tonight."

After unlocking your cell, you rush in and get back into your work clothes.

"Where are you going?" she asks.

As an answer, you hold up the key. Turning to Angelica's stall, you pass it through.

"Here, take it." you say, "I'm going to find a bike and get out of here while it's still dark. I'd recommend you get going too."

"I'm coming with you."

"No, no way."

"And we need to let the others out."

"Go ahead, I'm out of here."

"Cooper, please…."

Her eyes shimmer somewhere between hopelessness and despair.

You look back to the others. Part of you thinks you're all in this together; the antithesis of these male *Mad Max* survivalists. That you'll have better chances escaping the compound together. Then again, part of you doesn't give a shit.

➢ Tell her, "Good luck," and make your escape while she's busy freeing the others. Go to page 258
➢ Help her release the others. Tell her, "You can follow me out of here, but it's on you to keep up." Go to page 61

Well-Mannered Meal

You knock softly on the door, but there's no response. After a moment you rap harder, offering a "Sir?"–but still nothing. Slowly, you turn the knob and push the door open. Just as you step in, the man is upon you.

He heard you all right, but it took him a minute to get out of bed, and his dead hands couldn't open the doorknob. But now his instincts turn to frenzy as he brings you to the ground. You thrash against the man, but he's twice your body weight and doesn't have an ounce of hesitation left in his instinct-driven urges.

Jason's shotgun turns the Zulu's head to pulp, but it's too little, too late.

You're INFECTED!

What an Asshole

"Just what I thought. Put on that dress and I'll stop," he says. Bud takes a key from his pocket and opens the door to Angelica's stall. She steps away and you take a step forward, right up to the bars. "You're gonna put it in your mouth until I'm ready."

"Anything he puts in there—bite it off!" you shout.

"Shut up and put on the goddamn dress! You do as you're told, Blondie. I so much as feel a nibble and I'll blow your brains out."

"You'll do it without a pecker," you say.

That gives Bud some pause. Instead, he unzips his pants and plays with himself. Angelica looks away. "Look at it!" he shouts.

"Don't. You don't have to do what he says," you say.

"Shut your damn mouth! Just remember, if you would put that dress on, none of this would be happening."

Bud drops his pants and turns his back to you as he prepares to defile Angelica. Your eyes go to the dress and you think, *There's always a choice.*

So you make a choice: You take the spear and shove the business end through the bars and up Bud's exit-only chute. The man howls in pain and reaches back to free himself, so you shove harder. In fact, you grab the bars between stalls and use the extra momentum to kick the base of the broom handle as hard as you can. Bud loses consciousness and falls to the floor, blood pooling.

"Get the key!" you shout, but Angelica doesn't hear you. She simply shivers, huddled in the corner. "Angelica! Grab his key. Let me out! He got what he deserved. C'mon."

"He was…he was really going to…"

"It's not your fault. Not…not *everything* is a choice," you say, realizing the truth in the words.

"Is he dead?" she says in a mouse's voice.

"Doesn't matter. If you don't get me out of here, we *will be* when someone comes looking for him." She nods, steels herself and takes Bud's key ring. She lets herself out, then unlocks your stall. "Atta girl. I'm going to find a bike and get out of here while it's still dark. I'd recommend you get going too."

"I'm coming with you."

"No, no way."

"And we need to let the others out."

"Go ahead, I'm out of here."

"Cooper, please…."

Her eyes shimmer somewhere between hopelessness and despair.

- ➤ Help her release the others. Tell her, "You can follow me out of here, but it's on you to keep up." Go to page 61
- ➤ Tell her, "Good luck," and make your escape while she's busy freeing the others. Go to page 258

Wheel in the Sky

The Ferris wheel sits in the center of the park, but you can see the monstrosity from almost anywhere in the city. All you have to do is walk down Main Street and *all Rhodes scholars go to Rome*, as they say.

From the looks of it, the staff and the day's tourists abandoned the park when the crowds grew cannibalistic. Tumbleweeds made of flyers and park maps drift across the asphalt. Several displays are knocked to the ground. Carts lie overturned.

And a giant rabbit moans and stumbles your way.

Or, to be more precise, a fleshie in a bunny suit moans and stumbles your way. Looks like the little ankle-biters decided to take their nickname literally and infected the poor stiff. It's just you and the *pay-me-a-buck-a-photo* mascot, so you move in with Isabelle to put the thing down before its moan draws in more.

You stab into the cartoonish, oversized mask, bleeding tufts of cotton into the air, but missing the meat. The fleshie lunges and grabs your shoulders, bringing the rabbit-head in to kiss your gasmask while it chews at you from inside the costume.

In an effort to break the hold, you pull the giant rabbit-head off and finally get a sight of your target—a fifteen-year-old girl. For the briefest instant, you stand in shock and the ghoul snaps her jaws, spitting cotton balls like someone on a bad high after wisdom teeth surgery. You push the blade through her chin and into her skull and she drops.

Shit, she was just a kid... Your head spins. Catching your breath, you continue towards the Ferris wheel without incident. Onesie-twosie corpses line the street, but nothing like you'd feared. This place must have held ten thousand, maybe even twenty thousand, people on any given day. Now it's abandoned—but the wires are still hot!

It takes about thirty seconds to figure out the ride's controls (dumbed-down for high schoolers and carnies), then you set it to run a cycle and hop aboard. The wheel rotates slowly enough, but with the hundred-plus-foot diameter, your individual carriage moves fairly quickly. Knowing how high this thing goes, you bring down the safety lap-bar.

Each unit has its own viewfinder, the kind you'd find on top of a building or at the end of a pier. The wheel is truly gigantic; it must be one of the largest on earth. No wonder it's the centerpiece.

When you look around, the first thing you notice is just how empty the interior of the park is. Which is great news. As you get higher, however, you see the bad news. The area beyond the wall is crawling with fleshies who stumble your way.

The city beyond is devastated. You didn't realize just how bad it was from the ground level, but now that you've got some distance, you can see dozens of buildings on fire. And thousands—perhaps even a million—squirming masses in the far, far distance.

There's no way I'm going to live through this, a voice of doubt says. You look over the edge. If you were to jump now, it'd be at least two hundred, maybe even three hundred, feet down. An instant, easy end to the apocalypse. Your palms start to sweat. You get vertigo being so high up, and you close your eyes hard to get a grip on yourself. It takes a moment to register the last image you just saw down there—someone *running*.

Then the screaming starts. It's a woman, her scream perfectly evolved to pierce the cave-man part of your brain into action. When you open your eyes and look down, you see a blonde running from a pack of three crazed admirers.

As the wheel begins its descent and the distance between you shrinks, she grows larger by the second. She's wearing *heels*, for Chrissake.

"*Please!*" she shrieks. "Mr. Army-man! Help!"

So she's seen you, but have the fleshies? You could just stay up here and contemplate your mortality for another pass of the wheel while the woman below loses her own. Or you could leap off the moving wheel, dispatch the three ghouls, and get the girl. What'll it be?

➤ Maybe I'm afraid, maybe I get a kick out of watching people die, what's it to you? I'm keeping my seat! Go to page 194
➤ Leap into action! Caveman save girl, ugg. Besides, the more living people here, the greater my chance of getting rescued. Go to page 187

Whistling Dixie

You lick your lips in preparation. Then, with a deep breath, you place your forefingers in your mouth, curl your tongue, and let out a piercing whistle. The shrill sound pierces through the prison and when you finish the full lungful of air, the whistle continues echoing.

All the while, dozens of nutters pour out from the hospital and surrounding buildings. The nearest guard tower spotlight envelops you in its glow. *Shit.* Just as you start to run, the tower sniper hits you squarely in the back. No warning shots this time, and the frantic horde is all too happy to help finish you off.

THE END

Wild

You're back out front just as the fastest members of the growing horde arrive. Nothing you can't handle, though. With all the parked cars, newspaper bins, trash cans, and other urban obstacles, you're able to outpace them with relative ease. These ghouls are unthinking—they just chase you in a straight line. So when you hurdle a bicycle rack, the undead rack themselves against it.

The bad news is that you're afforded plenty of time with your thoughts. You try to keep busy, to keep vigilant, but no matter how hard you try, you can't get the images of mama out of your head. Her face appears on any wandering dead that even vaguely matches her appearance. Even the young black women with two arms become your mother in your head.

What's the point anymore? She screams. *How can you live with yourself after this?*

You shake your head to clear it. It's not her yelling at you. Still, you feel hollow. If you didn't have this funeral idea, you'd probably still be back home, numb, not sure what to do next.

The miles tick by until you make it to a service station on the outskirts of town. You could use some water or a sports drink, so you turn in. The front window is smashed in, and the place is looted, but they didn't get everything.

"Hello?" you call. "Knock, knock?"

These things aren't smart. If one is inside, it'll come when you call.

Seems like the coast is clear, so you head in. Most of the drinks are gone from the case, but there are a few bottles of unsweetened tea that were left. It'll have to do for now. On the way out, you see the racks of generic pain-killers, anti-allergens, cough medicine, and various medicinal products. How hard would it be to wash the whole rack down with a couple bottles of tea? End the pain once and for all. Rejoin mama.

No, you tell yourself. If you go now, who will bury her? So you continue walking, trying not to listen to the voice that says, *But maybe after…? Wouldn't it be nice just to sleep and never wake up?*

By the time you arrive at the outskirts of the mall, the sun is setting. You'll probably have to stay the night here, especially with that crowd still following. It should be defensible, though, because this mall sits outside of town, purchased while land was still cheap. Several construction sites are under development and just beyond that awaits the shopping mall with a large "Grand Opening!!!" sign. Brand-spanking new.

The nearest part of the mall happens to be a department store, and you figure they're all basically the same, so long as they have a menswear department for your suit and a place to get mama a nice dress.

- ➢ Go for the main doors. The double-wide glass doors should let you see if anyone's inside. Go to page 301
- ➢ Go for the service entrance, where they unload new items. It's out of the way and should have less chance of trouble. Go to page 324

Winner, Winner!

Celly takes the chicken dinner from the guard, but you have the man's attention.

"You can pay me?" he repeats.

"Handsomely."

"Yeah? With what? I need something right now, not promises."

You hold up a "wait a second" finger and go for your lotto ticket-hiding spot. With your back to the guard, you quickly scratch the other three tickets. Twenty bucks isn't likely to sway him, but if you can get a $50, you might have a chance. Three tickets left. First one? Dud.

"I ain't got all day," the guard says.

Second ticket...dud.

"Quit pullin' your pud and show me what you got."

Third ticket—*no way*.

"Mother fucker!" you shout.

"Asshole," the guard mutters, then turns to leave.

"Ten thousand dollars!" you shout, voice cracking.

Two years of daily scratch tickets has left you deep in the red, and the most you've ever won on a single ticket is a cool $250. Your hands tremble as you hold what you have before you—ten thousand goddamned dollars.

"A lotto ticket?" the guard asks, unsure.

"Ten grand. It's yours, all I want's a ticket outta here."

"Two tickets," Celly corrects.

You nod, holding the golden ticket just out of the guard's reach. He thinks about it, weighing his options. After what feels like forever, he finally puts out a hand and says, "Fuck it, give me the ticket."

"And you get us outta here."

"You'll get your door open, but that's all I can do. Hell, I'll open *all* the doors on my way out. This place is fucked anyway. We called for riot support, but the police said they're *busy*. Tried a state of emergency with the Governor, but he already declared one for the city. Gonna give me that ticket, or not?"

➤ Hold out for a better deal. Tell him you want a ride out with him, *then* you'll give him the ticket. Go to page 108

➤ I'm just lucky this poor bastard thinks somebody'll be around to cash that ticket. Hand it over, then wait for the doors to open. Go to page 260

Working Late

The rest of the house has the same rifled-through appearance that comes from looters hoping to make a quick score: Most of the food and medicines are gone, but that's about it. Can't eat the flat-screen TV. Still, you close and barricade the front door to prevent unwanted visitors from wandering in during the night.

Nolan's parents don't return. It obviously frightens the boy, but you're not sure how to comfort him. The only comforting thought you have is, *if we haven't seen their bodies, they might still be alive.* But for a child, that might just make his nightmares worse. Instead, the most you can offer is a smile and assurances that everything will be okay.

The next morning, you decide that if they're not back by now, they probably aren't coming back.

Haley's house might be "on the way" to Nathanael's, but it's certainly not close. It's in a newer development, one that backs up against the marshes, so you follow the long road away from suburbia and into swamp-front property marketed as "Gladedale Estates."

Stomachs rumbling, you hope that whether or not you find Haley's parents, there will at least be something to eat. There's a greasy spoon restaurant just off the road and you watch as each of your students lock onto the diner, their heads moving in unison. Your own salivary glands tingle at the prospect.

- ➢ It's worth a quick detour. Someone passing out from hunger would be a longer delay. Go to page 300
- ➢ Keep moving. Her house is out of the way, but only a few hours of walking remain. Go to page 175

Worn Out His Welcome

The house remains unmolested by looters, so you key the deadbolt and head inside. It's perfectly calm and quiet, like the annual after-Thanksgiving pre-football nap. But that could all change in a minute. Better hurry. Jason hangs back behind you, the same way he used to during a stormy night on camping trips.

The door is closed, presumably with the wounded man still sleeping inside. You listen in, but can't hear anything. Hmmm. When you look back to Jason, your brother simply nods.

Probably best to:

➢ Slowly open the door, rifle at the ready, just like Dad showed you.
   Go to page 360
➢ Knock on the door. Wouldn't want to barge in on a delirious stranger.
   Go to page 398

A Wretched Hive

The gunshot echoes through the range with painful reverberations. In such a small space, everyone flinches involuntarily. Everyone except for Mr. Ford. Then the next few seconds fly by as fast as the bullet shattering *The Fugitive's* kneecap.

Harrison Ford's security team moves to act, hands diving into suit jackets with practiced ferocity, Glocks pulled from shoulder holsters. Law and order still prevails in the land, and vigilante justice is not something these guys are paid to allow. You realize, not without a look of dumbfounded stupidity, that they're drawing down on you. You drop the Galil and raise your arms in surrender, but it's too late.

As two more gunshots ring out, you close your eyes and wince, ready to feel the pain. But when it never comes, you open your eyes to see the two security agents before you clutching chest wounds. Dad holds the smoking Galil.

Gunshots pound out around you in stereo as the remaining four agents unload their Glocks into your father. You scream out with Jason in unison, so your pain melds together into one mournful cry. The nearest agent trains his pistol on you, bringing it within arm's range—big mistake. All the rough-housing with Jay, all the holds, grapples, and techniques dad taught you… all for this moment.

You lash out, knocking the firearm askew, the resultant gunshot barely missing you. Then, in a completion of the movement, you torque his arm around by the wrist and slam your full weight upon his elbow, bending it the wrong way.

In the wake of the confusion, Jason drops down to your father's body, claims the Galil, then drops the other three agents. You turn toward him, his eyes growing wide at something behind you, and turn back just in time for Harrison Ford to bite down upon your neck. Jason shoots the immortal movie star, but the damage is done.

You're INFECTED!

Yes, We're Open!

You motion for the children to stand back, putting yourself between the door and the group. Master Hanzo hands you a wooden *shinai*, just in case. As soon as you open the door, a man runs in, and after a perfectly executed evade and counterattack, the man sprawls out onto the floor.

"Dad!" Christian yells, running to the man's side.

"Wait, stay back!" you cry, just as another man rushes in through the open doors.

The second man wears cycling spandex, and one of his calf-muscles is torn open to the bone. The wound does not bleed. His skin is deathly pale, and his mouth hangs open.

In instinct, you go for this second man, fending him off with the wooden sword. A cacophony of boots slapping against pavement announces the arrival of the National Guard troops, led by Captain Delozier.

"Get the biker!" Master Hanzo yells.

The National Guard soldiers detain the man from the rear, and it takes four men struggling to drag the crazed ghoul out of the dojo.

"Who's that?!" Delozier yells, pointing at the man on the floor.

"I'm sorry, I—I just came for my son, for Christian," he replies.

"How did you get past the barricades?"

"I stayed low. The cars, I used the cars as cover and came straight here."

"Dammit," Captain Delozier grumbles. "We'll have to tighten our patrols. Okay, sir, I need you to come with us. We'll need to get you looked at by the doc, just in case."

"I'm coming too," Christian says, rising from his father's side.

Captain Delozier nods, then motions for the pair to follow him.

"You'll keep the boy safe?"

"Of course," the captain replies, though he doesn't meet your gaze. With that, they're all gone.

"Back to sleep," you tell your students. They obviously want to talk about what just happened, about what *is happening,* and so do you, but what would you say? There is an old saying your father used to say when people were hasty to judge: *A frog in a well does not know the great sea.*

Lying awake in the dark, you simply listen to the children breathing around you. Salvator is gone, and now Christian. For the better? Who can say? Eventually, you come to the conclusion:

➢ I will ask about the other boys tomorrow. Captain Delozier should be reminded of his responsibilities, too. Go to page 388

➢ My responsibility is to the tadpoles in the well with me. Hard as it may be, I must push the others from my mind and live in the here and now.
Go to page 342

Your Call

A moment later, Sam Colt slides the panel closed and turns back. You pull out your cell and dial home, but nothing happens. A closer look at the screen shows no service. Not even one bar.

"What was with that 'Daisy' comment?" Lily asks.

"He was seeing if we were under duress. If I'd said 'Daisy's fine,' then he'd know that Tyberius here was holding us hostage and they'd be looking for a back way in right about now."

"Smart," she says.

"You guys got signal?" you ask.

"Network's down, or taken into emergency control, or some such nonsense," Sam says. "But there's a landline at the returns desk. This way."

Crossing your fingers that it'll work, you follow Sam to the store's phone. When you dial this time, the call goes through. Three rings, then she answers.

"Mama, thank God."

"That you, Tyberius? What's the matter?"

"Mama, I need you to stay home. Don't answer the door for anyone."

"Don't fool about, you scarin' me, boy."

"This is serious, you have to stay put. Lock the door. I'll come for you, mama. I don't know when, but just stay inside. A day, two, I dunno, but—" you stop yourself when there's a strange *click* on the line. "Mama? Mama, you there?"

A computerized woman's voice cuts in. "We're sorry, all circuits are busy now. Please try your call later. This is a recording."

"Goddammit!" you roar before throwing the phone across the room.

You can feel Sam and Lily staring at you, but can't bring yourself to meet their gaze. You press your knuckles into your eyes and fight the pain in your chest.

"Ty," Lily says, putting a hand on your shoulder. "She's alive, right? Help us defend this place, then make it home to her once the quarantine is lifted. Survive—for her."

Standing tall, you clear your throat. "What do we need to do?"

Sam nods. "I'm working on defenses, while Lily is on supplies. We're going to make it, Ty, together."

➢ I'll Help Sam with defenses. Go to page 132
➢ I'll Help Lily with supplies. Go to page 134

Zombies in Mirror May be Closer than they Appear

Dad insists that you bring the wounded man along, which will make this journey all the more treacherous. The man from your room stays comatose, and even with Jason's help, it takes twenty minutes to lug him outside and get him strapped into the back seat. Dad is at least conscious, and can walk on his own, but he's delirious and stops to vomit in the front hedges.

Two men stalk the neighborhood, but turn the other way when they catch a glimpse of Jason's 16-gauge. Looters, most likely. Best make sure the Jeep is filled to the gills with supplies and food; odds are, you'll never see home again. *There's a sobering thought.*

The sky is red at the start of the setting sun and the city is already in far worse shape than you could've imagined. Sirens wail, seemingly from every direction. Black smoke billows on the horizon, signaling the harsh, chemical burn of a car fire. The unmistakable *pop* of gunfire echoes from neighboring streets.

A sign up ahead shows "evacuation route" in the blinking marquee of a construction detour. *Thank you, Jesus!* The speed limit here is 45, and the evacuation signs say reduce to 25, though everyone's going 65. You keep with the flow of traffic.

As the route leads out of the city, the police cruisers that provide security on the side of the road give way to National Guard Humvees. You wave at the gunner on a turret mount, and he nods. Eyes back on the road, you slam on the brakes as someone two cars ahead *smashes* into a pedestrian and flips their Kia.

The idiot came out of nowhere, and the next car doesn't have time to react. They slam into the overturned car. The jeep skids to a stop only feet from the accident. You brace yourself, but the car behind you manages to stop before rear-ending you.

"Everyone okay?" you ask.

Jason nods. "Should we get out and help?"

"Go around," Dad croaks. He sounds terrible, but he's right, and you know it. Getting out of the city is a time-sensitive operation.

You bring the jeep onto the shoulder and into the grass median before coming back onto the road in front of the wreck. In your rear-view mirror, you can see others follow your lead. Everything you've been brought up with says you should help those people, but you know you've got to pick your battles.

Flipping on the headlights, you enter a tunnel. About halfway in, traffic thickens, then comes to a standstill. Cars pile up behind you, and you're smack dab in the middle of a full-on cluster-fuck. Dammit. Horns blare, but no one's moving.

- ➤ It'll clear. Stay in the car, no matter what. Who knows how many of those things are piling up outside the tunnel? Go to page 192
- ➤ On foot—now! There's little time to get out before you're trapped for good. Go to page 221

Zombieworld

The park wasn't far off in your memory, but your memory traveled by car. On foot, it's several hours away. In that time, you've successfully outpaced your undead fans, but you can be sure they're still following in the distance.

It's getting dark by the time you arrive at the amusement park, and you're not one to explore an unfamiliar battleground solo at night. Truth be told, this is your first visit to *The Funtastic Rockencoaster Adventure Park*, the carnival that couldn't settle on just one portmanteau when two would do. Your family didn't have the money for it when you were growing up, and with no kids of your own, there was little draw as an adult, until now. Guess that's just the way of the crumbling cookie.

The ticket counter is open and abandoned, with a rolling security gate window. Good a place as any to bed down for the night. You hop in and pull the security gate closed with a mighty metallic *squeal*—sending every bird within a three-block radius squawking into the sky. Sprayed over the ticket-pricing menu is a graffiti message stating, "The world is over. Amuse yourself."

Though its castle walls are forged from plaster and her moats flow only waist-deep, the walls surrounding the local amusement park are real enough. With security measures designed against an array of intruders—from a terrorist attack, to teens trying to sneak a free ride, to midnight looters—the theme park is ready for invasion.

Heading inside, you don your gasmask and lock the carousel-style entrance behind you. It won't stop the dead, but it might slow them. You'll have to find something to barricade the front if you're going to stay here long enough to signal rescue.

Posters at the gift shop show what you missed out on during childhood. Gleeful cherubs captured in time on various rides, as well as ads for merchandise for sale inside such as the brand new *Blender Ride* and accompanying "I got Blended at *The F.R.A.P.!*" t-shirt.

Time to have a look around. Where to first?

> - The park's most famous attraction—*The Chariot of the Gods* Ferris wheel. At the top, I'll have a great view of the city and park. Go to page 400
> - There's a tram that encircles the park grounds, and if I can start that up, I'll get a full VIP tour. Go to page 343

The Book Club Reader's Guide

If you want a true Monet Experience (no spoilers), avoid these questions until after you've read through the book several times. Take 1-2 weeks, progress through as many iterations of *PATHOGENS* as you can, while keeping the following questions in mind. Then, meet up with your reader's group and discuss:

1. Which character did you read first? Did you read the other characters in the order presented by the book, or did you jump around? Explain your choice.
2. Which characters did you most empathize with? Likewise, which characters did you feel the least connected to? Why do you think that is?
3. Each character had a diverse background before the zombie apocalypse started. How did this affect the types of decisions you were offered once placed in that characters shoes? Were some more or less prepared than others? Did that effect their chances of survival?
4. Did you read *INFECTED* before you read *PATHOGENS*? If so, did it change your viewpoints on the characters?
5. The group of "Preppers" known only by their tattoo *Ad Vitam Paramus* ("We are Preparing for Life") were perhaps a little *too* prepared for the apocalypse—to the point where they were immediately ready to take advantage of a crack in societal structure. Do you think there really are people out there waiting to take advantage in the event of a societal collapse?
6. The book is sometimes hilarious; sometimes disturbingly dark. How did you feel about this type of gallows humor? Was an appropriate balance struck between the two moods?
7. By its very nature, *Gilgazyme* ® takes out the wealthy and influential first. Does this make an apocalyptic scenario worse (no world leaders)? Or better (salt of the earth people most likely to survive)? Discuss your reasoning.
8. Were you able to fully immerse yourself as another person and think from their perspective? Or do you think you still made decisions as you yourself would? What does this say about our capacity for empathy?
9. What served as the book's most difficult obstacle? The zombies? The National Guardsmen? Or the roving bandits? What does this say about humanity and our ability to join together under a common threat?
10. Share an experience in the story that really stuck with you. Perhaps a spot where you thought you were going to "lose" but didn't, or a section that resonated with you for any reason. Discuss.
11. Each character had to make sacrifices in the name of survival. Some literally had to sacrifice loved ones. Others their pride or sacrifices of character. Is it possible to go through a survival ordeal unchanged? Do you really survive if you "become" someone else as a part of that experience, for better or worse?
12. This, more than any other of Schannep's works, is a character study. His other three books leave you with a blank slate from which to experience the story world, while this book gives you a clearly defined character as your guide. How do these experiences differ? Which do you prefer?

Printed in Poland
by Amazon Fulfillment
Poland Sp. z o.o., Wrocław